To Do

# Booms and Busts
## ...another Harry Spittle Adventure

### Geoff Le Pard

*With all my best*
*Geoff LePard*

## *Acknowledgements*

This book is the third in the Harry Spittle Saga, following the journey of Harold Spittle from hapless youth through nervous trainee solicitor to senior lawyer and potential partner. While in some ways his journey has mirrored my own, the firm at which Harry works and the characters depicted here are figments of my imagination and anyone who thinks they recognise themselves in this book should wonder at their own self-image.

Several people have been involved in reaching this point and to each of you I owe a debt of gratitude. My wife Linda and my children Sam and Jenni most of all but there are countless others. I just hope knowing that you are loved and cherished is sufficient.

If not, and you expect something more tangible then I fear you will be disappointed.

## *About the Author*

Geoff (not Geoffrey, save for legal documents and to his Mother) Le Pard is a former lawyer, novelist, enthusiastic blogger (at https://geofflepard.com), someone who enjoys walking (especially with his dog) and lover of London. He has published a few books and a memoir, all of which can be found on Amazon.

## *Copyright*

Copyright © 2020: Geoffrey Le Pard
Publisher: Tangental Publishing

The right of Geoffrey Le Pard to be identified as author of this Work has been asserted by him in accordance with sections 77 and 78 of the Copyright, Designs and Patents Act 1988.
All rights reserved. No part of this publication may be reproduced, stored in any retrieval system, copied in any form or by any means, electronic, mechanical, photocopying, recording or otherwise transmitted without written permission from the publisher. You must not circulate this book in any format.
The characters and situations described in this book are the product of the author's imagination and any similarity to actual persons – living or dead – and situations – past, present or future – is entirely coincidental.

For more information about the author and upcoming books online, please visit https://geofflepard.com

# Friday, 4th September 1987

## Chapter One

"Harry? Are you skiving too?"

I'm nearly 30 and a 'senior' lawyer at Newe Waters, one of a select group of solicitors' firms in the City of London (self-selected, naturally) that consider themselves a cut above the exceptional, let alone the average. Yet while others use this status to give themselves confidence their talents barely warrant, I have still to master that trick. Consequently the emotion I feel right now is guilt at being caught away from my desk rather than the expected effrontery. Which is very galling, especially as it's gone 5:30 which is the official going home time at Newe Waters and I've nothing to feel guilty about.

"Getting something for the weekend?" The speaker is Greg – Gregor Princip – a close colleague. He has fully embraced the firm's ethos and is not lacking in self-confidence. He nods at the pharmacy counter adjacent to where we are standing. Greg is taller than me – six feet something – with ridiculously white blond hair and blue eyes. He's wearing his raincoat, which means he's going home, and that riles me even more. We've worked together in Newe Waters' Property Department for four years as occasional rivals and colleagues but more recently as friends. I'm still never quite sure when he's teasing me, which is probably why we get on so well. It makes him look sharp and quick and me harmless and gormless.

"No, not skiving. I'm collecting some snaps that I forgot to pick up at lunchtime."

He almost nudges me. "Candid, huh? You going to let me see? I've got some boring ones of a family do to collect. My Father had a party for business contacts at the weekend – you know he has this place on the West Sussex coast near Chichester? Anyway, he insisted I was there and took group shots of all these old men. Sooo tedious. Are yours from your holiday? Skinny dipping with the delightful Penny?"

How does he know? Not the skinny dipping, well not me but...

Just then the woman in front of us steps away from the counter, having collected her prints and an assistant peers over the sort of horn-rimmed spectacles that suggest disapproval is her default setting. "Name?"

"Princip, Gregor." It's natural for him to go first even if he arrived after me. "Do me a favour Harry and grab some paracetamol, would you? I've a thunderous headache. I'll get your pics if you give me the receipt."

A stronger man would resist, but that isn't me. "Oh, okay." The assistant waves over a younger, prettier junior assistant as I begin to move away. I guess I'm flummoxed that anyone as in control as Greg can have something as mundane as a headache.

Even though he is a friend I really don't want him looking at the pictures so watch him carefully as he speaks to the new girl. It seems he knows her as her smile is definitely friendlier than you usually get in Boots. Or maybe that's just me.

She glances at me and smiles warmly. Do I know her? She says something to Greg, giggles and blushes and starts sifting through the packets of prints in front of her, her white gloved hands expertly hunting out the name he's given.

She holds up the packets; he says something and she lays them on the counter. I watch like a hawk. If he opens either he'll see my girlfriend Penny, heavily pregnant and topless trying to do a handstand or some other ludicrous piece of gymnastics. It seemed funny when I took it but right now I'd be happier if it was a group of old boring men like he says his are.

The assistant has her hand on top of the packets as they keep talking and I pray she keeps it there. She says something while looking rather shocked, but Greg just laughs. I suppose she knows what's in mine – the last film I brought in also featured Penny topless (she has few inhibitions) and it had the senior assistant moaning about their policy on inappropriate imagery – and I bet she's sharing her concerns with him. I pay for the tablets and head over to where he is waiting. Shit, my face must be burning like my 12-year-old self when Jolly Jobbing, my reed-thin P.E. teacher, caught me trying to look through the keyhole of the girl's changing room. I was caned for that; right now, caning would be preferable to the humiliation I feel certain is coming my way. I try to control my breathing by not breathing; I don't think he's looked at anything. Yet.

"Here you go." He pushes my packet at me. "Show me later; I need to get back." He has his own set that he slips inside his coat pocket.

I exhale deeply and feel slightly faint. "Thanks." I push the three pound coins to him, which he tries to wave away but finally takes. "I still prefer the notes, don't you? I'm sure I spend more of these bloody coins."

As we head for the front of the shop, he says, "What do you think about Crispin's latest cock-up? Sounded pretty stupid to me." He leads me past a bored-looking security guard, who is picking his nose and waiting for us to go so he can lock up.

"Cock-up? Crispin?"

"I know. Mr Perfect makes a mistake. Hold the front page. He forgot to pay the Land Registry fee, despite a reminder and the priority period elapsed. Lucky no one tried to register another interest. And to do it on Old Grant's purchase? Hardly going to help his chances is it?"

Crispin Muddle is another colleague in the same department as Greg and me and we are all in the race for partnership, not that I think either Crispin or I are the front runners. In fact in any normal year Crispin or I wouldn't be in with any sort of chance without the property boom that Mrs Thatcher's Conservative government has engineered with the Big Bang and Property Owning Democracy and tax cuts. And that's before you factor in the mountains of property work that continues to come out of the nascent privatisation programme. As a result of this perfect storm of legal work, there is a real prospect of two partners being made up, hence Crispin's and my continuing hopes of promotion.

Maybe I'm being hard on us. We each have our strengths, I suppose: I'm diligent and… well, that's about it. Crispin is technically excellent and Greg is brilliant with clients, helped in part by his Father's wide-ranging contact book. I've tried to ignore all the fuss around this partnership stuff, telling myself that if it happens, it happens, while pretty sure there's more chance of me being an undiscovered violin prodigy or award-winning portrait painter.

Greg, though, is patently ambitious and it is his intelligence-gathering that has led us to believe there are two spots available and he and I should get them because of our 'complementary skills.' Not that he's especially complimentary about either Crispin or me, but having him on my side does feel like it may help my chances. The result is he is always keen to hear about anything that might set back Crispin's hopes. Such as the aforementioned cock-up.

"You going home or heading back to the office? Penny got something lined up, maybe?"

"I wish." Why did I say that? I hurry on. "She's nearly due, you know. Only a couple of months now."

"So?" Gregor says he is from White Russian stock and often holds a pose like some Cossack painting, which he does now. "Aren't pregnant women meant to want even more sex than usual?"

I glance around, praying no one is listening and lower my voice, both not wanting to be overheard yet not wanting to look like I can't indulge in some risqué banter. "Someone forgot to mention it to Penny." I'm hating my indiscretion – why am I dragging her into this? "Although things are obviously fine in that department." Well done, Harry. Utterly lame.

He squeezes my shoulder. "No need to be coy, Harry. You two love birds have it all sorted out. Everyone says so. You both know how to maintain a mature relationship. Trust." And if he's not making himself completely transparent he starts humming 'Pretty Flamingo' by Manfred Mann, before adding, "…whatever ups and downs there may have been."

That is an unsubtle reference to a bar in Mayfair called The Flaming Flamingo run by Natalie Pendant, a close friend of both Penny and me from way back. She named it after the gambling club her ex ran, which in a way paid for its namesake. "You promised not to say…"

He puts a finger to his lips. "Soul of discretion, old chap. Mum's the word."

Lying toerag. After a particularly fraught afternoon last Friday, Greg and I ended up back at his flat – what he calls his 'pied-à-terre,' which belies how huge it is – and drank too much vodka. His Father's vodka apparently, much like the flat. During one of those confessional conversations where I seem to have spilt lots of beans and he didn't, I told him about a short and stupid liaison I had with Natalie. Why oh why did I tell him of all people? He promised to keep quiet, but will he? I mean, it's not that I don't trust him because I do, kind of. About work at least. But he's the sort of completely loyal friend who will keep all your most personal secrets unless the occasion arises when keeping quiet would be to pass up the chance to tell a really great anecdote and reinforce the fact that he is the natural centre of attention at all social gatherings.

I've spent the week wondering if his promise to keep schtum is worth anything and here he is teasing me about it. If he tells Penny – it'll be mentioned subtlety, full of apologies about how he was sure she knew, etc. – then I'm toast. Naturally me having sex with anyone would be grounds for Penny to send me packing, but we had split up at the time so there is an excuse except... except this dalliance was with Natalie, Penny's best friend and someone she knows I've had a thing for since we all met back in a hotel where we worked as students just over 10 years ago.

He goes on. "Natalie is a cutie though, isn't she? And she likes you a lot."

That's the other thing; we often end up at the Flamingo after long tiring days so he knows Natalie fairly well. It would be just as bad if he told Natalie that I'd told him. "Have you spoken to her? Tell me you haven't," I say. Now he's worrying me.

"Not about that, of course not. We had a couple of cocktails on Wednesday. Anyway, she's a trooper; she'll have your back, old man. So? Back to the grindstone or home?"

"Er? Yes, the office just to pick up a couple of things."

"Do you want a quick drink? I could really do with a pint. It's going to be a pretty heavy Friday night otherwise."

"Oh? Why's that?"

"I've got a meeting with the church elders at eight and then I'm off to meet Pater at his club. There's someone he wants to introduce me to. Some potential new client." That sums up Greg – even though he's just shy of 30 he's already something impressive in this church he goes to – I think it's Baptist or Evangelical of some such with an odd name but since Penny is a red-blooded atheist, which means that I am too, I never ask.

"I'd better pass. Maybe next week?"

We've reached the front door of our office. "Have a lovely weekend and give my love to your darling wife."

"Girlfriend," I correct.

"You're as good as spliced. And aren't you going to make an honest woman of her before the sprog emerges?"

I've tried to ignore that too, since the one time we talked about marriage Penny said she didn't see herself as a prize heifer so why did I think she needed a ring to keep her? However, there have been some recent hints and I'm not sure if I misread the signs. I keep quiet this time.

"Yes, let's have a beer next week. We should coordinate our strategy for the conference. Big opportunity there."

Yet another thing I've been dreading. Each year the partners and all those who are in the running go away for a weekend, ostensibly to talk about strategy and the future but everyone says it's the equivalent of a cattle market where we have our legal fetlocks squeezed and assessed. I know Greg has been quizzing the junior partners about what goes on and he has dropped a few hints, mostly of the sort that makes it sound like having your appendix out without anaesthetic while someone whips your backside with barbed wire is to be preferred. "It's just another initiation, Harry. If someone tells you to jump, just make sure you end up in the most influential lap."

With that he spins and walks away. Strides. He strides away. Nothing as prosaic as a walk for Gregor. His raincoat – Burberry, of course – flows out behind him like a sail. The sky is clear, yet as with most things with Greg it's all for show. A woman approaches him and he steps to one side, bowing slightly as he lets her pass. She smiles and turns to watch his retreating back. He has that effect on people. If anyone is a shoo-in for this partnership, it's him.

In truth, I could actually do with a drink. Penny told me to go for one as she's having her hair done and it will be take-away night when we both get home. But everyone who might join me will have gone for the day and I hate drinking on my own. Why didn't I accept Greg's offer? I'm such a twit.

When I push my way into the office reception, Ronnie O'Porter has taken over controlling the incoming and outgoing traffic as night porter. The combination of his almost job-appropriate name and a Northern Irish accent that makes Iain Paisley's consonants sound almost mellifluous causes no end of confusion when he introduces himself. Ronnie is aged, or at least his craggy face, historic acne scarring and a large chunk of missing nose suggest a life fully and rather harshly lived. The cause of the space previously filled by a nostril has been the subject of a fair degree of speculation, ranging from a bullet at Arnhem through to a bomb experiment in the Bogside gone wrong to the mundane of an ill-timed sneeze and an unfortunately angled propelling pencil. Ronnie never says. He rarely says much to be fair.

Standing next to Ronnie is his antithesis: Gloria Eagle the day receptionist, a full-busted force of nature whose garrulous cheery nature and love of gossip makes her perfect for one of the part-time receptionists. I've known her on and off for several years. She was the receptionist at the firm of solicitors in the West End where I trained and she joined Newe Waters sometime after me, much to our mutual surprise. She used to terrorise me with her faux-flirting and initially I feared I'd receive more of the same, but so far she's been friendly, cheeky certainly but staying just the right side of totally embarrassing me.

Where Ronnie is small and rather desiccated, Gloria is in full bloom – everything about her is large or larger than life: eyes, hair, shoulders, teeth, embonpoint and especially personality. Even though she's only been here a relatively short while, she seems to know everyone and is possibly the best-known person in the firm. Everyone sees her as they come and go; she's always got a kind word for the nervous, flirts with the confident men and indulges in highly indiscrete and supportive gossip with the women.

We share a smile. She knows things about me that I'd hope she'll keep to herself and she knows I know about the affair she had with a junior partner at my old firm who she was believed, certainly by the other secretaries, to have targeted and that ended messily when he resigned after a scandal involving some injudicious gambling debts. Naturally neither of us has spoken about these things.

Ronnie follows Gloria's gaze and sees me. "And a fine evening it is, Mr Spittle." Ronnie is old school and however much I try he will only call me by my surname as he does all the qualified solicitors below partner status. If I make it to partner I will be upgraded to 'Sir.'

Gloria is the opposite. "Hiya Harry." She reaches across and kisses me on the cheek, no doubt leaving a huge smear of bright red lipstick. Ronnie looks on indulgently. "Fancy a drink? I'm meeting some girls in the West End later, but you can buy me a glass of bubbles first. If you're not dashing home to the broodmare of course."

Gloria doesn't like Penny; Ronnie, however, doesn't approve of the slight to my girlfriend, tutting and wagging his finger at her.

She shrugs him off. "You'll not catch me blowing up like a barrage balloon, thank you. Come on, Harry. One drink. It'll be fun. Like old times."

I'm about to make excuses but I do want that drink and if she's headed for the West End we could pop in on Natalie's club – it will be quiet this early – and maybe I can test the water about Greg and what I told him.

It will be better if Natalie finds out about my loose talk from me and not him.

"All right. Okay if we go to the Flaming Flamingo – Natalie's club, you remember? I just need to pick up some papers. I'll be 10 minutes at most – well, depending on the lifts of course."

Gloria snags a copy of the *Evening Standard* that Ronnie buys on his way in and which sit on the reception counter for any partner who wants one when they're leaving. "Don't be long."

I manage a nod and press the button for the lift. As I wait I begin to relax at last. It is now gone six o'clock and officially the weekend. No partner worth his or her salt will still be in the building, so all disasters and confrontations can wait until Monday morning.

## *Chapter Two*

I'm not the tidiest lawyer. My desk suggests a paper volcano has erupted all over it. I have many plans to tidy it up and Chloe Sparring, my secretary, does her best, but it will take someone with more determination than the twittering Chloe to change my appalling habits.

Despite its pretensions to be a – no, scrap that: the prestige law firm – Newe Waters is currently housed in a building that even Prince Charles cannot find the adjectives to describe. Built in the 1950s over 10 floors, it has a hot and a cold side (depending on the time of year and position of the sun) and the windows are meant to open but if you do they may fall out and decapitate the netball payers who have a court on the podium deck below. Alternatively you will be caught by the wind howling in from Essex and pinned to the wall while every sheet of paper in the room (and that includes everything in the filing cabinets) is caught in such a ferocious vortex that it has been known to turn the next person to enter into a very realistic impression of an Egyptian mummy. A lot of the windows have therefore been screwed shut, which is a neat metaphor for how I generally feel by about 10 o'clock every Monday morning until 5:30 on Friday evening – imprisoned.

The property department occupies the top floor, which has its pluses and minuses. On the plus side the views are pretty good (when the windows aren't boarded up because they've fallen out again) and no one from other departments 'just passes by' to give you work or pick your brains or generally bug you. On the minus side the lifts work on their own version of a constant motion principle and thus rarely reach the top floor before someone has entered and pressed 'down,' which overrides all previous instructions to ascend. I'd like to say this makes us feel like some sort of elite outfit, but in truth it's more like we've been put in the attic and forgotten about. There are two sets of stairs but since they both double as the home of the sewerage risers and are scented accordingly, no one other than we happy few walks up to join us.

My little piece of this real estate empire is a three-person room that I share with my two colleagues: Jonjo Frampton, an Irish ex-pat from somewhere near Cork who isn't qualified to practice English law until he passes some exam but does so nonetheless, and Erica Twombly the articled clerk who is brain-achingly bright, myopic and incontinently eager to please. As such she is almost guaranteed to fail.

This Friday evening they have already left; indeed the whole floor appears to be abandoned. After all it is just gone six and who in their right mind works later than 5:35 on a Friday? Apart from the goons on the third and fourth floors that house the company lawyers who think of themselves as utterly indispensable – the self-styled 'Spitfire Pilots' on whom (or so they think) everyone else depends to succeed. Their dedication might be genuine, but the fact that the senior management team (comprising the senior partner and managing partner) have their offices on these floors may have something to do with their enthusiasm not to be seen as the first to leave.

It's a truism that if you believe somewhere such as an office to be empty, you feel you are being watched. I'm as paranoid as the next man so cover my nerves with a reedy whistle. That's when a door slams and I just manage to suppress a whimper. Probably a cleaner or something, I tell myself.

This little surge of adrenaline has me hurrying to my desk and grabbing the file to stuff in my briefcase. Having done that I pull out the photos from my jacket pocket and have second jolt in the space of a couple of minutes. The giggly assistant in Boots has made a major cock-up and given me a packet of photos in the name of Barry Tritewell. Barry happens to be a partner here. A more fortunate person than me would be confused with some total stranger. I will have to return the packet on Monday and the assistant will apologise (oh sure she would), hand me mine and that would be the end of it. But sadly I know Barry only too well. He is the head of the Private Client Department – these dinosaurs service the residue of the ancient blue bloods who once made up the backbone of the firm's client base but since the imposition of 98% tax rates during the Labour governments of the 1970s, their wealth – and commensurate ability to afford our fees – has dwindled to a trickle. Barry and fellow partner Florence Dawb continue to work for a sad group comprising has-beens, maybes (but highly unlikelies) and never-wases. And Barry really doesn't like me.

In an ideal world my contact with the likes of Barry Tritewell would be limited to those office social functions where I would be introduced, listen to some sad story (or 10) so he might think well of me when it comes to a vote on my partnership and then never speak to him again. But life isn't ideal. We, the minions in the Property department, are regularly called upon to assist with some Lord or Earl or Right Honourable and the last vestiges of their once glorious and extensive landed estates. And recently I have had three such jobs with Barry as the partner, none of which have gone especially well.

I could leave the packet in my desk and do the swap on Monday but because I know Sod is my patron saint, to do so would mean Barry would be collecting his prints as I'm returning them, or worse – he already has mine and is waiting on me to give him his. The very idea that he'd come to me for this purpose is about as likely as Penny saying she doesn't mind that I've had sex with Natalie and not mentioned it (I don't want anyone to think that is playing on my mind right now).

Barry, sad to report, is one of the very few partners who actually likes working late (or so I've heard), so with Sod running the show he'll almost certainly still be at his desk. However, if I'm going to take this partnership malarkey seriously, occasionally I have to act like an adult and this is one of those moments.

Another door slams. I need to go. Gloria will be sending out a search party. As I step out of my room and turn towards the lifts, I see the unmistakable back of Greg, his mac still draped over his shoulders. He's facing the lifts and hasn't seen me. I really can't face him again so spin round and head for the back stairs. A small part of me wonders why he's come back when he said he was heading off, but I'm not going to dwell on the eccentricities of faded aristocracy in the guise of Gregor Princip.

Barry's department is on the seventh floor (the Private Client team have half the floor and the rest is occupied by some of the litigators who also occupy the eighth floor) and I'm down the stairs, breath held against the festering miasma of a week's sewage backing up in the pipes, and out of the fire doors quickly. But just as I emerge at one end of the corridor, the lift stops at the other and the door begins its laborious opening. Bloody Greg. It's like he's following me. Some stupid instinct has me darting into the nearest room, which houses a photocopier. Were Greg to walk all the way along the corridor and find me I'd have no explanation that would make sense. Not that that is likely to happen but I'm not paranoid without reason, or so I often tell myself.

He must be dropping something off, although I can't imagine what that might be. Greg has done everything he can – and he is an arch manipulator, which makes him ideal partnership material – to avoid doing any work with the Private Client team ('no hopers Harry – why waste time with them when their endorsement may well hold you back?'). Maybe he's doing something with a litigator? Still, I count to 100 and cautiously stick my head out. The lift doors have shut and as far as I can judge there's no sound coming from the floor. He must have gone.

Still wary I move slowly past the rooms. Most have their doors shut except one – Mervin Toogood's office is open and there's a light on. But a quick peek shows he's not there. It could be Greg had something for Mervin. I have a vague memory that he and Greg's Father are friends or neighbours or something like that. But like most of the rest of the building the floor seems deserted.

The demarcation between Barry's empire and the litigators is very marked and suggests Barry has something very damaging on the office manager. Otherwise how do you explain the opulence of their décor and furniture? Even the most junior lawyer has a proper oak desk, not the MFI tat that we have to put up with, as indeed do most of the rest of the firm (that said, Mervin's room is like something out of a Sunday supplement). Barry's own room is only two away from the lift lobby and I can see the door is open. Taking a breath I approach it, determined to find out if he is there to just drop off the packet and make an excuse. If he isn't then I'll leave a note. What I'm not doing is getting dragged into yet another debate about Lord Portobello's copyhold problem. I'm meant to have researched it, but it is so abstruse I could feel my buttocks fossilizing as I dug around in the library trying to find something on point. I intended to ask Erica to take on the task but it's a long way down my ever-lengthening to-do list.

An alternative strategy occurs to me. If I sneak past to his secretary's room I can leave the photos on her desk with a note. Perfect. Worth a shot if he's still hanging around.

It's the shoe that stops me. A black brogue, lying on its side by his door. Why would a shoe be lying there? If I'd overlooked it I might have just walked past and not looked inside. But no such luck. Having taken in the rogue shoe my gaze is drawn inexorably into Barry's room and I am turned to stone. However complicated my life might have seemed a moment or two ago, it has just been stuffed inside a tumble dryer and set to the fastest spin possible.

I can't help staring – goggling might be nearer the mark. The backdrop hasn't changed: there is still the same large bookcase stuffed with tax tomes and a few gifts from clients; the coat cupboard in ornately carved dark wood with a door that has to be kept shut with one of the weighty books sits to the left, while two huge oils of his wife and daughter, who both look gorgeous but which is utterly unlike the actual people they portray, hang on the wall to the right. In the centre of the room is his wide, highly polished desk on which at all the other times I have visited I would expect to see his desk light, a Rolodex of contacts, a telephone and a blotter.

Today all of the above has been swept aside and instead Barry is on the desk. To be completely accurate his top half is sprawled face-first across it, his arms outstretched with his hands hanging limply over the edge nearest me, between which I can see his totally bald pate reflecting the unforgiving strip light above. Barry's head appears to be turned to one side, as if he's admiring his family's portraits.

Naturally my mind is in some turmoil; few partners in my experience hold a Superman pose across their desks. Furthermore – and this stops my already erratic breathing completely – middle-aged male partners rarely wear dresses in the office; in this case a silver and blue sequined number. Barry is not moving and for the first time I wonder if he is breathing.

Taking in some air, which is surprisingly tricky for such a hardwired instinctive action, I step forward and then abruptly stop. The dress has been pulled up, sort of tucked under him, exposing a pair of saggy and unappealingly pallid buttocks. For some reason the fact he is wearing no underwear is more shocking than the strappy dress. I circle carefully, trying to ignore that bare bottom, to check on his face. My mind is already playing tricks, wondering if there's any way I can justify not trying mouth to mouth if that proves necessary. I should try his pulse, I should—

"Harry?"

Jesus F Christ. I'm sure I leave the ground as I spin and come face to face with Sebastian Crout. The Senior Partner. The SP. A pompous narcissistic know-all who ultimately holds my career in his fine bony fingers and who has just found me in the most awkward situation imaginable. Actually, I don't think anyone could imagine this scenario.

"Harry? What the hell's going on?"

Where do you start? A partner dead at his desk? Possibly a transsexual? He may have been rogered by person or persons unknown, but none of the possible candidates includes me – does it? In any case he has no taste in evening wear, and why he is only wearing one brogue jars as much as any sartorial infractions – should I go with that?

Whether the SP understands any of my dilemmas is moot as he moves past me to Barry's head, checking for a pulse in his neck. "This is a fucking mess, Harry." Some people swear all the time; some use swearing judiciously for effect and some never ever swear. I would have put the SP into that last category.

Maybe it's the fact that even he can be driven to such extremes breaks through my mute torpor. "I found him a moment ago, Sir. Like that. I think, that is I haven't checked, but it looks to me, well maybe, you know, you've checked. He… is he dead?" Saying that word does something to my stomach and I feel its contents began to froth and roil in preparation for an assault on my oesophagus.

"Yes, he's very much dead Harry. His face is nearly blue. He… here." The SP moves quickly to grab the wastepaper bin and thrust it under my chin.

I heave once, twice, but nothing comes out. I heave again and dribble something sharp and acidic into the balls of screwed-up paper. When I look back at the SP, he's holding an apple. A Golden Delicious if I know my fruit. "Poor Barry. Not a nice way to go. At work, like… this."

The apple reminds me of something that I can't immediately place. I'm still trying to focus when I feel his hands on my shoulders and look at him. "Harry, can I trust you?"

"Sir?" I really do want to be sick and clutch the bin ever tighter.

The furrows on the SP's forehead deepen. "You need to sit down for a minute. You look like you might faint. Go and wait in Gladys' room and I'll be along in a moment."

In a way I'm very grateful to go. The knowledge that I'm in the presence of those exposed dead buttocks is making me feel ill. Gladys is – well, was I suppose – Barry's secretary. I take the seat next to her desk and do as I'm told. How on Earth can this be happening to me? Is someone going to suspect me of some sort of foul play? I shudder involuntarily and dry heave again.

It's only then I wonder about Greg. Did he see Barry? Surely he must have, unless he was dropping something off for Gladys. Otherwise he had to have walked past his room. How could he not see?

The SP is a tall skinny man with hair that is always the exact same length and style whatever the day. It never moves, is never out of place. Normally his complexion is so bland as to be unnoticeable but when he reappears there are red spots blooming on his cheeks. He takes Gladys' seat and stares at her typewriter.

"Harry, we have something of a dilemma here. On the one hand we must, of course, involve the police as well as the ambulance service; on the other, as you know, Barry is married – happily married with a beautiful daughter just off to university. And a stellar reputation as a man of the highest integrity and standards. Goodness, he was secretary of his golf club last year. We, that is you and I – and the firm, of course – need, for his sake – for all our sakes – to handle this with the utmost discretion and superlative sensitivity. Do you understand me?"

"I… I think so."

"Good. And I don't think it helps anyone at all – not him, not you and not your, erm, prospects – that we broadcast it was you who found his body."

"Sir? Mr Crout…?"

"Seb."

Did he really just ask me to call him by his Christian name and a diminutive version of it to boot? I mean, I can't. It would be…

"Call me Seb."

…very flattering.

"This is what will happen. When you have suitably composed yourself, you will collect your briefcase from where you dropped it and leave. You will do whatever it was you were going to do this evening as if nothing has happened. I will call the police and deal with this. You don't need to be involved at all."

"But… is that right? I mean, I've seen him, found him – Barry. Won't they want to question me?"

"Did you move anything? Touch anything?"

"No, but—"

"And you weren't there when he died, correct?"

"I… no."

"Then you've seen nothing that matters and I can deal with this and any embarrassment better than you. If I say I found him, it's not like you have anything more to add than I can, is it?"

"No sir. Mr Crout. Seb, I mean."

"Good man. Harry, there are times when we need to trust each other. If we are to be partners, then having that trust is crucial. Do I have your trust?"

Of course I say yes, but all the while I'm wondering at what he's saying and why. In the end, I'm not in a position to argue and in truth I'm delighted to get away as soon as I can.

"And Harry?" he calls out as I'm leaving the room.

"Sir?"

"If for any reason you feel the need to say any... any more you will do me the courtesy of telling me first, won't you?"

I take the stairs slowly, stopping on the second floor to splash a lot of water over my face in the cramped bathroom and finally copiously vomit. I'm still feeling queasy when I eventually head down the stairs to reception. Gloria is behind the desk, looking peeved. "Thank Christ. I thought I'd be here all night."

"Where's Ronnie?"

"No idea. On his rounds, I suppose. Time to go."

"Can we leave the front desk unmanned?"

In reply she rummages in her leopard-print bag and extracts a bunch of keys. "We'll lock the revolving door on our way out. If anyone needs to get in or out they can ring that bell and Ronnie can sort it out." She points at a small doorbell by the inside of the door, which I have never noticed before. "How do you think Ronnie survives if he needs a pee in the middle of the night? Come on, I need a drink."

As we stand on the kerb and hail a black cab she asks, "What took you so long anyway? I thought you might have died." She checks her watch without waiting for an answer. "If we're lucky we've time for one drink before I need to meet the girls. God, you lawyers are soooo boring."

I nod as is expected. Being boring would suit me down to the ground right now but somehow I feel my life has become anything other than uneventful.

## *Chapter Three*

The Flaming Flamingo doesn't advertise itself very well beyond a rather sad-looking Olympic-style torch on the wall with a flame effect light twinkling forlornly. When Natalie acquired the lease from her former husband Miles Tupps as part of their divorce, the unit was a shabby art gallery on the ground floor and basement that Miles used as one of his many outlets to launder money – at least that's what Natalie and all her friends thought. The landlord, a Mr Prentis, had wanted the ground floor back for ages but had had a rather depressing experience trying to persuade Miles to hand it over, which ended with Prentis naked and chained to the hoarding around the Eros statue, sporting a sign around his neck offering himself as a love token. Nasty as Mr Prentis was, he more than met his match in Miles in terms of ghastly business practices.

Natalie is many things but she's no mug when it comes to commerce. She didn't try to disabuse the landlord of his conviction that Miles and his sick streak were lurking somewhere in the shadows. She had become fed up with advertising and decided what she really wanted to do was run a bar-cum-night club. She did a deal involving her keeping the basement and adding the one next door while surrendering the unit on the ground floor. The landlord pulled some strings with Westminster Council and soon enough she had her planning, building regulation approvals and licences sorted. The only stipulation, which she didn't really mind, was the outside of the basement mustn't actually look like a club.

She opened about a year ago, insisting that she would only employ female staff; and ideally women who had been part of the recent grim past of this area as a high-class red light district and who wanted to move on. I helped with the legal work, Penny trained up the bar staff and Natalie did the marketing. We used some of our late friend Sven Andersen's money (he left me a ridiculous amount that I've pretty much given away now – sometimes I regret that, but really I'm just doing what Sven wanted, and that didn't involve him funding my life of indolent luxury) to fit the place out and waited to see if people would come. To begin, the trade was either slow or comprised of former clients of the female staff hoping, I suppose, for a different offering. But gradually the newly-monied younger professionals – lawyers, accountants, advertising and PR executives and people in the booming banks and finance houses – heard of this club where you could drink until two, and then be thrown out by a six-foot blonde called Cindy. As a selling point, it worked.

When I first took Gloria there, having taken several colleagues from Newe Waters already, Natalie offered her a job. Much as Gloria was tempted and fitted the criteria – stunning, flirtatious and ball-crushing – the pay didn't match the role at Newe Waters. "I may just be there for my teeth and tits Harry, but it pays the bills." Such a waste.

"Hi Spittoon, how's Pen? Developed a fine set of udders yet?" Natalie, as is her custom, greets guests by the entrance, partly to put them at their ease and partly to assess the likelihood that they may cause trouble – having married a psychopath, she's pretty good at spotting nutters. And Spittoon? A nickname I allow only my closest friends to call me; well, them and anyone else who might cause me any physical discomfort. She only occasionally uses it and when she does it usually means I've done something to piss her off. Which, given all that has been running through my head in the last few hours, is not good news.

I suddenly feel very tired. Coming here was a mistake. I can't seem to get the image of Barry out of my head. Maybe Natalie realises because she hugs me, holding me close and whispers, "It's good to see you, Harry," in my ear before turning to another customer who has just turned up.

Given the chance to fade to one side I enter and sit at a table where I can just about watch Natalie at work. She is entirely at ease in what has quickly become her natural environment. As I mentioned, Natalie and I have history. I first fancied – and fantasised about – her in the summer of 1976 and for years after. But always from afar – Penny is the true love of my life, however hard that is to remember sometimes – until the recent... there's isn't really a word for what happened that does such a historic moment justice. It was the classic one-night stand, we had both recently split up from our partners, we were drunk and... I try to block out what actually happened; reality, as ever, being the death of fantasy.

Today she's wearing a shimmering blue sleeveless dress that has a Chinese look to it. It clings to her, although not like it would have done a few years ago. Then she had generous curves; now her new found love of jogging and the addiction she has developed to dancing at the Pineapple Studios in Covent Garden has left her pretty much straight up and down. Mind you, the running has been a Godsend in terms of reducing her stress levels and it has pretty much put paid to an increasing ciggie habit too. She started running when she left Miles – I think she initially saw it as preparation if she ever needed actually to have to run away. Now she's done the London Marathon twice and once in Berlin and has the sparse build and chiselled features of the committed long-distance runner. In the low light of the club tonight, her taut skin seems even tighter than usual.

While we hugged, I felt every bone in her spine; is she skinnier than usual? I should say something but she'll just tell me not to nag. Natalie waves at me from the basement door and indicates I should grab a drink while I wait to speak to her.

She understands Penny better than anyone. She knows Penny hates being seen out, especially in a club like the Flamingo since she began to expand in every direction. While Penny expected some sort of neat bump, in the last couple of months of pregnancy she has begun swelling like a record-breaking pumpkin and it took her by surprise. Penny's biggest fear is she'll not be able to get back to something approximating her pre-pregnancy figure because, she said, I'll leave her if she doesn't. And Natalie will ensure that doesn't happen.

A party of four men in the widest braces and with the loudest voices stumble down the stairs. Natalie may be five foot five and she struggles to maintain seven stone even in the wet but they stop immediately when they see her. Each one bows their head slightly.

She takes a moment and then tugs the garish tie of the one on the right – a tall, floppy haired man of about 21 I guess – down to her and gives him a lingering kiss on the lips. "These are the 'boys', are they?"

Mr Floppy grins stupidly and begins introductions. From their expressions I can see they are all hoping that at some point they will reach Mr Floppy's status as the kissee. I head to the bar where Gloria is in deep conversation with a woman with cascades of dark red hair and some pince-nez balanced on the bridge of her nose, a strange affectation even for this place.

"Hi Harry. This is Sandra." She smiles at her. "Come and join us." She turns back to Sandra. "What did you say you did?"

Sandra has a scowl that suggests she's not happy at my interruption. "I used to be the secretary to the Astronomer Royal until one of the directors suggested something wholly inappropriate about black holes and taking me to the Event Horizon so I left and came here. I believe you drink this." She hands me a lager with evident disdain.

"Thanks. I need a word with the boss, Gloria. I'll leave you in Sandra's capable hands, okay?"

Gloria's expression suggests it's the worst thing I could say but Sandra's face suggests I've done something equivalent to landing on a newly discovered planet and named it after her. I squeeze out a smile, snag up my drink and head over to Natalie. She has the foursome eating out of her hand, sycophantically laughing at her well-practised school-ma'amly bit. I take her arm. "Come on Mummy, time for your medication. Sorry lads. She's mine."

Natalie lets herself be led away to the corner table permanently reserved for her. "Get you." She studies me carefully. "You look like shit. Penny told you it's not yours or something?"

"Ha ha. Thanks, and I do need a word about we three, but my head is exploding and I want to tell someone about the weirdest thing that happened tonight. I found a dead partner in the office this evening."

She leans back as if pushed. "Didn't see that coming. Although I understand that must be a shock. What was it? Heart? Brain embolism?" She lurches forward and grabs my hand. "God, not suicide?"

I manage to shake my head. "No. I don't know. I don't think... he..." I lose my thread, but she gives me time to describe the scene.

After I do she says, "Bloody hell. What do you think happened?"

"You remember that old boy, Sir Penshaw Grimsdale? The one who was at Miles' club on the night Sven died?"

She nods. "I remember his sister more but yes, of course."

"He died during some sex game gone wrong. It involved an orange. Autoerotic asphyxia while trying to heighten sexual arousal. Seeing that apple reminded me of that."

"Is the type of fruit important?"

"God knows. I'm not sure I did the right thing."

Her shoulders slump like this isn't unexpected. "Tell your Auntie Natalie."

"Do you think I should have stayed while Mr Crout called the police?"

"I think Sebastian is too calculating to do anything that isn't going to be in his best interests and probably yours too in this case."

"You know him?"

"He's been here and I've met him at other functions."

"You never said... I mean, why would you?"

She takes my hand and massages the fingers. "Dear Harry, if you knew how many of your colleagues come in here to talk to some of the girls," she looks down and lowers her voice, "after hours, if you know what I mean, you wouldn't be surprised if I said I knew a damn sight more about your firm than you can possibly imagine."

That floors me. "Like what?"

She puts a finger to her lips. "I – and they – wouldn't be in business long if I blabbed. Even to you."

"Do your girls…? You know, I thought they stopped that sort of thing…?"

Natalie rubs her face. "That's what I encourage but it isn't always so easy. I try not to judge and just be here for them. No propositioning, no pimping and no drugs. Those are the rules. And Cindy is brilliant but for some… well, it's a work in progress."

"But what about the firm? Just generally I mean, no details."

She's shaking her head. "Sorry Harry. I'm sure you are the soul of discretion… not. Bang goes my business if anyone knew I'd said something. Same with the girls. They understand pillow talk is only useful as a defence."

"Like estoppel."

"What?"

"Sorry. Legal joke."

"Isn't that an oxymoron?"

"I think I'm the moron. I think I should tell him I want to tell the police that I found him."

"Why?"

"Because… I…"

She smiles, a real smile this time. "You haven't stopped worrying since birth, have you? I bet you came out of the womb checking you had a full set of fingers and toes. Look, he was probably trying to protect you. You and his firm. He really doesn't need any more bad news just now."

"Doesn't he?"

"See what you made me do? One minute I'm telling you I'm as mute as the confessional and the next I'm giving away secrets." She holds my gaze and narrows her eyes. "I'll say this. There are a few rumours swirling just now about your firm having some problems with its image. I expect they'll blow over. Let's face it, most do. By the time you get in on Monday it'll just be some sad death of a middle-aged man in the office, everyone very upset for him and his family, blah blah. If he was indulging in some weird sex game and had a stroke, then it'll probably serve everyone if Crout smooths it over. I imagine he'll be able to sweet talk the cops."

"Will he?"

This time she half-stands and reaches over to kiss me. "My darling Harry, of course he will. He's a bloody mason, isn't he? They all are. If you get to be a partner, I expect you'll be asked to buy an apron as well. And if you want to make it to the top you'll accept, just don't tell Penny."

"God no. She'd have me castrated on the spot."

"What was it you wanted to say about the three of us?" Her face is expressionless although she is concentrating on her drink rather too hard.

"Do you know Gregor Princip? He's my—"

"Greg? Of course. Not exactly my cup of tea."

"He's okay. Bit full of himself I know, and technically my rival for this partnership malarkey but actually he's been a good friend." I see her expression and raise an eyebrow. "Why don't you like him?"

"It's more the people he associates with…" She takes another sip. "Never mind. Just another rumour, I expect. So what about the cocksure Mr Princip?"

"He knows about us. About that night."

"You told him?" She glares at me. "What was it? Some penis competition thing?"

"No. I… I was drunk and… look, I wanted you to know he knows rather than hear it from him."

"Oh yes, well that's just dandy." She squeezes her eyes shut and then smiles, looking tired. "It hardly matters, does it?"

"Doesn't it?"

She frowns at that. "No, it doesn't Harry. You know it was one measly fuck that we should both regret."

"Do you?" I'm not sure why I'm asking. "Sorry, that's a stupid question. It's been a difficult night and…" I look at her hand holding mine.

"No, I don't regret it. I wanted it, we both wanted to – didn't we? And we had the chance, all guilt-free and everything and, well, that's that. Penny had tossed you out and I'd broken with… what was his name? Whatever. That was the moment. It's over. We've ticked that box and moved on. Now it's about time you went home to your very pregnant girlfriend who we both know you love to bits and give her the biggest hug from me. I've a club to run so unless there's anything else…?"

She right. Of course she is. She steps in close to enable her to whisper to me, "Stop feeling guilty. You weren't with her at the time, she wasn't pregnant and she'd dumped you."

"I… it's… I…"

"Go home." She looks very tired and, once again, rather ill in the half-light of the club. She picks up her drink and disappears swiftly to the office she has behind the bar. As she passes Sandra she says something. Sandra looks at me and nods. It's not a look that suggests I've retained the goodwill of earlier when I left her with Gloria.

I think I love both her and Penny. What does that make me?

## *Chapter Four*

Home is... well, not very homely. When we bought it, it needed some TLC – so said the rapacious estate agent. By that he meant it was just about still upright, courtesy of the fact it sat mid-terrace and so was held up by the properties on either side. It looked like it could well have collapsed despite this. But we bought into the dream – the young couple in matching dungarees flicking paint at each other as they turned a damp piece of dereliction into a home of warmth and charm – and we moved into a freezing cold bombsite in January 1985. Since then any spare money has gone on stabilizing the walls, re-roofing and putting in essentials like a flushing toilet. The fact that it took the best part of 15 months was one of many gripes between me and Penny, leaving aside the fact that I managed to so bugger up the door that it remained an open plan loo for 12 of those months. It was only when a passing Jehovah's Witness got a fit of the vapours on peering through a broken pane in the front door to see if anyone was in and caught a flash of Penny's pubes that we had a new one installed.

The terrace is, apart from our house, well maintained – Herne Hill in South London is on its way up, apparently, and I am moderately consoled to see when I pass Grimes the estate agent by the station how much houses such as ours have risen in value. If only they saw inside the place, I often thought, then the market might self-adjust in ways the Bank of England can only dream about.

Tonight it feels like a sanctuary. I know that at some point I will have to tell her about me and Natalie, but it's the height of cruelty to do it while she's so pregnant. And I'm a coward, so there's that as well. Having decided to avoid the subject yet again, I imagine the scene of domesticity that awaits me: Penny on the sofa, trying hard to get comfortable while watching TV; I'll make tea; we'll debrief our respective days; I'll give her a sanitised version of the Barry thing and she'll be horrified and consoling; I'll tell her I've seen Natalie; she'll read between the lines and... my mind goes into meltdown as I practice a few calming techniques before letting myself in.

I can always bribe her. I'll do some more DIY; we'll go on another holiday somewhere warm; I'll agree to get a nanny so Penny can get back to her acting career. The trouble (which I try not to admit to myself) is that I've tried all of these already for other perceived crimes and rarely do they carry much weight. Still, nothing ventured I think as I open the door and call out as cheery an 'halloo' as I can manage.

"'arry? Iz zat you?"

The voice is familiar but I can't initially place it. Then the chiselled face and powerful frame of Magda Kleinkopf appears from the sitting room. Penny and I worked with Magda at Hemingways Hotel in the New Forest, which is where we first met back in 1976. She was on reception and one of the main reasons the hotel functioned at all. Initially we all thought she was terrifying – she was from East Germany, some sort of refugee and reminded me of those female athletes who seemed more muscled than the male competitors. We soon learned that behind the gruff exterior lay someone who was both kind and loyal. She used to flirt with me back then and I had no way of dealing with her other than to run away, but after the hotel was taken over and run by Ravi Ohja, whose family stayed with mine for a while and quickly became firm friends, we had a better, more even friendship. Occasionally when I go home to visit Mum and Dad I meet up with her and exchange news but that's it. To see her in my house is discombobulating.

"Come 'ere and kiss your Magda."

She sounds like a maiden Aunt but the way she pulls me to her and kisses me on the mouth is the antithesis of any of my Aunts. She stops and holds me by my arms, studying me; her smile is – as usual – lacking warmth on first impression. Over her shoulder I see Penny who has just managed to reach the door and is leaning on it while one hand supports her belly. She lets her eyes rise to the ceiling. Having Magda visit is clearly not her idea I'd guess.

Magda puts a finger to the side of my mouth and wipes my cheek. "Vot iz zis? You 'ave already been snoggink? You iz a bad 'arry, vot with your Penny zo full of baby. Who iz zis floozzee?"

I can see a smear of Natalie's coral pink lipstick on the tip of her finger. I can also see Penny begin to smile.

"She's Natalie. Remember her?"

"Owe iz she? You cheat with her?" She grins at me and then turns to Penny and I assume does the same to her. "You promise me sex, 'arry. If you cheat of Penny, then you cheat with me, ja?"

Penny begins the tortuous manoeuvring that takes her back into the sitting room. "Let him try Magda. After I've ripped his balls off you can make them into a novelty desk ornament."

Magda emits a strange noise that may be a laugh or she could be mimicking a donkey being inseminated. She takes my arm and leads me into my own sitting room. Penny is already back on the sofa; Magda makes a thing of pouring me a glass of wine – which I really don't want – and making me sit in the free arm chair while she pulls up a stool.

"Zo? How iz you?"

Penny is trying to attract the cat we acquired a year ago – Pettifore is black and white, tiny, ruthless and inclined to bouts of projectile incontinence, which had I known would happen I would have chosen a different colour for the stair carpet. I can honestly say having fresh cat faeces oozing between your toes first thing in the morning is in my top three worst things to happen immediately on waking, alongside finding there is no milk for my tea and catching my foreskin in my fly, which is a talent I seem to have mastered recently.

"I'm fine. What brings you here?"

Penny struggles to her feet. "While you two catch up, I'm going to make some hot chocolate." She looks at Magda. "It was so nice to see you again, Magda. I'm sure you understand but I'm knackered, so I think I'll go to bed early. You get to have really exciting Friday evenings when you're heavily pregnant. Sitting in front of the TV and not able to drink wine. Unlike Harry." She sticks out a tongue at me to show she doesn't mean it but I'm sure I detect a tiny weeny edge to her voice.

We watch her go. When the door has closed, Magda stands and goes to the recently vacated sofa. "Come. Sit and ve talk. Tell me vhy Penny iz bitch to you."

Pettifore, who has been skulking by the curtains – he has this thing about trying to rip them down – jumps up and snuggles into Magda's lap. She begins stroking him. "Come, zit here and pour me vine."

I join her and top up her glass. "She's hating being pregnant. Well, not pregnant per se, just being huge…" God, I sound like an arse. "She hates being constantly uncomfortable."

"She zay two more months. Poor Pen. And 'arry? Vot about you? You okay? 'appy at vork? Good sex?"

I burst out laughing. "Christ Magda, I'd forgotten how bloody obsessed with shagging you are. Yes, my love life is fine thank you very much."

She shrugs. "Mine iz scheisse." She surprises me by leaning across, putting a hand on the back of my head and kissing me again.

Of course Penny's head appears around the door. "I didn't mean to disturb your… tête-à-tête." There's a laugh in there. I think. "I told Magda she could stay so I've put out some sheets. Perhaps you can show her where before you come to bed."

When she's gone, Magda giggles. "I am zorry, 'arry. You okay?"

"Come on, tell me what brings you to our part of South London. I spoke to Mum on Tuesday and she mentioned you were leaving Hemingways. Do you have a new job?"

"I need your 'elp. As lawyer. I need become British citizen. Quick."

"I don't understand? Is this for some new job?"

"I 'ave no job."

"Okay. Why…?"

"You are lawyer, ja? You 'elp?"

"I'm not sure you need a lawyer. You just go to the Home Office and apply – you've been here for, what, 15 years?"

"Is 14."

"Right. Well, you should be fine. Although that's assuming you're not illegal?"

"I am not criminal." Back comes the old Magda, the one that sounds ferocious.

"No, sure, of course. What I mean is, when you entered the country it was on a visa? You were given asylum or whatever it was, right?"

"Iz complicated. Zat is vhy I need lawyer."

"Hmm. Well, I don't do that sort of law."

"Vot you mean? Zat sort? You not 'elp Magda. Dina zay you 'elp."

"Dina? What's my sister got to do with this?"

Magda looks uncomfortable.

"When did you speak to her about it?" She seems determined to keep schtum. "Magda, why is my sister involved?"

"Iz complicated."

"If Dina is involved, I bet it is."

## *Chapter Five*

Dina is the brightest person I know. After a bit of a false start when she got herself pregnant at 16 – okay, that rather belies the 'bright' assessment – and had a son called George, she took herself to university (Imperial College) and then she joined the Civil Service on a fast-track entry. I thought she worked for the foreign office, but Mum let slip last Christmas that she had moved to MI5, not that Dina confirmed or denied it. She is alternately indispensable and a total pain and sometimes both at the same time. She and Penny get on far too well and have a habit of ganging up on me, although since Penny became pregnant Dina has been largely absent from our lives, instead spending time in the West Country somewhere near Cheltenham.

"Why is Dina involved in your application for British citizenship? And why apply now? You could have applied a long time ago."

"Dina, she zay I must be client before I tell you. Iz privilege."

"Privileged? Like client privilege?"

"Ja, so you not say."

I shake my head. "Magda, I have no idea what Dina has told you but you don't... hang on, what about Noor?"

"Noor Ohja?"

"Yes, the very same. She's just started her articles at a firm that specialises in employment and immigration law. I'm sure she could help much more than me."

"I vant you."

"Yes, well, you've made that very clear, but since I really do not have the expertise and neither do any of my colleagues, unless Noor—"

"But she tell her Father. Ravi. He not find out." She is beginning to get distressed, so I take the hand that isn't stroking Pettifore, and say, "That's the point with privilege. If you become a client of her firm, she cannot tell anyone without your say-so. Even her Father. Look, I can call her on Monday, ask her if she'll take on someone – no names until her boss says yes – and, if you like, I'll sit in on the first meeting and act as a liaison. And meanwhile I'll ask my darling sister what she's up to."

Magda shakes her head hard. "No, you not zay. Not speak Dina. Privilege."

I decide that if I explain she cannot just say 'privilege' and I have to keep things to myself, she will force me to agree to keep my own counsel. Since my curiosity has been piqued, that isn't an option I want to pursue, not that it makes me feel good about myself. "I will help if I can. Where are you staying, by the way? After tonight," I add.

Magda shrugs.

"How long did Penny say you can stay?"

"Maybe a leetle longer?"

"Let's see what the morning brings. Now, I'm starving; have you eaten?"

"I okay."

"I'll check the fridge."

In the kitchen, Magda stands behind me as I consider the options. In the fridge there's a tray with what look like charcoal on it. "Mum's sent another food parcel. These," I push at the lumps, "are Scotch eggs I think."

"Zey look awful."

"Indeed. Mum is to cooking what Mrs Thatcher is to European goodwill; there's nothing she can't ruin while certain what she's doing is good for everyone."

"Your Father iz like Ravi. They love the Thatcher voman."

"So I've heard." I glance at her. "Maybe an omelette?"

"Vhy does your Mother zend food?"

"Believe it or not, Penny seems to love it. We had a macaroni cheese the other week that doubled as a trampoline for Pettifore. Every bite damn nearly dislocated your jaw. And she doesn't send it. She comes to London every week and pops in to check up on Penny. If there's one thing she is more anxious about than the B&B, it's her grandchild's welfare. I thought it would send Penny bonkers, but she loves it. Now she can't get out much it gives her some company."

"Ravi zays the B&B iz doing good."

I can't suppress a sigh as I begin the process of cracking eggs into a bowl. "When I gave them Sven's old house and some cash to start off, I wasn't sure they'd make a go of it, but they've been amazing. Helped, no doubt, by Ravi and Pritti. And thank heavens they hired in staff for the gardens and the catering. What I wasn't expecting was for Dad to become a card-carrying capitalist cheerleader for Maggie or for Mum to take to the marketing so assiduously." I glance at Magda; she's staring at the backs of her hands; she seems oddly vulnerable, which isn't how I would ever have described her in the past. "Maybe you could work there? Now they've converted the garages there must be tons of admin they need doing."

She fails to say anything, and it takes me a moment to realise she is crying. I hate anyone crying because I can't be doing with raw emotion. I should feel sympathy, but it tends to make me annoyed, like it's a trick or a manipulation. "You okay?" Which of course is both a trite and stupid thing to say but is generally the best I can manage in the circumstances.

When she looks up, her eyes are red ringed. "I am in zis much," she indicates the ceiling, "trouble. I don't know vere to go or who to trust. 'arry, can I trust you?"

"I don't know, Magda. It sort of depends on what's happened. Is my sister part of the problem?"

It takes her a moment to nod. Then she shakes her head hard. "No. Zat iz not fair. She has her reasons. She vant to 'elp but iz no zo easy for her."

"Really, can't you tell me what this is all about?"

I give her a few moments that stretch into minutes, but she says no more. In the end we eat in silence and after we've washed up I show her to her room and where the bathroom is. Only then does she hug me again and thank me with the saddest eyes imaginable.

When I creep into our bedroom, I can tell Penny is still awake from her breathing. I change into my pyjamas and slide in next to her, resting a hand on her hip. The room feels huge, like the distance from our bed to the walls has grown. With a grunt she flips onto her back, the pillow that has been supporting her stomach falling to the floor as she does so. "What's going on? She wouldn't tell me."

"Something to do with Dina and a British passport."

"Typical Dina."

"I'll try to call her. How long did you say Magda could stay for?"

"Tonight. She didn't say she needed to stay longer. Why, does she?"

"No idea. Hopefully Dina will explain."

Penny makes a noise like a blocked vacuum cleaner as she reaches down the side of the bed for the pillow and stuffs it into place. "Nats called."

"Yeah?" I feel a cold finger run down my spine.

There's another heaving grunting sound and I'm conscious Penny has rolled over to face me. I can just make out her open eyes in the thin light from the window. "I know about the fuck, okay?"

"She told you?" I know I'm squeaking but I really can't help it.

"I knew as soon as it happened. She called to apologise. She said you were both drunk and you slept together. You both regretted it and it never happened again."

Three out of four isn't bad. "You never said."

"And neither did you. Which I took to mean what Nats said was right. It's why I called you and told you to come back."

"Really?"

A hand sneaks across the gap between us and pulls me to her. "I love you and realised I'd made a stupid mistake. Okay, it would be nice to think you had some spine to 'fess up, but it was more my fault than yours. And I realised something else then. I realised that if I didn't act fast she might finally take you from me and, love her to bits as I do, I am not giving you up for her to get you, okay?" A hand moves down and slips inside my pyjamas, squeezing my nob. "I often wondered if you'd say. In a way it was good you didn't. It showed you cared about me enough not to want to hurt us." The hand disappears, leaving a pole and no handler. "I did wonder why now but she told me about you and Greg. Harry, I... are you getting fed up with me? Christ, I'm fed up with me. I lay in the bath today and you know what I thought about? A cottage loaf. That's what I look like. A fucking great dough ball."

I roll over and wrap an arm around her waist rubbing her stomach. "Let's make love."

She sighs. "We've tried and it doesn't work, does it?"

"But I want to. You are the sexiest thing and—"

She flips over. "No I'm not. I know I'm not. I'm a fucking whale. It just won't work. At best you'll come all over the back of my legs and at worst I'll fall out of bed and my waters will go two months early."

"Is that such bad news?"

She laughs. "Maybe not."

Without asking I slip my hand between her legs. She shifts to accommodate my clear intentions. She's soon breathing heavily and a moistened palm reappears inside my pyjamas. After we've both come and I'm cleaning up she grunts, "We are now officially a pair of sad wankers," then she turns onto her side and falls asleep.

True, but I'll take that for now.

# Saturday, 5th September 1987

## *Chapter Six*

The next day Magda leaves after one cup of coffee, promising to be out of our hair by Monday. She says she has an old friend who lives somewhere near Earl's Court who might put her up while she gets herself sorted. When we're alone, Penny studies my face while I potter around making toast and more coffee. When I finally sit down, she says, "You will say, won't you?"

"Say what?"

"If you get fed up with me. I know I've not been great in the rumpty-tumpty department."

"Rumpty-tumpty? You need to get away from the TV and soon or you'll turn into my Mother. On second thoughts, I never said that."

"But you would, wouldn't you? Say it, I mean."

Her face is so serious it's completely unnatural. It's only used to expressing delight, anger and frustration so to morph into an adult must hurt.

"I'm trying to get a partnership. If you think I've got the energy for an affair—"

"I knew it."

"What? Penny, you're being—"

"Joke. Come over here and kiss me."

I do as I'm told. She takes a hand and places it on her stomach so I can feel the movement that is followed by the most almighty thump and an expression like a party popper has just gone off in her undercarriage.

"Was that Wigglet kicking?"

She manages a nod.

"Geez. I think that one was rifled into the top corner."

"I think you meant that she just completed a rather fine jeté."

"I never mentioned Wigglet's sex."

"But you're thinking boy, aren't you?"

"No. Yes. Maybe. It doesn't matter. He or she will have to play football and cricket. I'm not choosy."

She lets go of my hand and I sit opposite her. "Natalie said you had some problem at work? Was that about Greg knowing and—?"

"No, no it wasn't that. But I was worried. And I should have said before."

"Hey Buster, if you're going to practice your scales on my clit as a way to say sorry, well, you just keep feeling guilty. Believe me that's a damn sight more my cup of tea than promising to redecorate the hallway. And let's face it, soon enough you'll have a job finding it, so we might as well make hay."

"It was good, wasn't it?"

"Seven out of 10. You need practise. How did Natalie look by the way?"

"The usual. Bony. Chiselled. Lacking her previously delightful curves…"

"Careful, you're dribbling. Do you think she looks ill?"

"Maybe. It's probably all the exercise. She's something of a health Nazi these days."

"I'm going to have a go at her."

"Rather you than me."

"You are such a wimp. Actually on the subject of exercise, I had a surprising call yesterday. You remember Ida?"

"Ida…? Oh, Mrs Soderberg. Did I know she was called Ida? Confidante to Lady Izzy Grimsdale. What about her?"

"She's left Isabella's employ, oh, ages ago. These days she runs a video production company. She rang to say she was talking to some old contacts, one being Maggie and—"

"The lesbian?"

"No, she was never a lesbian. What's your problem with the Sapphic sisterhood anyway?"

"Nothing. My memories of her involve you nearly going to prison for murder or have you forgotten?"

"Tish and tosh. That was never going to happen. She's a class act at directing, whatever else you might think about her. It seems she'd come across some rushes I did for a fitness video Maggie was promoting back then and wondered if I'd be interested in reprising my role. When I told her I thought performing whales might be a better bet she got really excited. She thinks there's a big market for new Mums both pre- and postpartum and what better than to make the videos with a real live new Mum-to-be as the star. I'm going to see her next week."

"Can I watch?"

"No, you sordid little man, you can't."

"But please, pretty please." I kneel on the floor in front of her and nestle my face into her breasts while she giggles and tugs at my hair to try to get me away. "Just the thought of these being released into the wild and bouncing free makes me want to drag you back for a second go at that piano concerto."

"We need to do some cleaning and shopping."

I rock back on my heels. "You are sooo dull. What say we clean the bath together?"

"You're obsessed."

"Desperate." I see her expression change. "I didn't mean—"

"I get it but I can't, okay?" She twists and stands, letting out a weary sigh. Fuck, why am I such a twit?

While she's digging out a bucket and floor cleaner she asks, "What else went wrong then?"

As I mop the kitchen floor and she cleans the work tops and cupboards, I tell her all about Barry and Sebastian Crout and my not telling the police that I was there. She listens carefully. "Do you think this will this scupper your chance at partnership?"

My mind is on the police issue, so I speak without engaging my brain. I don't intend to sound petulant but I do. "How do I know? That's not the point, though, is it? I should have admitted I'd found him and..."

That's when Penny stands and tells me to fuck off. "I don't care about the partnership but you do. Don't make this about me."

I watch her go. I should follow her, mollify her but I've just realised that when I turned round and saw Crout last night he was standing on the wrong side of the door if he had only just come in as he said he had. I try to remember what he actually said but I can't, although I'm sure it was some expression of surprise. If he was shocked by what he saw – and his words certainly suggested that – why would he walk into the room behind me and move so the door itself was between him and the corridor? He wouldn't, not unless he was already standing behind the door when I came in and found Barry. No, that couldn't be right.

I don't even notice Penny return and stand in front of me until she says, "Harry, are you listening to me give you a bollocking because I don't like wasting my energy if you're just going to blank me?"

"Sorry, I was thinking about Crout and what he said."

"God, you are so irritating. All I was trying to say was I expect Mr Crout was trying to help you. I mean, why wouldn't he?"

Why indeed?

"There's nothing to stop you telling them, is there? You said he just asked you to tell him first."

"I think that's a recipe for disaster, frankly. They'd probably still give me a hard time for not saying anything up front and Mr Crout would definitely take a dim view, having asked me to keep out of it. It hardly looks like I trust him if I don't do what he asks." I think about sharing what Natalie said concerning the rumours but decide against it.

"Listen to me, Harry. I know you pretend this partnership doesn't matter and you'll be fine whichever way it goes but no one puts themselves through the pain and uncertainty that you, Greg and Crispin are going through right now without wanting to win. If you did, you would be some kind of legal masochist. I want you to win, because I know deep down you want to win. But if you don't you're still my hero."

"Hero?"

"Oh, stop fishing for compliments. Sure there's the money and the kudos but mostly it's because I really don't need Harry Spittle after he's been confirmed in his opinion that, all along, he's been fooling everyone and now he's been found out."

"I'm not that pathetic. Am I?"

"Oh sure, you are this decade's Mr Self-confident. Everyone knows Greg would kill to be a partner and Crispin would run naked around Whitehall singing one of the Twats greatest hits if it helped him win. You, though? You pretend to be above such patent ambition when it's obviously eating away at you."

"No, you're wrong. It's not like that at all."

"Let's go and get some fresh air and you can buy me lunch."

"Okay, then I think I'll make a start on painting the hallway."

As she waddles to the door to get a coat, she says, "Then you are definitely having an affair."

# Monday, 7th September 1987

## *Chapter Seven*

As I'm leaving Penny reminds me we have a NCT antenatal class in the evening. "Don't you dare be late. There's no way I can drive and if you think I'm walking all the way to Crystal Palace like this you can dream on, sonny. And no, I'm not interested in trying to cope with the bus."

"A cab?" I volunteer as she turns away. Her dismissive wave of the hand tells me this isn't about transport but commitment – specifically my commitment.

In truth I'm dreading going into work given what happened on Friday, but in the initial skirmishes that comprise a standard Monday morning there are no suggestions that anything untoward has happened. Greg is already on his way out to a meeting as I emerge from the lift in my tracksuit, having decided to start cycling again. He says, "New client. Busy, busy, busy. I saw Natalie. She is something, isn't she and she still carries a candle for you, you know?"

He swans off and I watch him go. When he's gone, I turn for the loos. One of the consequences of my Mother's method of child rearing is a regularity that is both a comfort and an inconvenience, and which if I'm honest has become more predictable as I've aged. It's almost as if entering the office flicks a switch and if I've not 'been' inside the first 20 minutes I'm in a fair few problems, most of which comprise an internal dialogue of the 'I've not been yet, am I constipated? Why am I constipated? Have I got a blockage? What sort of blockage have I got? Oh my God, I must have cancer' type.

I've just settled to do this most important first task, trying to remember exactly what's the next post-poo priority, when the door to the gents slams open and a voice carries to me. "Morning comrade. Thought I'd find you in here."

Crispin Muddle. He's the sort of person who if he was in a group of two people you'd instantly forget him. The only feature that even begins to stand out is his hair, which is a bit of a throwback to university days in that it drapes over his collar, giving him a sort of forlorn academic appearance, like someone is trying to pretend he is still a student when all the other evidence says he's well past it. "You hear about Barry?" He pauses, by the sound of it wrestling with his fly. I'm sure he's going to say he's heard I was there and the police want to see me, but he carries on, "Poor old sod. Died at his desk. Heart they think but the drink didn't help."

"Drink?" I hate talking while contemplating my future and evacuating my bowels, but this conversation is unusually relevant.

"Alchie. Full-blown breakdown, AA sessions and everything. Seems the cleaners found him with an empty bottle of vodka in his wastepaper basket. Still, at least we'll not have to put up with his niggling about our draft letters any more, right? You going to this weekend thing?" The sound of running water lets me know he's washing his hands.

I'm still trying to process what he's said about the cleaners and the drink when I realise he's standing right next to the door of my cubicle. "You have said you'll go, haven't you? It's crucial."

It takes me a moment to realise his reference to me 'going' isn't an allusion to what is about to transpire but the upcoming away weekend. "Yes, yes of course. Can you leave me in peace?"

"I bet that White Russian pillock has been spreading his usual bollocks. We both need to be there, maintain a united front or he'll shaft us both."

"Can we talk about this later, Crispin? I am a little busy in here." At which point the sound effects tell him of the obvious truth of that statement and, in the next moment the door to the gents bangs again.

He's waiting outside. That man is really weird at times. "I didn't mean to snap. I had a bit of a frantic weekend. You know, what with Penny so close to popping, so I haven't really got my work brain switched on yet."

"God, how is she? She'll be a brilliant Mother, you know? Just wonderful. Such an empath. Spiritual."

Penny and I decided ages ago that Crispin secretly fancied her. I'm not sure he does but he often says these things, just like the load of old bollocks he usually spouts.

"I'll get on. Catch you later."

Fortunately that seems to be the extent of our conversation; I leave him fantasising about Penny as I head for Chloe's desk to check that I have in fact accepted the invitation to the partners' and candidates' away weekend; it's just the sort of thing that between us we're likely to forget.

As I exit her room, Crispin catches me up. "You know I'm on holiday shortly? Could I leave something with you? It's a job for Caldera Properties. A harbourside development in Barrington on the Sussex coast."

"Probably, but it depends how much of a mess you've left it. When are you off?"

"Ha bloody ha. You'll be a name on the file only, nothing that actually needs to be done. I'm off after the weekend of the conference, which is a bugger. We'll have to leave on Monday and that didn't go down well with the Mater." Crispin still lives with his widowed Mother, the Hon Daphne Muddle, and each year they holiday together once in Capri and once in St Anton. I've not met her, but it always sounds like she still treats him as if he was seven. Mind you, when he talks about her he tends to sound like he's still seven.

"How was your holiday? I don't think we've spoken properly since you got back."

"Holiday? Oh, it was lovely. Relaxing, you know? Penny didn't want to do much, so we lounged about, read, ate too much. The usual."

"Any photos?"

The creep. A couple of years ago I found him rifling through a packet of holiday snaps that mostly comprised Penny in various topless poses – not that I only take pictures of her boobs you understand – after a holiday that comprised a lot of sangria, sand and shagging. Happy days. Oh nostalgia, be my sword.

"I suppose it'll be kids' clubs and all that awful malarkey in the near future. Poor you."

"Not necessarily."

He's not going to miss the opportunity for some considered schadenfreude. "Kids' clubs, water parks, Pontins – that sort of thing. God forbid one day it'll be Disney in Florida. Makes a week with Mater and her whist-playing geriatric pals feel positively exciting. So, any pics?"

"I…" It's then I remember I still have Barry's packet and mine is… I don't know where mine is but I let go a silent prayer it's not in Barry's room but languishing in Boots. "Damn, I need to pick them up. Thanks for reminding me. Maybe we can grab a coffee and I'll show you the highlights?"

I leave him staring into space. Yep, he definitely has a thing for my pregnant girlfriend.

What am I going to do about Barry's bloody photos? Still, first things first – I'll never concentrate until I make sure I have mine and Barry didn't somehow manage to pick them up on Friday. I'll have to pretend I've lost the receipt or something.

I give a second prayer – Penny will have something to say about this religious conversion if I tell her – that the same fearsome assistant isn't doing a shift when I get there; for once the stars align. The assistant is the younger and prettier one who took over, the one joking with Greg. Now she seems so young, about 12, very smiley and helpful. She checks my name, jokes that people are always losing the receipt, makes me swallow hard when she adds that they often give the wrong packets, looks anxious like she's said the wrong thing and apologies profusely although it's not clear why and eventually she pushes my packet at me before turning to the till. It's only then I realise I have to pay again, because I'm not seeking to swap mine for Barry's and I don't have any money; I left it in the office. We stare at each other, both unsure what to do when a familiar voice says, "Embarrassed again, eh?"

It's bloody Greg with his wallet already out and open. "What does this crook owe you? He's always trying it on Tina."

"It's £2.98 Mr Princip."

I'm surprised that they know each other by name. As we turn to go, he says to her, "See you on Sunday?" She nods. Then to me he adds, "You must have taken a lot of pictures for one week's holiday. I rarely fill a whole film but then I don't have a gravid girlfriend. A lot of women wouldn't want to be caught on camera at their most fecund, so I congratulate you and Penny on refusing to bow to convention." He waves at the assistant. "She's lovely, but her family... Jesus." He shakes his head without offering any more. "Don't worry about the money. I'm sure they'll be a time when I owe you and we can call it quits. It's always good to be a little in credit, don't you think?" He says this in such an oddly knowing way I briefly wonder what else he has on me. I also remember with a jolt that he was there on Friday. What if he knows I was in Barry's room? Oh shit.

Outside we pause as he looks towards St Paul's Cathedral, shading his eyes against a low sun.

"I thought you were off to see a new client?" I say.

"I am. I was following you. You see, it's an estate agency that could go far. If they decide to use us I'd like you to meet them. Frank suggested I involve you or Crispin and, well, I'm not sure his social skills are quite what this one needs. Your everyman approach should be perfect. So can I mention your name?"

After I nod, he strolls away. He's such a difficult one to read. One minute I'm on edge he's going to drop me in something; the next he's offering me a new client. More credit in the bank, I suppose. I only realise I'm still watching him when he turns and comes back. He says, "Oh, Frank asked if you could pop in when you're back. Something about talking to the police?"

Somehow I maintain an upright posture until he disappears and then slump against the glass of Boots' frontage. An old lady offers me a Fisherman's Friend and tuts when I wave her away without a word of thanks. I can feel my Mother's disapproval in the way she tugs her coat closed, but I can't find even a mumbled apology. I'm sunk; I've been sussed.

Frank Pomeroy is the head of the Property Department. He's in his early fifties, overweight, mostly cheerful, congenitally work-shy and good to work for because he's eternally grateful someone else is shouldering the burden of doing the work while he fends off his wife who wants to know where he is and why he hasn't left for home yet. There are stories that partners will be getting one of the new mobile phones that everyone is talking about, which horrifies Frank. Once he's connected his standard excuse – 'I couldn't find a phone to let you know where I was' – will need to be updated. I've no doubt he'll soon have one ready to launch. Time spent with Frank is usually uplifting except most visits to his room end with you having acquired at least one and possibly more new jobs to do.

"Harry, sit, sit. How are you? Not too much pressure I hope? Penny okay? Not popped yet? No, you'd have mentioned it, wouldn't you? Or Chloe would. I think she's more excited than anyone. Did you know there's a sweepstake on names?" While Frank may try to avoid a mobile phone, he has embraced the conference call with aplomb. Sadly, he hasn't mastered the fact that it cuts out if either party to the call makes a noise while the other is speaking so most of his conversations tend to involve a lot of repetition. "Tea?" He presses a short dial button to be connected to his secretary. "Charity? Can we… sorry? Did you…? No, I…?"

"It's okay Frank. I—"

He waves me quiet in a rather irritated way and barks, "Tea. Two. Now. Ple… Oh for goodness sake." He jabs the off button. "I'm never going to get the hang of this bloody thing. I thought the fax was bad enough. Did you hear what happened on Friday?"

"About Barry?"

"Barry? Oh God, yes. That was awful. How could I forget…? Sorry, look, before I forget, not Barry but… I had a call about this shop in Chelmsford we bought for Arctic Investments. When I say we... well, I was the partner but I never... thing is, it was my ultimate responsibility, wasn't it? As partner. I should have taken more of an interest and... Barry, bloody hell. You heard, did you? At his desk too. Arctic Investments. Let's finish that first, shall we?"

"Please."

He focuses on me at last, rather surprised or so it seems to realise I'm sitting there listening. "Right. Turns out there's some right of way issue, or rather a lack of. They started quoting these faxes at me that I'm meant to have written or approved or something - not that that's likely, is it? Ha! Long story short, Charity dug out the old file and bugger me if they haven't all faded to a blank sheet. I have no clue what I said. Or anyone said, come to that. I pride myself on keeping up to date with the latest kit and then I'm made to look like a total tit because I, we – whoever – failed to copy the faxes. And I..." He stops abruptly. "Damn, the police." He pushes a file at me bulging with correspondence. "Any chance you could have a look and see if you can work out what's going on? Charity's typing a note of their Finance Director's call. He's a bit... well, you can imagine. Let me know how you get on, okay?"

I nod and pull the file to my side of the table; he audibly sighs, the burden having been passed on at least for now.

"Maybe you could close the door?"

Oh shit. There's an odd code about doors in our firm. The encouraged policy is an open door; that way everyone can feel they can raise their concerns with management, aka the partners. But everyone knows some partners can't stand to be disturbed so whether the door is open or not, you're not meant to go in uninvited. Then there are those who sign up to the policy but if you go in and the door closes, everyone assumes you are getting a right royal bollocking. The staff prefer the partners who keep their doors closed; that way, once inside no one knows why.

"So you heard about Barry? Awful. Tragic but no surprise given his lifestyle and... well," he looks around as if we are being spied on, "the recent," he lowers his voice to a whisper, "strategy document." He stares at me, almost begging me to nod, to show I know what on Earth he's on about even though I have no clue. I nod.

"Good, good. Can't be too sure who knows. Crout mentioned it... well, sort of implied really. Anyway, a death in situ requires an inquiry, you know, sort of preparatory to an inquest and Crout says the police will want to talk to people who were here on Friday night. Not sure why. Ronnie says you popped back?"

"I needed a file."

"You shouldn't have to work your weekend, Harry. You need to recharge the batteries. What does Penny say? Doreen's dead against me… you know. So, you'll speak to the police?"

"Of course. Will they call me or should I call them?"

"I… I suppose Gladys will organise it." Gladys is the SPs spectral secretary. "Just routine. That's what they always say, isn't it?"

"Was it his heart?"

"Not sure. I heard that's a possibility. It's Crout. He called them in. Can't afford any more…" Frank stops, almost as if he's surprised at himself. He shakes his head and manages a smile. "Okay then. Probably best not say anything, you know, any more than you have to? Leave it to the weekend, yes?"

"Weekend?"

"The wretched conference. Doreen is seething. Her Mother had 'plans' apparently. Crout will say something I expect, tell us what's party line is and so on and so forth."

Frank rocks back in his seat. It's a disconcertingly fast action and I often wonder if he's ever thrown himself over backwards that way. But it does signify that he's finished. I'm about to pick up the file and go when the overhead light, which is always on despite it not yet being 10 o'clock and the sun is out, suddenly goes out. Then the fire alarms go off.

"Oh, bloody hell. Those sodding kettles again."

As we leave his room, I'm sure I'm receiving more than my share of the curious looks from the other associates, all wondering what I've done. Sod it, let them speculate. I probably look as guilty as all hell. I fall in with Erica and Jonjo. Erica says, "Jonjo reckons this is a kettle break but won't explain."

"The secretaries can't be arsed to go to the seventh-floor kitchen to make an extra cup of tea, so some bring in kettles to make a brew at their desks. The only problem is this building and specifically its power supply is so much a heap of alligator's doodahs that if the load put on it is increased by an infinitesimally small amount, the trip switches go and all the power cuts out. The fire alarms are set so that a total loss of power assumes it must be caused by a fire and so they go off – they are on an emergency supply – and we all have to leave the building and congregate on the netball court. Six months ago management sent round an edict – no more bloody kettles – which the secretaries ignored. Or rather they have a rota of who can use theirs and when. Someone has broken ranks and they'll be blood to pay. I imagine one of the cabal is currently walking the floors and testing the kettles to find out which one is hot when it shouldn't be."

"Shouldn't they clear out, just in case it's a real fire?"

"In theory yes, but abiding by the code of secretarial practice is far more important that an unfortunate death in an inferno, so an expendable junior will have been delegated the task. Expect to hear about some poor soul who's been ostracised or had their typewriter ribbon cut or something equally traumatic."

Erica's face begins to show her annoyance. "Management ought…" She is silenced by a hand on her arm from Jonjo.

"You're making an understandable but erroneous assumption, dear Erica."

"How?"

"By assuming 'management' and the cabal to which Harry alludes are distinct bodies."

"Well, if I find out who they've picked on, I'll… I'll…"

"Show moral support? Get up a petition? Organise a food parcel pushed out the back of a Hercules? By all means, but don't expect to get any work done either on time or to an acceptable standard."

"That's outrageous. I'll complain. I'll…" She stops herself. "They'd do the same to the partner's work?"

"Possibly. Some partners would be exempt but enough are cowards."

"Well, it stinks."

I look at Jonjo, who shrugs. "She'll learn."

"I hope not. Most of us have sold out."

She frowns at me. "Surely Chloe's not like that?"

"Chloe? She'd have a breakdown rather than go against the Coven. Anyway, I'm not about to interfere with the secretaries, so Chloe needn't worry. Bloody nest of vipers that lot, cross them at your peril."

We have reached the fire door on the ground floor. I take over from the last person to leave and hold it for Erica before relinquishing it to an aged Legal Executive called Norman. We cross the windswept podium, weaving through clusters of lawyers and support staff from other departments – no one speaks to the other groups, though a few nods are exchanged. We might be one Firm, but each department is a village and the other 'villages' are our sworn enemies and arch rivals. When we reach the netball court we stop next to other Property lawyers and staff. Jonjo rubs his hands. "Frank giving you the heads up on the partnership race?"

"Hardly. I don't even know if they've put me into the starter gate."

Erica looks confused. "Makes you sound like a horse."

"Exactly. All possible partnership candidates are thought of as thoroughbreds so a horse racing analogy fits well. Those put forward are said to be in the paddock."

"Really?"

"We are expected to take the jumps, eventually we might enter the final furlong, winning by a short head."

"Well, if you win I hope you sort out this nonsense with the secretaries."

Jonjo laughs. "No chance."

"Thanks for that vote of confidence, but he's right. I'll not be poacher-turned-gatekeeper. The power balance at Newe Waters has taken years to settle and everyone is happy with it. It means that everyone is invested in the success of the business. A partnership is an odd commercial model with the 'management' and ownership residing in a flat structure. Anyone below partnership level can feel like they have no power at all. Therefore allowing the secretaries to feel in control suits everyone. After all, everything we do is based on words and those words need to be typed. That gives them power, which means the likes of you and me, associate lawyers and trainees, are the lowest form of pond life. Welcome to our world."

Erica is clearly taking in the realpolitik of law firms, outfits in the City of London generally if truth be told. I take a couple of steps away, aiming to catch a quick word with another colleague when I catch sight of Gloria standing under the hoop talking to two men and scanning the crowd until she sees me and points. The men stare and nod. It's then I recognise one. The police. I smile and the man on the left smiles back and holds out a hand as he walks towards me.

"Harry. Long-time no see."

"Jan! Ditto. Still one of the boys in blue?"

"Indeed. How's...?" He looks away.

"Dina is fine. And single." Do I detect a brief look of hope? Jan Kruis is a large ruddy-faced man, with a thick neck and a thicker South African accent. He and my little sister had the steamiest of affairs five or so years ago. At one point it looked like they might become a real item, but she thought he broke her trust and then he had to go back to South Africa to see his Father and that was the last I heard of him.

"Do you have a moment for a quick word about Friday's events? You know that Mr Tritewell passed away at his desk?"

"Yes, terrible business." I managed to keep the urge to swallow my head under control and add, "Frank, Frank Pomeroy, he's my boss. He said you… the police, not you per se…" Another swallow and another breath. Hold it together, Harry. "He said you might want a word because I was in the office latish on Friday. I'm guessing that's when it happened?"

"Yes. This isn't a formal investigation, by the way."

"Was it a heart attack? That's what I heard."

"There is a post mortem that will establish the cause and approximate time of death."

"Frank said Mr Crout called you in. Is there…" My throat dries up but I ride the feeling of sandpaper in the oesophagus, "…is there a reason?"

"He felt it was important that things were done correctly. And, well, the thing is Harry, there are some anomalies."

Shit. Fuck. "Amon… anon… anomalies?"

"It looks likely that the body had been moved post-mortem. We'll know more when the forensic team have finished their investigation. It's also not yet been established who found the body."

"Oh?"

"Yes. The night porter said he was called, or rather a message was left, asking him to check on Mr Tritewell. He found him and called the ambulance. That's why we're tracking down anyone who may have been in the office and left a message when the porter was away from his desk. He told us you left when he was on his rounds?"

I manage to stand upright as I confirm it wasn't me who called. Right now, I could do with about a dozen Fisherman's Friends to keep me from fainting.

"And did you see anyone else when you were in the office?"

## *Chapter Eight*

I'm on the platform at Blackfriars waiting on my train when I remember the antenatal class. On the positive side I'm not yet late; against that I'm on the wrong platform at the wrong station and unless I'm incredibly lucky with the timing of the buses I will be hung, drawn and quartered. I'm trying to do a calculation when Frank appears, sees me, clearly considers pretending he hasn't, decides he can't and walks over, all smiles. Frank, being a partner, is heading for the next station after mine – leafy West Dulwich where the posh and pretentious live; I've heard that Maggie and Dennis have bought some new mock Georgian pile near the park, which is enough to make me consider breaking one of London's inviolate rules – if you start living south of the river you can never move north, and vice versa.

"Harry, I'm glad I caught you. There's a client I need some help with. I was going to mention it earlier, but, well, what with everything that's been going on it must have slipped my mind."

Does he emphasise the 'everything'? Is his look what you might call a gimlet eye? Am I utterly paranoid?

"He's American and he's planning on launching a residential mortgage business. Have you heard about these things? They depend on something called 'securitisation.' Sounds a bit fancy-pants to me and it'll probably never take off."

"Isn't that more Crispin's area? Finance?"

"He asked about you. Said he'd heard good things. And you'll need to work with a Finance partner, which will be good exposure for the final straight while you're all jockeying for position. I said you'd call him tomorrow." More horse analogies. Frank begins to turn away and then stops. "Chuck. He's called Chuck. I didn't think anyone was really called that. Must be an American thing." He leaves me, shaking his head at such an absurdity.

The train is late, which gives me time to find a phone box and ring home to tell Penny to get a cab. Magda is there and tells me she already has. Bugger.

When the train eventually arrives, I'm in so much of a daze that I jump into the smoking carriage. It's always awful but today I'm really offended; why do they allow these places to exist? And then I feel guilty that I'm sublimating my frustrations onto these misbegotten excuses for humans. The smoking carriage is the travel equivalent of the Faustian Pact: you're guaranteed both a seat and cancer. It's too late to get off, and of course being a commuter cattle wagon this train doesn't have a connecting door, unlike the InterCity 125s. I spend the few minutes to the next station leaning as far out of the open window as I dare without risking a mobile nose-job, garnering glares from the four hapless, addicted inmates who huddle in each of the far corners, like everyone else is a pariah except them.

The bus is little better and once again I'm stuck with the smokers upstairs at the back. Consequently, when I reach the concrete box that is home to Priscilla, our NCT midwife, I stink like I'm a 40-a-day chain smoker. The door is opened by Priscilla's husband, whose name I have still to learn and/or remember. He has eyebrows that are quite magnificent – things of feral beauty that always make me speculate on whether he has to comb and trim them. Tonight, I'm straight into trouble – his glare could be the result of the stench from my clothes or the fact that once again I've forgotten to take off my shoes before I cross the threshold. As I stand on the coir mat, my way barred until I'm de-shod, I realise I'm beyond caring.

NCT antenatal classes are evidence, if any were needed, of the burgeoning of the yuppie generation: sharp suits and shoulder pads; Filofaxes in hands that are creamed and manicured (both men and women); and conversations dominated by salary increases (in percentages), house price increases (ditto) and bragging about some delicate burgundy or original camembert that only the cognoscenti know about. Penny, lumpen, dressed in a velour tracksuit and with her hair interfering with radio signals, is something of a treasured anomaly – an out of work actress with no aspirations to be rich, despite being shacked up with a despised lawyer. Why she feels comfortable among this lot beats me.

"Harold!" Priscilla is jolly with short hair harbouring an asymmetric green stripe and multi-coloured framed spectacles that are so huge they might better be described as a facial shopfront. She bobs cork-like across the room and pulls me by the hand towards Penny who looks like she is being eaten by a tangerine beanbag and is not at all happy. "Busy, busy! Keeping the wheels of commerce turning I suppose? Penny is looking wonderful, isn't she everyone?"

The other participants are a mixed bunch. At one end of the spectrum are the over-exuberant socialists Paul and Clarissa – both teachers. Then there are Donald and Pet, who want to be as keen as Paul and Clarrie but somehow seemed weighted down by other's expectations and rarely speak. They are, respectively, a social worker and importer of Belgium chinaware. After them come Mark and Maddie – an upmarket car salesman and an estate agent who like to project a sort of 'loads-of-money' cynicism but are just too nice to either manage it or, I guess, be any good at their jobs. And then there are the true cynics, Mo and Chrissie – a bond dealer and handmade lingerie maker – who look horrified at each new agey exercise but are actually willing participants in ways the inhibited Don and Pet would like to be but can't quite manage.

I shrug off my jacket, lie it over the arm of the sofa and sink down next to my partner. We are all 'partners' here; only Mark and Maddie are married. "For Harold's benefit, we are explaining to the group how we want the big day to go: our hopes and our fears and our plans. And while we hear from each other, your supporter is giving a calming massage to their lover. I'm sure you know what Penny likes Harold, so carry on."

I don't, in truth, beyond playing itsy-bitsy spider with her vagina. She is either so ticklish that simply getting close to the wrong part can trigger at best giggles and at worst a punch to the head, or so indifferent that she usually tells me not to bother. I think back to Friday and bringing her to several orgasms and wonder what she'd do if I tried for a repeat. The fact I don't know if she'd go for it or split my lip says a lot about our relationship. All I can be sure is the reciprocal handjob is out of the question.

Maddie has just finished explaining about a cassette of music they have put together to keep her calm and 'in the moment' and 'centred' when Priscilla's husband appears with a tray of cups. He hands them round. When he gets to us, he gives Penny some camomile and me the same. "You weren't here so I copied what she wanted."

I take it. I hate it. It looks like urine and smells like, well, pretty much the same. There's not much space to put it down so I balance it on my stomach, grateful there's an excuse not to attempt any massage while I have my drink.

"Why don't you tell us your plans, Don? Pet?"

These two are probably the youngest here. They glow with joy; everything is wonderful. They hold hands, stroke each other and finish the other's sentences. They are utterly irritating.

Pet starts. "Whatever else happens we are having our blessing at home and Priscilla will be there seeing us through." The two women beam at each other. "We've hired a birthing pool that will be in the centre of the sitting room. Our Feng Shui sensei has advised on the location and orientation and the correct correlation of lighting and scents – the candles are a mix of lavender, cardamom and baby breath. We are aiming for an ambience of Jupiter in Mars, dominated by Venus rising. The day before a seven monk Buddhist chant, which we have specially commissioned, will be performed around the pool, while Don and I release the baby's aura after which we will rebirth each other, under the tutelage of Hom, the pre-futurologist…"

In comes Don. His eyes are sparkling, and he is patently so excited I think he might burst. "On the day we will have our intimates around for a special…" I think he says 'vegan homunculus' but I could be wrong, "and fast, ending with mantra exchanges. Everyone is welcome, and we hope as many as you as possible will be in the pool with us to offer a hand as baby emerges through the divine waters. Then there will be singing and dancing and celebration."

Don looks at Pet and they each slump against the beanbag, exhausted. I'm bemused as I'd guess are most of the others judging from their expressions. Priscilla, however, can barely contain her excitement. She looks at each of us as if willing us to applaud or something. "Is anyone else aiming for something similar? It is such a wonderful plan. Wonderful."

Mo snaps his red braces against his shirt. "Can I ask a couple of questions?"

"Of course Mo," Pet's gaze stays on Don, her face radiant.

"Great. What is rebirthing?"

Both of them eye Mo with the zealotry of evangelical Baptists. "It's so exciting. We take each other back to our birth moment and re-experience the pain of parturition and the joy of life. By confronting the good and moving beyond any legacy of distress we are in the best place to welcome our child into the world. As such, we will be able to offer the most soothing start to a long and happy life."

"Great. Yep, that'll be just dandy. And how do you release the baby's aura while the monks are doing their chant thing?"

Hands held, they turn to each other and say, as one, "We will copulate and masturbate each other." Pet goes on, a serious expression on her face. "Semen is a powerful trigger to enable the baby to be born naturally and in the full loving presence of the Father. We try to make love two or three times a day as we approach the due date."

I don't think I'm the only one to be gobsmacked, but I am the only one to absently take a mouthful of pisswater as I let this news sink in. As the still hot and disgusting beverage scalds my tongue I cough, splutter and choke, spraying the couple next to us.

Chrissy looks at Mo. I know exactly what she's thinking. She sees me looking and turns to Don. "Not wishing to pry but are you two having much sex these days? I mean, we're finding it a bit awkward what with the imminent birth and whatnot."

Don looks at Pet. "We've never stopped our exchanges, however hard it is."

Pet nods and giggles. "And sometimes it is very hard."

She is the last person to indulge in a smutty double entendre, so I really think she just means difficult but when I look at Don – who's definitely changed colour – I wonder.

Priscilla turns to us and changes the subject. "Penny? Harold? And you? Your plans?"

Penny shifts on the beanbag and says, "I want as little pain as possible and I'll take whatever intervention is going to keep me from screaming. I want Harry to be there so he can share my agony in a very real way and if he doesn't show up or he's late he'll not be capable of being the Father of my second child. Or anyone else's." She looks at me and winks. I love my girlfriend. The others appear less than impressed, save for Chrissie who discretely and silently claps her hands so only we can see.

Priscilla has lost something of her joie de vivre. "I do hope you experience the natural splendour of childbirth, Penny. Interventions can be so depersonalising and many a Mother has regretted a hasty decision. What do others think about pain relief, C-sections, epidurals, et cetera?"

I force myself to zone out; this will get way too medical for me and the risk of my fainting will be increased exponentially. My mind wanders to Dina and Magda, wondering how long Magda will be with us. I said I'd call Dina about this citizenship thing but it's slipped my mind.

Thinking of Dina makes me think about Jan Kruis. Should I tell her about him? They seemed to be good for each other; a more suitable match than her and Jim – George's Father – ever were. And what the hell is going on with Barry's corpse? I don't get why Crout asked for an investigation or what he did after I left. Moved the body? Anonymous calls to Ronnie? I managed to say little to Jan about being in the office by the convenient but stupid expedient of lying. What a bloody mess.

And then it dawns on me. I need to talk to Dobbin: Gary Dobbs, my best mate and also my wealthiest friend who has become very successful as an independent financial adviser and someone who's utterly trustworthy. And since he has acquired his money and as a consequence lost his girlfriend he has become easily the most miserable person I know.

He'll be the ideal person with whom to discuss my new life of crime.

# Wednesday, 9th September 1987

## *Chapter Nine*

I'm at my desk, sticky with sweat and still in my T-shirt and shorts from cycling. I try to make sense of the to-do list I wrote yesterday but I can't.

"Are we friends?" Greg asks. I wait for him to elaborate.

"I offered you the chance to help me with my new client and you then go and muscle in on this great opportunity with the Finance team."

"Sorry." I wipe my forehead on my sleeve. "I only recently avoided catching lung cancer on a double-decker, my to-do list seems to have rewritten itself in Serbo-Croatian and I'm pretty sure Chloe has stolen my trousers. Can you start again and avoid the bloody riddles? What am I supposed to have or have not done?"

He plonks himself in the chair on the other side of my desk. "Frank told me he's earmarked you for some new mortgage deal where you'll work with a couple of senior finance people and get some great exposure. And he – Frank I mean – says if you need help you should ask Crispin because he's got the best knowledge of the area. Come on, Harry. You know fuck-all about finance, so you had to have asked him for a favour to get this. Are you trying to steal a march on me? I thought we were working together to get the two slots and here you are in cahoots with Crispin."

I manage a couple of blinks. "As far as he's told me anything, Frank said the client wanted me. And no, I have no idea why either. Also, he's not mentioned what I should do if I need help. I was the one to mention Crispin and that was to ask why he wasn't doing the job, given that he knows more than I do about this stuff. If you like, I'll put in a word to get you involved. Then—" I stop because he's stood up and walked out. "Arse," I say to my empty room.

His head reappears. "Probably. Sorry. It came from an apparently reputable source. And thanks. About the mention. Now, are you going to stay like that or get into a suit?"

"I don't know where my trousers are until Chloe arrives and—"

"For pity's sake, Spittle. That new client is here. Come down as soon as you can." And with that he disappears again.

I stare at the empty door frame. "Oh Christ. Why didn't you...?"

Once again Greg's face reappears. "Because he's just turned up. Quick as you can old chap, arseholes and elbows."

I'm still sweating and can smell my BO when I make it to the conference room a while later, having found the errant trousers in a box marked 'Office Party.' Greg has his back to the window and a corporate associate, Tony Crescent – one of our vintage that Greg likes and is probably the nearest to a shoo-in for this partnership round but who I've never really got on with – is seated at the oval table, pen poised. The client has his back to me. He's broad shouldered, wearing a blue suit with an extra wide chalk stripe weft and gold cufflinks that peek out of his sleeves. I know him instantly. It's Natalie's ex-husband, a man I sort of exiled to Newcastle back in 1981 and someone I really hoped I would never see again: Miles Tupps.

When he turns to face me his smile is wide, his teeth are enviably straight and dazzling and the handshake firm and not as bone-crushing as it used to be. "Harry, mate. Long-time no see. How's Nats? Haven't heard from her in a while but she sounded chipper when we last spoke." He snakes an arm round my shoulder. "I told Greggy here I knew you, but for your benefit Tony, this young man is a genius. He stopped me getting up to my neck and beyond in the wrong sort of business and set me up. I hated him, you know? You don't want some snotball lawyer putting you right, do you? But I came to realise he was right and I'd been wrong. I found me a niche, worked hard and it's all legit, Harry, although I guess you'll have a ton of questions. Anyway, here I am ready to crack the London market with the help of you fine gentlemen."

"Are you... will you be moving back to London?"

Miles wrinkles his face. "Nah. The wife and kiddies are settled and I'm used to the wet and the shit beer. I even follow their bloody football team, you know? You and me need to have lunch to catch up properly. Greggy says Penny's in the club? Go you! Now, since all of you are charging by the second and I'm paying for it let's get on with it, shall we?" He lets me go and then says, "Oh, and I'm glad to see you're still the same old rebellious eccentric."

"Sorry?"

"Smell like sewerage and wearing mismatched shoes. One brogue, one plain. Not many people can carry that off. Kudos, Harry."

I sit down and listen to Miles drone on just as I remember, in so far as he's full of himself and he's not really changed but there is something different about him. Back when I first knew Miles he was an unreconstructed thug who'd use a fist before words. Natalie was seriously at risk of being beaten senseless but through the generosity and brilliance of Sven Andersen, Miles' threat was neutered. They divorced – although not very quickly and not without setbacks – and he disappeared, initially to Leeds and then on to Newcastle. At the peak of stress, while I was trying to piece together Sven's plan – Sven had died and left me in charge of his estate – Natalie and I had one day when, well... when we nearly fell into each other's arms. It never went beyond a couple of very passionate snogs (later things went further) and we managed to step back before a line was crossed but at the time part of what stopped me was the thought of what Miles would do if he found out. For once, Penny's retribution for this illicit encounter seemed mild by comparison.

Sitting down with Miles brings so much back to me. It also reinforces the notion that there is unfinished business between me and Natalie, which I need to finish if I'm to be a proper Father to our unborn and partner to Penny.

"Shit."

I'm suddenly conscious I've said that out loud. Tony raises an eyebrow and says, "It's actually a rather good strategy." He looks supercilious and smug and since I've not heard a thing about this plan I'm not in a position to argue.

Miles looks annoyed then laughs. "Nah, Harry's right. It's okay; it'll do while I get a foothold but it ain't the USP I need. What do you think, Harry? Where'd you set up first?"

It belatedly occurs to me that they are discussing where the new Tupps Properties should start trading. It is hardly something lawyers are usually asked to think about and I begin to blather on about following the transport links, but I'm only partly concentrating. I've just realised, perhaps for the first time that I do actually want to marry Penny – make us legitimate and solid and therefore harder for us to split and reform like amoeba, which is what we seem to do a lot. She's made it pretty clear she thinks marriage, and specifically weddings, are a waste of time and money, but that was before she got pregnant. Do I want to marry her? Really? And if so, is that to stop me turning over in my head the idea that I might in fact be destined to be with Natalie? I really do need a session with Dobbin to sort this out.

The meeting ends with Greg talking about the finance Miles will need to effect the expansion, something that Greg's Father is apparently helping with. "My old man says he hopes to have some ideas this week." Greg is in his element, dealing with the business side of things. Anything to avoid the grubby legal details, I think.

Miles holds his gaze. "I'm going to need a decision soon or we'll miss the wave."

As I walk back to the stairs, heading for my office – Greg is seeing Miles out and, happily, he hasn't repeated the suggestion that we have lunch – I think how different it would have been before. Miles raising the money from legitimate sources would never have happened. I know I'll have to tell Natalie and Penny about his reappearance; I wonder if they'll buy the idea that it was Greg who introduced him to the firm and not me. There's no reason why I would, but these sorts of coincidences create lots of suspicion in my experience.

Chloe is waiting for me as soon as I return to my desk. "Mr Charles V. Streib has been waiting for you. Mr Pomeroy says he told you about him?"

"Who?"

She looks more nervous than usual and double and triple checks the note she's holding, from which she re-reads slowly. "Mr Charles V. Streib. Gloria spelt it for me. He's a little, erm… angsty."

A snort of laughter escapes before I can stop it. Chloe looks mortified.

I say, "Sorry. What do you mean 'angsty'?"

She looks at the note again, her hand shaking a little. "I'm quoting, okay? He said, 'If that goddam limey piece of shit isn't here in five minutes I'll fist-fuck his pretty boy ass so hard he'll be shitting bagels.' That was 17, no… 18 minutes ago."

"He said that? To you?"

"No, he screamed it at Gloria but I heard and wrote it down. It's not easy to forget."

"No, it's not. Okay, I'll go and see what I can do for Mr Streib. I expect he's the Chuck character Frank mentioned."

One thing you soon learn in law firms is that the partners employ junior lawyers for two reasons: to do lots of work that they don't want to do because it interferes with the golf club and to stand in front of apoplectic clients while they harangue you to within an inch of your life about various infractions, misdemeanours and/or incompetencies. It doesn't matter that you don't know the client, the piece of work they are complaining about or the reason for the complaint: you merely have to take the beating and console yourself with the thought that one day you will have a herd of cannon fodder below you, waiting for the moment when a futile sacrifice is required. It is possible the reason why they employ so many products of the private school system is that these young men – and it is still mostly men – learned from an early age that to be abused like this is just the way life is. I went to a grammar school so missed the buggery training and it remains a wonder I've survived this far.

Gloria is waiting by the lifts when I exit. "Hi. First room on the right. Take care in there." Her face looks like she knows it is a far, far better thing I'm about to do. She holds up a letter. "And I thought I had it bad."

"Why? What's that?"

"A by-hand special delivery for Mervin Toogood that I must deliver to Mr Wandering Hands himself apparently." She steps into the lift and the doors slide closed. As they do so, she winks at me, making me feel infinitely better. Toogood may be a partner of much importance, but not everyone gets the personalised Gloria Eagle 'by hand' service and I doubt he's about to join the exclusive list.

"Mr Streib? I'm Harry Spittle."

Charles Streib is a man of bulk; 250 pounds if using American units of measurements and built to stop a stampeding bison. He stands with his back to the room, arms behind him and his feet about 18 inches apart, rocking from foot to foot. When he turns, his face is round, sweaty and he looks like he would prefer to have his tonsils sucked out by a vacuum cleaner rather than meet with me. He says nothing for a moment while he stares at me, his gaze going up and down and eventually stopping at my eyes. Then he hurries to the door. "Come on."

No handshake, no greeting, no confirmation he is in fact Mr Streib. A briefcase and light raincoat are grabbed from the table as he passes and then he yanks open the door. It is clear he is used to being obeyed. By the time I exit the meeting room he's in the revolving doors heading for the street. The person minding reception while Gloria is being pressed into service by the Head of Litigation watches open-mouthed as I follow Chuck outside. I join him on the pavement where he's clearly intent on hailing a cab. At some point in this blur of activity he's managed to light a cigarette.

"Are we going somewhere Mr Streib?"

"Are you always this fucking obtuse? No, I'm hailing a cab so we can have a meeting in the back."

"Quite. Now we have that established I'll see you when you return and—"

"Listen you piece of shit. You and your fairy bosses are this close…" he holds his thumb and forefinger an inch apart and two inches from my face, "…to getting sued to kingdom-fucking-come. I need a lawyer. You're it, God help me."

"I need my jacket and wallet and—"

His whistle, which in a more enclosed space might shatter glass, has drawn a black cab alongside the kerb. In moments, he's inside and glaring at me through the open door. "Get. In."

"Mr Streib, I really…"

I'm not that old, not yet 30, and while I've had some strange life experiences being kidnapped in broad daylight is not one of them. Yet that is how this situation feels to me. Charles V. Streib grabs my tie, and in a way I would not have thought possible until it happens to me he drags me into the cab, pushes me back into the seat next to him and slams the door. "Grafton Street. Number 103," he barks at the cabbie who if he is surprised at this behaviour hides it with a cheery, "Right-o guv."

There's an awkward silence that I feel I have to break. "Are you Chuck? My employer – Frank Pomeroy – said I would be meeting a Chuck."

I glance at my captor. He's watching me and smiling. When he sees me looking, he bursts into laughter. "You should see your face, kiddo. A fuckin' picture. Look at you. Yeah, I'm Chuck and it's good to meet you Harry Spittle. You come highly recommended."

"Do I?"

"Yeah, they said you'd do that shit too. Self-defecatory."

"I think you mean deprecatory."

"Nah, I saw your expression when I grabbed your tie. I know what I mean. You shit on yourself. Okay, here's the deal. I need somewhere to stay. This agent has found me a flat and I need to sign today if I'm going to get it. The agent – a real ass-wipe named Claude or some such shit – says the tenant has to be a company but I don't have a company over here, so between this place and the agent's shop you're going to come up with a solution to that and we're going to sign."

"Okay."

He raises an eyebrow. "Really? It's that easy? You're happy to commit some sort of felony, are you?"

"No, not at all. First, if you are who you say you are, what is the business you're planning on setting up?"

"You don't trust me, huh? I'm hurt."

"You're hurt? I think I'm the one who can claim with justification to be hurt since you just kidnapped me by my tie. The business you had in mind?"

"A home loans business of the sort the Mortgage Corporation and National Home Loans are considering. The idea is to use the money markets to raise the finance and sell off bonds backed by the mortgages to create liquidity. What we Yanks call securitisation."

"Okay Chuck, this is what we'll do. First up, what do you want to call your company?"

## *Chapter Ten*

I watch the estate agent explain the paperwork to Chuck. Before he began it took me a few minutes to satisfy him that, as a lawyer from a reputable City firm, the lack of any detail about the company that was to be a tenant wasn't going to be an issue. That and the £400 offered by Chuck as both deposit and first month's rent. After the formalities we all head for Half Moon Street near Green Park.

The building where the flat is located was once classy and expensive but now it looks in need of some love. The flat itself is on the third floor. It surprises me that Chuck is delighted with the place, claiming that it is better than he hoped. Has he really signed sight unseen? "Who are the other tenants?" Chuck asks.

The agent, a man who could be Miles' skinny older twin, bows a little and smirks. "Oh, they're very quiet. Usually out a lot, hard-working, er, people. Friendly too when they're around. I doubt you'll know they're even here."

Just then a door slams somewhere in the building and I hear colourful swearing from the street. I look down from the widow; a bald-headed man in an expensive camel-hair coat hurries across the pavement and steps into a Daimler, whose door is held open by a blue-suited be-hatted flunky. I'd guess the man in the coat is of Middle Eastern origin. Maybe all the tenants are from oversea. The agent says his goodbyes and leaves me and Chuck alone.

I'm also about to say my goodbyes and suggest I go back to the office to sort out the company that is to be the tenant but Chuck sits down at the table, waving me to wait and picks up the phone receiver. He taps to check for a line and dials a number. "It's Chuck," he says almost immediately, quoting the address. "I need a full sweep and the kit in 30." With that he puts the phone down and sits back. "We don't want to be here when the removal men turn up. Let's grab a beer."

"It's a bit early."

"Shit, are you always this unenthusiastic?" He leads the way outside onto Piccadilly and checks each way. "Where can we get a beer round here? And a quiet table?"

"I have a friend who owns a bar nearby."

"All right," he says quickly, "I want privacy. That work?"

I nod. "She'll be setting up at this time but I'm sure she'll let us have a corner table and a free drink."

He lets his bottom lip jut out, appraising me. "You're clearly the right man to know."

I lead the way. When we reach Flamingos Natalie comes to the door, dressed in a too large T-shirt and tracksuit bottoms. Her hair is tied up in a scarf. She looks surprised to see me, gives me a quick kiss on the cheek and listens to my request, studying Chuck all the while.

"Of course. I've been changing the barrels so no beer but help yourself to a shot. You know your way."

Chuck watches her go. "This is her place?"

"Yes. It's very popular."

"She's a doll."

"Indeed. Come on. What do you want to drink, other than beer? Scotch?"

"You are a perceptive man. Show me what she has."

The bar smells of last night's cigarettes and stale booze, although Natalie has opened the windows – in truth they're just glorified pavement-lights – and through the office I can see the back door is propped ajar revealing a set of narrow stone steps that curve up to a small yard. A slight gale is whistling through the place but it's not too cold. We take the same table Natalie and I sat at the last time I visited and clink glasses.

"Let's see what I've found out about Harold Spittle so far. One, my sources say you're a good attorney despite an inclination for the negative; two, you're capable of showing initiative; and three, you know where to get a drink and are friends with the cutest little bar tender in London. What else am I missing?"

"You're easily seduced by my naïveté and charm."

"Bullshit." He offers his glass and we clink again.

"I'm a country bumpkin at heart. Parents still alive. One sister. I live—" He cuts me off.

"What does your sister do? Parents?"

"Dina works for the government, you know: a civil servant. Mum and Dad run a B&B."

"What part of government?"

"Something to do with… why are you interested?"

"I'm not. I trying to be polite but fuck that. Let me tell you about my proposal and you can tell me what we need to do to make it happen."

"Wouldn't it be better if we did this at my office?"

"What, and have some limey bastard listen in and steal my ideas?"

I look round the club. "Natalie might be a spy."

He shrugs. "If she's a honey trap, then hey – I've got a very sweet tooth."

"Lovely image." I'm suddenly aware that bringing Mr Charles V. Streib here might not have been the best idea.

He laughs at his own joke. "In future we'll use the apartment if we need to discuss anything confidential, otherwise I'll come to you. Yes? Okay?"

For an hour we discuss his ideas and drink more whisky as I list the other specialists we will need. He argues against each one saying he just wants me and I can speak to them if I need to. He wants what he calls a 'point man' and that's to be me – I'm flattered and terrified in equal measure. By midday I'm back on the street, slightly pissed, thinking I should have stopped to tell Natalie about Miles' reappearance and unsure what to make of Chuck V Streib.

# *Chapter Eleven*

I've been friends with Dobbin - Gary Dobbs if we are being formal - since university. For four interesting years we shared a flat that his parents bought and rented to us at less than the market rate. During that period I fell in and out of my relationship with Penny several times, but I only had one other brief fling that went beyond what my Father used to call 'heavy petting' and I've still not recovered from the image that accompanies that description, redolent as it is of cute and bouncy farm animals. In contrast, Dobbin had maybe a dozen to 15 girlfriends, only one of whom lasted more than five weeks. That was Brenda Silverman, a law student, daughter of a sweet lady called Zenda and step-daughter to a bastard crooked judge, Reginald Rother. She was the love of his life.

When she and Dobbin got together she was fronting a punk band called the Twats and using a stage name Vera Copula. She had seriously infected nipples from some unhygienic piercings and a fixation with al fresco sex. Actually all sex in truth – to say she was rapacious makes her sound almost demure. That she was compensating would be an understatement. Eventually the ferocious rebel persona faded, Brenda went back to finish her articles and qualify into a small firm that specialised in advising women, mostly in connection with domestic abuse issues, custody and divorce. The newly serious Brenda (I used to be unsure whether she preferred Vera or Brenda but these days it is definitely the latter) decided she didn't need anything sporting a penis, dumped Dobbin and moved with Zenda and three other women into a large house in Hampstead where she declared she was a homoromantic asexual. The only thing that remained consistent in Brenda's life was her vitriolic and unswerving hatred of Maggie Thatcher. Last I heard she was running a refuge for victims of domestic violence and thinking about standing as a local councillor in some north Islington ward as a member of the newly formed Electra Party, a name that sounded neat but rather ignored its mythological context.

I meet Dobbin in a pub in Covent Garden. If Eeyore were a man, he would be Gary Dobbs. "Hi Spittoon, why are you so happy?"

"I've left the office and I'm not yet home. This is the one part of the day that's just about me."

"Great. I suppose that means you're going to moan at me about the state of your life to try to cheer me up."

"You first. Any specific reason why you're glum or is it just because the sun rose today and you wish it hadn't?"

He sips his beer and says, "I'm quite chipper, actually. I've made a decision. I'm selling my business. Well, merging it."

"I didn't know you were thinking about that."

"Oh, don't sound so peeved. You'd never act for me, even if I wanted you to. I had an unsolicited offer from an American outfit who want to take advantage of the opportunities for private pension and personal investments that will flow from these privatisations. I have to stay on for six months – longer if we mutually agree but otherwise I'm out of it."

"What are you getting?"

"Two and a bit million."

"You're kidding?"

"Nope."

"I understand why even you might be chipper."

"Christ, I thought you knew me. It's because I can exit without my Dad saying I'm running scared. The money is awful, although at least I know how to invest it."

"Awful? Are you serious?"

"On normal returns the P:E ratio should mean I get three, maybe more but I wanted a clean break, not some indentured servitude. Six months was the minimum."

"Tough break. I wish I knew how to make money from investments. Just seems a lot like gambling to me."

"I've told you countless times that I'll look after your finances, especially now you're a rich parasitic lawyer."

"I know, it's just…"

"What?"

"I don't like to impose."

"Rot. But since if that's your reason, once I've sold up you'll no longer have that as an excuse not to take advantage of me."

"No, you're right. Thanks. So why do you look suicidal?"

"I don't know what to do with the money beyond make more of it."

"So invest it and wait for inspiration to swamp you."

"That's the point. I'm done with all that. I've had it with the thrill of the next success. It just means more dosh I don't want."

"Give it away then. Find some good causes to support."

"I don't know any."

I take a moment to study his pained expression. "You're serious, aren't you?"

"I don't want people taking advantage of me."

"Set up a trust, a charitable one. Then you can go looking for what seems worthy."

"Maybe. Later."

"What do you care about?"

The look he gives me echoes the look Natalie gave me when I last asked about her love life, like it's the most stupid question I've ever asked. Then a sort of forlorn regret settles on his expression. Love is bloody cruel. I know what he's thinking the gormless puppy. "Have you spoken to Brenda recently?"

"Bren? No, but I saw Zenda last week."

"Oh? That's good. Does that mean—?"

"It means nothing. She – Zenda – calls from time to time and we have tea. Sometimes in town, sometimes at their place if Brenda's away."

"Right..."

"Don't sound so suspicious. She needs help with her investments following her divorce and I give it to her."

"Does Bre—?"

"Of course she bloody doesn't. She doesn't even know Zenda has any investments. Christ, that woman is wilfully blind to how they fund their operation. She's full of all this anti-capitalist crap yet without some readies she'd have no shelter, no ability to fund court actions, no security, no real plan – none of it." He looks straight at me. "It's amazing what they do there. Even their house is secure and I have to come in via a side door. Some of the women who're there – they're the ones who are probably ready to move on from the shelter – can get very twitchy about seeing a man. Christ, it's awful what some men do just to get sex, to wrest control."

"So there you go: that's your charity – support them. Just imagine what they'd do with the extra funds."

"Yeah, well, if Bren knew it was me she'd go ape-shit and probably blackball her Mother for polluting their operation with the stain of the patriarchy. Let's talk about something else. What about you? All set on weakening the gene pool with a new baby Spittle?"

I'm suddenly hit by a thought. If we aren't married why would the child take 'Spittle' for his or her name? It could just as easily be

Grover. And then the thought that caught me earlier. Marrying Penny. To make the birth legitimate. Is that what I want? We want?

"You okay? For a moment I thought it might be your brain working but that's impossible, so I assume that pained expression is merely trapped wind."

"Ha ha. Yes, all's good. The last scan showed legs and arms and what appeared to be an enormous arse – her side obviously – but turned out to be the head. We're doing NCT classes – all a bit Earth Mothers and pot pourri sandwiches for me – and Penny is huge, poor thing."

"Sex?"

"Non-existent."

"Not thought about Natalie?"

Dobbin is the only other person who knows about my stupid dalliance.

"Fuck off. That was a mistake. We both know it."

"Really? I saw her on Saturday. She asked me outright if you were okay. She cares."

"She's a good friend. Like you."

"Yeah, but you've never ached for my tits."

"Lovely. I saw her on Friday and found out she'd told Penny about that one off… what?"

"She said. We had a laugh about the fact you were the only one who didn't know she'd told Pen. And I know you're good with Penny. All I'm saying is you can give off ambiguous messages. Just be careful."

I give him a hard stare but he doesn't blink. That's almost perceptive of him so someone must have told him to say it. "Natalie?"

"Penny. She's very unsure, okay? She needs you to be demonstrably in her corner and on her team."

"Have you been wining and dining my girlfriend behind my back, too?"

"We had a coffee, that's all."

"Geez. Although I do understand that. It's tricky just now, what with all this partnership guff. It means I can't be at home as much as I probably need to be."

"That sounds like an excuse."

"Yeah, well. I'm dealing with some crap at work too."

"Is that what this is about? I didn't think a Spittoon pint could just be social. You always have an ulterior motive."

"I do not. I… Oh ha-bloody-ha. Very drole."

"Tell Uncle Gary and make him smile."

"I'm not sure anyone has the drugs to achieve that Herculean task. You remember that colleague at work? You met him at ours last year. Gregor Pri—"

"The posturing Romanov?"

"Yes, that pretty much sums him up. Though he's okay. As a colleague I mean. Still, I had really the weirdest day of my life on Friday and I bet he's involved. Maybe."

"Coming from the man who helped wind up a criminal empire, bought off a couple of gangsters, gave away millions and still won't admit he's got the hots for his girlfriend's best friend, that must have been some day."

"Yeah, well, I've not got the hots for Natalie. Friday, where do I start?" Quickly I tell him about Barry, the dress and the apple, Crout's instructions, the police investigation and Greg's odd appearance in the office. I go on and tell him about Magda coming round and her strange request and Dina's unexplained involvement. "So you see a lot is swirling around me, which does mean I'm a bit distracted with Penny and the baby stuff. Any idea what I should do?"

"I'd not sweat any of it. Just let it play out. There's no one who knows what you saw beyond this Crout and why would he say if he hasn't already? And right now you want things to be smooth at work, don't you? How is work, apart from the perjury?"

"Pretty good. I've just seen a new client who specifically asked for me."

"Why?"

"Thanks for the vote of confidence. I never asked. Maybe I will next time I see him. Oh, and guess who turned up as another new client introduced by Greg? None other than Miles Tupps."

"Bloody hell. Did he try to remove a body part?"

"He was very complimentary, saying I saved him from a life of crime. Greg seems to want me to help with his new business line of estate agents."

"Laundry shops you mean."

"According to Greg he's very kosher and the money he took from Sven's estate gave him almost enough legitimate funds to get started. I'm not going to rush into helping. Actually, I'm not really sure why Greg wanted my help. Other than I know Miles and aren't likely to be seduced by his olde worlde charm."

"Sometimes you're the least suspicious person I know. Is that a good trait for a lawyer?"

"Probably not."

"At least the surprise person wasn't McNoble."

I do a theatrical shudder – Stephen McNoble was my nemesis for years although in the end he helped me sort of Sven Andersen's Will and see off Miles. He had as many problems with his Father as Sven had with his. I'll never really feel comfortable around him, but there was a kind of sense of finality when we settled everything and he left.

"When did you last see him?"

"Not for at least three years. He did call me out of the blue a few months ago to say he'd lost track of his Father – you remember Charlie Jepson? – and was worried about him and asking anyone who knew him to keep an eye out."

"I thought he wanted his Father dead."

"Yeah, well, once. There's a bit of unfinished business there I expect."

"Why did McNoble think you'd know anything about his Dad's whereabouts?"

"Not me. My parents."

"Oh, of course. Your Mum?"

"More unfinished business. Anyway, he sounded genuinely worried about his old man."

"How are your Mum and Dad by the way?"

"Fine."

"So this has nothing to do with who exactly is your Dad?"

"Why did I ever tell you that?" My Mother had an affair with Charlie back in the 1950s and I feared at one point he might in fact be my Dad as well. That fear has never entirely gone away. "No, it doesn't. And my folks are very busy with the B&B. They are making a real go of it. Less good is that Dad is becoming an active member of the local Tory party and he'd probably mortgage the whole business if he had the chance to buy a set of Maggie's knickers at some charity fundraiser."

"Dina?"

"No idea. I do know she joined MI5 and works down in Cheltenham a lot. She went on some fast track thing after Imperial and I hardly see her."

"George?"

My nephew, Dina's boy with Jim. "Oh, he's fine. He lives with his Father and his parents and my Mum and Dad look after him a few days and some weekends. Jim works for my Uncle Norman, you know?"

"Yes, I think you said. Dina happy with that? She always seemed to flip-flop between wanting to be a proper Mum and working."

"I think she'd probably cut out your kidneys for suggesting she's not a 'proper Mum' but yes the dilemma remains. He's 10 this year and I know she and Jim were discussing where he might go to secondary school. He wants him to go to the local state school in Lymington, but Dina was thinking about him moving in with her and going private."

"Have you told her you've seen Jan? She liked him, didn't she?"

"She did but I'm not sure that's up to me. I mean they're grown-ups and—"

"Man, you do talk a load of old bollocks at times. If you don't I will. Has she had anyone since him?"

"Have you since Bren?"

"Low blow, Spittle, very low."

"Well? When will you move on? Or try again?"

"I'm not sure I want to do either."

We sit for a while contemplating our respective feebleness of spirit before I ask, "Are you serious about helping with my finances? Someone at work said I should start a pension."

"And you not even 30. How very grown up."

"It's just that if I do make partnership – unlikely as that sounds – then I'll suddenly have a load of wonga and nowhere to put it. Someone said I need to make sure I don't waste my RAPs, whatever they are."

Dobbin smiles for the first time. "Retirement Annuity Pension. And you being you and hating to look ignorant never asked, right?"

"Well, I thought… oh do shut up. No, I didn't ask. So?"

"The nice people at the Inland Revenue give you back tax if you contribute to a recognised pension. Which it's true is great but right now there are some even better schemes than that, even if you are paying a full whack of tax. Do you want Uncle Gary to nurture your nest egg?"

"Well, it's more a small bit of broken shell right now."

"No reason not to start. I'll send you some ideas. If it makes you feel any better I'll be investing in the same stock."

"Coming from the man who wants to give everything away, I'm not entirely sure that sounds like a great idea."

"What have you got to lose?"

"Erm, everything?"

"Apart from everything? We can set up a trust if you like, do it offshore."

He begins to witter on. I know he's good at what he does and I should be more interested in what he's saying, but my mind keeps rolling back to Penny and Natalie. He catches my attention again when he says, "...and how's the partnership thing going? Last time we spoke you said you didn't think you had a chance."

"I still don't. It's like electing a new Pope, it's all very secret. We get told nothing at all so we have to guess. Greg's convinced there are two places available in our department but there are three of us that meet the criteria."

"You have criteria? How exciting. Shall I guess? You need to be white and have a penis?"

"How very 1950s of you. That's the unspoken piece. There are three of us be-dicked whitey-boys who have served our time and, it appears, convinced a few people we have the necessary talents – nice hair, own teeth, an ability to tie our shoes and properly furl an umbrella, that sort of thing. If I'm honest I'm the safe candidate; the other two are, on the one hand exceptionally bright and on the other a genius at attracting new business. If I was deciding it wouldn't be me."

"You might as well give up then, mightn't you?"

"You are really a help, you know?"

"You don't have to losten to me."

"I won't then. This weekend there's a conference where all the candidates across all the departments get to stay with about two-thirds of the partners in a posh country house hotel in Hampshire where we'll be put through a rigorous set of relevant tests – how to order a full room-service meal on expenses, what is the correct spoon to use for your quince jelly, how to address the senior partner if you find him bonking his secretary across his desk."

"I'm fascinated. What is it?"

"'I'm sorry, sir. Shall I wait or do you want me to come back?'"

"Sounds awful."

"Probably. Those who've survived say it's usually great fun because there are all sorts of factions between the partners you don't know about and this will be the first time you'll get an inkling of who hates who, who's screwed who and who wants whose job. I can't wait. One more for the road?" I say, pointing at his empty glass.

"I suppose so."

## *Chapter Twelve*

Dobbin leaves me with a new business card that identifies him as a consultant. He promises to let me have some ideas for investment opportunities – 'it will give me something to do' – and tells me to try to not screw up the weekend away. As I open the front door when I get home, I'm still wondering about our parting. He was pretty drunk and sort of lurched in for a hug, which is most unlike him. "I think I'll call Brenda. See how's she's doing. Maybe she'll take my money," he slurred. I know I should have tried to sound encouraging, but I was put off by his attempt at a hug. Maybe he thought I was Brenda.

Magda and Penny are both in the kitchen drinking something green and foul smelling. I don't ask. Penny says, "Have you spoken to anyone about Magda's application yet? She's getting anxious about it."

A glance at Magda suggests she's completely relaxed and rather it's Penny who's anxious, presumably for her to move on. "I'll call Noor in the morning, fix an appointment with someone from her firm. This week." Looking at Magda I add, "Did you speak to your friend? About staying?"

"Iz not good idea. He iz having domestics. With boyfriend. I see him and all he speak about iz boy."

"He's gay?"

"Ja, of course. Iz Amos."

Amos Rodgers. Goodness, now there's a name from the past, another link back to our time at Hemingways. Last I heard about him – and that was a while ago – he had climbed up the greasy pole of waiting and was well placed at the Savoy or the Dorchester or similar. "How is he? Did you know it was Amos, this friend?" This last is addressed to Penny.

She nods. "I've been meaning to see him. We agreed we'd have tea sometime, but you know how things slip."

"You've spoken to him?"

"You know I have."

"I don't. Do I?"

"Browns. Beginning of last year. I asked if you wanted to come."

"Last year?" It dawns on me that was when during our last hiatus when Natalie and I finally managed it. "I don't remember."

"I'm sure I must have said. Didn't I?"

There's a noise like a boiler about to explode. Magda is laughing. "You iz like old married couple. I love you two."

Penny smiles and reaches out for her hand and then mine. It may just be me being paranoid but I'm absolutely bloody certain she rubs my left ring finger exactly where an engagement ring might sit.

"He has a boyfriend then? That's new. He was always one for the regular change of bedmate."

"Amos zay he not in good health. He zay he need get better but zis boy, he zay he vant throw him out. He zay zat he argue vith boy – Pascal. Pascal iz young, likes random sex. I'm not sure I cope with zis stress, ja?"

Both Penny and I look at each other and do well not to laugh.

"Iz all right I stay? For bit more time?"

I look at Penny who nods. "Maybe a week?" I suggest.

# Friday, 11th September 1987

## *Chapter Thirteen*

I don't cycle today because this evening we are decamping to Pyrell Hall, a smart five-star hotel just outside Basingstoke. Frank is giving Crispin and me a lift; Greg is taking his Mazda and says he will be late because he has to see a client after work. It is probably bullshit but it always seems to impress Frank.

Frank calls us to his room at 11.00 and is in a really good mood. "I am so proud of you three," he tells us over coffee. "You are so much better than the rest of the candidates put together. I'd not want any of them, you know, and I will do everything – and I mean everything – to ensure you all..." He peters out, clearly embarrassed and we all know why.

He has nearly done something he has not yet done in the six years I've worked at the firm: acknowledge publicly that someone – in this case us three – are up for partnership. This code of silence is the same with all the partners. Everyone knows who is on track – 'in the paddock' to use the horse racing analogy beloved of law firms – but the game we are brought up to play is never to publicly acknowledge anything so grubby as who might be a candidate. Goodness that might smack of ambition, which is all rather non-U. Individually he is happy to talk about our progress but not in a group. There is an awful, awkward silence before Greg says, "You think it's going well?"

"Fine. Good. I—"

Charity Perfume – Frank's secretary – appears at the door. Charity is a uniform grey (both complexion and clothes) and when moving makes no noise at all. Her voice is so quiet it is in an aural range that only bats can hear. It has been said that she can slip through the flimsy partitions that separate our rooms to catch out unsuspecting associates and pass over a file from Frank with a new matter to undertake. I think I hear her say, "Mr Pomeroy." She could have said anything but since she bows slightly in Frank's direction, it's a fair guess it is his name, "a message."

The message in question is a telephone attendance. You can tell because it is on an A5 sized sheet of yellow paper. Internal messages from other partners come on blue sheets (indicating their superior importance) and those from other ranks are on white paper. Super-secret, super-important messages are in cerise envelopes. Faxes come in brown envelopes. It's a wonder anyone can do any work immediately after they join us, as they have to spend two weeks trying to unravel the code of working here.

The other thing about notes are the initials. Partners use their initials and it takes a while to work out who's who. The use of initials on notes is one of the three visible ways of identifying a partner. The second is the entitlement to have a speaker phone. The third is a less apparent sign of that exalted status (there is the eye-watering wealth we all assume they accumulate but rarely see) and is only known to a privileged few (which somehow includes Greg). Each partner is given a napkin ring with his (or, if somehow a Y-chromosome slips through the sifting process – three have to date – her) initials on it, to be used in the hallowed halls of the partners' dining room.

Frank reads the note, looks at me and grimaces. "Chaps, Harry and I need to call a client. See you later for fun and games." He sounds a bit concerned which, given that Charity has just saved him from having to explain to us our status in the partnership process, is a mite worrying.

Once we are alone, he indicates for me to shut the door, adding to my anxiety. As he begins dialling the number, he says, "Your American. Chuck. Seems like he's…" he squints at the note, "pissed, which I believe is American vernacular for a touch put out."

The call is answered on half a beat loud and clear over the speaker phone. "Streib."

"Mr Streib, Frank Pome—"

"What in God's good name is your monkey playing at Pomeroy? I'm stuck in a tart factory and I'm not getting any peace."

"Tart factory?" Frank looks at me, bemused. "What sort of tarts? Mr Kipling? Bakewell?"

"What are you on about? Whores. Hookers. Titbait—"

"Yes, right, I see. Ladies of, erm, ill-repute. You say you're in a factory?"

"I thought you Brits were meant to have invented irony? Do you always take everything so damn literally?" Chuck begins to talk slowly as if explaining something to a halfwit, which is shrewd with Frank. "The flat he signed me up to is a brothel. All the other tenants are whores, right? Their pimps hang about by the entrance, which isn't nice either. I need to get out of here and this lease and I need it done today. That goon Spittle isn't at his desk so—"

Frank almost leaps at the phone. "He's here. He's here. Fear not, Mr Chuck… Streib. He will be with you post-haste."

"When?"

"Shall we say inside an hour?"

"No –10 minutes." The phone rather obviously goes dead and Frank sighs.

He sits back and puts his hands behind his head; his armpits have suppurated leaving blots on his shirt – to me they look like, respectively, a frog trying to escape a blender and a man crushed by a large rock, both of which could be prescient. "This is a good test, Harry. I know he chose the flat and that it isn't your fault, but Mr Streib is potentially an important client for you. Of course in other circumstances I'd take charge, but I rather think we should see how you handle the rebarbative Mr Streib. I'll see you at five?"

## *Chapter Fourteen*

I try Chuck and someone picks up who tells me I'm expected at the flat and then rings off. Given what Frank has just said, I decide to take a cab and I'm outside the place in 25 minutes. There are no signs of pimps or anyone else. It is 12:15 and nobody is about. When I ring the bell and am admitted I'm surprised to be greeted by Cindy, one of Natalie's staff."

"Where's Chuck? Was that you on the phone?"

"He's at the bar."

"Christ. Okay. I…" I've half turned for the door when I stop and look at her. "Why are you here?"

She laughs. Cindy has a tinkling laugh that rather counterpoints her gruff, smoke-scarred vocal chords. "It's not what you're thinking. He's handing the lease back today and I'm just making sure he gets all his deposit back."

I must look confused.

She adds, "I know these crooks, Harry. I'll make sure he gets his money and the lease is torn up. Poor man has been shabbily treated."

"Has he found somewhere else?"

"As I said, he's at the bar."

"The bar?"

Another laugh, this one is more like breaking glass than a tinkle. "Nat offered him the use of one of her rooms."

"I thought she used the flat for supplies?"

"You need to come round more. She had it made over and is staying there. The box room is his for now. He seemed delighted with it."

"Really? Why's she being so nice? Never mind, I'd better go and find him. You sure you can sort everything out here?"

She offers a look that suggests I was right when I said I needed to leave.

When I arrive Chuck is leaning on the bar nursing a Scotch. He's also exploding out of a grey suit. "You look smart," I say.

"Yeah, well, I can look the part when needed. Your gal is the business, Harry. A real saviour."

"Cindy says she's going to sort things out for you. Hand the lease back?"

"Yeah, can you believe these broads? They knew exactly which buttons to press. She's certainly started pressing mine." He is shaking his head, smiling at the surprise of it all. "I may take another place but just as a working space; staying here suits me just fine."

"I'm not sure Cindy is a press-button girl if you understand what I mean. I think her tastes are more discerning?"

"Sure. She's into broads, that right? Or maybe she prefers the each way bet? Anyway, I was thinking more of Nats. Some piece of work, eh? If she's just a 'friend' then your good lady must be pretty special. Whatever."

Natalie appears looking tired. Her hair is tugged back into a tight ponytail and her parting is wide and severe, making her eyes seem like they are migrating round her head. She kisses me and then Chuck. I decide not to read too much into that.

Chuck, though, voices what I've been thinking. "You eating properly, kiddo? Coz right now you look like you need some meat inside you."

She tries a smile. "If that's an American chat-up line, then it sucks. And thanks for the concern but I'm just dandy."

He shrugs and lifts his tumbler, chinking the ice against the sides. "I owe you Ms Pendant."

Natalie goes behind the bar and pulls me a half pint. I take the stool next to Chuck. "Sorry about the flat. I didn't know it was a knocking shop."

"Yeah, sure. Don't sweat it."

Natalie puts a drink in front of me. "Cindy says it's a standard tactic by the owner – put in an unknowing tenant when all is peaceful, ramp up the action making it intolerable, have him complain and want out, offer a deal at a price to buy off the lease and rinse and repeat. Cindy knows a few things about Mr Crossbow – he's the landlord's agent – that the vice squad would love to hear. She's quite an asset, working around here. I suspect she'll have you moved out soon. She called a few minutes ago to say the corner flat on the ground floor is available if you want it, although it's unfurnished apart from a bed. Or you can stay here, but this place is pretty noisy when we're open and it isn't exactly spacious."

Chuck looks at me approvingly. "Do all British women have such balls?"

I manage to keep a straight face. "Some, though I'd suggest you don't try one who has. They are an acquired taste."

It takes him a beat before he bellows with laughter. "Harry Spittle, I'm so glad I found you."

After we've finished the drinks (which over an hour grow from the half pint into two Scotches and something sweet and cloying), I feel woozy and I take my leave. Natalie sees me to the door. "I wanted to talk to you. Penny called. She said you'd spoken to her. About us."

"It would have helped if I'd known you two had spoken," I add with an emphasis I'd normally bottle but which the alcohol enables, "about us."

"How would that have helped? Really? We know it meant nothing, or it can't mean anything, not now. Can it? And she'd have worked it out anyway so I thought it best to tell her and then leave you two to work out what to say and when. Anyway, she was the one who insisted I kept quiet and let you confess."

We have emerged into the sharp daylight, which does her complexion no favours. "You're working too hard. Can't you get away for a bit?"

"Where? Why would I want to? I've no one to go with, have I?"

"I… we're worried about you."

She puts a hand to my face and rubs the bristles. "Don't be. I'm looking forward to being a wicked and corrupting influence on Spittle Junior and teaching your little wiggle all the bad habits I can think of. Go on, go and look after your beautiful girlfriend."

"I met Miles, by the way. It looks like he's becoming a client of my firm. Not my idea. Greg's."

Is her hand shaking as she taps out a cigarette? "You gave up."

She shakes her heard. "That's what you wanted to believe. It's just a stress reliever."

"It's a killer."

She waves smoke in my face and ignores me. "Greg told me. He's a piece of work, isn't he?"

"Greg or Miles?"

"Both." Her laugh is not a happy one. "He's clever, the way he gets you talking. My fault, in a way." She holds her face to the sun and closes her eyes. "Maybe I should go somewhere warm." She shakes her head and looks at me. "It may surprise you to know we stay in touch, Miles and me. He's remarried and settled. I'm pleased for him. I fell for one version of the man not realising there was another, but time away and Marion's influence seem to have worked wonders." She takes my arm. "Let's walk to the tube and I'll explain. He mentioned he needed to raise some capital and I was telling Greg who said he knew people and, well, it seems like it's all worked out. Be nice to him

Harry. I know you think he's a shit but there is some good in there somewhere."

Sure, I think, buried very deep. "I didn't realise you see so much of Greg."

"He's pretty regular with Tony and Raymond. They're all from your firm, aren't they? He speaks highly of you." We arrive at Green Park tube station. "You will help Miles, won't you? I think marriage suits him. This one anyway. And I'd like him to make a go of something." She kisses and hugs me and lets me go.

As I descend into Green Park station, I can't help thinking yet again that she should be saying 'your wife' when she refers to Penny. I'm halfway down the escalator when I realise Magda is coming up on the far side. She's not seen me, but when she looks up I start to wave. Somehow she fails to register it's me and sails past without showing any sort of recognition. I feel stupid for no real reason. Maybe she's very short-sighted? I also wonder where she's going. Maybe to see Amos again? He probably works in one of the large hotels nearby. Seeing her reminds me I still haven't heard back from Noor or spoken to Dina. More items to add to my growing to-do list.

## *Chapter Fifteen*

There are two messages waiting for me. One is from Chuck, thanking me again and asking for a meeting on Tuesday at 10.00. The second is from my sister Dina asking me to call. It's just gone four and I need to brief Chloe to organise the meeting for Tuesday and sort out a room. She's very efficient, and suggests that it would be polite if I asked the finance and tax partners to join in rather than her making the first call. She's right but I know I'll end up grinding my teeth. Our department isn't, by common consent ('common' as in the rest of the Firm but not us) peopled with what might be called those with the most get up and go, the epitome of the modern thrusting lawyer. Thus, finding it is a property lawyer leading a meeting with a new client can be psychologically challenging for partners in other departments, and it is bloody irritating for us. It might be thought of as paranoid on my part if it didn't always happen. Frank has left me a couple of names to speak to, both of whom make it more likely that I'll be accelerating some dentist's retirement plan. I also need to sit down with Crispin to sort out the handover of his harbourside transaction. Knowing Crispin it will be both a mess and extremely complex. Even though I've never worked for them, Caldera Properties have a reputation for making things difficult so being well-briefed is essential if I'm to avoid a hellish week while he's in France.

    I call the tax partner – Dermot Malloy – first. Dermot is a little eccentric – he wears a deerstalker for starters – and confounds my expectations by being delighted to be asked. He's very bright and on this occasion sounds ever so keen. As I'm explaining what I know I hear him light a match and remember he smokes awful cheroots. Damn. By the end of this deal, I'm going to end up smelling like an ashtray and getting grief from Penny for subjecting her/the foetus/the new born to a version of passive smoking via my clothes.

    Because I'm an optimist at heart – well, compared to Dobbin – I am already making assumptions about the reaction I'll get from the finance partner I call. That mirage is soon put in its place as Sonia Porcelaine isn't taking calls. Even her secretary communicates via a series of patronising sniffs, telling me that Ms Porcelaine has already been briefed by Mr Pomeroy and someone will attend. When I try to prompt her to tell me a name, I'm rebuffed with a 'you will be informed when appropriate.' I'm about to challenge this and say it needs to be someone senior – I'm trying to imagine what Chuck will do to someone wet behind the ears and with the sort of concave personality that he will shred – when she says, "The Finance team will of course lead the transaction."

As the tell-tale click tells me my time is indeed up, I lean back in my seat. Well, that would suit me down to the ground in truth, although the presumption is entirely typical of finance partners and Sonia especially.

The phone rings; it is Sonia's secretary. She asks, "Who will be providing tax assistance?"

"Dermot."

There is a strange sound that might be disapproval or she could have just decapitated a live chicken. "Sonia will require you to ensure Mr Malloy avoids being anti-social."

Ah yes, and that's the other thing with Dermot – 'anti-social' behaviour being an office euphemism for someone with debilitating BO. "Of course." The lies come easily these days. "The client has asked for names so if Sonia has a chance to let me know who—"

"Ms Porcelaine is engaged on a delicate family matter as I'm sure you will appreciate."

"Sorry?"

"Mr Tritewell's demise? She is consoling her husband."

This takes a bit of mental gymnastics. Sonia's husband is some junior government minister in charge of obliterating small dusty parts of the world in the name of free trade or some such. If seen on the TV, it is with hair like an oiled otter and a smile that would, on other mammals, indicate the presence of carrion. The idea someone so crepuscular might need consoling is beyond my small imagination.

My silence must give away my continued confusion. "He is the late Mr Tritewell's brother?"

Oh, ah – yes, I did know that. I begin an attempt at an apology but it is cut off. "As I said, you will hear when Sonia deems it necessary."

*You handled that well, Harry.*

It's now nearly 10 to five and I should be heading for the car park – Frank hates tardiness – but I decide a quick call to Dina is warranted. She's left an 01 number – a London code  which is a surprise given she works in the West Country. The phone is answered after a single ring. No one speaks. "Hello? Is anyone there?" There's a hollow noise like the receiver is in a cave or a large basement. "I'm trying to get hold of Dina Spittle."

Moments later a familiar voice comes on. "Dina here. That you Harry?"

"The one and—"

"Where's Magda?"

"I've no—"

"Did she say where she was going today?"

"No. Look what's go—"

"Shut up Harry, will you? What exactly did she say?"

"Nothing, though I saw here about an hour or so ago in Piccadilly. Green Park tube to be precise."

"What did she say?"

"Nothing. Actually she acted as if she'd not seen me."

"Where did she go?"

"I said I don't know." I can't help sounding irritated. "She was going up and I was going down. I—"

"Hang on."

There's a muffled conversation that I can't make head or tail of before she comes back on the line. "We'll speak next week and sort this out." Then the line goes dead.

Well, that was really helpful. What on Earth is this about? I scribble a note and leave it on my blotter as a reminder for Monday: '1. Call Noor, re. Magda. 2. Call Dina, ditto.' And then head for the door. Time to go and impress the partnership with my sparkling banter and repartee. As for Crispin, well, I suppose I'll have to take a briefing over the weekend.

## Chapter Sixteen

The drive to Hampshire is uneventful. The reason Crispin didn't brief me earlier is he had to rush to Tommy's to have a boil in his ear lanced. He shares some unnecessary details about pus sacs and yellow-red blood that almost has Frank driving off the Twickenham Bridge as he gags.

To be fair, when he does begin the briefing he makes the job sound interesting, especially when he explains the cast list. "The main man, not that I've met him, is this Scot called Gerald MacThing—" Crispin stops when Frank snorts with laughter.

"MacThing? Really? Surely that's made up?"

"No, that's his actual name. I asked and apparently it used to be MacTin, but so many people got it wrong Mr MacThing's great grandparents changed it."

I pipe up with, "I did a holiday job once and there was a couple there, the MacThings. Maybe they're related."

No one comments on my interruption. Crispin continues, "He's ruthless apparently, built the company his Father started into this aggressive property developing business specialising in waterside schemes. Old canals, harbours, former docks and coastal resorts – even lighthouses and an old radar station. Oh, and those Martello Towers they built during the Napoleonic wars. Often they include marinas and leisure facilities, including shopping."

"They get all that in a Martello Tower?" Frank asks, sounding bemused.

"No, of course not."

Frank looks across at me and winks. "How did we get them as a client?"

"I believe it is through Caen Montreif's Edinburgh office. Caen's have acted for Caldera since they began but they don't seem to have ever had regular English lawyers. Some employment issue needing London expertise. Then there was a financing of an English scheme and we did the property work. Martin agreed to be the partner. Naturally it didn't end well."

Martin Grubways is the most junior partner in our Property Department. He was elevated to the partnership three years ago and that is generally recognised to have been a mistake. If he wasn't in situ then all three of us would have a stab at partnership. Not that any of us are bitter. Not yet, anyway.

Crispin carries on. "When this job came up, they were going to put it out to another firm but because of a recommendation from Greg's Father it came to us as long as Martin wasn't involved. Greg recommended me because it falls within my particular skillset."

Frank glances across again and this time the wink has a degree of sympathy added.

When I glance back to where he's sitting, he gives me this sly grin – very un-Crispin-like – and adds, "Greg's a team player, isn't he?"

Frank nods. "Indeed so." Oblivious to the foul look Crispin has sent in my direction, he adds, "Martin talks highly of your work, Crispin."

Crispin is positively preening. "He's a better judge of a lawyer than many think."

Frank laughs. "True. And I'll have a word with Greg about passing this to you. Very pleasing." I can see him frown briefly. "Who's the partner if not Martin?"

"You."

Frank's shoulder's slump. "Really? I suppose I should read all the memos Charity gives me. Can you brief me, Harry? Next week will do."

I can see Crispin begin to bob around, clearly anxious to show off. "I haven't briefed him yet."

"You haven't? That's a bit remiss, isn't it? You're off aren't you? After the conference?"

Ah, I could sit and watch Crispin sag like a punctured balloon for hours but I'm not that spiteful. "I've been in and out with Chuck, Frank. Not Cris' fault." Crispin loathes that diminutive; I'd didn't say I wasn't childish. "Maybe we can get briefed now? Kill two birds and all that?"

Crispin's sigh is a thing of beauty. He is capable of Olympic-standard sulks but he's not really got any choice. He coughs. "Really you need to do as little as possible. We're working through some solutions to the extension of the original scheme that involves reclaiming some land. According to the client, the sums didn't add up initially but if they can extend then it'll be a game changer. It's pretty complicated and I don't think you'd have the time to get your head around the issues, Harry. No offence, of course, but all that technical law isn't really where your talents lie."

That's true but he's still a bastard for articulating it in front of Frank. And Frank is equally a shit for doing nothing other than to chuckle slightly. "None taken," I say, "I'll just ooze charm and keep the client believing we have humans who work for us rather than machines." No, of course I don't say this but I know he can read my thoughts because he says, "There will be a meeting at the end of next week – a board meeting – and you might be asked to attend and give a briefing. I've done a note and that's all you'll need – they won't have any technical questions; I've attended three board meeting to date and they never ask anything legal. You'll be able to rely on that famous charm, as usual." He mimics Frank's short laugh. "That'll probably go down well as they're not very intellectual, either."

Another laugh from Frank. "We all need to be shallow and frivolous sometimes Crispin."

I love you, Frank Pomeroy.

"Not often, though, eh Harry?"

The sod.

Frank gives it a few moments before he says, "Okay, now before we get there you just need to be aware of a few possible bear traps. And this is the one time when acknowledging you are both possible candidates is acceptable. Given the point of the weekend it would be a bit bloody stupid not to."

We both nod as if this last point is obvious. As if anything in the Byzantine organisational edifice that makes up the modern law firm is obvious.

## *Chapter Seventeen*

After checking in – my room, even though it's right up in the eaves, is spectacular with its own en-suite and minibar; it's certainly not the usual type of place I stay in on my holidays or weekend breaks – I head for the bar. The early arrivals are there surrounding the senior partner. A group of nervy-looking associates have gathered at the other side of the room and I begin to head over when the SP calls me to his group.

"How are things Harry? I was just saying to the others that Barry's inquest is next week. Have you been called? I heard you were in the office that evening?"

"No sir, I haven't."

"Oh, it's Seb, Harry. I think we established that the other day."

I can feel a couple of partners look at the SP curiously, and I'm even more aware of my fellow associates hating me with every snatched glance.

"Did the police interview you? Poor Ronnie was most put out about it all. I think they gave him a hard time for being away from his desk for a period. That and being Irish, possibly. Not that they should worry about Ronnie." The SP glances around and leans forward causing those in his circle to lean in for what is clearly intended as a confidence. "Though don't say I said so to the Managing Partner."

One of the other partners (not that I know his name – I think he may be a Terrance) asks why. The SP closes his eyes, like this is a topic he really doesn't want to talk about. "Roly has a son in the army and is terrified he will come to harm. I think he's currently in Enniskillen, not that anyone says as much. Having Ronnie's Londonderry accent greet him on the way home tends to set his nerves on edge. Not really fair on Ronnie, of course, but it's understandable."

The self-same partner does the decent thing by changing the subject to the Inquest into Barry's death, not that that evinces a better reaction from the SP. I think he may be a litigator (the least empathetic of the partners) from his huge watch – the litigators are all show-offs and have the sharpest suits and plushest offices of anyone, the SP included – in the firm, even better than the Private Client group (who because of their aristocratic clients tend to go in for ancient antique furnishings). If ever they become the most powerful department then the rest of us had better look out. If having company lawyers lording over the rest of we pond life is bad, it'll be a tea party compared to the raptors amongst the litigators. After all property lawyers are the vegans of the City legal firms, known by some as the gardeners but more recently as the Neighbours, the joke (ha ha) being that we are the only lawyers in the firm who get away from our desks early enough to catch the Australian soap, which currently airs at 5:35 every evening.

"It's happening soon. They are sure he had a heart attack, though of course they are still a little coy about that. I asked them to carry out an enquiry purely because the initial police report suggested he'd been moved post-mortem. The woman in charge – an Inspector – said she was happy to wait until the autopsy but given recent…" he stops and looks around; the other partners give knowing looks and nods, "…events I thought it prudent to have them look into things anyway. I doubt it's suspicious. Whoever found him probably was in shock when they called reception and may have moved him for perfectly understandable reasons – checking how he was or to see if they could try mouth to mouth, that sort of thing – and later, having not come forward they feel, I don't know, foolish. There is usually a perfectly simple explanation for these things."

I'm wondering if most of this is for my benefit, but from the rapt look of the other partners it could well be for them.

"Just make sure we keep any speculation to a minimum, eh?" He blesses us with a smile although I doubt I'm the only one who notices the lack of any warmth.

"I think your friends are waving you over, Harry. Don't let us detain you. We'll speak later, I'm sure. Have a good weekend."

Dismissed, I move away and the partners close ranks as the SP continues to hold court. I join the fringe of the group I'd noticed on entering. There are 10 of us so far – in total, in this year's paddock, there are 15 that we know about but some departments are even less forthcoming than the Property department so none of us are actually aware of the true number. All the rumours are that the explosion of City work since Maggie's Big Bang and the privatisation programme has generated a huge need for firms to expand, which means more partners – cannon fodder, really – in every department except one: Private Client, the former home of Barry Tritewell. They have a talented associate who has been passed over four times already – Cynthia Maxwell – who may be added to the list now that Barry has gone. That seems to be the main topic of conversation.

Tony Crescent is the main talker, as per usual. "What did the old prick say? He looked very chummy."

"Just talking about Barry. Poor sod. I was in the office the night he was found and he wanted to know if the police asked me any questions."

"Yeah, and? You see anything?"

"Not me."

Tony isn't really interested in my reply. He's addressing the group in low, conspiratorial tones. "I bet he's bloody nervous. The firm doesn't need more scandals just now, not while the government are working out who to have on its panel of lawyers for all the sell-offs."

A slippery shrew of a man, who could double for the chap who sold Mum life insurance once when he came knocking on our front door – I think she was so surprised someone would venture out as far as our isolated cottage that she bought a policy as a sort of prize for persistence – frowns. I'm pretty sure he's a tax associate and is as certain as Tony is to make it into the winners' paddock, even with his zero client-handling skills – asks about the scandals. To be fair, he did join the firm late on – maybe two years ago – and has probably not seen much daylight since. I have no idea what his name is.

Tony is happy to take centre stage. "Christ, it's amazing the whole edifice didn't collapse. About two years ago one of the litigators drove into a supermarket when drunk and sent one of their displays of special offer baked beans flying – the headline in the *Evening Standard* was 'Legal Eagle Spills the Beans.' Very droll until you realise he put a four-year old into a coma. He'd just left a group of partners celebrating some deal and it didn't read well, especially as the partners closed ranks and he stayed put."

"Who—?"

Tony stills the question with a finger to the lips and smirk. "Not for me to say. Said partner then made it worse by trying to buy the silence of the girl's parents. Even Crout couldn't defend that so he left to pursue 'other opportunities.'"

I suddenly realise who he's talking about. And I thought he had genuinely decided on a change of pace and that the plan to set up a fly fishing school was a positive choice, not some last resort.

The tax nerd – what is his name? – asks, "What happened next?"

"Next?" Tony leans back against the bar, as adept at holding court as Crout. Yep, he'll go far.

"You said scandals?"

"I did, didn't I?"

"Go on."

This is gross. The little gremlin is fawning. Still, if I'm truthful I'd like to know what else. Odd, when one comes to think about it, that we are hard wired to flee or fight, to eat and breathe and also to gossip. I suppose there's no point fighting nature.

"The sex on camera fiasco. Classic. Some misbegotten tourist was apparently trying to take the perfect picture of St Paul's, which our beautiful building hides, and by accident snapped a couple of very clear images of a man, totally naked, taking a woman from behind over a desk on the fourth floor. It was a Sunday so the loving couple probably didn't expect to be caught."

"Are they still with us?" Nerd boy – Colin I think – asks, his eyes gleaming with prurient interest.

"They are. The man is Patterson O'Blick – to Crout's left in the tweed jacket – and the woman is standing by the bar ordering a drink – Sonia Porcelaine. The tourist must have been pretty shrewd because he offered the pictures to the papers. Apparently they were a bit too full-on even for the awful *Sunday Sport*, but even so it took a lot of string pulling for the story itself to be spiked."

"It was Sonia?" I join in. "Are you sure?"

"Well, I've not seen the prints but Patterson isn't shy about his 'conquest.' Who did you think it was?"

I shake my head. I've not heard anything, but it doesn't do any harm to make Tony think I might have. That said, how does Tony know all this? As usual I feel well out of the gossip loop.

He goes on, "When you factor in the collapse of Minters after we acted on their bond issue and the Bank of England investigation, another unfortunate headline, whether in the business pages or gossip columns isn't what we need right now."

"It's a wonder you stay to try to nab a partnership, Tony."

Greg has come up behind me and is smiling. Anyone else and Tony would have gone straight for the jugular but he knows – we all do – that Greg is the last person to cross. Tony laughs. "Someone has to keep this place going, eh Greg?"

"Indeed."

"Surely it's just poor behaviour by a couple of partners, maybe three out of what, 35?" nerdy boy says.

"Hmm, hardly." Tony's supercilious smile gives away how much he's enjoying this. He looks at me, "And Harry, it really was Sonia. If it wasn't then why did her husband – a member of the current cabinet, let it be noted – storm into Crout's office demanding that the 'cuckolding shitebag' who'd just serviced his wife in the fucking office window be sacked immediately or we'd see none of the upcoming legal work that is about to flood us all? And of course said cuckoldee is also the brother of the recently deceased head of the Private Client department… or rather was. Crout, to give him due credit, told the Hon Leon Tritewell MP that—"

Greg stops him with a hand on the arm.

"Gentlemen," it's Crout, tapping a glass, "it's time we adjourned for a briefing on this weekend's activities." He looks at Tony, or rather straight through him. "And we can continue our little office stories later."

We turn to face Tony who is looking everywhere but at Crout. Tony might be suffering from a sort of instant anaemia given how pale he's suddenly become. I shouldn't smile but it couldn't happen to a more deserving pillock than Tony Crescent.

# Saturday, 12th September 1987

## *Chapter Eighteen*

I never realised how much partners drank until last night and the aftermath is reflected in the first session. It's 9:30 am and it comprises a briefing on the financial performance of the first half of the financial year from the Chief Cashier, a man of impeccable hangdog credentials. Neil Grey manages to make Dobbin seem like a natural-born optimist. Having Neil speak this early, after the skinfull imbibed by the vast majority of attendees last night tells you all you need to know about Neil's standing. Even the dead would baulk at trying to function in this graveyard slot.

Looking around the room, waiting for Neil to get his papers organised, I would estimate that there are about 15 partners from an expected 27 attending plus all the 15 associates, none of whom would dare to be absent. That said, two associates have turned green and one is albino. I may not have many skills but being able to avoid too much drink is one I learnt from numerous evenings out with Dobbin. The only others who seem alert are, naturally, Greg – who has probably been for a run, so glowing is he – and the tax associate who is actually called Daniel. It appears he is teetotal, a characteristic that, according to the litigator in front of me, would normally count against him. As he puts it, 'Can you trust a dry-boy?' but he then answers his own question with the most obvious explanation, "But then he does tax law so he's hardly what you'd call normal."

Before Neil begins, the SP takes to the podium. "I think I should update everyone on the situation pertaining to Barry and his department. Of course we are all devastated by his death at such a young age, but as he would be the first to acknowledge the firm must go on. We will have a memorial service in two weeks and the funeral will follow the inquest." He takes a deep breath. "I don't want to spoil Neil's thunder, but you will be pleasantly surprised at how well we are doing this year, which continues the progress we have made over the last two years. I think the case studies we will be working on, which are based on real transactions, will be stimulating and revealing, showing us to be at the top of our game and a match for any law firm in the City. I couldn't be more proud to call each of you my partners and," he looks at our group, "that will include all of you, should you make it through the challenging period ahead."

Neil isn't the only one to think he has finished because he begins to stand only to be stopped, mid-crouch, by a flat hand. "That said, the success is not uniform. Barry's loss is untimely in many ways, but not least because the figures for his department are..." He pauses, looking away over our heads at the large crittall windows behind us as if seeking inspiration, "...less than adequate. I was in a process with Barry – highly confidential, of course – to decide on the future of his department. That discussion will continue and I fully expect to bring a proposal back to you by the end of the calendar year."

To say the room is speechless underestimates the coma into which this silence has fallen. Even the most unaware of attendees can't fail to understand he is effectively saying the Private Client department is for the chop. Behind me and to my right there is a sort of gurgling sound. I'm not the only one to turn and look at the double doors that are the main entrance to the conference room. Standing there, framed in the sunlight, is Florence Dawb, the de facto head of the Private Client department. Florence is lovely, a real star who makes everyone feel welcome. She does dress a bit like a hippie, but she's very clever, easy to work with and always makes me feel wanted. Right now she looks fit to explode.

"You utter bastard, Crout." She doesn't wait for a response but turns and heads for the door to the reception.

When she's disappeared, we turn back to the SP. If I can put any sort of interpretation on his expression, it would be 'See what I have to deal with?' He makes the briefest of nods at Neil and retakes his seat.

Neil's presentation generates no response, no tricky questions and ends early. We are given extra time for a coffee break before reconvening in groups for our first workshop. The associates form a gang at one end of the break-out room. Tony checks no one is nearby before saying, "I knew that was coming. It's been the hot rumour ever since Tritewell snuffed it. He's been fighting a rear-guard for ages and no one knows how he's fended Crout off for so long."

A few others from the larger departments, Company and Litigation nod knowingly. I glance at Greg. He seems to be more interested in a painting hanging over the mantelpiece. I'd lay a small bet that he knew as well. Maybe he feels me staring at him because he looks back sharply.

"It's beginning to look like Barry's death is perfectly timed for our SP."

Tony looks excited. "Are you suggesting he was involved?"

Greg looks at me. "What did that policeman say to you, Harry? You had a good long chat with him, didn't you? Do they think it's all innocent?"

How did he know I'd spoken to Jan about Barry? Was the sod watching me? "He just wanted to know what I'd seen."

Greg shrugs. "That's odd, isn't it? If it was simply natural causes, why would the police be involved? And why would your evidence be relevant? After all, you weren't the one who found him, were you?"

Someone, I'm not sure who asks, "Why were they talking to you anyway?"

Greg holds my gaze. "Harry was working late. Typical Friday night, eh Harry?"

I want to ask what he was doing back in the office but instead say, "Just grabbing a file for the weekend. You know how busy busy we property lawyers are Greg."

Another shrug. What's he playing at? As we break up, another thought occurs to me. Well, two in quick succession. First, why hasn't Crout ever asked me what I was doing in the Private Client department that night? I'm sure I never gave a reason. Maybe he was already there and felt so guilty about it that he forgot to ask. And the second thought is that the reason I was there was to return the packet of photos that I still have in my desk. I need to get rid of them first thing Monday.

# *Chapter Nineteen*

We are all split into teams of six with a hierarchy of partners and associates in each one. Mine comprises Sebastian Crout, Mervin Toogood, Sonia Porcelaine, Doringo Pelmetio, Vicky Wisteria and me. We are dispatched to a small windowless room on the ground floor where all except Sonia, who is tied up elsewhere apparently, convene.

I only really know Vicky and to a lesser extent Mr Crout. Vicky sits next to me on my left and is short and ruddy-faced like she's more used to working outdoors. She is a possible candidate from the Litigation Department and is by common consensus fantastic at her job and far too nice to be any good at it.

Next to her is Doringo, another finance partner in Sonia's team although she specialises in banking while he's what is called a structured finance lawyer. It makes a change that it's not we ignorant real property lawyers, whose work is often contrasted unfavourably with intellectual property lawyers (they must be the brainy ones, naturally) who are the butt of the jokes for once. After all, if there is structured finance, what is unstructured finance? Some sort of informal lending where you just give the money away and ask nicely for a bit of interest? These are what are considered to be legal jokes but they tend to fall very flat at dinner parties. I know of Doringo by reputation (fussy, self-important and clever) but have yet to work with him. He's swarthy, like he's from Southern Europe and wears sharp suits and button-down shirts that Frank calls 'Wanky-Yankies' for reasons I don't understand.

At the far end, facing Mr Crout, is Mervin Toogood. I worked on a job where he was the partner, not that I imagine he would remember as I was very junior at the time. Otherwise all I know is his reputation (litigation Rottweiler, not too worried about either the law or professional ethics so long as he gets the right result. Likes to throw his considerable weight around; he is also 'hands on' in the sense Gloria meant when she went to deliver him a by-hand letter). He is staring at me and making me feel very uncomfortable. It is not a face to snuggle up to; someone once said that if you imagined what a face would look like after sitting in the afterburners of a *Saturn V* rocket on take-off you would have imagined Mervin.

Our allotted task is to consider a strategy for negotiating the disposal of a brewing business following its acquisition as part of a large listed conglomerate company. There are six teams, two each acting for the seller, the buyer and the buyer's financier. We have to come up with the 10 most important issues that we would want to take into account in the negotiations. On the table in front of each of us is a fact sheet; we can ask up to five questions before we provide our list. Our ideas will then be subject to scrutiny by the other teams, after which we will vote on the best list. The winning team will not have to pay for any drinks that evening and they can choose whatever they want from the bar's comprehensive selection – the losing teams will split the bill. Of course you cannot vote for your own list.

Inevitably the SP takes the lead. "I think we should agree it will be a sign of weakness to ask questions so we will forgo that. Then perhaps each of us can put forward a couple of ideas and we can prioritise them. I suggest we leave the last 20 minutes or so to discuss what we think the other teams should have on their lists, so we can challenge them if they aren't there. Yes?"

We all nod.

"Good. Harry?"

I assume he wants me to take notes so I lift my pen obligingly and smile. He smiles back. "What are your two best ideas?" I think he's actually being kind, giving me first go but my mind immediately empties.

The silence isn't long but Mervin grinds out his cigarette and says, "And for fuck's sake don't say the terms of the lease of their premises or I might have to kill you."

Everyone looks to the SP who effects a laugh. "Harry?" His tone is more impatient.

The truth is I was just about to mention property, given that most large brewers have thousands of tied pubs, but my chance has gone and I'm stumped.

Vicky fills the awkward silence, "What about outstanding litigation?"

I love Vicky. She knows it's not likely to be front and centre and I'm sure she's doing it to help me. I say, "Size of their debt?" and smile at Vicky, who nods once.

At that point Sonia appears. She's wearing a tailored two-piece suit with a skirt that ends just below the knee and is cut so tight she can barely swing her legs. To sit, she has to slide in almost sideways. She only makes eye contact with Mr Crout who nods and waits. Deliberately, she slips off her jacket revealing a frilly blouse, opens an enormous bag that she perches on the table in front of her and pulls out a pad and gold pen. Having moved the bag to the floor she looks round at all of us. "Well?"

Mervin lifts his eyes to the ceiling but Mr Crout summarises briefly. She makes quick notes and looks at Vicky, then me. "Litigation and debt?"

Doringo leans forward and makes a funny snorting noise. "Exactly. That's all they've managed in," he looks at his watch, "25 minutes. Anything else or just the amount?"

Sonia sighs. "Doringo, don't be an arse and give him a chance. When you came on your first conference you nearly got sent home for upsetting Craig. Remember Seb? When Craig was explaining about a disastrous meeting he'd had with Chamberlain Bank's Chief Executive?"

The SP smiles. "Yes, that bloody stutter of his." He mimics Craig Parsimon's broad Suffolk accent, "Those clients were so sh-sh-sh-sh-sh..."

Sonia giggles, a sound I thought her incapable of making, "And Doringo has to finish his sentence 'so shitty'..."

The SP is barely capable of finishing the story off, wiping his eyes. "Yes, yes. And old Craig shook his head for about a minute and eventually said, 'No, no, sh...ambolic."

Sonia's face suddenly changes. "So sad he's gone."

The SP follows her lead. "Yes, God rest his soul."

These mood changes aren't easy to keep up with and both Vicky and I are late laughing and even later stopping. Doringo, however, eyes me with undisguised malevolence, like it's all my fault that he has been made the butt of a well-trodden if rather feeble joke by Sonia.

Time is now getting away and the SP takes over, teasing ideas from us. I'm conscious that Mervin hasn't said anything, nor has he been asked to. As we head back into the meeting room he falls into step with me. "What on Earth have you done to Crout? A feeble answer like that would normally see you humiliated yet he lets you, a fucking gardener, get away with it. You his new squeeze, are you? You Mellors to his Lady C?"

He moves away, heading over to where Greg is standing. It feels deliberate, how he holds out a hand and shakes Greg's, clearly smiling throughout. Sod him. The SP is gay? That fits with the rumours although no doubt it would be strenuously denied. And thanks for picking on me, Mervin, and not Vicky even though her answer was also pretty feeble, even if she only did it to help me. At least I can be fairly sure I'll not get his support.

# Sunday, 13th September 1987

## *Chapter Twenty*

Sunday morning is the most terrifying part of the weekend. Once again, we have been drowned in alcohol the previous evening; it is uniformly expensive and almost forced down our throats. One candidate has been taken to hospital though whether because of liver failure or some other unspecified complaint isn't clear. The rest of us are trying to imbibe enough coffee to see us through the first session and I expect I'm not the only one who's thinking that being on a drip in A&E feels like a canny alternative to what the rest of us face. In the next two hours, each of us will be interviewed by a panel of partners. It is meant to be informal and carry no weight in the eventual decision, or so we are told, not that any one of us believes it. I am fifth, immediately after Crispin, who has taken to sitting in a corner and rocking very slightly. Most of the candidates have gone outside for some air – it is a beautifully crisp and sunny morning, the sort of day I can remember as being the first day back at school for a new academic year. Those memories include nerves and excitement and sweating in the new pullover Mum insisted I wear whatever the temperature. Today I easily reprise the nerves and sweats.

About five minutes after Crispin disappears into the interview room my stomach makes a decided flip and I head for the toilets. To my horror every stall is full, no doubt of other candidates. A maid points me to the bar – even though it is shut, she says the toilets are open.

To my relief they are empty, so I take the end stall. I've barely sat when the doors bang open and then shut. Moments later I hear a familiar voice though I can't immediately place it. "What did he say?"

To my surprise the voice is answered by a woman who may be Sonia. "The police are suspicious. I heard he'd just had sex, there were sequins stuck to his head, around his privates, he'd been moved and there were signs his nostrils had been blocked. He may have had a piece of fruit in his mouth."

I'm desperate to hear more but also want to release what I came in to release and I won't be able to hold out for much longer.

"Does Crout know about this?" the male voice asks.

"Of course. He's trying to cover it up, saying we knew he was gay."

"Did we? I didn't."

"Oh don't be a prick; he wasn't gay. Ask all the women he fingered at the Christmas parties over the years. He always had one on the go."

"So not gay?"

"Bi-sexual, I imagine. They're trying to ascertain his movements over the previous 24 hours, just to see if they can find any real evidence. At the moment it makes little sense and anyway he definitely died of a heart attack. It's just the scandal that worries the partnership board. Especially now."

At that moment my sphincter gives way despite my manly and manifold efforts to hold on. The rush and the splash can no doubt be heard 10 miles away in Basingstoke. The two partners go quiet and a moment later the door opens and shuts. When I emerge there's no one to be seen.

I still have 10 minutes to wait and pace the lobby area making myself worse rather than better. I've tried and failed to convince myself that a partnership is in the 'nice to have' category of career ambitions but at this point it is all-consuming. Right on the dot of 11 o'clock Crispin appears from the meeting room, looking sombre but otherwise fairly relaxed. He isn't someone who hides his feelings well, so this sangfroid is unexpected. He nods at me as he passes and hurries away.

The door to the conference room remains firmly shut and I have one of those dilemmas that always strike the unsure and feeble-minded: do I go in to see if they want me or wait to be called? What is the etiquette? On the one hand, my slot is now and Crispin has gone; on the other, if I was expected to go straight in wouldn't Crispin have been charged with the task of telling me? Maybe he was just forcing himself to hold it together until he reached a toilet and forgot to say? At that moment I catch a glimpse of Crispin's frothy hair through the window to the gardens. Standing I see him approach Greg, who is reading a Sunday paper on a bench. Crispin sits and they begin an animated conversation in which both smile and laugh. Why does this feel like a conspiracy? Because you're paranoid, echoes the answer inside my head.

Just then Roly Cuthbert, managing partner, appears from the conference room followed by three other partners. The last is Doringo. As he passes he says, "Go in and wait."

Inside, the room is bare of features beyond a large oil painting behind the bank of four seats, clearly set for the panel. It shows a hunting scene with a stag being savaged by dogs while a hapless gamekeeper – he's in tartan so I suppose he's a ghillie – does his best to call them off. I expect it's famous, but it rather feels like an apt metaphor, except I'm not aware who will be playing the ghillie in the scene that will shortly unfold.

I don't want to be caught out pacing around as it will only emphasise my nervousness, so force myself to sit. In front of me is a pad of notepaper, a pen branded with the hotel's name and in front of that a tray of stationary bits and pieces: a rubber, a couple of pencils, some paperclips, a mini stapler and a small heap of those push-through-bend-back thingies so loved on children's TV shows.

Absently I pick up one of the paperclips and unwind it. Why would Crispin go and find Greg? I'm his closest friend so why not speak to me? If he's briefing Greg – whose slot is second from last – on the panels' questions, then why not tell me too? Greg is always saying we are the favoured ones for the partnership slots and, of course I believe him, but what if the two of them are trying to outflank me?

"Harry? Sorry for the delay. You okay for another five minutes?"

It's Roly, a chubby man who favours wide red braces that frame his belly like the rind of a cheese.

"Gpher. Ptrank-olaiop." The sounds I make, which are intended to be a confirmation that I'm happy with the delay, are caused by the fact that the unwound paperclip is now stuck between my incisors. It appears that I have absent-mindedly tried to chip away some plaque from my teeth and the little metal wire has become jammed.

"You all right?" He does sound genuinely concerned and since I'm facing away from him, he can't see my problem.

I nod rather frantically and hear him withdraw, at which point I begin a panicked tugging and twisting, trying to free myself from my self-inflicted impaling. The little bastard thing appears to be completely jammed. After a minute that seems like a weekend, I can't fix it. In my desperation I stick my head out of the door and check the lobby area. No one. Covering my mouth with a handkerchief like some Victorian heroine suffering a fit of the vapours – which isn't so far from my actual mental state right now – once again I head for the toilets next to the bar. In the mirror I can better see the problem but my horror is compounded by the fact I appear to have become a late flowering punk by piercing my lip and have dripped blood down my white shirt. How did I not feel that?

I'm now on the verge of tears. If I could open my mouth I might scream with frustration. And then, to my horror, the door opens and Greg appears. "I thought I saw you. They... what have you done to your face?"

It's too late to hide the damage. I stand and let him inspect me and my paperclip-pricked hopes and begin to sag at the knees.

"Right, let's fix this." Before I can protest – like I could if I wanted to – he steps forward and in a swift, albeit excruciating manoeuvre twists and removes the wire. He grabs a wad of tissues that he dampens and hands me to stop to blood while getting a second wad that he offers for me to sponge away the stain on my shirt. In under a minute he stands back. Then he takes off his pullover and hands it to me. "Put this on. It'll hide the stain."

I do as I'm told.

"Good. Come on, they're assembling. You'll knock them dead. And if they ask about the lip say you missed your bed last night having had too much Scotch. It'll make them laugh."

We're now outside the room. I can hear a murmur of conversation inside. He gives my arm a squeeze. "Go kill 'em, cowboy. And if they ask about overseas expansion tell them to focus on Japan and China, not Europe. Tell them the opportunities there are better and you need a long run in to build credibility." With a shove I'm inside and facing my doom.

## Monday, 14th September 1987

## *Chapter Twenty-One*

The interview turned out to be fine; sure enough they asked about 'our global reach' and then something about corporate governance that not only mystified me but also another panel member, which caused Roly to have to intervene and end the session as we were at risk of running over. They laughed as I elaborated on my lip damage and started telling tales of their own debauched evening; I guess the fact that you don't make it to partner without both a huge ego and enjoying the sound of your own voice means these sorts of things are as much a test for the panel to keep quiet as they are the interviewee to speak.

Back at my desk there is already a message from my sister offering to buy me lunch; that's a first. There's also a message from someone called Olga who works at a firm called Howard Kitchen, which I've never heard of, and two more: one from Greg suggesting coffee with him 'to debrief the weekend' and a second from Crispin who wants to speak to me before I speak to Greg. Crispin is flying to Capri or some such with his Mother this morning and says he'll call again.

I have Chloe ring Dina to sort out a time and place and then call Olga. She sounds like she went to a finishing school, so embedded are her vowels in the back of her throat. I'm having difficulty understanding what she's saying when I'm put through to another person.

"Hi Harry. Good to speak to you."

It is Brenda Silverman, Dobbin's ex. She and I haven't had much to say to each other for some time, and nothing since she and Dobbin split up. That's mostly because our interactions are coloured by the fact she acted as a spy for Stephen McNoble some years ago and nearly got me repurposed as reinforcement in the concrete footings of some office development or motorway flyover. I tell myself that I have forgiven her in principle but that thought is contradicted by the anger that immediately surfaces on hearing her voice.

"Brenda. You must want something to be calling me. Whatever it is, the answer's no."

"Ha! You always were a joker."

"I didn't know you'd thrown in your lot with us merciless capitalists. When did you start at Howard Kitchen?"

"It's just to make some money for the shelter. I've something for you."

"Really? How unusual."

"Hear me out. I know you're shooting for a partnership and I'm sure you'll get it, but if you don't…"

"I'm not working for a women's rights firm, Brenda."

"You'd be great! Seriously probably the only man I know who'd try to understand."

"Thanks."

"You have been well trained by your sis and Penny."

"You did have to go and ruin it. When have you been talking to them?"

"I know you're busy so very quickly, I was speaking to an old contact of ours and he wanted to be put in touch with you in case you needed his services. He's a headhunter, helps run a business that deals with all sorts of professional placements and you're the sort of chap they'd really be able to assist."

"If he's a contact of mine as well as you, why not call me direct?"

"I think he felt I'd know your situation better than him. John Thomas from the College of Law? Remember him? He and Karen got together and set up an agency about two years ago. Going great guns, I believe."

"John with Karen Himcol? How'd they get into business together?"

"Bed first, business later."

I can't help squeaking. "They're an item!?" Karen was a sophisticated star in our year group, a bit severe perhaps but a real genius who was destined for the highest position in the law; John was not and was in fact an utterly unambitious klutz whose only hope of making it was to marry well. It looks like he succeeded.

"They have two kids now as well. Karen had a huge amount of prejudice against her when she got pregnant and was side-lined from an obvious partnership, so they set up a business that specifically caters for women professionals but recently their more thoughtful and caring approach has appealed to a wider constituency. You interested?"

"Not really. It's full-on just now; hunting season has opened and I'm trying to dodge the bullets. I'll know by the end of October if previous years are anything to go by. Maybe if it goes pear-shaped I'll call him."

"Would you mind if I gave him your number, just so he can follow up?"

"Yes, but on one condition."

"Which is?"

"You call Gary and—"

"Harry, we're over."

"Yes, but he still cares and he has a proposition for you."

"I bet he does."

"Stop it. You loved him once."

"I still do."

"Sorry?"

Her sigh is deep and comes from a long way back. "What has he told you about why we split up?"

"You needed to explore your feminine side; you wanted to focus on helping woman and you'd become a lesbian—"

That causes a burst of laughter. "Me? A lesbian? Oh, come off it. You had a bedroom next to ours. It wasn't me who couldn't keep it up if you recall."

It's my turn to laugh. "The chilli up the arse?"

"That was a bit of a myth but yes. No, it wasn't to do with sexuality but more, oh, political I suppose."

"Gary doesn't do politics."

"Exactly; I do. He wanted to make money, a real Thatcherite poster boy. He had to, didn't he, given his parents… especially his Dad. It was all about showing he could be successful, all about proving his bastard Father wrong. He never had your guts to break that familial umbilical cord. I couldn't stand the way he was going but if I'd told him to stop, it would have crushed him. It felt easier to tell him I'd moved on from him."

"You are serious, aren't you? He loves you."

"Not any more. Not if the last two times we've met are anything to go by."

"Are your politics more important than—"

"I've got to go. I'll let John have your details."

Damn. I thump the desk in frustration. Just then the phone rings and I snatch it up. "Spittle."

A slow quiet Scottish voice says, "Are you the same Harold Spittle who worked at Hemingways in 1976? You sound rather flustered."

"Who is this?"

"Gerald MacThing. My family stayed there and you made quite a hit with my parents. My Mother especially."

Christ. All I can remember – or rather the thing that I immediately remember – is seeing her sunbathing nude, her pubic hair apparently dyed bright orange. I still shudder at that image; there are some things that you can never unsee.

"How are you, Harry? I hear from my people that you've taken over from that cretin Crispin Muddle. What an apt name."

That is a great start.

"Hello, Mr MacThing. Yes, I remember your parents. I'm sorry but I can't remember if you were there."

"Briefly Harry, briefly. And it's Gerald, please. I assume Mr Muddle has spoken about our project and the setback? I'd like to meet on site to discuss it before we have our board meeting. Can you make that? I'm free on Wednesday afternoon. It will take you three hours by train, so you will be out most of the day. Billing me, of course, so I doubt that's a real hardship."

I flick through my diary. "I think that should be fine, I just need to check with my secretary."

"Call mine and confirm. The number will be on your file. I do hope you have a more solution-based approach than your colleague."

I'm staring at the phone, wondering about Crispin when it rings again. Goodness I'm popular today.

"Spittle."

"Harry. I've been holding for ages. I have 10 minutes before we're called to our gate."

"Crispin, just the man. I've just had Gerald MacThing on and—"

"He rang himself?"

"No, he rang me."

"Don't be a twat, Harry. Why?"

"To quote him 'I assume Mr Muddle has spoken about our project and the setback?' What setback? You didn't mention any setback."

"It's in the briefing paper."

"Which I don't have because your secretary is incompetent."

"They want to build out into the water, reclaim some of the seabed. Legally it's fascinating but, well, they didn't like my advice much."

"Which was?"

"They'll probably need an Act of Parliament."

"You're kidding? How do you do that? And how long does it take?"

"I spoke to a Parliamentary Agent. About two years and it costs a fortune."

"Oh yes, that would explain the, quote, 'I do hope you have a more solution-based approach than your colleague,' unquote. Thanks for that."

"Look, I'll sort it when I'm back, okay? Just don't go making things worse. And don't tell Greg or Frank or Martin."

"Why did you call? Why before I speak to Greg?"

"He said you were trying to shaft me by getting him to agree to a strategy that sees him and you as partners. Is that true?"

"Not exactly. But he suggested to me that 'we should look out for each other because we were the ones most likely to succeed…'"

"When did he say that? This weekend? The shit is trying to play us off against each other."

"It was a week or two ago."

"Really? Why didn't you say something?" There's some sort of public announcement in the background that drowns him out, then he says, "I've got to go. Don't you dare agree to anything with him. I don't trust him. Or you for that matter." Then there's a click and he's gone.

When I look up Greg is at the door. "Coffee?"

## *Chapter Twenty-Two*

Greg says nothing about Crispin, focusing on the weekend. He tells me that everyone – which I think means the existing partners – were surprised by what was said and, more pertinently, implied by the SP's words on the future of the Private Client department. Apparently a lot of time and energy were wasted on people taking sides, although the consensus seemed to be that it was inevitable after Barry's death. I wonder if I should mention the conversation I overheard in the toilets but decide that I'll keep that to myself for now. Once again, I'm reminded about the photographs in my desk drawer. I really need to do something with them. I wonder if he's going to mention Crispin's conversation with him in the gardens on Sunday or his, Crispin's conspiracy theory but our fellow property lawyer barely rates a mention. Overall Greg expresses himself satisfied with the weekend. "We're on track, Harry. Mark my words."

The photos have to wait as I need to go and find Dina for lunch and to sort out what is going on with Magda. The restaurant she has chosen is underneath the office, a grubby place where they bring the dish of the day on a metal platter, all cold and congealed. If you choose it they shove it in the oven, overheat whatever it is and return it, only this time on a plate. If that sounds unappetising then it pales in comparison with the set menu, where the emphasis is on the 'set' rather than the 'menu.' But it's obviously close by and cheap so tends to do a decent trade. When I arrive some 10 minutes early she is already there with Magda.

As I take my seat I say, "You found her."

"No thanks to you. Are you going to help?"

"With her citizenship? I explained—"

"I've ordered. Chicken and chips. No wine."

"Fine. I don't have the expertise to help. I suggested—"

"Noor. I know. She's not qualified so she'd need to bring in someone else. This needs to be, erm, handled with discretion."

"What's going on, Di? You know I don't have the relevant skills or the contacts, and neither does Newe Waters. And it's a pretty straightforward matter if she's been here long enough. So…?"

The conversation around us is growing, and it makes us lean in close to hear each other. She says, "Do you remember the German group who stayed at home just before you sorted out Sven's Will?

They had originally been going to stay at Hemingways, but Ravi sent them to Mum and Dad?"

"Were they the gay ramblers? Dad thought they were boy scouts or something?"

"They were from Leipzig in East Germany. One of them was a spy and he recognised Magda. It may even have been set up so he could get at her."

Magda has been resolutely silent and now looks down, seemingly ignoring everything but I suspect she's listening intently.

"He approached her and told her that her sister was doing well at her school – she is a teacher – but that 'might not continue if Magda didn't help the DDR.'"

I try not to look like I'm about to laugh. "He wanted her to be a spy in the arse end of nowhere?"

"You'd be surprised at some of the secret establishments hidden in places like Lymington."

"Too right I would."

"The thing is the Germans knew of it. Some of the visiting scientists stayed at Hemingways because of its proximity and that gave Magda opportunities to collect whatever intelligence she could."

"Bloody hell." I look at Magda, not trying to hide my scepticism, and she nods. "This is all a bit James Bond. We're talking the New Forest here. It's hardly a hotbed of international espionage."

Magda smiles. "You remember ze man with the sunglasses who vore ze tveed suit in ze heat?"

"Him? We thought he was just a nutter."

"Izz big 'ead from Oxford. 'e 'ad zese black prints."

Dina touches her hand and she leans back. "Blue prints. Dad must have told you about the man with the expensive cameras who wanted to know how he could access the water tower. He was sure he wanted to take pictures of Doris Feldstein."

"Really?" My memories of Ms Feldstein are of a woman with shoulders like a prop forward and a penchant for smoking with a cigarette holder. She also had to be close to receiving her telegram from the Queen.

"A spy. When I joined MI5 they knew about her, knew about what was going on and had been feeding her misleading information for about a year. But they wanted to up it and to do that they needed to recruit her as a double agent. They knew I knew her and, well, it was a test, you know? Asking me to get close and work with her. I had the perfect excuse to be there so if she was being watched, my presence wasn't suspicious…"

"This is so exciting."

"Shut up Harry. Magda's sister is at real risk here, but no one is taking it seriously. They know they have enough to deport Magda but if that happens, neither her nor her sister will be safe. If she uses Noor, then when the Home Office ask awkward questions, as they might well do, no one will be able or more to the point willing to feed them the right answers."

"I don't understand why you need me? Why this citizenship business?"

"We need an impeccable character to back up her story, to work for her – someone who will pass on what I feed them and not ask dumb questions. Someone who knows her, not a stranger who they might suspect. You, in other words. When she gets that passport, it can be taken to Germany and smuggled across the Wall and her sister can use it to escape. All quite legal. Ish. They are twins, you see. Not identical but close enough. All you have to do is sign the forms, send them in and chase them up. And answer any queries they raise with my help. She doesn't even need to be a client. You're an old friend doing a favour, that's all."

"I just have to swear I've known Magda since I worked in the hotel? Okay, that's not difficult."

"It's a bit more than that. You'll need to vouch for her reasons for being here, how you knew her at university and then at Hemmingways. You know her as Matilde Grummann, though you've always called her Magda. That's who you have to say you know."

"Who's this Matilda Thingy?"

"She was a German student who disappeared. We've kept her actual disappearance secret and this is the perfect chance to utilise her identity."

I google at Dina. "Did you kill her?"

"Now who's being a bit James Bond? No, of course not. Just taking advantage of circumstances."

"What happened to the real Matilde?"

"Does it matter?"

"Er, yes."

"She's joined a cult in Penzance. Rejected all material things in favour of a cabbage diet, hemp clothes and free sex."

"Seriously?" I hold up my hand; I don't want the answer. "The point is this is all beyond shady, I have a career and life and child to worry about and... what?"

Dina raises a hand to still my rejection.

With the other she extracts a VHS tape and hands it over to me. The cover is blank. "You need to understand this is serious, Harry. Have you wondered why Noor hasn't answered your calls? Because I've made sure she doesn't want to."

"How? And what is this?"

"Has Penny mentioned Ida Soderberg and a fitness video?"

"How do you know about that?"

"Penny's excited, isn't she? Something to do that's not just her being a Mum. What's she heard? They know she made a fitness video before and now want her, as a pregnant woman, to be the lead in a series showing how to get back to full fitness, postpartum? They want to break into the new Mums' market, to tap the current pressure for new Mums to get back into shape."

"What are you trying to say, Di?" I turn the box over. "Is this a copy of the original video?"

"At the time Penny made the fitness video, she made two other recordings. A music video... and this." She reaches across and taps the tape. "It's porn. A sex tape."

I google at her. "Penny? When?"

"Doesn't matter. I—"

"It fucking does matter. When?"

She rubs her face. "Listen, I don't want to do this, okay, but it's not my decision. If you don't help us – and we need this to be as independent as we can make it – then a copy of this tape will find its way to her parents and then to the senior partner of your firm. It will be made clear that it will also be sent to the *Evening Standard* and all the rest of the gutter press if you're made a partner."

I can barely speak let alone breathe. "Why tell her they're making a new video then?"

"You know what Penny's like about stripping off. They'll get some new shots and, well, with careful editing it'll look like she's still at it."

"I'll warn her. Tell her—"

"Really? And how do you think that conversation will go?"

I really think my brain is melting.

A waiter with a fake French accent brings me back to the present. "Who is having the breast? They are lovely and juicy, no?"

# *Chapter Twenty-Three*

Being at home is rather awkward. First, knowing Magda is there in her room is bad enough. But second, knowing she knows about this tape is appalling. And what do I think about it? And Penny? Does it matter? Penny and I have had other partners during our various times apart – at the last count there have been five 'pauses' of different lengths since we first started dating – actually we had sex first and then went out, which sort of sums up the oddity of our relationship. I know it shouldn't matter and, let's face it, I've been agonising about my behaviour with Natalie, who is her closest friend and not some mechanical 'sex for cash' piece of celluloid. Is that better or worse? Is the fact she's kept it from me making it worse? Is it true? I have the tape and could watch it, but can I? And what the fuck is my sister doing blackmailing me? Of course, given the circumstances I signed the papers for Magda's citizenship and have them in my briefcase with the tape. I say I'll send them off tomorrow.

Penny is sitting on the sofa, watching the news. On her lap is a bowl of what appears to be anchovies. She is dipping each one in honey and then delicately laying it across a water biscuit. Before I speak she says, "It's not a craving; they ended months ago. It was on the radio today. Apparently these are good for Mothers-to-be. You don't think I'm weird, do you?"

"No, not at all. You like Mum's cooking so in culinary terms you're in a select group of one anyway. How's your day been?"

"I think I dislocated a rib while pulling up my pants. Mr Gruber next door was treated to an absolute rifter when I reached up to get the washing off the line – I think he was peeping again but the heavy breathing could be him sucking up oxygen after my outburst – and I spent an hour on the phone with Natalie who told me I need to make sure I'm not neglecting you." She looks straight at me. "Sexually I mean. Am I?"

My mind lurches to the idea of Penny starring in a porn movie. "You've been talking to Natalie about our sex life?"

"No, unlike you boys we girls don't fixate on sex. But we haven't done it for weeks, have we? Apart from a bit of solo sexing, that is."

"That was great."

"Was it? Really? I saw how you looked at the NCT class when Pet said they still had lots of sex."

"Actually, they said they still exchanged fluids or some such which isn't quite the same thing."

"I'm not sure I can right now. I want you to know it's, just, well, it really doesn't appeal at the moment. With me like this. I want to, but every time I think we should do it I picture myself, and, well, it's such a turn off. Does that make sense?"

"Of course."

"Are you, you know, managing?"

On the television Trevor MacDonald is talking about Zimbabwe and a visit by some government minister. I can feel his gaze boring into me, much like Penny. Why does he care what I do to relieve myself? Would he do a report on the new sex tape?

I'm not sure if I should admit that I have been pretty good at not overdoing the polishing of Percy but I did have a sneaky little hand-shandy in the hotel at the weekend. Before I can say anything, her fingers – still a bit sticky from the honey – begins to tug at my fly. Michael Heseltine is on screen now talking about the success of a development project in Liverpool. Her fingers ease me out and with what I assume is anchovy oil she begins to encourage a growth spurt. At T-minus not many seconds, the screen cuts to a forlorn looking football manager who has already been given the heave-ho and Penny hisses, "Hanky," before Big Ben appears – some feature on resetting the clock – and as it erupts into its familiar ding-dongs so do I, as harmoniously an apt a metaphor as any I could conjure up. As things begin to subside the weather man warns of imminent downpours and recommends a brolly. Penny looks at my hand, hanky cupped to catch the mess, and giggles. We kiss for a while before I'm dispatched to make tea.

When I return with two cups and a chocolate Bourbon each, I ask, "So when do you think you might fancy it again?"

She looks worn out. "I don't know Harry. I'm so worried about how big this baby is going to be I'm not sure I'll ever be fit for it again. My fanny will be so huge you might fall in." She puts the tea down and kisses me. "I do love you. Here," She holds my hand on her bare, beautifully brown stomach and instantly I feel a kick. She is utterly sexy and if I could only find the switch I'd willingly take any position to make love to her but that ain't going to happen for a while. Instead I kiss her belly button.

She pushes me away with a sad little sigh. "How was your day?"

"Me? Oh, you know. Just the usual routine same old same old."

"Magda seemed a bit withdrawn. She wouldn't even look at me. I hope things work out for her."

"Yeah, me too." If they don't then I'm not entirely sure what my darling little sister is capable of.

I sip my tea and watch Penny fall into a deep sleep. She is unutterably gorgeous so who cares if she's in a blue movie? Maybe I can use that to... no Harry, stop it. I kiss the end of her nose and she stirs a little but soon resumes her rhythmical breathing. "Maybe," I say to her as I give each breast a small kiss, "we should get married and make our child legitimate." I plant another kiss on her stomach.

She doesn't move. I toy with leaving her there, but in the end I ease her awake and help her to bed where we go through the rigmarole of propping up her engorged stomach with extra pillows. As she slips back to sleep I chastise myself for my cowardice; I should propose properly. When she's awake. Wimp.

# Tuesday, 15th September 1987

## *Chapter Twenty-Four*

At just before 10.00, Chloe is by my desk with some post to sign. As I'm reading the letter through – it's pretty good although I do say it myself – she asks, "Did you like Mr Tritewell?"

"Barry? I didn't really know him well enough to say if I liked him or not. He was probably the most irritating partner to work for – talk about picky. But he was okay, I suppose."

"Oh. I must have misunderstood."

I look at her then. "Why do you say that?" My chest is suddenly tight. Has someone said something?

"It's just you have a packet of his photographs in your bottom drawer – I was looking for my stapler that someone has taken, and you had it before so... Anyway, I saw them. I'm sorry, I thought it might be holiday snaps but then I saw the name. I just wondered."

Before I can stop myself, I say, "But the drawer – the drawers – were locked."

"I've always had a spare key, didn't you know?" Her look morphs from confused to beady. "Is it a secret?"

"No. No, of course not. I picked the packet up by mistake on Friday, the Friday before he died, and I would have given it back to him but for that. I should pass them on to Gladys."

"I can do that."

"It's all right. I'd better explain to her why, you know, I have them."

She nods. "Your client Mr Streib called and said he'd be 20 minutes late and Miss Porcelaine said she won't be able to make it. Mr Pelmetio will be there instead."

Doringo. Great. The man thinks I'm a muppet. Why couldn't Sonia tell me herself?

At least the delay gives me a chance to do something with the photos. As soon as Chloe has disappeared back to her work station I open the drawer and pull out the packet. It is immediately apparent it has been opened. Nosy woman. She said she saw the name but that was after she looked inside.

I slide out the inner folder and flip it open. I can see the top half of the first picture. It shows Barry from the rear, his bald head gleaming and his shoulders bare. It takes a moment to realise he is wearing the same dress that I saw him in the night he died. Shit, did Chloe see that? Is that why she wondered if we were close?

My hands are shaking as I ease the photos out. There are only six or seven. After the back view of Barry standing in his room at night in the dress, there are other shots of his room, one with an apple in the centre of his desk. I take a deep breath and study the image with Barry in it. This time I realise the dress is unzipped; he's standing as if he's waiting for the cameraman – or woman – to zip him up.

The last picture is in daylight. Still in Barry's room but this time he is in his suit, smiling at the camera, almost a formal pose. He's holding a fat pen and the composition makes it look as if he's about to sign something important.

Only seven photos. I fumble for the negatives. There's only one strip in a grease proof paper sheaf. When I slip it out and hold it up to the light, I nearly lose control. The images are all of Penny on the beach. Eight or nine and in three she is clearly topless, her boobs splayed across her bump and her areolas huge like saucers.

"Mr Spittle?" I drop the strip as Chloe adds, "Mr Streib is here. Conference room four."

As soon as she's gone I put the negatives in one part of my briefcase and the photos in the packet in another and lock it up in a different drawer. Chloe doesn't have a key to that. Having done that, I detour to the toilet, splash water on my face and head off to see Chuck.

He is dressed in his suit that looks about two sizes too small. He is frothing out of the shirt collar too. "This won't take long, will it?" he asks irritably.

"Hope not," I say, not really knowing. "I'll introduce you and if you can then explain what you're after—"

"Didn't you do that already?"

"I did my best, but we've discussed this once and I want to make sure we have it clear. If I've missed something, then it would be dumb to assume. Yes?"

I'm not normally so forthright – the worry about the photos has disabled my polite gene – but Chuck seems content with the answer. He sits down, eases back and lights up a Marlboro. "What's with your girlfriend?"

"Penny?" How does he know about Penny?

"Nah. The broad who runs the bar. Natalie. She ill?"

"No, I don't think so."

"I ain't seen anyone so skinny in ages."

"Oh yes, well, she's become something of an obsessive runner and has lost a fair bit of weight." He eyes me carefully. As the door begins to open and Doringo enters he adds, "I think it's something more than that, Harry."

## *Chapter Twenty-Five*

When I emerge from the meeting, Doringo is delighted and thanks me for the introduction. "This is so exciting Harry. There's a lot of research needed here. This stuff is right at the front of the financial changes. If we get this right, it'll be a huge boost for the banking practice. And property, of course."

Chloe stops me and tells me the SP wants a word. "He said there's no rush but to make sure you got the message as soon as you were free."

That's pretty clear, then. I don't bother to ring to check if he's busy, but simply change direction and head for the fourth floor. As I walk along the corridor from the lifts, his secretary sees me and points at his door, indicating I should go straight in.

"Close the door, Harry. And sit."

Sebastian Crout is a vain man. His hair is a thick bouffanty affair that touches his collar. It's a mix of honey blond and grey and is, I suppose, distinguished. It is also never changing; every hair is in exactly the same place at all times. Talk about obsessive grooming. Rumours about a hairpiece have yet to be substantiated.

"I thought the weekend was a great success. Did you?" He wears half-moon reading glasses and looks at me over the tops of the lenses.

"I suppose that depends." I'm still in the new decisive Harry mode, which may not be a good thing.

"Depends? On what?"

"On how I get on in this partnership round."

"Oh. Ha! Yes, of course. Your perspective is inevitably a little different to mine. What did the associates think about my announcement?"

"Was it an announcement?"

"I think so, yes. Florence certainly thought so."

"The mood amongst those from the larger departments was 'inevitable.' Smaller departments were more circumspect."

"Really?"

I don't elaborate and he doesn't ask, which immediately begins to undermine my newfound self-confidence.

He looks quite pleased. "For what it's worth, I thought you did well. Confident without being arrogant. Still," he puts a yellow telephone attendance note in front of him, "I don't suppose you care what I think."

What? Is he potty? The senior partner says I did well and I don't care? Ha!

"Turning to more, erm, sombre matters, the police have been in touch. They are becoming increasingly, ah, *focused on* Barry's death and some apparent, erm, inconsistencies. I need you to tell me exactly what you told them. Just so we can allay any suspicions."

"Suspicions? But he died of a heart attack, didn't he?"

"We await a formal decision on that, but yes it looks likely. It's the other things…"

I mirror his earlier silence but it seems to annoy rather than undermine him. "Well?" he says.

"Sir?" He doesn't correct my mode of address. Bang goes the cordiality.

He squeezes his eyes shut. "Harry," he pops them open and stares at me unblinking. "You will say if you find yourself being compromised in any way, won't you?"

Oh shit. "Compromised?"

"We need to do what is best for his family. It would be unfair on them to allow him to be mired in scandal."

A thought occurs to me and before I can weigh it up I open my mouth. "You moved him?"

This garners a wince. "Only so far as I needed to, to make it seem, erm, natural. I don't want you to think – if the police speak to you again – that there was any ulterior motive. Just bear in mind I did it for the benefit of the firm. And Barry's family, of course."

I nod, although I'm not sure what I'm agreeing to. His reasons sound well-intended but surely he should know better than to interfere with a real life corpse.

He seems to echo my thoughts. "It's a strange feature of the human condition, Harry, that you can do something for the right reasons but which only causes more problems, or at least different ones than those you were trying to remedy. All I wanted to do was avoid a scandal for his family. So far as I know, or rather knew, Barry didn't dress in women's clothes, nor, I think, did he have a proclivity for strange sex games. But I could have been wrong. By removing those features, I seem to have stirred up… something else."

It occurs to me that it is rather odd that he is confiding in me.

"The police? What did they say?" he asks me again.

"Not much, sir." I repeat what Jan Kruis said and he seems satisfied.

"Let's just keep it between us then."

I'd like to ask why he thinks that's still a good idea and maybe mention the conversation I heard in the toilets, but just then his secretary knocks on the door.

"Mr Crout, your appointment is here."

Dismissed, I decide I need some air so head outside. There's a sandwich bar behind our offices and they make a really good milky coffee and occasionally I buy a fruity bun to accompany it, although recently they have been oddly flavoured.

It's as I'm queueing that I see a face peering through the window, one that is vaguely familiar. He is clearly a vagrant, with wild unkempt hair and goggling eyes. He appears to be staring at me.

Behind me one of the two brothers who run the shop – they are Italian – swears in his native tongue and limbos under the counter flap to rush outside and shoo the homeless man away. I feel a little sorry for the old boy, but the proprietor comes back in, full of profuse apologies. Up close – I'm usually separated from him by the wide serving counter – I realise that his hair is heavily oiled and smells of lavender. I turn and gawp at his brother who has the same thick, slicked-back thatch. As I watch, horror layered on disgust, he runs his fingers through his hair and then presses down on my bun while he cuts it in half.

"I give you extra butter to make up."

I take the paper bag with my disgustingly well-oiled bun and polystyrene cup of coffee and hurry outside; I can't get away quickly enough. As I reach the nearest bin and am in the process of dumping the bun, a hand stops me. It's the vagrant. "Can I have that if you don't want it? I like buns, even the scented ones."

How did he know? I hand it over and he looks directly at me. I am immediately struck by his body odour and his eyes, which are a piercing blue.

"Hallo Harry. The Men of Barrington are always on your side. Take good care of yourself. Godspeed."

For the second time in a minute I'm gawping. The dishevelled beggar is none other than Charlie Jepson, my Mother's ex-lover, Father to my long-term nemesis Stephen McNoble and a congenital crook. Last time I saw him he was cursing me from pillar to post as I had just handed over his share of Sven Andersen's estate to his wife Monica, who had no intention of sharing any of it with him.

What's he doing here? And since when did he become a homeless person? And who on Earth are the Men of Barrington?

I'm rather shaken as I walk slowly back to my office.

There's a message from Gerald MacThing with details of our meeting in deepest darkest Sussex tomorrow. "I'll pick you up at Barrington town station, 12.45 pm." This is too weird. What did Jepson say about Barrington? The Men of Barrington are on my side? Did I hear that right?

Why is it that my life spirals out of control just when things were settling into a boring normality?

# Wednesday, 16th September 1987

# Chapter Twenty-Six

Magda and Penny seem to have had a disagreement and Magda has moved out, or so Penny says. I'm now worried about her but Penny won't answer any questions. It takes a night's sleep and me bringing her a cup of tea in bed, coupled with massaging her shoulders to loosen her up. That wins me a huge sigh and a sort of smile.

"She said the weirdest thing about our sex life. Or lack of. I rather assumed you must have said something and that led to a row. Do you care that she's gone?"

"It's nice to have the place to ourselves, but Dina told me some odd stuff..."

"Yes?"

"You know where Di works?"

"MI5? Seriously, they're interested in Magda? And there was me thinking you might have decided to get your end away with a bit of East German disciplinarian sex."

"You know... oh, ha ha. No, only you oh light of my life."

"You don't fancy her, do you?"

"Hardly. I'm concerned, that's all."

"She's very touchy-feely for a Communist."

"That has to be up there with the top three strangest things I've heard in the last twenty-four hours."

"What are the others making the short list?"

"Number two is Charlie Jepson telling me the Men of Barrington are on my side and the Senior P—"

"You've seen Jepson?"

I briefly recount the circumstances. Penny can't stop shaking her head.

"Number one has got to be a humdinger."

"Crout telling me he was impressed with me this weekend?"

"Yep, that's clearly weird."

"Thanks."

"He's cleverer than he appears if he's sussed that out."

I give her a kiss on the lips. "Magda is in trouble and Dina needs me to help. I'm not exactly happy but, you know..."

"You'd do anything for your sister."

"She's saved my bacon enough times."

"And you hers."

"Not really."

137

"She thinks so."

"Does she?"

"If you stop being so self-deprecating then I'll stop asking if you still fancy me."

"Done. Did Magda say where….?"

"Sorry, no – and no forwarding address left by her bed."

"Oh well."

***

The journey to Barrington is torturous, comprising a cancelled train at Victoria, a lost driver at East Croydon and a broken bogey at Three Bridges. The extra time gives me a chance to read the file thoroughly and fully understand the dilemma. Partly this is because of Crispin's patent excitement at such a complicated problem landing in his lap. Words such as 'uniquely difficult' aren't reassuring to any client.

What is clear is that Crispin has explored all the angles and the only solution appears to be this Private Members' Act of Parliament. It's not something I've come across before and it's not something they taught us at university so I have to rely on the note left by an articled clerk. The train has slowed to a crawl, so for want of anything better to do, I begin to read the attachments to the research note. One is a 'Short History of Barrington' that appears to have been written in the 1920s. One of the chapter headings catches my eye:

### *The Men of Barrington*

> *It is often claimed that ancient rights to encroach on the foreshore exist here in Barrington, originating in the uncertain times before the Norman invasion of 1066. The local Lordship of the Manor appears, from authority established in the case of Primrose v Dugdale 1874, to possess rights that are probably unique along this stretch of coast, including the right to moor without payment, to establish footings for a pier from which passenger boats may arrive and depart and to dredge sand and shingle for three days in every calendar year…*

How interesting. There is no copy of the case referenced nor any indication that Crispin was aware of it and the possibility it might assist. What's most intriguing is how on Earth Charlie Jepson knew about it and was aware of my upcoming involvement. That really is too weird.

The meeting itself is fascinating. I may be a bit of a nerd but I love wandering around development sites, imagining how my legal work might translate into something tangible like a new harbourside scheme. All my colleagues in other departments work on paper, never seeing their work in 3D. How do you see a loan? A company takeover? Other than as a series of contracts? Gerald MacThing isn't around so I'm shown the proposals by his project manager, a windswept ruddy man called John (his surname is, I think, Polish or Czech and full of consonants) who looks like he's spent a long time staring out to sea. I'm tempted to mention the article, but I don't in case there is no merit in pursuing it.

The final part of my tour is to the point where the scheme needs to extend into the bay. John sighs deeply. "If we can't sort out the extension then this whole thing won't be viable. See there?" He waves to a spit of land that juts out of the coast a quarter mile or so away. "If they can persuade the council to grant them planning, we're dead in the water." Symbolically he kicks a pebble that flies into the sea and sinks without trace. "If we have to tell the Board about this Act of Parliament thing, we might as well give up." Suddenly he grips me, looking rather manic. "It's up to your firm to save us."

Goodness that sounds dramatic.

He must realise how this looks because he lets go and steps away quickly. "Sorry. We're a bit tense just now. The company needs this to succeed, that's all. I'm sure Gerry explained."

Gerry, I assume, is Mr MacThing. "No, though he may have told Crispin."

"Oh yes. Well, I'll leave him to say at the board meeting on Friday. Are you going to be there?"

"I've been asked to make myself available."

It might be the wind that has picked up and distorted his words, but I'm pretty sure he says, "Rather you than me."

## *Chapter Twenty-Seven*

Having left Erica, my articled clerk, to research the Men of Barrington, I head home wondering about Magda. Penny is already in bed, her ribs especially sore today. I leave her to reading and trying to get comfortable. I'm pretty sure that if I say even the slightest wrong thing all sorts of shit about 'knocking her up' will be dumped on me.

There is a note, though, saying Dina rang and asking for me to call her back. It's the same 01 number as before.

The anger I felt when she blackmailed me the other day comes surging back. It's the same stupid rigmarole as last time with an echoing silence when the phone is answered. "Get Dina. It's her brother."

Moments later Dina comes on the line sounding like Mum used to when I demanded her attention during the Archers.

"Harry?"

"You rang. What do you want?"

"Did you send off the papers?"

"Yes."

"Will you chase them up?"

"Why should I?" Then, "I don't really have a choice, do I?"

"No, not really."

"Are you going to explain why you're doing this?"

"I'll let you know what to say next. Is Magda with you?"

"Don't you know? She's moved out."

There are voices in the background. "She'll be back. We'll make sure."

"Penny won't have her. She thinks we're having an affair."

"That might not be a bad idea."

"Oh, that's great. Improve her cover story, would it? Where do you live? Why can't she stay with you?"

"That wouldn't work."

"Why?"

"I don't live in London."

"What's wrong with Cheltenham? Too middle class?"

There's a hesitancy and another off-line conversation. "I must go. I'll be in touch."

"No hang on; you can—"

She's gone. When I try and ring back the noise suggests the line has been disconnected.

Moving to the kitchen, I begin to reheat some food Penny has left when I see a message by the breadbin. 'Ida, 2:00 pm'. That must be Ida Soderberg and the fitness video. Shit, I need to warn her off doing anything too outrageous. However, when I get to the bedroom she's fast asleep.

## Friday, 18th September 1987

## *Chapter Twenty-Eight*

The board meeting for Caldera Properties is this afternoon at four. Erica appears at 11.00, rather excited in her understated way. "I think I've found something."

Her research is first class. She has even been to the British Library to scour their microfiche records. "It's not a nice place and there are some odd men who seem to be there to keep out of the rain" – it is a foul day – "though one of them was very helpful. Strange wild eyes and equally mad hair and clearly he'd not seen soap this decade but he asked me if I wanted to find out about Barrington and its unique rights. Before I could ask how he knew he gave me the codes for where to find the books. They were spot on."

Bloody Jepson. He always did give me the creeps but not because of his supernatural powers. I think I preferred him as an out-and-out crook. Smiling at the absurdity of it, I describe him to Erica.

"Yes! That's the chap. How do you know him? Did you tell him what we were after?"

"More the other way around." When that triggers a look that suggests more questions that I really don't want to answer right now, I hurry her on. "What did you find?"

Momentarily she looks disappointed before she says, "I then went to the Law Society and found two cases, the one in the pamphlet and another. It's clear that the stretch of foreshore where Caldera have their property is immediately adjacent to the land giving the rights to the Men of Barrington."

"Who are these men?"

"Basically, the Court held it was the Lord of the Manor from time to time and anyone appointed by him by deed so long as the appointee or appointees have land that can benefit from the rights."

"And the rights extend to building into the sea?"

"Yes, though the use must have a 'common benefit.' In one case it was a ferry port and in another it was to collect cockles and erect a stand to sell them. The case implies that anywhere open to the public counts."

"And the rights are still extant?"

"According to the leading text book, Chaucer's *On Rights and Incidents*, they cannot be extinguished. Chaucer suggests the incumbent could from time to time surrender them by deed poll, but even that has no authority and there are some interesting arguments against that being possible, since they are a direct gift from the Crown." Her eyes sparkle; she's the new Crispin, enjoying the intellectual challenge as much as, if not more than, finding a workable solution.

"Mere disuse isn't sufficient?"

She shakes her head.

"All we need is a name then. How do we find out who's the Lord of the Manor? I don't suppose it says anywhere in your research?"

"In 1899 it was Edward Pengalin. The title and all rights attaching can be transferred for valuable consideration. The details are kept in the local records office – you have to register the transfer for it to be valid or the powers revert to the previous holder – but when I rang they said I needed to write in and it could take up to three weeks to reply as they are short-staffed at the moment and it may be longer as no one there likes rats."

"Have I missed a link between those two statements?"

"The records are kept in a room that is apparently infested with rats and they are awaiting a budget to get in Rentokil after which they can access the records."

"I don't suppose you'd fancy a rummage?"

If I'd suggested she runs around Eros' statue starkers and singing an aria she couldn't look more appalled. Mind you I'd pay good money to see that.

"No, I guess not. Take a minute. Do you need some water?"

"I'm musophobic."

"Er...?"

"Rats scare me witless."

"Oh. Yes. Of course. Sorry. That's not really helpful of me, is it? Are you sure you're okay?"

Erica has bent over in her seat and her head is between her knees. With one hand she fumbles in the top drawer of her desk, pulling out a paper bag into which she proceeds to breathe slowly and deeply.

"I'll be getting off then. Erm, I'll ask Chloe to pop by."

The Board meeting is a strange affair. To start with I'm never asked to speak, mostly because two members of the Board spend the whole time having a go at Gerald. It appears the company's finances are more precarious than the Board appreciated, and some important loans will fall due in the next month or so, which if not rolled over as was expected might prove difficult to replace. The banks, apparently, are expecting the announcement of another large development – the pipeline is all important they say – and if the Barrington scheme or one other isn't under contract before the end of September then the company will be in trouble – 'trouble' not being specified but the suggestion is it won't be much fun.

Gerald is quiet throughout the pummelling; afterwards he says little beyond thanking me for coming and expressing the hope that 'that prick Muddle doesn't get back involved,' which is rather annoying as I was hoping to hand things over. I nod, not prepared to say one way or another. He smiles and holds my arm, meeting my gaze with a ferocious one of his own. "My Mother always said you were the worst waiter she'd ever met but somehow you had a way of getting out of the messes you got yourself into. Like Napoleon and his generals, I like my lawyers to be lucky – skilled too, but mostly lucky – and she always assured me you were one of those types. Be lucky for both of us, Harry."

# Saturday, 19th September 1987

# *Chapter Twenty-Nine*

In a no doubt futile attempt to stay in reasonable proximity to Penny's good books I decide to dedicate Saturday to some much-neglected DIY. We have been meaning to lay some hard-wearing flooring in the hall for some time and the chosen surface is cork tiles. Bright and early I head to Sainsbury's Homebase store and am given a quick instruction on laying the tiles. The area isn't huge but the terribly youthful though extremely self-assured assistant tells me to lay hardboard first and then the tiles on top.

There was a time when I never thought I'd learn to drive but about a year ago, at the fourth time of asking, I managed to find a test centre (in Epsom) where the examiner was less than rigorous. We managed to mount the kerb twice (I had the sense I was probably okay when he said 'whoopsie' after the first jolt and 'here we go again' after the second) and stall three times, yet I still passed. Oddly the act of obtaining my license seemed to give my driving the confidence it needed and I am now merely incompetent rather than dangerous.

Between us the assistant and I load the car with hardboard, pins, tiles, glue and a cork tile cutter. I think I have all the other tools I need. I cannot actually see out of three sides of the car as a result of all the clutter but make it home in one piece with only one screech and crunch on my left side at some traffic lights on Brixton Road.

It turns out to be hard work but enjoyable and by 3:30 I have a cork floor. Penny decided to abandon me to it when I started spreading the glue. She seemed a bit uptight, although she didn't elaborate and moaned about the smell of the solvent and how it might affect the foetus.

While the glue hardens I go and make myself a cup of tea. As the kettle is boiling I realise that the three previous cups are filtering through and I head for the downstairs toilet.

That is when I relearn a lesson I've learnt many times before – there is always a consequence to me starting a DIY project. The toilet door won't open because of the increased height brought on by the new tiles. Short of ripping up my new tiles we now have a lovely new floor and no access to the toilet.

Just then the doorbell goes and my heart sinks; that'll be Penny with armfuls of shopping and feeling knackered.

I've prepared my apology when I pull open the door to Zenda Silverman, Brenda's Mother. "We need to talk about Gary and Brenda. But first can I use the loo?"

"Er, well. I seem to have blocked ours."

"Oh dear. What did you eat?"

"No, not like that. I've laid this floor and forgot to take account of the raised height. The door is jammed."

"Is that you're only toilet?"

"No, sorry, of course there's one upstairs. Second on the right. I'll make some tea."

When Zenda reappears, she's laughing. "You always were something of a klutz. Do you remember that mousetrap?"

She's right, not that I want to agree.

"You'll need to get it off its hinges and slice a bit off the bottom."

"I'd like to know how."

We both inspect the problem. Zenda gives the door a good shake. "If you can get inside you might be able to push it open far enough to access the hinges and take it off. How are your breaking and entering skills?"

"I guess I'll have to find out."

We leave it for the moment.

"I was just passing and thought it would be easiest if we had a quick word."

"How does someone who lives in Hampstead end up 'just passing' a terrace in the arse end of Herne Hill?"

She nods. "It happens, and this is a flying visit. The thing is Gary says he's told you about his new-found wealth and your idea to fund Brenda's work."

"What does she think?"

"I don't know. She won't see him and if I so much as mention his name she covers her ears and starts singing one of her old punk songs about Mrs Thatcher and her lack of genitalia."

"I remember it. I bet that pleases the neighbours."

"Yes, well, the point is she'll listen to you, Harry."

"Me? I doubt it. What about the women she works with? Can't they be persuaded to explain?"

"Ha! They're more strident than Brenda. They've also heard from her about what a capitalist pig Gary is—"

"Does she call him that?"

"And worse, though she doesn't really mean it."

"You sure about that?"

"Harry, we both know it's stubbornness on the part of my daughter that is keeping them apart, that and feebleness on the part of your best friend in not telling her to get over herself. It's different with you. She respects you for what you did with Sven's estate, how you gave it away. Okay, so you work for a money-making legal machine, but she's not forgotten how honourable you were. I think she finds you inspiring."

"I really don't think so."

"The fact you didn't try to punish her in any way taught her a lesson, I think. You are some sort of role model if you like."

That makes me feel very awkward. "These days the only roll I model is the Swiss variety." To ensure my sparkling wit and repartee hits home I tap my stomach and realise that, indeed, my waist line is an expanding enterprise. Another item for the growing 'to do' list.

"If you spoke to her, told her how he's changed, then… maybe?" she asks hopefully.

Zenda wants the same as me, but I don't think either of us really believes it can be fixed. "I spoke to her just the other day. I did try."

"Please keep trying. Neither of them are happy, are they?"

That's certainly true.

She finishes the tea and with the brisk manner I remember so well, snaps her bag shut and stands, leaning in for a kiss on the cheek. As I lean towards her she hugs me hard. "You're a good man, Harry. We're lucky to know you." She smiles and sniffs as she turns for the door. "I'd better go. Give my love to Penny and if I don't see you before the baby arrives, good luck. You'll be a super Dad."

Hmm.

# Monday, 21st September 1987

## *Chapter Thirty*

My cycle ride to work takes me up through Loughborough Junction, past Myatt Fields and on to the grim gyratory system at Elephant and Castle. This is a sclerotic piece of urban road planning that comprises some of the worst interlocking roundabouts anywhere in the country and, for a cyclist, the sort of lottery that ensures constipation is not a regular encumbrance. Depending on my mood I might hop onto the pavement at the top of the Walworth Road and coast through the underpasses, home to scuttling commuters and various archetypes from the underclasses. Today is such a day. As I freewheel around another blind corner I'm stopped abruptly by a wide-eyed madman, arm's raised and held apart, his once multi-coloured poncho looking like a pair of my gran's boil-washed bloomers.

"All hail, Harry. Guardian of the poor and downtrodden."

"Jesus, what the fuck are you playing at Mr Jepson? And how did you know it was me?"

"I've been given the gift of insight." His demonic stare softens into a wink. "And I saw you take this route a few days ago so decided to wait until you came this way again."

"What do you want?"

"Nothing but a small chance at redemption, and to tell you that you need to find your sister. She is a lamb in the wilderness, crying for her shepherd." Once again, he trains his glassy-eyed stare on me. "That's you."

"I don't know where she lives. Do you?"

I think he smiles. "You need to ask someone."

"I just asked—"

He walks towards the stairs. There he stops, turns and begins to whistle a piece of vaguely familiar music. "Know it?" He smiles, his face open and unquestioning.

"No, not really. A TV show?"

He lifts his hands in the air and shouts in an oddly squeaky sing-song voice. "It's a clue!" Then he runs up the stairs and disappears.

To try to hold on to it, I hum the wretched theme song until I reach the office and head for reception. Gloria is talking – flirting more like – with a corporate associate who I think is called Leslie.

"Harry, you hunk. Free for another drink? Although if you dare abandon me to a lesbian ball-crusher again I'll never forgive you."

"Any time, Gloria. But first, what the hell is this tune from?" I start humming it. Both Leslie and Gloria frown in concentration. She says, "It's very familiar. Oh, what is it?"

Behind me, Greg's voice cuts in, "I never saw you as a Waltons fan, Harry. It must be a decade since I last saw that God-awful rubbish."

Gloria beams. "Oh, I loved them. Elizabeth was a childhood heroine for me."

Leslie curls his nose. "My parents thought them trite and pastiche. I don't think I ever saw the show."

Greg is standing with us. "Saccharine, really. All that 'night John boy' crap at the end. I... Harry, you look like you've seen a ghost."

I smile. "More like I just heard one. Thanks everyone."

Greg heads out of the office and we watch him go. Gloria growls, "God I'd like a piece of that. He's gorgeous."

Leslie smirks. "Soon to be a partner and thus out of your league."

I catch Gloria's eye. "Oh, I think that takes him straight back into her league."

Gloria eyes me fondly. "When you're a partner, does that mean I have a chance?"

I'm not sure if it's a snort of derision from Leslie; whatever it is, Gloria turns on him. "You want to watch out or you'll be getting a Maxwell from me."

This time he definitely snorts but with laughter. He says, "We don't know who did that." He waves and heads for the lift.

Left alone I turn to Gloria. "A Maxwell?"

She rolls her eyes. "Don't tell me the juiciest piece of gossip to hit this place in years hasn't reached you up in your hideaway in property?"

I shake my head, knowing I'm about to hear.

Gloria checks for prying ears and leans in close. "After Mr Crout's announcement to you lot that Private Client was going to be shut down—"

"That's not exactly what he said."

"Will you not interrupt a very good story with facts, please?"

I hold up a hand defensively.

"Everyone thinks that's what he said. Especially Cynthia Maxwell. She's tried, what, four times to get a partnership and never made it so this rather destroys her hopes, the poor thing. We all thought she was a bit of a mouse and expected her to go quietly. Anyway, turns out she works fast, because she handed in her resignation last week. As Tritewell is no longer with us and Ms Dawb was away, she gave it to Mr Crout, only it came with a little gift." At this she checks again and leans in closer. "The letter was put on his blotter and it was weighed down with a small, firm but rather smelly… thingy."

"Thingy?"

"Number two." She exaggerates her lip movements as she whispers, "A turd."

I'm totally flabbergasted. "Cyn put a turd on Crout's desk? I squeak."

She waves me quiet. "Shush, shush. It's not meant to be common knowledge."

"Telling you was meant to keep it secret, was it?"

"I've only told you. And maybe some of the girls. Good for Miss Maxwell I say. That's one in the eye for those old dinosaurs."

Not a nice image. "Do we know it was definitely Cyn?"

Gloria shrugs. "She'd just resigned and felt completely betrayed. I heard she told her secretary she'd only stayed because she was on a promise. Anyway, who else would do that?"

Who indeed?

I head for the lift, smiling at the dreadful image. If that got into the hands of the tabloids, they would have a field day. Once inside the lift I'm humming that wretched tune again. At least Gloria has helped me work out Charlie's clue, although right now the importance of it seems rather remote as I contemplate Cynthia's graphic resignation.

On my desk there's a telephone attendance note – Crispin has called to say his flight has been cancelled, he's stuck in France and could I look after Caldera for another day. If I could just find out who currently holds the Lord of the Manor rights and hand things back all sorted out, then the extra day would be worth it.

# Wednesday, 23rd September 1987

# *Chapter Thirty-One*

Two things happened to upset the equilibrium of my day. First Crispin returned and dismissed my ideas about the solution lying with the Lord of the Manor as 'bunkum.' Who uses words like bunkum that hasn't been scripted by PG Wodehouse? Anyway, what do I care? It's his job and it's up to him. Given his instant sneering – 'of course we looked at this Harry, but it's a myth' – I omit to tell him about the financing issues when I give him an overview of what's happened. He can find out from my note when he gets it and if Gerald MacThing calls in the meantime and bollocks him, then all well and good.

When he's gone I curse myself for not defending the idea more strenuously. I'm always fighting an ingrained lack of confidence in my legal abilities – and those of Erica to research things thoroughly, too. Crispin is known as the department's brains and is so used to going unquestioned that it is easy to fall into the trap of his academic arrogance. Having washed my hands of his problem one minute, I'm plotting to try to think of a way to find who holds the Lordship and provide the answer the next. Truth is, putting one over on Crispin and his supercilious sneering would make my day.

After he's gone back to his room, it occurs to me that he's probably still cross at what he sees as my duplicity with Greg. Maybe I should just leave him to it.

Oh get a grip, Harry. We three need a heart-to-heart, that's all.

The second jolt comes in the guise of a call from Jan Kruis. I can't help the guilty feeling it triggers, but he says he just wants to meet for a drink. Maybe he's just being friendly; I'd rather not go but equally I don't feel as if I can turn him down.

We agree to meet at the King Lud, a large if careworn pub by Ludgate Circus popular with some of the more boisterous bond traders who are now flooding every drinking hole in the City. I tell him I need to get home pronto, so it will have to be a quick one – we have another NCT class, this time called 'the partner's role in the birth – present and patient.' Sounds bloody ghastly.

Jan has a voice that carries out the door so finding him is not too difficult. When he sees me he orders me a pint and points at a table in the corner. I want him to kick the conversation off but he just sits down, staring at his half-drunk pint and chewing his bottom lip.

Finally I crack. "Is this about Barry's death? Are there more, erm, complications?"

He looks up, confused. "Barry? Oh, you mean Tritewell. No, nothing complicated yet but it is getting to be a bit of a conundrum. Did I tell you he'd had sex?"

"I think I heard that, yes. Gay sex. And something about an apple?"

He frowns. "Gay sex? Not immediately before he died but he had had anal sex in the past. I meant he had recently ejaculated." He blinks. "Although we did find he was covered in sequins around his bits so God only knows. No one we've spoken to – not friends, family or colleagues – thought he was gay, but apparently he might have been. We found a credit card receipt from a leather fetish shop in Greek Street and the owner said he was a regular at some gay club in Hoxton. He definitely died of a heart attack but where was he when he had sex? And did that trigger it?"

"Not in his room?" The image of him bent over his desk, bottom exposed, won't go away. Surely that had to be gay sex? Or maybe he had a heart attack just before… if so when did he ejaculate? I stop myself, the images begin to pile up one on top of the other in ways that aren't conducive to my mental health.

Jan pulls a face. "Christ that would be pretty risky if he was trying to keep his sexuality a secret. And I'm guessing even partners are reluctant to have straight sex at their desks?"

You'd be surprised, I thought, remembering a few stories from the occasional department party.

"We won't be able to tell if sex was the trigger," Jan finishes his pint. "People are bloody odd Harry."

"Indeed they are Jan."

He seems to be thinking out loud, his gaze unfocused. "His secretary said he left the office about three – that wasn't unusual on a Friday, she said, as he'd go to his club. They said he'd not been in that day, and nor for that matter had he been in for the previous three or four weeks, which surprised his secretary. Our guess is he was in the habit of meeting someone, having sex and then going home to his family as if he'd just had a normal day at the office. Poor sod, that's not fair on anyone." He spins the dregs of his drink. "Do you know much about the politics at your firm? We keep hearing rumours of malcontents and how his department was under threat, but none of it takes us anywhere. At best it looks like someone might have moved him and put him in his office, but no one has come forward to say they saw anything and you'd think someone would notice a dead body being dragged around. Best we can guess is he had sex, came back, collapsed and died and someone put him at his desk – his lover maybe." He smiles thinly. "I shouldn't be telling you this. You will keep it to yourself for now, won't you?"

"Of course."

"If nothing comes to light then the inquest will find out that he died of natural causes and that will be that. That'll probably suit your bosses and neatly avoids any scandal."

That makes sense and it's a bit of a relief. I think about the photos. The photographer must be the mysterious lover and since the shots are in Barry's office it makes sense for him or her to be a member of the firm. I should have another look at those photos that I've been carrying around, see if they give any clues as to the photographer's identity. Although if they do, what am I going to do about it? Heaven knows.

Thinking about the pictures reminds me of those negatives in the same envelope. How did that happen? And the packet was open. Chloe said she looked inside but she's either a cooler customer than I give her credit or she never looked at the actual pictures once she saw Barry's name. If she'd seen the dress she would have to have freaked out, wouldn't she?

"Harry?" Jan looks at me oddly. "Are you listening?"

"Sorry, what did you say?"

He sighs, like he's making a major effort. "I asked about Dina."

"Dina?"

"After I saw you, I realised I don't just want things to end, you know – without us trying, if she wants to I mean. I don't know how to get in touch. She's not living with you still, is she?"

"No, she's not."

"Do you have a phone number or an address? I might call or write."

"No, but I'm sure that if you write to my parents they'll be able to forward it."

"Is she's seeing anyone? Not back with that guy from your home town, Graham or whatever?"

"Jim. No she's definitely not with him. I know she's been working in Cheltenham. I know she bought a small place in north London but that's rented out. I did have a London number, but it's a work one and I'm not sure she'd want me to pass it around."

He looks defeated.

I add, "Look, I'm going to try to get hold of her – I'm helping a mutual friend and I need to talk to her about a couple of things. Do you want me to mention you?"

He takes time but shakes his head. "I'd prefer to explain myself. If you feel you can let me have her address, if you find it, or her number, then I'd be very grateful."

"Okay. Do you want me to keep my ears open at work?"

He laughs, more a snort through his nose. "I wouldn't put yourself out. It's odd, sure, but I expect there aren't many gay law partners, are there? It's probably stupidity that lead to the body being moved, not criminality. If you find the gay lover or hear he's been murdered tell us, but I doubt we're going to spend much more time on it."

That is a relief.

I begin to relax and drink an extra pint, which makes me late. As I wait for my train at Blackfriars station, which is also delayed – everything hereabouts is a mess, with the development of the new cross London railway – I begin to sense I'm being watched. When I turn around, certain I'll see Charlie Jepson lurking somewhere, the platform is practically deserted.

My briefcase is on the bench next to me. Tucked inside, where I put it the other day, is the packet of Barry's photos. A sombre-faced businessman, probably my Father's age, is standing right on the platform edge, reading the recently revived *Evening News*. Otherwise no one's around.

The packet has slipped right to the bottom and is caught by a folder. It's only when it is out and on my lap I realise it is different. The covering envelope is blank – no mention of Barry's name or phone number. I dig about in my briefcase but this is the only packet.

Swallowing hard, I open the flap and shudder. Even with only half the top photo on display it is clear this isn't the same set I picked up. Somehow I take the photos out and look at each one. Seven. Three seem to be of Barry's room. Just the room, no Barry. And also no apple, which I'm sure was on a desk in one of the others.

The fourth photo is a man who at first I assume is Barry, standing in profile and looking out of the window. It's only when I look more closely I begin to wonder if it's him. The picture is at night; you can see the lights of other buildings through the window.

The last two pictures are somewhere else, a bedroom. The dress is draped over the door of a wardrobe in the first. In the second someone is wearing it. As before the wearer has their back to the camera but it isn't Barry. The shoulders are broader, the man is taller and the bald head is spiky with the odd wispy comb over, not the totally smooth pate that Barry had.

Someone has to be playing a game with me, that's for sure.

The rubbish fluorescent lights above the grubby platform are making it difficult to pick out the detail in the photos. That's why the other passenger is almost hanging off the platform edge so keen is he to cast light on his newspaper. Taking his lead, I head down the platform until I'm far away from him and I too stand on the edge, tilting the images towards a light source across the tracks.

Shit. Fuck. In my newly nervous state I almost drop them onto the tracks. Oh fuckedy-fuck. There's a reflection in the window of the photo of the man in the dress. It may be a man with no hair but it is also unmistakably Sebastian Crout. The rumours about him having a wig must be true. He's Barry's gay lover. He must have been in the room when I came in. Christ, maybe he'd just buggered Barry, whatever Jan says.

I stare at the other pictures. The man in profile is also Crout or at least I believe so. And on closer inspection the room may well not be Barry's. I squint at the reflections in the window that the photo has caught, trying to see if I can make out the photographer but without any luck.

A horn brings me back to the moment; my train is pulling in and my heart is pounding fit to bust. An odd thought hits me – given how sensitive Crout is about his hair, he may be more embarrassed about this shot of him without a wig than wearing a dress. I almost smile before it dawns on me – again because it hit me as soon as I opened the packet – that someone is playing me. I check. Again, no negatives.

I find a seat to myself and check in the better light of the carriage. I wish I'd paid more attention to the first set. It doesn't feel too much of a stretch to think both these and the previous set are from the same film. And whoever split them has been careful to make the previous set about Barry and these about Mr Crout. But for the dress which I'd swear is the same one, these could be two different films. Both show partners at Newe Waters as cross-dressers but any romantic involvement with the other has been neatly avoided. Why? And why does someone want to involve me in this strange subtefuge?

I spend the journey pouring over the pictures, but I can find nothing else to shed any light on anything. I wish I'd studied the other shots more thoroughly now. Maybe there was a reflection in one of them that might be a link. Who is playing around with these pictures and why?

The train journey to Herne Hill takes 15 minutes. For the first time in ages, I miss my sister. She's a pain and a smart arse and recently a blackmailer but she's bright and quick-witted and sees things that I don't. And for all her recent flirtations with criminality and all-round bastardness she's been loyal and immensely supportive when I've been at my most stressed. Like now. She'd know what to do.

The bloody Waltons' theme tune comes back to me and those irritating closing credits when the family all say goodnight to each other. Eventually they all call out to the youngest member of the family who they wake up. Jim-Bob. Jim. Jim James, Dina's ex and Father of George. That's who Jepson was pointing me at for her address. That's who I need to contact. Obvious really when you think about it.

# Chapter Thirty-Two

The NCT class is tense mainly because Penny refuses to engage with me as punishment for my tardiness. Mo comes up to me during a break to ask if she's all right. He's a nice enough guy but I barely know him so fudge the answer. He looks sadly at me. "If you say so, Harry. It's just that Penny rang Chrissie and said she felt vulnerable."

That's an odd choice of word. I manage a little nodding thing that he interprets as my way of saying: 'please share whatever cod-psychology you have in mind, it will be really helpful' instead of the intended 'that's utter bollocks; can I please have a Bourbon biscuit?'

On the way home, Penny says she's had a good chat with the girls and is feeling much happier. I say that's good but since I wasn't really aware she was so unhappy as to need a chat I feel a bit left out. She then blathers on about how all her friends said it was important to keep the 'marital bed' sacrosanct after the baby comes so we have somewhere for ourselves, but all I can focus on is the 'marital' bit. I suspect that's merely a Freudian slip but it makes me wonder if all the moods and silences and 'vulnerability' have more to do with my lack of a proposal rather than some spurious concern about her lack of attractiveness, which is of course groundless.

I try to ring Jim when I get in; he lives with his parents but there's no answer. I decide that I'll try the garage in the morning.

As we're lying in bed, Penny says, "I think I'll go home this weekend. I doubt I'll be able to soon. It'll give you a chance to fix the loo door. Unless you want me to call out Mr Rogers?"

Rogers is a slimy, unctuous man who does all sorts of odd jobs. Part of his fee comprises humiliating me for my lack of any nous when it comes to such things. Withering put-downs have included:

'It must be nice to be able to afford to pay someone for such a small job.'

'Have you never wondered how the water gets to the tap?'

'Boilers have a habit of not working when the pilot light is out,' and,

'Oh dear, Mr Spittle. That second flush was a mistake, wasn't it?'

The idea that he might find out I've rendered the downstairs toilet utterly inoperable is simply too awful to contemplate.

"Good idea. Night."

In response a hand briefly rubs my hip and then my penis but stops before either of us can get excited. Bloody tease. I love you, you silly thing, if only you'd believe it. Anyway, I'll take any sign as a good one just now and go to sleep smiling.

# Thursday, 24th September 1987

## *Chapter Thirty-Three*

"Hello, Harry. It's John. John Thomas."

"John. Good to hear from you." I try not to sound cagey, but having a headhunter call – albeit one who's in that grey area between friend and acquaintance – isn't ideal when you're meant to be showing the ultimate loyalty to the firm as the partnership decision looms. "Brenda told me you might ring."

"She's lovely, isn't she?"

Brenda is many things – vibrant, challenging, intense – but she's not really on any scale of 'lovely' that I know of.

"I hoped she'd mention I might call. She said she explained about our new business, Thomas Himcol & Co. Yes?"

I'd forgotten how strong John's Welsh accent is. It sings and soars through sentences. Little undulations of sound. I say, "I've heard you've been doing well."

"You too. I bet you'll love being a partner."

"That's a bit like the Scottish play superstition for actors – we don't mention the 'P' word in the office."

Immediately John sounds flustered, which takes me right back and brings a smile to my face. I can see him sitting in the Bear Garden, an area outside the Master's rooms in the Royal Courts of Justice in the Strand, waiting like a condemned man for his turn arguing some minor point on a Writ. He was utterly forlorn, the epitome of morose. It's hardly a surprise he packed in being a solicitor, a job he was never really cut out for. John needs optimism, the joy of finding someone a new and exciting job, to feed his soul.

"Sorry, Harry. I didn't mean, you know… it's just everyone says… well, we hear things."

"It's okay John. If it happens, it happens." When did I get to sound so sanguine?

"Karen and I wanted to invite you over for dinner. No strings or anything, more a brain-storming session."

"That sounds intriguing."

"Well, we're quite new in the recruitment business and so far we've had successes with the smaller and middle-sized firms who are expanding in selected areas – property mostly – but we know the major firms are an untapped opportunity. We wondered if we could maybe float a few ideas past someone who works for one and see what you think." He adds hurriedly, "No trade secrets or anything, just generalities. And if Penny's available that would be great. I heard you're about to become a Dad?"

"Yes, not long at all now. We're facing the last six weeks. I'll ask her but it's a bit of a strain, so she might prefer to pass on this one. When were you thinking?"

"Saturday? There's a restaurant in Kensington we'd like to take you to. I know it's last minute but, well, we thought there's no time like the present."

I manage a smile. It sounds like he's been let down, has a hole in his diary and needs to fill it.

"I'll ask her and let you know."

"If she's happy to let you come on your own then that's fine too."

And I suspect he's paid a deposit he might be about to lose.

As I put the phone down I remember Penny said she was going to see her parents. I toy with calling John back immediately but decide that making sure Penny's plans haven't changed is a wiser strategy right now.

About an hour later, Chloe brings in some post. My room mates are out, one at a meeting, the other in the library and this is the first time I've managed to get her alone. "Close the door please, would you?"

She looks terrified. "What have I done?"

I point at the spare seat. "You know those pictures I picked up by mistake. Mr Tritewell's? You found them in the bottom drawer."

"I didn't mean any harm." She starts crying.

"Did you open the packet or just look at the name?"

"The packet was open and... he'd died, here, and, oh I don't know..." She's miserable. "I was interested, that's all."

"It's okay, Chloe. It's not a crime to be curious. They were strange pictures, weren't they?"

"Yes, yes they were. Wearing a dress. Poor man. No one knew."

"He has – had – a wife and daughter."

"Oh God. Yes, of course. How dreadful."

"I need you to be totally honest with me. Have you told anyone? Even a hint? We really want to avoid his family hearing about this at such a dreadful time. His predilection wasn't common knowledge."

"I... no, not really."

"Not really?"

"Greg... Mr Princip. He asked if you had given them back. He said he knew about them being given to you by accident. Well, not the pictures themselves just that you'd collected them by mistake. From Boots?"

"Greg?" What the hell is he playing at? He was there when I got them but he can't have known I'd picked up the wrong packet or he'd have said something at the time.

"Was that wrong? I've not told anyone else."

"No, that's fine. But please keep it to yourself. You understand?"

"Yes, of course." She hops from foot to foot. "Is that all only I need to get to the supermarket for some jelly during my lunch hour."

I nod. Jelly. Like my insides.

## *Chapter Thirty-Four*

I have a meeting with Chuck and Doringo, plus a phalanx of associates from around the departments – tax, intellectual property and competition. Doringo takes the lead and commands the room. It's complex and fascinating and Chuck is equally impressive – happily dressed in loose trousers and a lumberjack shirt without a tie. After four hours, we have a list of technical issues to look into. Chuck asks me to wait for him. As he sweeps up his file and shoulder bag, he stretches his left arm and pulls it behind him, grimacing. He sees me looking. "Recoil. Too many unsympathetic guns in my life."

There's a lot about Chuck Streib I don't know and don't really want to.

"Let's go get a drink. You know anywhere open? I never realised what a pissy narrow-minded city this was until I tried to find a drink at three pm.

There's a bar at the back of the Fox & Anchor in Smithfield meat market that the articled clerks visit because it still feeds the needs of the traders. It looks shut but will let you in if they're in the mood. Today it's mostly empty. We both nurse pints of Guinness and stay silent.

Eventually he says, "It's great you put me in touch with Natalie. I'd be pretty lonely without her place, you know. She speaks highly of you, says you saved her bacon a few years ago."

"She's a good friend. It's what you do."

"You know she's ill?"

"Ill?"

He shrugs. "She won't admit it but yeah, ill. I said she looked bad and like you she said it's the exercise, but I've seen healthy skinny and I've seen dying and—"

"Dying?" I say in alarm.

"Maybe not technically dying. Look Harry, in New York we've lost good people to AIDS, right? I watched them go. She needs to get checked. She's in total denial."

"Christ, you think so?"

"I ain't a fucking doctor, okay, but I've got eyes. If she's had unprotected sex, then yeah, it's a possibility. She's still got the hots for you…yeah, yeah, don't look like that, it's obvious even to a dick like me. You tell her she needs to see a doc. She might listen."

I let this sink in. It's not a total surprise if I'm honest.

"Tell me about your sis."

"Dina?"

"That her name? Natalie says she's really something. Kid at 16 and now some whizz in government."

"She's pretty much the reason my mistakes don't usually cost me a body part or instant dismissal. I don't see much of her at the moment but in the past she's always been around when I need her."

"You see Harry, thing is I need bright people for this operation. Okay, right now it's me, scouting out the possibilities but before long they'll be an army of folks over and I need bright locals to make sure we don't let brash Americana fuck up a perfectly good idea. Maybe someone like your sis."

"You'd be taking a risk, Chuck." I manage a hollow laugh. "She takes handling."

"Why?" He doesn't reciprocate the humour. "You think I can't cope?"

"I think you have no idea how hard it could be. Anyway, how do you know her skill set would suit your needs?"

"Three of your A levels to A grade, first class degree from Imperial in politics and history, fast-track civil servant and now with MI5. She's got the sort of mind I like the sound of and I'll pay her at least twice what the government bozos manage to scrape together."

"You have done your homework. Okay, if you're serious I'll ask her. Assuming I can get hold of her."

Some 30 minutes later back at my desk, I call the family garage in New Milton in Hampshire. Thoroughly's Motors was established by my grandfather in the 1930s and taken over by my Uncle and Aunt in the 1970s. Uncle Norman nearly lost it through some injudicious – no, let's be honest, downright fucking mental – loans and only my Mother's generosity held them at bay until they were finally cleared as part of the Sven Andersen legacy. In another life, Uncle would express his gratitude either expressly or at least implicitly in some way. Not Norman. If anything, knowing I had a part in his rescue makes him even more antagonistic towards me.

"Thoroughly's."

"Hi Uncle. It's Harry."

"What's he done now?"

"Who?"

"Your berk of a Father, of course. Haven't you heard about the latest embarrassment? Veronica" – that's my Mother – "is seething."

"Nothing new there then. I know you want to share so please don't spare me the details."

"He bid at a Tory fundraiser. 'A night with Maggie' or some such bollocks. Actually I think it might have been a night with Dennis. He paid £100 for whatever it was and it was a hoax."

"A hoax?"

"Christ, you still do that, like all your side, don't you? Repeat everything."

The days when I'd apologise at this point in the conversation are long gone. "Maybe if you explained yourself clearly then I wouldn't have to."

"You cheeky little shit."

"That's me. But I've been working in an industry where I get called a lot worse every day so—"

"I'm not surprised."

I rub my ear. He's laughing.

"It's about bloody time you bit back. There's a touch of your grandpa in you after all. Not just those weedy Spittle genes. What are you really after? It sounds like it isn't just to be insulted."

"I need a word with Jim. About Dina."

"Christ, be careful will you? He's never going to get over your sister, you know. It's not that I blame her. He's not in her league but he'll never stop hoping. And this schooling malarkey – he wants him to go to the comprehensive in Lymington, but Dina is talking about going private somewhere – well, let's just say it isn't helping. I'll put him on."

I'm mulling over this change in Norman and wondering if, going forward, I might in fact develop a different relationship with the old sod, when Jim's tinny voice rings in my ear. "Hiya Harry. How's the Big Smoke? What's it like being a Big Shot lawyer?"

"As boring as any job. How's my nephew?"

"George is doing really well. He's got the lead in the Christmas play. He plays a detective."

"Very apt."

"Sorry?"

"Given Dina's a... look, sorry."

"That's okay. Yes, she'll be pleased when I tell her."

"It was about Dina that I called. Do you have an address? Or a phone number? I want to drop something off."

"She calls me, Harry. You know, because of her job."

"You don't have contact details for emergencies? If something happened to you? George?"

He goes quiet. For a long time.

"Jim?"

"Is this important, Harry?"

"Yes. Yes, it is."

"Only she said I mustn't tell anyone, especially your parents."

"Tell me Jim. I think she needs some help."

"You do? So do I. I've been so worried. It started in the summer when that woman from the hotel came round."

"Magda?"

"You know her?"

"Yes. What happened?"

"She was terrified. Absolutely desperate. I called Dina then and she came and got her, took her off. I didn't hear from her for a week, maybe 10 days. That was odd because she always calls at least every other night to talk to George. He was very upset and wouldn't speak when she finally rang. There were lots of tears. I then got this letter, saying if I needed her I was to place an ad in the *Bournemouth Echo*. It was an offer to sell a Fabergé egg with a blue ormolu centrepiece."

"That sounds like Dina. Not many of them in the *Echo*."

"I was so concerned I tried it and she called me. She got really angry when it turned out there wasn't anything wrong. Since then she rings every other night at about seven, speaks to George and that's it. She refuses to say what she's doing, where she is or what's going on. I'm worried she's in danger. Do you think she is Harry?"

"I don't think so. I had lunch with her a few days ago. She seemed all right then."

"Did she? That's good, isn't it? I mean if she has time for lunch things must be all right."

"Yes, look don't worry. I'll call her at work or something—"

"You have a work number? I wonder why she didn't give it to me."

"Oh, it's an old one. It may not even be connected. I'll give it a try and if it's current I'll let you have it. Give George a hug, will you?"

"Of course. And thanks. It's good to know you're looking out for her. And Harry?"

"Yes?"

"I'm happy about his school, if that's worrying her. Whatever she wants. It's my Mum, really. She doesn't want to lose him."

"Right, of course."

When we break the call, I sit back in my chair. Shit, what is going on?

# Saturday, 26th September 1987

## *Chapter Thirty-Five*

Yesterday I put in the ad for the Fabergé egg as suggested by Jim, instead leaving my number rather than his to call. Part of me wonders at the weirdoes who might take the bait, but I trust that this scheme will work. There's nothing I can do in the meantime. Just in case she calls me, I checked with the Home Office for Magda's application. They spent an age finding the forms, then asked me who I am and took my details. To be credible I said I'm her lawyer (given more time, I might have thought of something as believable that didn't involve me giving away my true identity or link it to the firm – like I'm her boyfriend and speak better English or something). After all that they say it is still being dealt with and, no, they can't say when it might be ready.

Last night, Penny left to see her parents. I accepted the dinner invite with John and Karen, not that I really want to go, but I'm not keen to be on my own with the bloody cat. John was delighted and understood about Penny when I told him she wouldn't be joining us. "Not a problem, Harry. We will find a four to make up the numbers."

"A blind date, is it?"

"Oh no, although if that's... I thought, you know... you and Penny but if I've mis—"

"Joke, John."

"Ah-ha! Of course. Ho ho. See you at 7:30."

That just leaves the toilet door to sort out. I manage to get in through the side window by the cunning expedient of breaking the glass. I also manage to avoid lacerating myself on the jagged shards that stick out of the frame. Inside I check things. I try pushing the door into the hall, but it is no better than pulling it from the other side. I have a go at prising it up with a crowbar but all that does is lead to an awful cracking sound. And when I go into the hall, the crow bar has badly dented the new cork tiling. In the end I concede I have to hack up five tiles that are causing the jam and set to with a Stanley knife and a will. They come away surprisingly easily, which is a bit of a concern in its own right. After an hour with a destroyed window and an equally butchered floor I can take the door off its hinges.

I check my watch. I have enough time to go and buy some glass and putty and at least fix the window before I need to leave. That way I might avoid handing some local jobbing burglar the opportunity of a lifetime and with it any credibility I might have left with my girlfriend.

I can pick up some more cork tiles and glue at the same time; fixing that, though, is a job for tomorrow.

What a pillock I am.

## *Chapter Thirty-Six*

The restaurant is in a mews in Knightsbridge close to Harrods. A gold-braided flunky looks at me with the sort of disdain reserved for French teachers when I attempted anything so complex as my name. "Are you expected?"

Before I can answer, Karen appears. When I knew her as a student she hid inside a monstrous cardigan thing that smelt like the family loft and not in a good way. The next time we met she was working at the prestigious law firm called Middleton Priestly and had on both a severe suit and equally severe expression. At no stage did I think her beautiful. Terrifying, indifferent, ferociously bright, but not like she is now. The word 'slinky' comes to mind and not the coiled spring sort. She kisses me warmly – another change – and holds me by the elbows as she inspects me. She could be an aunt – an unexpectedly sexy one, true – with masses of hair and a vertigo-inducing cleavage. If she says, 'my, how you've grown' I'll know I've slipped into a parallel universe.

"My, aren't you the smart City type!"

Close enough. "You look pretty fabulous yourself. Life treating you well?"

"Very. Come on. I was on my way to the loo but I'll hold on until we've done the hellos."

I can see John standing up as we approach. He's as weedy as I remember him, but the moustache and tidy hair at least make him look slightly older than 15. The other guest is Brenda. She smiles, not fully, and says, "You don't mind if I'm your date for the evening?"

Now that's a loaded question but for the moment I let it pass and give her a kiss on the cheek. I think she's relieved I don't snap and hugs me tightly, saying into my ear, "It's really good to see you, Harry. Really good."

When we part, John is beaming and Karen is releasing unspoken questions into the atmosphere like party balloons. She turns away, apologising while we all take our allotted seats.

The meal is adequate, for what it is – too small and lacking taste but it gains top marks for artistic presentation. As we start on the main course, which may or may not have a smear of duck jus somewhere, I say to Brenda – who has been laboriously explaining about a programme to support victims of domestic abuse with training and the provision of crèche facilities and needs more cash – "I have someone who's looking for a home for cash. For a good cause."

She smiles at me – I remember that smile, which used to presage one of her punk bands more outrageous antics – and says, "I hope the source is feminist."

"Impeccable credentials. The donor has just sold their business, having had a change of heart…" I pause on 'heart' thinking myself rather clever but, of course, without the context the others don't notice it – sometimes I'm such a clever dick – "…about the direction they want to take and they've decided to give their money away, well – most of it."

"Send them over."

"No, that wouldn't do. You'd have to call, introduce yourself. I can give you the number if you like; just say I sent you and they'll listen."

She smiles and holds out her wrist, like she used to do to take down numbers.

Karen laughs as she hands me a biro and I write down Dobbin's direct line at work, hoping Brenda doesn't know it or remember it. When I go to hand the biro back, Karen tells me to keep it. One of their firm's branded pens.

"This mystery donor, he – I assume it's a he?"

I nod.

"He's giving up on his capitalist ways?"

"Something like that."

She turns to Karen. "That's good to hear."

Karen nods. "Give him a go, Bren. You never know."

The conversation moves on as I wonder if I've done the right thing.

Maybe not. Maybe it will be a disaster, but it can't go worse than the current impasse between her and the man she's meant to be with.

It's about 9.30 when I need a pee.

I'm just about to enter the men's when the stone-faced flunky of earlier approaches me. "I've been asked to give you this."

"Who by?"

"They asked not to disclose that information."

"Are they still around?"

"No, they left shortly after you arrived, sir. They impressed on me the importance of providing you with a note when you were not with your friends."

He turns back to the door as I turn over the note.

The handwriting on the front – 'For the Eyes of Harry S only' – is Dina's. Inside it says, 'Sven's end, 10.30. Tonight.'

## *Chapter Thirty-Seven*

Whatever is going on with my sister, it doesn't feel great that I'm playing along with this cloak and dagger stuff. I know where she wants to meet – we called Wandsworth Bridge 'Sven's End' after his body was found there, having been moved by Stephen McNoble following Sven's collapse at a gambling club owned by Sven but run by Miles Tupps. Thinking about Miles brings back all sorts of memories but mostly of Natalie and what Chuck said about her. Maybe I should try to see her tomorrow, find out what I can do to help.

The cab drops me off and I cross over to the squat frontage of the Ship Inn. Dina and I drank here a few times when she lived with me for a few months before starting university. The wind has picked up and I'm regretting my choice of jacket. I wonder if Miles' business is taking off; Greg hasn't mentioned him since that first meeting, for which I'm very grateful.

The tide is on the way out. From the lights on the bridge you can see the currents flowing fast around the supports. It's an intimidating sight for a non-swimmer like me. A hand on the small of my back startles me: Dina. She keeps walking and says quickly and breathily, "Walk a bit behind me and then overtake and head for the Hurlingham Club. I'll catch you up."

The road to the classy Hurlingham Club, home to a croquet and polo playing elite (which counts me out), takes you past some rather sad industrial units. I walk slowly but there's no sign of her. Finally, I reach the point where to enter the club you need to turn right and walk alongside a tall wall. The street lighting here is broken and it's very gloomy.

I've just stepped into a shadow when she appears from across the road and hurries me through a gate that looks closed but is on its latch. As soon as we're through she shuts it firmly behind us. For a moment she leans back against it, apparently getting her breath. Then she lurches at me and pulls me into an even tighter hug than Brenda gave me earlier. "Christ, is it good to see you." She lets me go. "Well done for sorting out the code."

"How'd you get the message? It doesn't go in the paper until Monday?"

"I get called if anyone puts in that ad. They give me the details and I can decide what to do. Using Charlie Jepson was neat, eh?"

"You sent the message through him?"

"I saw him talk to you the other day and I tracked him down. He's in a state but pretty compos mentis still. Trying to avoid his son."

"Aren't we all? Is he unwell? Jepson I mean"

"Not sure. All very religious but there's something desperate about him too. And I expect Stephen will be in touch with you soon enough."

"Why would he do that?"

"We really don't have time to talk about them right now. I'm being followed and although they know I like to lose them I'll have to be 'refound' soon or they'll get suspicious."

"Who's following you?"

"My employer."

"Is that normal in your line of work?"

"Yes. My boss is playing a strange game; he may even be working for the other side, although that could be one of a number of entities, both friendly and not so friendly. Magda is something of a coup, or at least her sister is, and because they are pretty much nearly identical they are an incredibly valuable resource." She checks the door and moves us away onto the manicured grass and further into the gloom. "I trust you can keep this entirely to yourself."

"Of course you can."

"I know. I said."

"Ha! What is going on?"

"Magda's sister, Matilda—"

"I thought Magda was meant to be Matilda, the missing student?"

"Magda is Magda, but she came here on Matilda's passport."

"But how could she if Matilda is a missing student?"

"Matilda is Magda's sister."

"The missing student?"

"No, that's still who Magda is meant to be."

"I wish I hadn't asked."

"It's easy enough. Let's keep it to Magda and Magda's sister."

"Please do."

"Magda's sister is the mistress of Kurt Orik, a high-ranking official in the General Commissariat of the DDR—"

"You shouldn't really be telling me this, should you?"

We've wandered so far away from the lights that I can't see her head let alone her expression. "I trust you with my life." It's a simple statement but one that stuns me. Some days I forget what we've been through together and simply remember the Great Sibling Wars of 1964–1980.

"Di—"

"Just listen will you?"

That's better; I prefer tetchy. I know where I stand with tetchy.

"She's now under suspicion, or at least there's suspicion of Orik and Magda wants to get her sister out. But she's providing so much good information, so much gold and right now things are in such flux there…"

"So pull her out or whatever it is you do. Or isn't it that easy?"

"There are two plays currently. One is a straightforward extraction… not that any such thing is actually that easy. The other option is a swap."

"Like people crossing at Checkpoint Charlie at midnight?"

I can feel rather than see her shake her head. "Magda's idea was to go there, as a visitor – but also a British citizen – and let her sister return on that passport. She'll then claim she was tied up, mugged, whatever and ask the British consulate to help get her replacement documents, assuming the passport application goes through okay. Meanwhile her sister claims asylum."

"That sounds mad."

"It is. They'll keep her. And the 'simple' way doesn't appeal to my side. They've spent a lot of time, money and effort training her up." Dina shuffles away so that I catch a glimpse of her profile as she walks across a faint light that emanates from the direction of the river. "I'm trying to help her do it her way, but they have other ideas. They want her to stay for a period, set up a listening operation and then they'll heave her out. Or so they say."

"I'm still not clear why you need me in any of this."

"My bosses think I'm just running with the idea of a swap and an immediate extraction to keep Magda sweet; I have a reputation for being tough – mostly because of how I'm thought to have abandoned George in service of the job – and putting pressure on you merely adds to that reputation. If Magda gets a passport through someone she trusts – i.e. you – she'll not suspect until it's too late what they have lined up for her."

"Why wouldn't Magda just do it her way, once she's there, if they're identical?"

"Nearly identical. Because at the last minute it will be explained to her that if she tries to pull out too soon, she'll never get out. Without papers she'll need consular assistance."

"But then she'll just not go."

"Matilda is pregnant. In Magda's eyes she has to come out."

We stay silent for a while. Then I say, "You wouldn't really show anyone that tape, would you?"

"Of course not. Not Penny or your bosses, but others might."

"This film – it's real, is it?"

"It's nothing Harry. It's like one of those soft-focus things. Yes, she's naked and cavorting around but that's it, only these wankers can manipulate things, you know. Any caressing is more down to faking that reality. And, anyway, you weren't together, she was young and she needed the cash."

"How on Earth did you get a copy?"

"My boss gave it to me; made me watch it too. God, he's sick." She turns away, not wanting to look at me, even in the dark. "All I ask is you proceed with the application. It'll go through fine and then we will sort it out. Somehow we'll get her out with her sister."

"Can't you find another way to get a passport out there? Some sort of courier? Dead letter drop?"

"Get you. We don't have the influence. There's only one country with that sort of espionage infrastructure and it isn't us."

We have circled back to the gate. She stops me just before we reach it. "I'm up to my eyes in trouble and I'll probably get sacked over this, maybe locked up. But I wanted you to know I'm not really out to ruin your relationship with Penny. Do you believe me?"

"Yes. By the way, where is Magda? In case I need her for anything to do with the application?"

She reaches up and kisses me on the cheek. "I'll find you. Give my love to George if you see him soon."

"Jim said you mustn't worry about the school. He'll support whatever you want to do."

I can sense her hesitation, like she wants to say something but moments later before I can react she's gone.

I decide to walk back to Putney and catch a bus home. It's as I turn onto Putney Bridge that I catch a familiar sight ahead, hurrying towards the far side. He disappears as he crosses the midpoint and by the time I reach it he's nowhere to be seen. His face remained hidden from me but I'd know that uncomfortable American in a too-small suit: I'm sure it's Chuck Streib.

# Sunday, 27th September 1987

## *Chapter Thirty-Eight*

Most of Sunday is spent worrying. What has Dina got herself into? I want to help but feel helpless, which isn't an unusual situation. She wants to support Magda but how can she if her bosses will just take away the passport and string Magda along? I'll need to do some serious thinking to see if it gets me anywhere. It usually doesn't.

To take my mind off the complications in my life I set to with the downstairs toilet problem. The good news is my glazing seems to have held up well and that is probably where the overconfidence sets in. I take my time smoothing down the putty and repainting the window and frame. When it's had one good coat and is drying I turn to the door/floor conundrum.

This is how the process goes. With the door and floor the way they are, the door won't open with the new floor laid. I can (a) leave it the way it is, with a nice new cork floor save for an area the size of five tiles that looks like it's been eaten by termites; (b) try to lower the floor, so the door will swing over it or (c) increase the amount by which the door clears the floor by planing the bottom down. I plump for (c) because, well, I'm apparently a bit of an idiot savant at this DIY game.

I even have an epiphany when I'm making a coffee. If I put the new tiles down with the door off I can then work out how much I need to reduce the door by. God, I'm good.

I'm rather pleased that the area where I replace the tiles is tucked near the back door because it turns out that the somewhat bruised edges of the tiles I left in place when I took up the Famous Five aren't quite so visible.

By 2.30 and with some afternoon play on the radio, I've fixed the floor, put a second coat on the window and have measured the amount I need to shave off the bottom of the door. It's then I have my first setback. I can't find my saw and my plane is more plain than edged. Penny said she'll be back by four so I head off to Raphael, two doors down and a man with the ultimate collection of shiny power tools, to try to borrow something. This proves to be a shrewd move as Raphael lends me his jigsaw, having given me a stern safety talk first.

It's a doddle. I fix the door to the kitchen table with clamps, measure off the strip to be cut, plug in the saw and zip across the wood. Time is getting on and if I'm going to impress Penny with my new-found carpentry skills I need the door rehung by the time she walks in. It is therefore with some haste that I carry the door to the loo and present it to the frame. With barely minutes to spare I have the two hinges back on and tightened.

Behind me I hear a key in the lock so push the door back in place – it's still a bit sticky so I probably need to take a little more off, but it will do for now.

Penny enters and puts down her bag as she massages her lower back. She straightens up and looks at me. I stand to one side of the door and indicate the toilet with a flourish. "All fixed," I say with supreme confidence.

She looks confused and then frowns deeply. "Why is there light flooding out of the top?"

When I look back and up, she's right. A line of light from inside the toilet – I left the light on when I closed the door – is playing on the ceiling. My brain, which works slowly at times, subsides to a glacial crawl. Before I can move, let alone articulate to myself the fear that is building in my chest, Penny is next to me, hand on the door knob. She pulls and tugs but the bugger doesn't move.

When she looks at me, a silent question sitting between us, I say, "I fixed it," but even to my jaundiced ears it sounds hollow.

She narrows her eyes, checks the door again and then looks at me. "Have you cut the bloody top off rather than the bottom?"

The unspoken fear has unfurled its wings and taken flight.

"You utter pillock." She heads for the kitchen and I hear the kettle go on. I also hear laughter, lots of it. Oh well, every cloud…

We sit and have tea while I tell her about last night and setting Brenda and Dobbin up. She's pleased. She tells me about her parents, how her Father has been offered early retirement and will take it and how her Mother wants to come and stay when the baby is born 'to help out.' Penny's face says what she thinks of that idea. "I'd prefer your Mum, in truth."

"That bad, huh?"

"You know what she's like with Dad. It's the way she criticises through apology. With a baby and me having zero experience she'll be playing the 'I'm sorry Penny, but I really think you need to do this or that' card. I will have to kill her, although it will be justified."

We stare at the door, now back on the table.

"Can you fix it?"

I sigh. "Yes, but it'll be a bit more work and I'll need to borrow some more of Raphael's tools, which will mean I will have to explain what happened, and so on ad infinitum. But I will sort it out tonight."

She struggles to her feet. "I'll work out dinner, then."

"That's sorted."

She smiles at me. "You cooked?"

"I defrosted."

"Oh well, that's a step in the right direction. By the way, did I say I have a session with Ida tomorrow to see if the fitness video will work?

The note in the diary. I had forgotten about that. As I begin to mark where I need to cut - something I should have done the first time - I say, "Um, have they said much about how it'll go? What they expect you to do?"

"Not really. I think they'll take a few stills, see what I can manage, which isn't a lot right now, is it? There may be a bit of filming, I suppose."

"What will you wear?"

"I wondered about that. It's not like I've got any exercise gear. I imagine they'll want me in something specific. There are maternity brands but they're so expensive. Still, if it gets me the role I'll do it naked."

"NO," I say in a strangled yelp.

"Sorry? I was joking."

"Yes sure. I... it's... ignore me." I go and give her a hug. "I don't want other's sharing your beauty."

She pushes me away. "Bollocks. You want a screw and the answer, sadly, remains no. You'll have to see to yourself, Buster."

# Monday, 28th September 1987

## *Chapter Thirty-Nine*

At breakfast, Penny mentions seeing Natalie for lunch.

"Do you think she's ill?"

Penny doesn't reply immediately. Then, "I wondered about that the last time I saw her. She said not, said she'd seen the doctor who told her to reduce the exercise classes and running as he's worried about her joints."

I'm relieved. I'd been dreading raising the subject with her in case there was something wrong and then I'd have to deal with all the emotions. And I'm really not great with emotions.

Just as I'm getting my backpack ready to cycle to work, Penny adds, "I tried the window. In the loo. It's stuck. Is that you as well?"

I need to retire from DIY. It's a shame it's not the New Year so I can make it a resolution.

Later, as I wheel my bicycle through the underpass at Elephant and Castle and approach the junction where Charlie Jepson stopped me, I wonder if he'll be there again. He's not but I'm still brought up short by another familiar and frankly wholly unwelcome sight. Leaning against the stained tiling and smoking a rollup is his son, Stephen McNoble. As he sees me, he pushes himself off the wall.

"Morning Harry. Mind if I walk with you for a bit?"

Of course I mind but don't, or rather can't, say so. Anyway, these days I'm not so much terrified as intrigued by his presence.

"Odd how your family likes this spot."

"So you've seen him, I hear."

"Who told you?"

"Brenda. She said she'd been at a meal with you."

"I didn't think you'd be speaking to each other."

"We don't. Not usually. She doesn't like me, but she understands my worries. About Dad."

That's a turn up. Calling him 'Dad.' "I thought you hated him? I didn't see you as the worried son."

"It's a long story, yeah? Did you hear my Mum died?"

"No. No, I didn't. I'm sorry."

"Yeah, well. Cigarettes; cancer. It was quick, that's about all you can say. Two, nearly two and a half years ago now. She and Dad..." there it is again, something like affection or am I mishearing? "...reconciled. He was good in those last weeks. Attentive. He's been good with Monica too."

"Is he after her money?"

He shrugs. "That would be the obvious explanation. Actually, I've come to think his change is genuine. He found God. Well, his version. Long story short, after we cratered his stupid plan to rebuild his crooked businesses he disappeared for about a year. Ended up on an island off the coast somewhere near Liverpool. Probably Sodor I expect, given he lives in a fantasy world these days. Or the Isle of Man. Wherever, there's a sect on the island where it is, not sure if it's Christian or more a sort of Buddo–Christian thing. I don't get it, frankly, but he bought into it all. Gave everything away, even did some missionary work. In Redditch. Yeah, weird I know. I lost track but he kept Monica in the loop, even though they'd divorced. Next thing I hear from Mum that he's with her in Hampshire, caring for her. I hightail it down there, sure he's trying to screw her or something but he's this longhaired hippy creature who just smiles and lifts his arms a lot. Skinny too, though he looked well enough for it."

We've reached the junction where I usually cycle again so I stop and wait for him to finish.

"I didn't believe it, not really. But Mum was adamant he'd changed for the better. He was there right to the bitter end. Then, while I'm sorting out the funeral and stuff, he upped and disappeared. For some months we heard nothing; then Monica got a message that he'd decided to join Mum in a better place."

"Suicide?"

"Sounded that way. She was really worried. We tried everywhere we could think of to find him – the retreat, the Redditch facility, but all we heard was he told everyone he was leaving and had said his goodbyes." I watch his expression; he looks pained and confused. Not terrifying at all. "I wanted some of that."

"What?"

"What he achieved with Mum. Reconciliation. I'm not that bright when it comes to people, Harry. I often judge too quickly, too harshly. I don't regret what I did to him to make him stop, but I could have done it, you know, a little less…"

"Violently?"

"Thoughtlessly." He smiles. "I'm not the thug you think I am."

"Maybe, but the evidence back at uni was pretty compelling."

"Was I that much of a shit?"

"Do you need me to answer that? My nipple is still in rehab."

He winces. "Fair enough. It took me six months before I heard – Miles as it happens – that he was living rough somewhere around here."

"How did Miles know?"

He manages a smile. "Whatever you've heard about Miles Tupps turning over a new leaf is a load of old bullshit. He still has the same contacts with the South London underworld, and this new business he's bringing here is just a more sophisticated scheme with a better front for the money washing."

I file that away.

"Some contacts of Miles who use the homeless community as eyes and ears told him about Dad. Miles promised to keep an ear to the ground and there have been a few sightings. But every time I hear of him he's nowhere to be found."

"What do you want me to do? If I see him again?"

"How many times have you seen him?"

"Twice. And both times he found me."

"He's helping you, isn't he? Trying to make up for things, I guess. If he does find you again, just tell him I want to see him, would you? Please?"

How odd is this world of ours? Stephen McNoble almost begging me for help.

"Of course. So how do I find you?"

He hands me a card. 'Impressions, discreet inquiries guaranteed'. I shake the proffered hand and watch him walk away. Why was I ever scared of that man?

# Chapter Forty

"You little shit." Crispin isn't usually quite so Anglo-Saxon in his language.

Jonjo looks up, his lazy eye trying to catch up with the rest of his expression. When he realises the epithet is directed at me, he shrugs and looks back at the lease in front of him. He's one of the most laid-back people I know, and I doubt he's even interested in why Crispin is so riled.

Crispin glares at me, then Jonjo, the wall, the open door and back to me. I wait for the punchline, but apparently it is up to me to continue the conversation.

"Is this 20 questions or are you going to elaborate?"

"Caldera."

I pull a face of mock concentration. "Nope, I need more clues."

"Why didn't you fucking tell me?"

"That your advice was as welcome as a fart in a lift?"

At last he moves, his balled fists resting on the desk and his chin, such as he has one, pointing at me. "Their board decision to give Gerald MacThing until the end of the month to sort out their debt restructuring. He just gave me an almighty bollocking for not coming up with a solution to the harbourside problem after you'd indicated there might be one." He leans in even closer. "And if you say it's the Men of Fucking Barrington I'll shove that telephone so far up your anus you'll take calls via your spleen."

"Graphic. I don't suppose that's original. Is it something Gerald said to you that you're currently recycling?"

"No, he said it to Martin who told Frank who told me. Greg said you'd try to ruin my partnership chances, that you were trying to gang up with him against me but I didn't actually believe him. I didn't think you'd sink so low."

"I did a note—"

"I've seen nothing."

I watch him as I pick up my phone and press the extension to reach Chloe. "Hi. That note I did to Crispin on the Caldera development. He says—"

"I've done it. I'm sorry, I missed it and didn't realise—"

"Okay, just bring it in." I put the phone down and spread my hands. "Sorry, but you can see—"

If anything, his anger has ratcheted up. "Don't think I can't see through that. You set that up, you shit! When you lose this race, you'd better get a move on and leave because staying here will be hell on Earth for you." He storms out of the room.

I meet Jonjo's gaze; he is listening. "That went well," he says.

Chloe's head pokes round the door. "Mr Muddle took it from me. I said you hadn't checked it but he insisted."

"It's okay Chloe. I expect we will all survive." As I say it, I'm not entirely sure I agree with my own propaganda.

About an hour later the phone rings. "Spittle."

"You shit. You utter shit." It's Brenda.

"Are you laughing or is that just indigestion?"

"Why didn't you say the newly moneyed donor was Dobbs?"

"Would you have listened?"

"No and I rang off when I heard his voice."

"Brenda—"

"No, you listen to me. What's he done? The truth now."

"He got sick of the cut and thrust and sold his business. To do so he's had to agree to a handover period but once that's done he wants to get rid of his money and there's a lot of it."

"And he wants to help me?"

"Honestly, I don't know but he was always hugely supportive, wasn't he?"

"Well… yes."

"It's up to you if you want to explore things but I know both of you have unfinished business with each other. You didn't like his apathy and he didn't know how to deal with your zealotry…"

"Oh, come on. I'm not a zealot."

"Is Zenda there?"

"Yes, she's front of house."

"Put her on and don't say why."

"Harry…"

"Do it."

While she fetches her Mother, I look at Jonjo who is watching me. He raises an eyebrow. "Matchmaking. Another sideline I'm exploring," I say with a weak smile.

He nods and turns away.

Zenda's voice brings me back to the call. "Harry?"

"Zenda. What three words would you use to describe your daughter when it comes to her politics?"

There's a pause, then, "Passionate, didactic and zealous."

"Thanks. Put her on please."

"You bastard. You fixed that."

"You're the second person to accuse me of being a duplicitous bastard in the last hour."

"Well, you are."

"Thanks. I am, but not in that way. He has changed, Brenda. Really. Just talk to him. No strings but give it one evening and try to keep an open mind. If you still think he's totally shallow, then you're a pretty good judge of character. But you might like this new version."

"Okay. Oh by the way, I was talking to Karen yesterday and she said she had an idea about that thing you mentioned at dinner. The Men of Huntingdon thing?"

"Barrington? What idea?"

"She didn't say but apparently her Uncle lives down that way and she called him, and he knows someone who might know who the Manor Lord chap is."

My heart takes a skip. "Really? I'll give her a call right now."

When we've finished with the usual reciprocal promises to keep in touch, I call Karen's number. Even though I'm calling for personal reasons I still feel a mite guilty that it's a headhunting business. When I get through she's straight to the point. "My Uncle knows the local historian, Thaddeus-something, Melpot I think. I'm sure if anyone knows he will. Do you want his number?"

A head pokes round the door. Greg. He sees me on the phone and makes a sign to give him a call.

"Thanks Karen. That would be great."

"Be warned: Uncle says he's an exponent of the debilitating word dump on whatever subject you raise with him. Prepare for the call to be at least 30 minutes before he gets to the point."

I can't help smiling; we've been waiting for the County Record Office to let us know what they know but if I can get a name quickly then we might still be able to help Gerald. And get Crispin off my back. I look at the corner of my desk where I'd put Karen's business card while I called her. It's no longer there. Shit. I head for Greg's office with my own anger building.

## *Chapter Forty-One*

Greg drags me to a vegetarian café, the Sense of Hummus. "Good coffee and falafels but skip the signature dish. Crispin's livid by the way."

"You set him up. And me."

"Prove it."

"You did though, didn't you?"

The waitress is wearing hessian dungarees and looks both sweaty and as if she's got some awful eczema. Greg pauses to order for both of us while she fidgets and scratches with her free hand.

"Why?" I ask when she's taken our order.

"I didn't 'set you up' Harry, but I do want to win. I will win, and I will do exactly what it takes. Harry, I regard you highly and you'll make a fine partner – we will make a dynamic team, really. But so would Crispin and me and you and he would be fine too. We all know it. The question is not 'why am I doing this?' but 'why aren't you?' And the answer is you really don't care, do you?" He slides Karen's card over to me. "And that makes you very dangerous."

"It's not what it seems."

"I don't care, Harry, but what about Frank? Martin? They'd see it as dishonest or at the very least a lack of grit, as if you were already throwing in the towel or thinking about doing it."

"I'm not. The owners are old friends, that's all."

He nods slowly. "And what about Barry's photos? Have you given them to the police yet?"

That stops my breath. "Did you swap them over?"

His smooth forehead develops a small wrinkle. "Swap? Swap what? You picked them up at Boots. The assistant there said it was a mistake."

"Why did she tell you? You checking up on me?"

He rubs his face like I'm keeping him up past his bedtime. "I know her. She said she thought you had them by mistake. When she mentioned Barry's name I thought I could sort it out but then Chloe told me the photos were, well, you know…"

"Someone swapped the packet I picked up by mistake with a different set."

"Who'd do that?"

"You tell me."

"You've got the wrong idea, Harry. I wanted to help."

"Oh sure. You wanted to help yourself." I can't stop sounding petty; I hate sounding petty. It's too much like my Dad.

"Do you want me to get rid of them? Is that what's worrying you?"

"Why would I be worried?"

"If you could see yourself. Look, I can slip them back to Boots, have a word with my friend and that'll be the end of it."

"Oh, sure it will." I begin to stand. "Don't worry, Greg. I can sort out my own mess, thanks. I'm used to it."

"We need to work together, Harry."

"No, we really don't."

He hangs his head in a way a teacher might when he's given a difficult pupil a last chance and he's not taken it. "I'm sorry you think like that."

I'm not prepared to argue with him. I lean forward. "You've made it clear this is a fight, Greg. Let the best man win and all that." I turn for the door and then come back. "Oh, and by the way if I were you I'd distance myself from Miles Tupps. I have an old contact who knows him from way back and he tells me he's not changed his methods much, just his source of finance."

"That would be my Father."

"Exactly. I hope he knows what he's doing."

Greg picks up a spoon and stirs his coffee. "I think you can be assured he is well aware of what he's up to."

"He's trouble Greg."

"I assume you don't mean my Father?"

"I don't know him, so I think he has nothing to do with this Greg. I've known Miles for years and—"

"Natalie's ex, yes?"

"Yes. So?"

"Maybe your vision is distorted through a smear of lust."

I goggle at him. He's not looking at me but is smiling slightly. I say, "You have no idea, do you? About Miles?"

"I know he made some poor decisions as a young man, got in with a bad lot and paid the price for it. Do you not believe in redemption, Harry?"

"Do you believe leopards change their spots?"

"That's very trite. I certainly believe in reinvention. Of course it might be for selfish reasons but that doesn't matter if the outcome is acceptable. My family is testament to that."

We're back on the subject of his Dad I suppose, not that I know much about him. A while ago I read this article from which I remember the following: Piotr Princip made money from the Nazi Soviet Pact in some way, but shrewdly knew which way the wind was blowing in 1942 and defected via Turkey to the Allies. He joined up with a Polish regiment and fought his way back through Europe, getting various decorations and commendations along the way. After the war he established himself as a backer of various businesses that exploited the uncertainties in Central and Eastern Europe, although there was the occasional whiff of scandal. When he focused on Britain, initially his reputation went up and down with what my Uncle Norman would have said was 'the regularity of a tart's knickers,' but over the last 15 years or so he's become something of an established, if not establishment, figure. At least that's what I think it said. It was in a copy of *You Magazine* that I idly browsed in a barber shop one day – always an accurate and trustworthy source of information. It didn't mention any specific scandals but if you want a whiff of something similar then bedding down with Miles Tupps is a good way of going about it.

Greg finishes his coffee. "I need to get on. We're all in this together Harry – you, me and Crispin. It may only be two of us up this year but those two can make sure Martin's tenure is shortened and then the third can join the party. We might not form a majority, but we will be the 'Young Turks' and it won't be long before we can set this department on a course that will make it the most successful property department in the most successful firm in the City. Please – if my behaviour seems, what, rather Machiavellian at times, it's really in all of our interests to stick together. I'll sort Crispin out; he's spent a week with his Mother and that is always challenging for him. The old bat thinks Crispin's a pale shadow of his Father and says so constantly; getting a partnership would alleviate that pressure a little. It's very important to him."

Quite the speech, I think. Unusual for Greg, who is normally sparse with words. It all sounds good and may well be true but I can't help feeling sure that, while he may aspire to have all three of us as property partners, the most important thing – the overriding rule – is that he is the first among we equals.

## Chapter Forty-Two

I call Thaddeus Melpot. He answers in a cheery, singsong voice. "Helloooo, Taddy here."

Taddy? Not a diminutive I would have chosen. "Mr Melpot—"

"Taddy, please, unless you're a tax inspector or work for the *New Scientist*. Then this isn't him, it's an entirely different person."

Briefly I wonder why the *New Scientist* is lumped in with tax inspectors, but bearing in mind Karen's warning I decide not to pursue that thought. "Karen Himcol suggested—"

"Thomas. She married that Welsh phantom and I don't have much truck with this modern way of nomenclature. Taking the male name dates back centuries and is well established—"

"Thomas, yes – sorry. She recommended you, as I—"

"She did? Now isn't that kind? It's her Mother, of course. The Himcols are genetically incapable of such a gesture. Why, my great grandfather once—"

"Barrington. The Lordship of the Manor. The current incumbent. She thought you'd know who it is."

"Barrington, you say? Fascinating piece of history, dating back a 1000 years, nearly. The default position is that the Crown, in Her Royal Person owns the foreshore, but around the coasts of England there are 17 exceptions through direct Monarchical Grant, in contrast to the numerous Acts of Parliament that have derogated from the Monarch's entitlement."

"And do you know who is currently entitled to the rights gifted by the Monarch?"

There is a sharp intake of breath of the sort my Aunt Petunia effects if someone swears in her presence. "Gifted? Gifted? Young man, it was not a gift, it was a grant and therein lies a significant difference in terms of enforcement. I managed to show this to the satisfaction of a rather stupid Judge, Mr Imperious Plonk or whatever his name was, when we took those dredgers to court—"

This had to be the other case Erica mentioned. "Featherstone v Angler and others?"

"Indeed, and one of the others – a significant other if I may be so bold – was me. A Person of Interest or some such."

He pauses, an actual taking of a breath.

"Was Mr Featherstone the Lord of the Manor?"

"Indeed, although he was funded by that charlatan Toogood."

197

"Toogood?"

"Damned man. He bought it, even though we'd raised the money to buy it for the benefit of the community. Rich bastard lawyer, you know the type. Couldn't compete with such a rapacious shark."

A cold shiver pitter-patters up my spine. "Can you tell me his first name?"

"I can, but I don't want to."

"Mervin?"

"Who are you?"

"My name is Harry Spittle."

"Well, Mr Spittle, Karen is a lawyer. Are you?"

"Yes."

"And do you have any connection with Toogood?"

"I…" What should I say?

Before I can answer, there's a buzzing in my ear; Taddy has put the phone down.

I lean back in my chair, conscious Erica is eying me with interest. "Am I to understand Mervin Toogood of this very firm is the Lord of the Manor of Barrington?"

"I think I understand why the record office is infected with rats. Shit."

"But surely that's good news? Won't he want to help a client?"

"A client of the property department who provides no work to the litigators? You have a lot to learn Erica."

I should tell Crispin. Instead I head off to find Frank. This may need handling at the highest level.

## *Chapter Forty-Three*

I need a drink after spending an inconclusive hour with Frank, who agrees to mull overnight what we should do with Mervin; I head for the Flaming Flamingo. Natalie is in her office so Cindy greets me. "Hey, sexy! Haven't seen you in an age. Your girl is getting 'busy,' if you get my drift." She grinds her hips to help explain, then grins hugely. "You want to be careful who you introduce her to."

I look at the bar and spy Dobbin who I agreed to meet here. "Gary?" I nod at Mr Morose; he looks like he's assessing the chances of drowning himself in beer.

She shakes her tresses and I'm enveloped in such a strong scent I think I might be suffocated. "The Yank, Harry-boy. The big fat rich dude at the end of the bar."

"He and Natalie…?"

She raises a rather splendidly pencilled eyebrow.

"…engaged in… you know?"

"Sexual congress? You'd better believe it." She sticks out a bottom lip, confirming my disbelief.

"You sure?"

"If a 20-stone elephant starts humping in a wooden-floored terraced house, the whole neighbourhood knows about it."

She leaves me to greet another guest while I head over to Dobbin. He eyes me briefly before returning to his 4.3% ABV hoppy suicide pact. I say, "Won't be a moment; I just need a word with the Sasquatch over there."

"I'm not going anywhere. Take your time."

Chuck watches me come over. "Cindy spreading rumours?"

"Rumours?"

He gives a perfunctory shrug. "It happened. It was nice. We both needed it."

"Geez."

"She said you'd had a thing but you're – what did she say? 'Spoken for?' How quaint. She don't need your approval."

The words sound aggressive, but his tone is light, backed by something that suggests a joke. Maybe I'm the joke. I ask, "How are things? With Doringo?"

"Good. He's barely got a personality, but he knows his stuff and especially the regulators. It'll take maybe a year to fly but when we launch it will be big."

"I believe there are a fair few issues to resolve."

"Sure, but my bosses are in touch at a pretty high level through the State Department and word is your government wants this extra fuel for their property-owning democracy thing, so if there are obstacles, they'll get rid. If we get the green light it'll change the way people borrow money for everything, not just houses." He waves at Sandra who is all smiles as he buys me a drink. "There's some crazy stuff going down in the next couple of years. The world we know will look very different in the next decade."

"All these computers?"

"Yeah, I guess. But I meant geopolitically. It will be nuts, you wait and see." He nods at my drink and I sip. "How's your sister? Asked about that job offer yet?"

I put my drink down. "Did I see you on Putney Bridge, what, this Saturday night?"

"Where's Putney Bridge?"

"In Putney?"

"No idea. Saturday? I had dinner in Fulham" – he pronounces it Full Ham – "and walked to the river to catch the subway."

"Fulham? I'd have thought if you were getting the tube you'd go to Fulham Broadway; that way you'd come straight back to Green Park. Did someone send you to Putney Station? If they did, they were having a joke."

He doesn't answer; rather he watches as Sandra moves along the bar and stops by Natalie. I'd not seen her enter and realise she is staring at me. When she sees me looking she walks across, bending to kiss me. "Hi Harry. You well? Pen?"

"Yes. Penny's sore and tired. She's looking after me, if that's your worry."

"She…? Oh," she giggles. "I see. Good." She's gone pink, or at least a darker shade of white. "Can we have a word? In my office?" She looks at Chuck. "Sorry to drag him away. I'll let you boys get back to it in a mo."

Chuck raises a glass and nods his consent.

In Natalie's office she sits behind the desk, looking stressed out. "What's up?"

She covers her face briefly. "I don't know how to say it. I… I… Harry, I'm worried. Have you heard about Amos?"

"Amos?" He was the friend Magda went to stay with, but he was having boyfriend issues. "No. Well, nothing specific. Penny mentioned seeing him not long ago. A year, maybe. Why?"

"He's in a hospital. In St Tommy's. He's got AIDS."

"God, is he…? Will he… die?"

"I think so. He looked awful. Oh Harry, I'm so sorry."

She's stood up and lets her hands hang by her sides. I go to her and hold her. She takes an age to respond and only manages to embrace me lightly. I say, "Come on, it's not your fault." It then occurs to me it's not what she means. "And of course it's dreadful. We're all sorry for him. I'll tell Penny. She'll…"

"NO! No, you mustn't. No, not yet. It's not… with the baby due, she doesn't need the stress."

She looks distraught at my idea, so I nod in agreement. She stares right at me, her brown eyes scanning my face for something. It's like watching her fight for something to say.

Suddenly she jumps. I turn and Chuck is watching from the door, a neutral expression on his face. When he's got my attention, he says, "Can we grab a quick word? I need to go in the next five."

Natalie moves away and walks around her desk. "I think I'll get a rest. We need to talk, Harry. Soon. Please?"

"Of course. We'll work out what we can do with Amos to help him. You know?"

Back in the bar, Chuck has a series of quick-fire questions about structuring a bond issue. I don't have a clue what he's on about but rather than become irritated by my ignorance it seems oddly to please him. After 20 minutes I mention his need to go. He makes a pretence of looking at his watch and strolls away without a word. It feels like our conversation was contrived, but I have no clue why he would do that.

## *Chapter Forty-Four*

Dobbin chinks his glass against mine. My mind is drifting to Natalie; maybe I should pop in to her flat and see how she is, but part of me worries about being alone with her just now. I'll not do anything – of course I won't – but what if word got back to Penny? What would she think? And why do I think she would think it meant something?

"I saw Bren. It was nice. We didn't argue."

I look at his profile for some hint that this is good news. If he'd been told he was going to have all his teeth out without any pain relief he'd have looked happier. "Isn't that good? A start, right?"

His head has sunk so low it is nearly resting on the bar. He peers up at me. "You know what made it so good with Bren?"

"The constant sex?"

He grimaces. There were times when I really feared for his sanity, so demanding in the bedroom – and indeed everywhere else – was she. "The utter ease we had with each other. And the passion. We sparked off one another. Today it was like meeting my accountant to discuss the specific Treasury bonds I should be buying. I prefer her screaming at me that I'm a fascist lackey with a soul as black as obsidian. At least it would mean she cared."

"Maybe it needs time."

"It needs more than that."

"Were you like this? When you saw her?"

"Like what?"

"About as animated as a used postage stamp?"

"I'd describe myself as wary."

"Do you want to get back with her?"

He pulls a few faces. "I suppose it depends on the 'her' that's prepared to try."

"What did she ask you?"

"How I voted in June."

"And?"

"I didn't. I never do."

It's my time to sigh.

He turns away. "That was pretty much her response."

"Why didn't you?"

"When there's a party that I agree with then I'll vote, but each one has policies and politicians that I loathe."

"Did you explain that to Bren?"

"No. She didn't ask."

"Try explaining. She thinks it's apathy."

"Then she asked why I wanted to invest in her shelter."

"Good. And?"

"I said I didn't know if I did."

"Oh fuck. But you told me you did."

"I said it was the sort of thing I'd invest in. I told her I had no idea how she ran it and what her plans were. She said they were hers and she wasn't about to tell me her 'trade secrets.' I told her I just wanted to be sure she wasn't going to fritter it away and as soon as I'd said 'fritter' she started on a rant – a polite, even tempered rant, mind you – about how saving women from domestic abuse wasn't 'frittering' anything away. We sort of ran out of things to say after that."

"Great. Oh well, you tried I suppose."

"I did ask her for a drink. I said I'd be here for a couple of hours. Not that I held out much hope."

"No, well, of course, it's not likely is it?"

Dobbin checks his watch. "I've given her an extra hour too. I'm off for a slash. Pint next week?"

"Sure."

Alone, I watch Sandra and Cindy ease a couple of sharply suited men who are slightly worse for wear to the door. They must have closed some deal as it's a bit early for most people to be ratted. It takes both of them to handle the punters, who appear to have lost the power to control their lower bodies. As they let the front door swing close it immediately swings open again.

It's Brenda, looking rather flustered. She scans the bar and seeing me, heads straight over. "Is he here? Have I missed him? Shit."

Her face is a picture of annoyance and upset. She puts down a hessian shopping bag on the bar. "He wants to know if my operation is sound. I was pissed he didn't trust me but then I thought why should he and he's right, it needs to be viable on paper. I thought I might get him to check it over, but I was probably too stubborn."

I tap the stool, hoping Dobbin will come back to the bar rather than leave. "How did it go?"

"I was so nervous. I really wanted it to work, you know? I almost jumped him when I saw him. Christ, he was such a good lay that man. I miss that, you know? That and his calmness. I could really do with a bit of that right now." She smiles at me, looking a little confused. "What?"

"I think you should tell him what you just told me but first kiss the silly sod or he'll dribble over the carpet."

She stands and spins. "I… oh fuck." Her face has gone crimson.

His expression hasn't changed, no sign he cares. "You're late."

From surprise mixed with hope, her brows suddenly knit together. "Fuck you." She pushes past him and heads for the door.

He looks at me. "I caught the end of that. Why on Earth can't she tell me all that rather than you?"

"Why the fuck can't you just kiss her, moron?" It's my turn to be angry. I push the bag she's left on the bar to him. "Here. I guess these are her accounts. She wanted to ask for your help and guidance. Do what you like with them. I'm going home."

## Chapter Forty-Five

I'm chuntering to myself – not a good habit and one that's genetic because Mum does it too – as I wait to cross Berkeley Street at the lights my gaze is drawn to a familiar figure emerging from The Ritz on the other side of Piccadilly. Greg Princip. Instinctively I step back into the shadow of probably the gloomiest building in London – the Aeroflot offices. Greg is with Miles Tupps and another man, taller than Greg and with even more ludicrously blond hair.

"Piotr Princip. One fuck of an operator that one."

It's Chuck. I smell his Marlboro before I see him emerging from the gloom behind me.

"How he gets away with it, God alone knows."

"What do you mean?"

"Look at the crooks around just now."

"Crooks? Like who?"

He holds up his fingers as if to count, then drops his hand. "Nah, why would you believe me? Some are your most prestigious clients who are the City's darlings. When the crash comes – and, Harry there's always another crash right around the corner – let's hope you guys don't get too burnt."

"You're making it up."

"You believe what you want. One thing I know for sure is that Princip floats like a happy little turd in a sewer, bobbing alongside all the other charlatans, stripping out this, saturating that with debt. You know he's a war criminal, a serial smuggler and a financier who's so crooked that mathematicians have named a shape after him?"

"I work with his son."

"Yeah, I know."

I glance at his profile. He's watching as the threesome hail a cab and head off towards Mayfair.

"That young man will come a cropper – that's what you say, isn't it? One day soon."

"He'll be a partner before then."

"You want to hope not, Harry. Don't stand too close when the shit hits the air conditioning." Abruptly, he takes my arm. "Come on, let's walk."

I don't know why but I follow his lead. We cross the road and head down a path that exits Green Park and leads onto the quiet roads between the park and St James Street, before heading in the direction of the Palace. When I catch up with him, I say, "Were you following my sister the other night? In Putney?"

"You. I knew you'd take me to her eventually." He glances across at me and smiles. "For a youngster, she's good. She lost me somewhere in Wandsworth. Or Battersea. One minute we're easy-peasy and the next she's gone. Must have entered a building, not that I saw. She needs me, Harry – although she doesn't know it yet."

"Who exactly are you Charles V Streib? Because I may be naïve and simple, but you aren't a financial whizz trying to front up any new mortgage loan business, are you?"

"That's all kosher Harry and it's my main business. It takes me to all sorts of places. Great cover. But sure, I also help out the Company when I can."

"The Company?"

"The CIA to you Brits.

"So you're a spy?"

"Not exactly; more their second cousin. Look, your sister is getting in deep and she needs a hand. Her boss is dodgy at best and probably playing both sides. He won't last long. But the agent she's running…"

He pauses and waits for me to catch up, both physically and intellectually.

"Magda?" I say eventually.

"Yeah, that's her current name. She's a great resource. She's very useful to us, as is her sister. The intelligence puts us in a really good position for when the Deutsche Demokratische Republik government falls and—"

"East Germany's government falls?"

"I give it five years, tops."

"Why tell me this? I could go and—"

He stops me, a hand on my chest. "And what? Your sister will be the one to suffer and if there's one thing I know it's that you care too much to let that happen."

"Why tell me this?"

"Because we are sure the Brits are planning something with Matilda and Magda and we need to know what. She's your resource so you guys control her, but we'd hate you to fuck it up."

"Bit harsh."

"Yeah, sure. Your sister is at the centre of this and I need to know what she's planning."

"Then you'll have to ask her."

"No, I know she's told you something, somehow got you involved. She even had Magda stay with you, just for appearances, and now she's hidden away. Why? What gives?"

"Isn't there a Special Relationship? Ask your counterparts."

"That's all PR and 'opiate of the masses' bullshit. What do the Brits want? That's what I need and you can help." He takes his hand off of my chest and walks in a circle.

"Why should I?"

He jerks his head back like I've said something really, really stupid and then starts counting on his pudgy fingers, "One, your sis; two, your girlfriend and unborn child; and three, this partnership crap. That's just for starters. And no, I ain't blackmailing you, just pointing out that you need waves like a flat-bottomed boat. Come on, what are you doing, Harry? You're not one of life's risk takers so what's your role in all this? Because I know you have one."

We're standing under a street lamp, an old-fashioned thing with a weak yellow light that seems to make it more difficult to see than if there was no light. "You can't expect me to say, Chuck. If I'll call my sister and tell her about this, you'll be on the next plane home."

He shakes his head. "Seriously? You want me to spell this out? Where do you want the squeeze to come first? Because it will and not necessarily from me. Whose squeals will bring you running?" To make his threat as graphic as possible he squeezes what could be an imaginary apple, momentarily reminding me of Barry sprawled across his desk. What is happening to my life right now? "Someone close to you will get hurt. Be sure of it. Take tonight to think about things and decide. Tell me what you're doing for her or get me to her. You decide. I'll see you tomorrow."

I watch him go, just another overweight tourist wandering around our capital on a quiet warm September evening. For fuck's sake.

# Tuesday, 29th September 1987

## *Chapter Forty-Six*

"What's wrong?" Penny peers at me over her reading glasses, a new habit that makes her look intimidating rather than stylish.

Breakfast should be a relaxing time, me reading the paper and grumbling at another retreat from Empire while Penny bustles/waddles about in housecoat and slippers, offering me lightly buttered toast and more tea. In practice, it's done at a canter, grazing rather than feeding with the news segmented by the presenters of Capital Radio and our movements paced by the choice of upbeat poppy ear-pap. Today she's wearing an extraordinary confection of colours – purple and cerise and something that could be turquoise but equally could be mould – that is stretched taut across her gargantuan form in a parody of exercise wear. She has another shoot today – a 'baby jog,' whatever that is. I'm hoping it involves minimal nudity because right now Penny is up there with the Pyramids and the Great Wall of China and easily visible from space.

"I've a lot on."

She kisses me on the top of my head. It's affectionate but it also feels, you know, rather too much like flesh on flesh. I touch my scalp and she laughs. "It's not that thin. Not yet, although given how your Dad is it can't be long."

Thanks for that. Male pattern baldness as well as a crap life; what else can go wrong?

"Ida's given me two tickets for a new Alan Ayckbourn play at the National. Can you make 7.30 this evening?"

"I suppose."

She snags up her bag, all smiles. "You're spending too much time with Gary, you miserablist. See you in the foyer."

As I cycle to work, my mind in a tizz, a white van pulls out in front of me. He's going slowly and the mini-roundabout has slowed me down so the collision, when it happens, is rather cartoonish. I manage to slam on my brakes but still thump into the front wing. The driver is staring at me, a mix of horror and disbelief on his face as my front wheel crumples. Meanwhile the momentum means that my back wheel, weighed down by my briefcase strapped to the rear rack, continues on its journey. It the words of the Otis Clay song, The Only Way Is Up and I'm propelled forward by the momentum.

Leaving my saddle is not a choice I make and nor is the way I am sent, in a less than graceful swallow dive, across the delivery man's bonnet. Somehow, through a mix of luck, physics and a grim determination not to look a total prat, I roll off the far side and come to rest standing upright.

An elderly gentleman standing on the pavement while his grizzled Yorkshire terrier does its business studies me for a moment. "Flippin' heck. You'll not do that again, lad," he offers before tugging his shitting pooch away towards the park.

The driver and I exchange details; I declare myself in one piece and hail a cab. Having deposited my bike at the bike shop near the office, I make it to my desk where I oddly begin to cry. My wrist is aching all to buggery and I'm shivering.

Jonjo takes charge, arranging for Gloria to call another cab and I'm dispatched to St Thomas' Hospital for an x-ray. Everything is moving oh so slowly as I wait to be triaged.

"Harry?"

I look up. The nurse standing over me is familiar although it seems more like a dream than reality. She sits next to me and takes my hand, bringing me jolting back to the present as pain sears though my arm.

"Fuck me!" I pull it away. "Jackie?"

She smiles a smile I remember well. "The same. What have you done to yourself?"

"Come off my bike and rolled over the bonnet of a van. Not sure about the wrist."

This time she inspects it gently. "Hmm. We'll get you seen to. Come on."

Jackie Preston is all efficiency as I'm seen by a junior doctor who looks terrified and then sends me for an x-ray. Jackie is a former girlfriend during a longish break from Penny back when I was sorting out Sven's estate. Sitting on a sweaty plastic seat, an image of Jackie naked comes to mind. Well, actually it's pretty much just her breasts that I remember. They were small and pointed out to the side somewhat, but when I fondled them it was like lighting blue touch paper.

"Spittle?"

I stand and realise I have the most enormous erection that is rather hampering my gait. God, why is my penis so disloyal? I'm about to be a Dad, for Pete's sake. Once again I start crying and the radiologist stares at me like I'm mad. At least it distracts her from my rampant Hampton.

Back in A&E, Jackie finds me. "What's wrong?"

"Aren't you meant to tell me when you've seen the x-ray?"

"Patti said you burst into tears. Since when did Harry Spittle do emotion?"

"It's complicated."

"That sums you up. Looks like you've chipped a bone. We can strap it – probably easier than setting it – and I'm due a break. You want to grab a coffee and tell me about it?"

"Not really. No, I'd love to only I can't. Part of it is feeling sorry I've not seen you more often."

For all her brusqueness earlier, the tender way she now takes my good hand and rubs my fingers makes me smile. "I miss you, too, but you decided – not me."

"How are you?" It's awkward, standing in the corridor, but I don't want to go.

"Me? Still a nurse, still in A&E. Married, deserted, divorced – an army regular who couldn't stay put. No kids, thank heavens. You?"

"Still Penny. One about to pop. Still unsure about everything."

"Why the tears, then? It could be shock from your accident, but there's more to it, isn't there?"

"Things are a bit crazy at the moment. I'm worried about my sister."

"You always were and you always underestimated her."

"True. Look, if you've time can you help me find a friend? He's here somewhere, pretty ill I believe."

"Of course. What's his name?" She leads me back to the main reception. When she's spoken to the man on duty she cocks her head as she looks at me. "He's got AIDS?"

"Yes. He's gay. I heard from Natalie. You remember her?"

"The flighty one who you fancied and who fancied you, but you could never make it with each other."

"You're laughing at me."

"Yep. Come on. Have you been to an AIDS ward before?"

I shake my head.

"Then you're in for a shock. It's been better since Princess Di shook hands with that poor soul at the Middlesex in April, but we still have people trying to get in and take photos to make salacious stories up for the press. We have to have a security guard on duty, but I can vouch for you."

The ward is in an isolated part of the hospital and, indeed, there are checks as we approach. The first two beds are empty, although one looks like it was recently occupied as there are personal things around it. I think she must realise what I'm thinking when she takes my arm and says, "They don't just come here to die, Harry. It might be because he's gone for some treatment – an x-ray maybe."

"But they will all die, won't they? I mean, at some point?"

She looks sombre. "Yes, probably. We just don't know enough about it yet. Look, here he is."

We have passed three men, all of whom are looking gaunt and ill. In contrast Amos looks much like he has always done, with ruddy cheeks. He has a tube in his wrist. He looks up as we approach and glares at Jackie. "Fuck, not another vampire?"

He always had an acid tongue and some of his caustic asides kept me sane when we were waiters together at Hemingways hotel near my family home in Hampshire back in the mid-seventies, but this hard edge is new.

Jackie, however, is made of stern stuff. She goes and takes his pulse and then tucks him in. "He'll live. I'll leave you to it. Call me." She gives me a kiss and holds me close. "If it doesn't work out with Penny, you know where I work. Or if you just need that chat?"

"You could come round. Meet Penny properly."

She pulls a face and then shakes her head. "Maybe in another life? I'd not be much good making polite chitchat while wanting to pull you into the loo for a quick fuck. Here," and as she did once before, she takes my wrist – the good one – and writes down a phone number. "Let's have a drink and reminisce sometime. And I promise you'll be safe."

Amos watches her go as I pull up a seat. "Who's the ghoul? Girlfriend?"

"Ex. I'm with Penny."

"Yeah, I know Harry. Natalie keeps me up to date. How are you?" He lifts his left hand and holds it out. I know it's okay, I've seen the clip of HRH shaking hands but this is my first time up close and personal with an AIDS sufferer. I take the proffered hand with, I hope, no obvious hesitation.

Amos squeezes it hard. "This is an absolute bugger. Total fucking nightmare." Tears roll down his cheek. Unlike female tears these just make my throat hurt.

"Why are you in here?"

"Didn't Nats say? I have an ulcer. I had to have a blood test and as soon as they diagnosed the gay plague they put me in Stalag 13."

I look around; it looks like any other ward to me. "Aren't you allowed to leave?"

"They pretend it's the same as all the wards but we're tucked away – supposedly to protect us from the tabloid vultures – and I bet if I tried to leave they'd stop me. You talk to the boys in here and they all say it's a matter of time before every gay is compulsorily tested and then we'll be locked away."

"Surely that's an exaggeration."

He turns his face away and slips back against the pillow. Then he looks at me, "I need to get out of here, Harry. Now. It can get you at any moment. A slight infection – nothing to you, but for me I can come crashing down in days." He looks distraught. "I don't want to die here, Harry. I want to see the sky, the grass, the sea again."

I take his hand back. "You'll be out soon, you'll see."

He grips me back. "You're a lawyer. You could do something, couldn't you? This is kidnap, enforced something or other."

I am well out of my depth, but fortunately he lets go.

"I know. I'm being silly. Did you hear about Craig?" He's the boyfriend, if I remember things correctly.

"He walked out?"

"Yeah. Bastard. He gives me this and then fucked off. Amsterdam last I heard. I loved him, you know? I've no one now."

Half an hour later I walk slowly to Waterloo and get the tube back to the office in a thoughtful mood. The last thing Amos said was how he longed to go back to Hampshire, to the hotel where we all first met. "The sea, Harry, that's what I miss. Those picnics on the beach. One last picnic. That's all I ask, you know? Just like old times."

Chloe has done wonders to sort out my diary and Jonjo has attended a meeting that I was meant to be at. The only black spot is that Frank is angry that I've missed a briefing about the latest on the partnership and he has news about Mervin Toogood that he needs to impart. I want to call Chuck but first it has to be Frank.

## *Chapter Forty-Seven*

Frank is standing by his window, looking down on the podium level below; we occupy a scruffy 1960s building in a group of five, all built on a pedestrianised podium deck under which sits a sprawling car park and service rooms and around the perimeter there are shops and restaurants. State of the art at the time of architectural conception, now it's just in a state. Frank is, as is his custom between 12.00 and 2.00, following the netball games played on the podium level by short-skirted, healthy young women.

"My daughter plays. For Westbrooks, the accountants. She joined as a graduate in the summer. She's just doing her first exam."

He sits at his desk and rubs his face, making the flesh slide around his skull. "God, I'm getting old." He looks up at me. "Do not have a daughter, Harry."

"Really? Why?"

He looks at the ceiling, like he's trying to find the right words in amongst the tired paintwork. "I realised last week that I'm a hypocrite. I've enjoyed these games," he nods back at the window, "for the best part of, what, 12 years, since we moved in. If I'm honest it's the legs that attract me – I don't even understand the rules. Then Cecilia asked if I wanted to watch her team. I went down and stood on the touchline – is it a touchline, do you think, or is that just rugger? Anyway, I was as proud as punch until I realised there were a group of three men – all in the thirties I suspect – making lewd comments. I gave them what for I can tell you, and they sloped off, as was only right. But it dawned on me today that they're like me, watching for all the wrong reasons. They're back there today, but because Cecilia isn't playing I'm not intervening. As I say, don't have a daughter. It's too bloody complicated." He pushes himself back in his seat. "Right, Mervin. I spoke to him and he was pretty clear where he stands."

"Yes?"

"Two words: how much?"

"And he is the Lord of the Manor?"

"He says so although I'm sure you can check if you really want to. I doubt he'll make it easy if you question his integrity and right now that wouldn't be good for your career. In any event, when I told him you'd asked me to speak to him, he accused you of cowardice." He grimaces and adds, "Sorry."

"Can he ask for money? I mean, this is for a client."

"If he has the rights then I don't see why not. I'd hope he would be reasonable…"

"Surely he'd have to ask for a fair valuation?"

"Toogood? He's a bloody litigator, Harry. He'll screw your client if he can. Do you have any leverage?"

"I don't know. I'll have to try and find some."

"Do that, and if I were you I'd find some before you enter into discussions with him."

"Did you tell him who the client was and why you were asking?"

"Nope, but knowing Mervin he'll have some articled clerk researching it right now. And lock the files away. I'd not put it past him to organise a night raid on this department to see what you've got."

"Jesus. Really?"

Frank just shrugs. "You missed the SP's briefing. He asked where you were – no one knew, and when I heard you'd been in touch with a firm of headhunters…"

Greg. The utter bastard.

"…which is a bit premature, Harry, in all honesty. All the other candidates were there, too. I suggest you apologise and make sure you're around for the next one on Monday, or alternatively you have a clear and relevant excuse that is communicated, in advance, to the SP. I'm sorry Harry, but things aren't looking so bright just now."

I shuffle my feet, hunting for words to convince him that I want this partnership much like I want to keep my elbows and knees, but nothing comes to mind or mouth. I'm annoyed that no one has told him I was at Tommy's getting patched up after the accident. Or maybe they did and he wants me to raise it. Well, sod them. In the end I drift away, a sort of mutual understanding having grown between us that I might just as well go and speak to all the ravenous headhunters.

My desk, strewn with notes and draft documents covered in different coloured amendments, no longer defines my sense of belonging or indispensability but rather emphasises my chaotic mind and hapless incompetence. My wrist is aching and my stomach hurts with anxiety. Jackie's number is burning into my skin and I still haven't tried to contact Dina.

Angrily I sweep part of the heap of papers onto the floor, grab my jacket and head for the door. I don't know where I'm going but in what seems like no time I'm crossing Blackfriars Bridge and heading towards the National Theatre. On the right as you cross is a grotty-looking pub called Doggett's Coat and Badge, named after a race on the river every July. My head tells me to walk on but my stomach says grab a pint.

I've never been inside and it's pretty empty as the lunch trade is wearing thin. There are maybe three people in the cavernous space, tucked away in corners when I head to the bar. Having procured a pint I turn and come face to face with Karen Himcol, who's staring at me and looking as surprised to see me as I am her. I don't really want to talk to anyone, but my politeness gene stops me from ignoring her and I go over and ask if it's okay to sit down. She nods.

"I'm glad, Harry. For the company. Not that I'll be much good."

"Me neither. Shitty day?"

"Not really. Just…" she pulls a face that suggests indecision, "…I don't know how to explain it, really."

"Try me. I'm not about to tell anyone. Given the way I am today, I doubt I'll remember what you say in an hour's time anyway."

"What have you done to your wrist?"

"Some misjudged cycling that ending with a triple Lutz across a Ford Transit's bonnet. Which reminds me, I need to go to the bike shop next and find out the damage."

Karen sighs, gulps what must be dishwasher Chablis if the grimace is anything to go by and says, "Okay, here goes. I was doing well at Middletons, on track and all that. Then John and I got together, a condom breaks and I'm pregnant. There's me, Little Miss Organised and I'm up the duff at precisely the wrong point in my career. Hero to the sidings in one burst of enthusiasm. I wanted that partnership, Harry. I'm a good lawyer but, boy, was I cheesed off. It was John's idea to move on, set up our own business and – don't get me wrong, it's been great – but…"

"Unfulfilled ambition?"

"I don't like losing. Or quitting. I've been looking at maybe going back into the City, but I know it's not the answer. Sure, I can get a partnership," she snaps her fingers – goodness I wish I had that level of self-confidence – "but I realised on Saturday that's not what I need. Listening to Bren about what she's doing, I know I want that instead. I want to make a difference. She's got a lot going for her but she needs help. Her skills, allied to mine – goodness we'd be good together."

"You'd be amazing. So why the agonising?"

She takes stock of her wine, knocks back the dregs – which don't seem to have been as bad as the first mouthful – and stands to go to the bar. "You want another?"

"Why not? Lager please. No, lager shandy. I need to stay upright."

When she comes back, I say, "It's John, isn't it?"

A nod. "The business doesn't fly without me. It needs someone… dynamic to keep it going in the right direction."

"There must be loads out there who'd fit the bill."

"Yes, but who'd have the business nous and allow John to be John? And while Bren's war stories made me see that is the sort of direction I want to go in, how do I know she'd want me or it's actually the sort of thing I'd want to get involved with?"

I manage a smile. "Can I ask you not to do anything with your agonising for 24 hours and then meet me at the Flaming Flamingo in Albemarle Street at six on Thursday? It's in Mayfair."

"That's very cryptic. And also precise."

"It may turn out to be a nothing, but I may have someone I'd like to introduce you to."

"Okay." She folds her arms across her chest, no longer the distracting cleavage of the weekend. What is it about breasts right now? My head seems fixated on them more than usual. "Are you going to tell me why you're hiding in this grotty hole at 2.40 on a school day? I have an excuse – our office is just round the corner – but you're a step or five from yours."

"I needed to do some thinking. And now I've done it and I need to find a phone box and make a call. Two in fact. Can I leave you to finish up?"

She spreads her arms wide and I keep my gaze on her laughing eyes. "Off you go Harry Spittle, and remember it's not your job to save everyone and neglect yourself."

Ha, as if!

## *Chapter Forty-Eight*

The phone box is tucked into a corner on Upper Ground, just behind Sea Containers House. I try the number Dina gave me but it's disconnected. Next, I try the classified department at the *Bournemouth Echo*. It takes a few minutes to speak to the woman in charge. "Hi. Listen, I placed an advert on Friday to sell a Fabergé egg with a blue ormolu centrepiece."

"Yes? Was there something wrong?"

"No, not at all. But you have specific instructions that when someone places this ad you need to call a number and give them the details of who's placed it before it's published."

"I really—"

"I know you won't say. Ideally, you'll give me the contact but as a second best will you please call them and give them this number? Now, please. It is a matter of the utmost importance."

"I'm not sure what you mean, sir."

"Just write it down. 017465984."

When I ring off I wonder how long I should give it. I imagine it depends on whether Dina is next to a phone for the message to get through. I glance out of the box, wondering if Chuck is still following me. It's then there's a firm series of raps on the glass behind me. Damn, someone wants to make a call.

I spin round to be confronted by the smiling visage and hand raising nonsense of Charlie Jepson. What does he want now?

I push open the door, about to tell him to bugger off when he grabs my wrist – the broken one – and gives it a little tweak. I'm in agony and have no choice but to stumble out of the box, groaning. He lets go; while I nurse the pain, he bends in close. "She's by the plane trees near the National Theatre. Third bench. Sit at the far end."

He steps away and I look up at him from where I've squatted, whimpering; his face is full of distress and sadness. "I'm sorry Harry, but you must listen to me. And if you're all at sea, then go and look in Martindale Cove."

I watch him skip away, his ragged poncho flying out behind him. There's an even stronger whiff of unwashed human left in his wake.

Martindale Cove? Where on Earth is that? It rings the vaguest of bells but how is that going to help me find Dina? Without thinking much about it, my feet take me towards the theatre and the plane trees.

Sure enough, sitting on the third bench along reading the *Evening News* is Dina.

"You wanted me?"

"You know Chuck Streib?"

"Of him, yes. American. CIA links. Bit of a maverick. He's been following me. A bit half-hearted like he just wants to make sure I know he's there."

"He wants information about Magda."

"How do you know him?"

I explain, omitting the bit about him and Natalie having a fling. I still don't really believe it. "He said he wants me to tell him what you've told me and if I don't then something nasty will happen to someone close to me. Is that likely?"

"It's not inconceivable."

"Great. That's really comforting. He says the Yanks are getting nervous about your plans for Magda and her sister."

"It's nothing. Tell him you're getting Magda a passport. At her request. Stick with the truth and let him speculate if he wants."

"He made it sound like she was also working for the Americans. Is that possible?"

"They'd love that. I don't think it's likely but in this business never say never. Mind you, if she was I doubt he'd be talking to you about it."

"Is she okay? I've not heard from her for ages."

"Harry, you don't need to know. Just leave it."

I've been staring at the churning brown water of the Thames and avoiding looking at her. I feel her hand rest on mine and look down at it. "Jan Kruis wants to see you," I say, apropos of nothing.

"Jan?" The hand withdraws quickly.

"He's investigating a death in my office. I've seen him a couple of times."

She lets out a rough laugh. "I've heard of sleeping your way to the top but please tell me you're not murdering your way there?"

"No, of…" I stop myself. Is that's what's happening?

"Good." She's not noticed my abrupt pause. "Maybe I'll find him. I thought he'd given up on me."

"He thinks the same about you. Do you want…?"

"No. Just tell Streib about the passport and then see what happens. Here," I turn and she's holding a pen, "give me your wrist."

219

Smiling, I hold out my good arm. She frowns at Jackie's number and then looks at me, confused.

"You're not the only one with secrets. Just put a D by yours so I don't get confused."

"I'm sorry I got you involved in this, Harry."

"Hey, my life is so dull, anything that adds some colour is welcome." If only that were true.

She nods and heads off towards Waterloo.

On my way back I call Dobbin and arrange to see him at the Flaming Flamingo tomorrow. Then I call Chuck. "Magda asked me to help her get a British passport. That's all; I can vouch for her too as I've known her for over 10 years."

"She say why?"

"Because she wants the certainty of being—"

"Come off it. Why now? Why leave her job? Where's she going with this?"

"I don't know." The silence extends to somewhere beyond uncomfortable and well on the way to intimidating. Finally he says, "You've been very helpful, Harry. If you speak to your sister, tell her the job's still open. She'll probably need it now," Chuck concludes.

"I…" There's a loud click and the line goes dead. What the hell did that mean?

I really don't have much time to think; I'm just glad the threats have stopped. Time to go and pretend to do some work before pretending I'm delighted to be watching some fluff at the theatre. God, I'm a good actor sometimes.

# Wednesday, 30th September 1987

# *Chapter Forty-Nine*

Today is all about grovelling, which is one of my strongest skills. As I splash water on my armpits to reduce the chance that I gas someone with my toxic body odour, I set my internal dial to maximum sycophancy. On my desk is a note. I head to the SP's office.

Mr Crout has a number of people in his room – a sort of war cabinet, I suppose. Roly Cuthbert, the managing partner, stands by the window, his hands behind his back, one squeezing the other. Mervin Toogood is on the two-seater sofa that sits at the far end of the room – the place for 'informal' discussions, as if such things could ever happen here. Gladys, his personal Cerberus of a secretary, is nowhere to be seen, hence my being able to just wander in.

When he catches sight of me there is a small moment – what a lawyer would call a scintilla of time – when there is a mix of fear and loathing in his face before normality and faux bonhomie is restored. "Harry, dear chap. Come – come and cheer us up."

Toogood eyes me with undisguised disgust, but Roly turns and beams. "Dear fellow. I've been wanting to tell you your interview was a gas. Made us all laugh, even Doringo. Most impressive."

The SP fidgets with an ornate paperknife and waits for Roly to finish. "What can I do for you?"

"I just wanted to apologise for missing the briefing. I will be at the next one."

"Not a problem. Busy busy busy, eh?"

I hold up my injured wrist. "I had an accident – came off my bike—"

"Christ, are you one of those bicycle terrorists? Not surprised. You lot ought to be thrown in the river, slowing down the traffic and hopping on the pavement whenever you feel like it and ignoring the bloody traffic lights." Mervin is watching the SP while he rants.

Roly makes a sort of growl. "What do you think, Harry? Are you all a menace?"

"There's good cyclists and bad cyclists." I wait for Mervin to look at me. "Much like litigators."

It takes a beat but almost at one, the SP and Roly laugh. Mervin can't do anything but nod. His jaw moves like he has a dozen pithy comebacks but for some reason he decides not to share them with us. I imagine my cheek will come back to bite me on the arse. What the heck, there's no way I'm winning him over.

There's a silence while everyone looks at me expectantly. "There was a note on my desk, sir."

The SP nods. "Seb, dear boy, but yes, yes. Okay gents, I think we've done what we can for now. It's contained, so let's hope that's it. Thank you, Mervin. As ever we're indebted to your sage advice."

Roly lets Mervin go first and as he begins to close the door, he looks back at the SP. "Thanks for that, Seb. The boy is safe but I really do hate this bloody awful uncertainty. I'd like to string up all the buggers, but..." He stops, looks at me and leaves.

When we are alone, the SP rubs his eyes. "Roly is getting a bit fixated. Did you know his lad was in the army?"

"I'd heard something like that, sir. I mean Seb."

"I tell you what Harry, it doesn't matter how grown up your children become, you never stop worrying. Or in Roly's case, wanting to fight their fights. I think if he ever came across someone from the IRA he'd lose all reason." He smiles and once more picks up the paper knife. "Changing the subject. Barry," he says, as if that explains it.

"Yes?"

"How... are you coping? I know I asked you to do something that... well, you've met with the police. Did they mention if there were some, erm, peculiarities?"

"Yes. They said the body had been moved. That was you, wasn't it? You removed the dress?"

The nod is almost imperceptible. "I know I shouldn't have. It was unprofessional. But," he looks at me, sadness the main expression on his face, "I was thinking of his family."

"I understand, sir. But wouldn't the police understand? I mean, why would they tell anyone?"

"Money, Harry. There are people who would love this, love to see it in the press." He drops the paperknife on to his desk. "Are you happy to keep up the pretence?"

I don't know what to say. I'd love to unburden myself. "There's something I need to tell you, sir." I note he's stopped prompting me to call him Seb.

"Yes?" He sounds weary.

"Thing is, there was a reason why I was on the Private Client floor that night."

"I assume you were dropping something off?"

"Yes. But not work. Photographs."

"Photos? I don't understand," he says, looking puzzled.

"I picked up a packet at Boots by mistake. They muddled up mine with his."

He pulls a face, suggesting he doesn't see what my point is. Oh dear. "I was going to leave them on his desk but after he died I was going to give them to his secretary. I forgot and then my secretary looked at them – she thought they were my holiday snaps – and… and…"

"Harry, I don't have all day. Get to the point."

"They were intimate. He was in that dress. And…"

"Oh, Christ."

I don't finish. Mr Crout looks ill, really like he might throw up. But he's not senior partner for nothing. He controls himself quickly. "Do you still have them?"

How do I explain this? "I have some and—"

"Some? What do you mean 'some'?"

"After I saw what they were, I tried to decide what I should do next. I locked them away in my briefcase. Then when I checked them again, someone had changed them." He's about to interrupt so I hurry on. "The first set I saw, there were seven or eight – not a full roll. I think someone split the packet up and then swapped them."

"What? Why? And who?"

"I… I don't really know. Not really."

"This is mad. Surreal. Why would someone do that?"

"I don't know, sir."

"You'd better go and get me the ones you have so I can decide what to do."

"I…" My throat is ridiculously dry.

"Well, come on? What is it?"

"There's one of you. In a dress. In the same dress as Mr Tritewell's."

To say the silence is profound doesn't do justice to its pitch black depths. His eyes seem to have become unfocused and he appears to be incapable of movement. I'm pondering whether to go and grab the packet when he almost leaps up. As I watch he yanks open the door to his wardrobe and pulls out a holdall. He's more animated than I've ever seen him as he tugs at the zip and sticks his hand inside. Whatever he's after he must have found it as he slows, carefully shutting the bag and putting it away. Even though I've not seen it, I know what it is: the dress. And I know because as he removes his hands I see they are spotted with the same sequins as I saw that Friday.

He retakes his seat, calmer now. "I probably owe you an explanation. Let me say that we... we – Barry and I – share a, erm, common history. Harry, you have been very loyal and I've asked more of you than is fair. I can't in all conscience ask more. Now, it is possible the police will re-interview you. I recommend you tell them what happened. But I do have one favour – if you can keep your counsel for 24 hours that would be enormously helpful. I'd be very grateful."

"The photos?"

He waves a hand dismissively. "I don't care about them. Show them to the police if you feel you must. Are you sure you don't know who might have changed them? Do you have any suspicions?"

"I... Greg."

"Princip? But why him?"

"He knew about the photos. He's friendly with the woman behind the counter in Boots who muddled them up. He was also there when I was given them by mistake." A picture of him talking to Tina while I'm buying paracetamol comes to me. "In fact he picked them up and gave them to me."

I realise Mr Crout is staring at me. "I thought you two were friends?" He pauses then looks away. "Rivals first, eh? You mustn't let this partnership race cloud your personal relations, Harry. It was unfair of me to ask in the first place. Now would you tell Gladys that I'm not taking any calls for the time being? And close the door on your way out please."

## *Chapter Fifty*

Before I finish for the day, I call McNoble to report on my latest meeting with Charlie. "He's looking okay, although all he seems to have to wear is a thin shirt and a scabby poncho. If it gets cold or this rain continues, well…"

"He had pneumonia a few years back. They said he had a weak chest." McNoble sounds really worried.

"He seems to be working with my sis…"

"Di? Really?"

"Yep. The last two times I saw him he's passed on messages from her."

"Bit cloak and dagger, isn't it?"

"That's the new version. Look, when I next speak to her I'll see if there's a way she contacts him directly and let you know."

"Thanks. Really."

"No, it's okay."

"If there's anything I can do, you know?"

"Funny you should say that. Miles Tupps."

"Christ. Didn't I say he was bad news?"

"Indeed. Thing is he's been introduced to my law firm by a colleague who I have reasons to wonder about."

"Okay. And how does that involve me?"

"You're in the investigation business, yes? I want to know what's going on. Gregor Princip is the colleague."

"Any relation? Piotr Princip?"

"Son and shining light."

"Got you. Well, Princip Snr is all above board these days but Sven had some dealings with him before you got involved. He had a small interest in one of Sven's Father's businesses and got out quickly once Sven appeared. Maybe that's how Miles knows him."

"If you're still in touch, I'd love to know what they are really planning."

"And knowing you that's as soon as possible, right?"

"Ideally."

"We should go into business together, you know? Your inherent lack of trust makes you the ideal partner."

I cut the call, laughing. Now that is a thought.

"You free?" It's Crispin. Shit, I hope he wasn't listening to my conversation. I was sure everyone else had left. It's after 6.30.

"Yeah, sure. What can I do for you?"

"Mervin Toogood came and saw me. Demanded to see the Caldera file but wouldn't explain why."

"Damn, I was going to say something. He's the Lord of the bloody Manor in Barrington, would you believe it? He wants to know how much he might screw out of Caldera for the rights to build into the sea."

"Well, now he knows. Gerald called. He's got an extension to the middle of the month. I told him we were still looking." Crispin looks sheepish. "I need to apologise. I read Erica's paper and your notes and the cases. You're right. It looks like it would work. I suppose we need to put Gerald in touch with Mervin and let them try to negotiate a price."

For some reason Charlie Jepson's comment comes back to me. After all, he put me onto the Men of Barrington. 'If you're all at sea…' "Does Martindale Cove mean anything to you?"

"It's the rival development. If Caldera can't secure the building rights then the local authority won't sign the section 52 planning agreement with Caldera and may well go with Thompson Greek's scheme instead. It's not the favoured one – it's a long way behind and I don't think they've even put in for planning yet."

"There's something familiar about that name. I know I've heard it recently."

"Why's it relevant?"

"I don't know but something in my water says it is."

"You looking at an alternative career as a mystic, Harry?" He's laughing.

"I'm not trying to screw you, you know. It's not me who's the Machiavellian slimeball here."

"No, probably not. Look, I'll speak to Gerald and pass on Mervin's details."

"Maybe give me a day. Let's say two. It can't hurt and we may yet be able to salvage something."

## *Chapter Fifty-One*

Before I go indoors, I head for the old lean-to where I house my bike, intent on dumping my pump, pannier and lights that I rescued from the wreckage. I've never bothered with any sort of lock, partly because I'm too lazy to fit one and partly because I had this fantasy it might be stolen so I could get a shiny new machine. Now I'm getting my wish but in a very painful way. Be careful what you wish for, Harry. Of course, thinking about it brings my attention to my wrist which throbs unpleasantly. My life feels like it's full of unintended consequences just now. I'm in the middle of releasing my frustrations with a gratuitous and incoherent bellow when a hand on my shoulder nearly turns me inside out with surprise. I spin round intent on defending myself to be met by a beatific smile.

It's the fuckwitted Charlie Jepson. Again.

I catch a couple of breaths and begin, "You know, Mr Jep—"

"Please. It's Charlie."

"What are you doing creeping around here?"

"Helping." As before he raises his hands to the sky and lifts his face. This faux-subservience to some omnipotent being – if that's what it is – is getting on my wick.

"Well, you can stop it right now. Unless you can tell me where Dina lives. Or how you two get in touch so quickly."

He shakes his head.

"Do you want a drink? Something to eat?"

Another shake.

"So why are you here?"

He just smiles.

"Stephen – Claude to you—"

"Stephen is what he prefers so Stephen is good for me."

"Stephen. He's worried about you. He wants to see you."

He lets his head hang for a moment, looking like a naughty child. It really is quite pathetic. "He needs my forgiveness when there is nothing to forgive. Tell him…" He pauses, looking rather as if saying this much has exhausted his vocabulary, "…tell him we will have all the time we need, I promise. Before I go."

"Go where?"

Suddenly he reaches forward, grabbing my arms in a surprisingly firm grip. His eyes have widened and in the crepuscular gloom his pupils seem huge and dark. "You must conjoin. Soon. Share your ecstasy with your soul mate."

"Do you mean Penny?"

He nods furiously.

"And when you say conjoin…"

He lets go, stares at the sky and cries, "Let the fluids combine!"

This is all getting a bit much. "Yes, well that would be great, but we're in a holding pattern at the moment," I point towards the west, "like that jet, waiting to land. It ain't happening."

"Her toes are the switches to her passion."

"Her toes?"

"HER TOES ARE HER GLORY!!"

Penny is watching from the kitchen window. Charlie turns and waves. Given her expression either she can't see him clearly or doesn't recognise him. He whispers in my ear. "Third car to the north. Your shoelace." With that he waves his arms and runs off back to the road.

I want to go and explain to Penny but first I need to check the cars. Sure enough there's someone in the third car along. As I reach it I bend to tie my shoelace and the driver's door opens a crack. I'm not surprised that it's Dina. "Is she here?"

"I assume you mean Magda?" I say with eyes down, fiddling with my laces.

"Is she?"

"No, I've not seen her for two weeks at least." I glance up.

Someone else is in the car but I can't see who. Neither Dina nor the other person say another word. The door closes and they pull away.

Back inside the house Penny says. "Who the hell was that? Some wino?"

"You know him."

"I do?" She pulls a face. "I honestly have no idea."

"A guest at Hemingways when we worked there."

"That MacThing man?"

"Funnily enough I'm working with his son just now, but no – not him."

"Not the ruddy-faced goon who was dribbling over Monica Jepson's tits?"

"Nope."

"Then I've no… Christ, not Charlie J?"

"Ta-da! He's found his God and he is dispensing wisdom to we small-minded mortals."

"But he hates you."

"Not any more. It's his goal in life to seek my forgiveness. Actually, I've no idea but I've seen him three, or it four times now… look, let me make you a cup of tea and I'll explain. Maybe you can make sense of it all."

"I'm going for a bath. Bring it along and you can rub my back if you like."

"I'll rub your—"

"I know you would, but I've said it just isn't happening at the moment. Sorry, but there will be others times." She looks doubtful when she says this, no doubt thinking of the baby's imminent arrival.

I know I am. I wonder if I should mention the toe thing, but suspect this is probably not the right time.

"Oh," her voice drifts back from the bathroom, "Don't forget it's the NCT class tomorrow. And it's at a different address. The details are by the phone."

As I wait for the kettle to boil I scribble the address down in my notebook. It's somewhere in Upper Sydenham.

Penny is stretched out with her eyes closed in the bath. Her stomach curves above the water's surface like a brown whale and her breasts float to one side, the nipples hidden amongst bubbles. She looks adorable and I put the tea down and kiss the one nearest me.

She groans slightly. "Stop it or I'll have to beat you."

"Promises, promises."

# Thursday, 1st October 1987

## *Chapter Fifty-Two*

Dobbin rings first thing. I'm staring at my to-do list sat in the middle of the blotter, hoping that I can spirit away some of the more adhesive problems as I pick up the phone. "I've sorted out the money," he says.

"Great. Have you told her?"

"Penny?"

We both fall silent. Then I say, "Are we talking about Brenda's shelter?"

"Your savings, moron. You wanted me to invest your paltry savings and I've sent you a schedule with my suggestions. You'll need to move quickly to take advantage of the opportunities. Have you sold up what you had as I advised you to?"

"Yes, it's all in the building society. But what about Bren?"

"I told you, I'm done. There will be some things to sign. God, you're losing a fortune using a bloody building society."

"I thought you weren't interested in money?"

"I'm not, but that doesn't mean I don't want you to benefit."

"You are very kind. Are you on for that beer? Just a quick one as I have an NCT class at 7.30."

"If you're trying to put me together with Bren…"

"No, I want you to meet another woman and help her out."

"She pretty?"

"Delightful."

"Is that a euphemism for 'adorned with quite spectacular boobs?'"

"Yes, I suppose she fits that mould, too."

"I'm your man, Spittoon."

"You are so predictably shallow."

"Indeed. That's why we're friends."

Crispin is waiting outside. It seems as if I've barely put the phone down and he's sitting opposite me. "Toogood is getting really shirty. He said if I don't introduce him to the client he'll do for me and if I lose him this opportunity I'm toast. You too, if you care."

"See that file?" I point to a faded blue folder of the sort we use for staff matters – we still do legal work for staff, unlike some firms. It is an utter pain. "Have a look."

Crispin picks it up and glances at the cover. "Toogood?" He raises an eyebrow.

I say, "I remembered what I was struggling with. Last year Jonjo had to deal with a right of way issue for Toogood. Some neighbour was arguing he had certain rights and dear Mervin wanted to tell them to eff off or at least screw them for some readies. This is the file when we acted for him on the purchase of his beach house in Barrington about 15 years ago. That's also when he bought his way to becoming Lord of the Manor. See where it is?"

Crispin pulls the documents and title papers from the pocket at the front and studies it. "It says Sea Crest Villa."

"There's a plan there. Open it out."

It is a bit of a struggle, but he manages it. For a moment he orientates himself with the map, but then he looks at me, a light in his eyes. "You mean…?"

"Exactly. Martindale Cove."

I leave Crispin mulling over this little nugget and head for the bicycle shop near Holborn tube. The walk does me good, except for the fact it's raining and I forgot my brolly. While I'm there I defer to the lugubrious mechanic who persuades me that if I'm essaying gymnastics across bonnets a helmet might be a good idea. I feel a fool - I mean, who wears a helmet apart for children of neurotic parents - but even as I think the thought I imagine Penny watching me and give in to caution. Maybe, for once, I should accept that I really do need to be sensible and a grown up. God, this is hard.

## Chapter Fifty-Three

The flotsam and jetsam of London life that finds its way to the Flaming Flamingo never ceases to surprise me. At the bar tonight are Dobbin, alone and morose but encouragingly accompanied by Brenda's files, Chuck busy talking to two men with their backs to me and leaning on the counter flap and chatting with Natalie is McNoble.

Chuck is the first to see me; he waves, and his guests turn around. I see that he has been talking to Greg and his Father Piotr, who looks distinctly uncomfortable. Greg hurries over. "Natalie said you were coming. Come, meet the old man. He's been saying he wants to meet you for a while now."

I bet. Inevitably Mr Princip Snr is all charm and graceful gestures, insisting on giving up his seat for me while Greg hunts for another. I'm aware that both Natalie and McNoble are watching; Dobbin, by contrast, has his head down and appears to be counting the bubbles in his lager.

"Mr Spittle," Princip Snr has a trace of an accent and draws out his words rather like a sleepy marsupial. "Gregor has told me how much he respects you. You will make a fine lawyer."

Nice dig, I think. Although he's hit the sweet spot since I tend to agree with the assumption that I'm yet to make any sort of adequate lawyer, let alone a 'fine' one. His enunciation ensures the sneering undertone isn't missed by those present. "I hope so."

"I hear your firm is…" his pause is extended, which makes me feel like stepping in; Greg shifts awkwardly while Chuck doesn't move a muscle, "…unfortunate," he concludes eventually. "Such silly stories can be so damaging, yes? And Mr Crout has tried so hard to keep everything looking perfect. How sad if all his efforts were to fail."

"Why'd you say that, Piotr?" Chuck's expression suggests mild interest only. "Sounds to me like it's going places, although I ain't any sort of expert."

Piotr adopts a reptilian smile. "Ah but Charles, the question always is…" another interminable pause, "…to which particular place is it headed?"

"Yeah, well, Harry here and his gopher Doringo are doing a fine job. Do you use them?"

"We," a short nod at Greg much like I suppose he might nod at a servant, "feel that it might be thought inappropriate while he is awaiting his elevation. Once he's made it in his own right, then we can begin to bring our operation to..." goodness this is getting irritating "... the party."

"Planning another take-over, eh? Poor Crout. Not much room for him if you do, I guess." Chuck eyes me briefly. "Be wise to stay on the right team Harry. Make sure you know which side your bread is buttered."

Just then the door opens and Karen steps into the Flaming Flamingo, scanning the crowded room. Natalie makes her way across and they speak briefly. By the time she's on her way over I've said my excuses. As I exchange kisses – oddly intimate from Karen – and head for Dobbin at the bar, I can feel other eyes on me. Why did I choose here for a meet up?

"Gary Dobbs, this is Karen Himcol. Karen, Gary. I was at the College of Knowledge with Karen – super bright, super scary and a super doll..."

"A doll?" Karen looks mock-offended, "You will pay dearly for your patriarchal assumptions, Harry."

"I withdraw my statement. Not a doll, more of a cuddly toy."

"You're going to have to try harder than that."

"Sounds like you'd get on well with Bren." Dobbin has at least stood up but his expression still suggests he's been told he has terminal scrofulous.

"You know Brenda?"

"Karen, this is Bren's ex, also known as the Dobbin. Former financial whiz and now a trainee patron of good causes."

Karen frowns slightly and looks at me suspiciously.

I address my friends over the hubbub of the noisy bar. "I'll just ask you two to bear with me for a moment. Karen told me a couple of days ago that she'd like to go back into law, specifically with Brenda or at least working in the same field. Currently she runs a headhunting business with her husband but to change direction right now would put that business under strain. Dobbin, on the other hand, has recently sold up and has a bit of cash to spend on good causes. He is Brenda's ex, but I know he has her best interests at heart and more to the point Brenda trusts his judgement. Those," I point at the files and folders that I now see are more neatly organised than when Dobbin collected them, "are the current state of Brenda's operations. You'd both like to help, but you both want to know if it makes financial sense. I think you might find you have some mutual interests and – here's the nub – that's why I've brought you here tonight."

Dobbin sighs one of his 'life-is-shit-and-then-you-die' sighs. "Nice try Spittoon—"

"Spittoon?" Karen's expression is an eloquent testimony to her revulsion.

"It's graphic but an accurate representation of his personality."

As jokes go, it's pretty crap but Karen giggles and Dobbin visibly relaxes. "Karen, he's trying to get Brenda and me back together. I… let's just say it's not up to me." He nudges the top file. "I have been through all these and, without giving away any trade secrets, I can give you a heads-up on how things stand, if that helps. But that's about it. If Brenda wants my help, she'll have to ask me herself."

"Thanks, Dob… can I call you Gary?" He nods. "That would be great and I'll avoid any suggestion of matchmaking unless and until I'm told otherwise."

He takes a moment to twig she's making her own feeble joke. He manages a 'cloudy with a chance of rain' type of a smile in return. I only hope she realises how much effort that takes.

I stand up and put a hand on each shoulder. "I'll be over there for another half hour, then I must get to my class. I'll say goodbye before I go."

Karen frowns a question. "Class?"

"National Childbirth Trust. Antenatal classes. I think we're learning about the clean and jerk for the pelvic floor tonight."

McNoble pushes a pint at me as I approach. "Natalie said this is your poison. Who's the woman?"

"An old friend from law school."

"Classy," Stephen says appreciatively, his eyes locked on her arse as she unsteadily moves around the table.

I watch Karen as she listens carefully to whatever Dobbin is saying. "True. Well out of my league anyway, even if I was back on the pitch."

He turns and leans on the bar, facing the mirror that reflects the rest of the room. "You undersell yourself. Always did piss me off that, you know. False modesty, yeah? Really? Bollocks."

I say, "I'm a hypocrite Stephen – I know it and it pisses me off too. Part of me thinks I'm this honest, loyal guy but…" I let the thought drift away as I watch Natalie sit down – more like slump – on a chair while looking exhausted. I know why I came here for the drink; I wonder if everyone else – especially Natalie – does? With a flash of insight, it occurs to me that my presence – my unexpressed longing – is part of her problem. I know she harbours some hope of… well, fuck knows what, really. By regularly coming in, being friendly, occasionally making her laugh, I'm letting her think, wonder, hope… I snap out of my thoughts and say, "I saw your Father again. At my house. He was offering me advice on my sex life."

"Bloody hell!" McNoble rarely smiles and when he does it's easy to see why he hides it. "Any good? The tips, I mean."

"I've not tried. Maybe later. I'm pretty sure my sister knows how to contact him. She's gone into hiding but you can get a message to her. It's a bit convoluted, but if you want to try take this."

I've written down the instructions for the ad in the *Echo*. He takes the paper and slips it into his wallet without looking at it. He says, "One of the good things about Miles is his gambling addiction. That and a propensity" – I'm still uncomfortable with the multisyllabic McNoble, it has always been easier to think of him as a badly-educated, unevolved simian – "to get very pissed very quickly on vodka. We had a little session on Tuesday. Princip is backing him, just as you thought. I asked if he'd seen you, knew you were screwing Natalie – I know you're not, but he doesn't and it's like catnip. He tried really hard not to growl at the idea, made a big thing of working with you and Princip at your shop and then said, with a laugh, that he'd then take even more delight in ruining your career. I asked how, given you're this kosher lawyer and all that and he said there were 'plans afoot.'"

I wait. McNoble waves over the waitress – I don't recognise her, but she smiles at me and asks how I'm feeling, which is odd and a bit uncomfortable, not that I know why. Finally when she moves away, I say, "I don't suppose he said anything about that plan?"

McNoble half-turns, resting on one elbow as he looks at me. "No. He did take me back to his office. Nice, very modern and minimalist. Turns out he's got this place in Princip's building and is spending a fair bit of time with him over these 'plans.' I said I'd come by, see if we can't help through my agency."

"Yours?"

"I work there. He's not taken the bait. Well, not yet."

"Thanks for trying. That's really helpful. It's good to know anyway."

"Oh, and for what it's worth I don't think his boy's involved in any of this."

"Greg? He must be."

"I didn't ask, but Miles volunteered that his Father didn't really trust his son, said he was too honest."

Just then Greg looks over at me, an odd look on his face like he's struggling to understand something. He nods towards the door and stands, making some sort of apology to his Father and Chuck.

"Thanks Stephen, that's really helpful. I think I'll have a word with Princip Jnr. If I see your Dad I'll let you know."

Greg is on the pavement; there's a light drizzle and he's tugged up his collar, making him look rather shifty. "My Father likes to do that. Test people, gauge their reaction. Don't believe him."

"I'm not sure I understood what he meant. What do you think of Chuck?"

"I can't really read him. He's that mortgage finance fellow, isn't he? Strikes me as an odd person to be leading the charge; he's not very knowledgeable about the market."

"I think he might be testing you there. He's a bit too cunning for my liking."

"Cunning? That's an odd choice of words."

"Yes, I suppose it is."

"You friends with the man at the bar? You know him, do you?"

"From the same pool of dodgy fish that spawned Miles Tupps. He's a nutter and someone I make the effort to be polite with, that's all. He's also got this thing about Natalie and as you'll probably understand I'm a bit protective of her."

"Is she okay? She's looking very thin and there's something missing, like she's washed out."

"I don't know. I've tried to find out but she's cagey."

"Tupps is on great form, you know? He's got a good business and it's nice to be bringing in clients just now."

"Does Frank know his past?"

Greg is suddenly right in my face, looming over me. "If you try to screw this up Spittle, I will not be responsible..."

"Hey, hey. Easy." I put a hand on his chest. "I'm only thinking about you. If it turns out he's bad news I don't want it reflecting on you."

"I don't know what your game is. Trying to undermine me, suggesting to Crispin I'm trying to screw him and those photos – yes, I know what you've alleged and you want to watch what you say about me. I don't know your game, but I'm not fucking playing it."

He storms back inside, leaving me watching the quick feet of the late leaving office workers hurrying for the tube and trying to stay dry. McNoble is wrong; the man is trouble. Although his anger about the photos can only have one source.

Crout.

## *Chapter Fifty-Four*

The NCT class tonight is hosted by a couple who recently had their baby. What hasn't been explained to me is that, firstly they used a birthing pool and, secondly everyone is 'encouraged' (in the sense that to fail to do so is the social equivalent of handing over the leadership of the Campaign for Racial Equality to Enoch Powell) to 'take a dip.' Everyone, including Penny, is sloshing about in cloudy warm water contained in some sort of inverted bell tent. They are all wearing swimwear and appear to be entering into the spirit of things. Why Penny didn't tell me becomes immediately apparent on being shown into the living room where this aquatic monstrosity is housed. "He'll sit this out. Not a water baby, are you darling?" Penny says.

There's something in her voice that jars. An implicit suggestion that I'm not really entering into the 'becoming a parent' enterprise in general. Priscilla, who is standing by the edge of the birthing pool, waves at me. "Come on Harry. Don't listen to her! No one minds if you're in the buff."

No one but me.

Penny floats over and makes eye contact. "Stop staring," she hisses under her breath. "Everyone else has managed to ignore them."

The 'them' in question are Priscilla's boobs. She has chosen swimwear sporting a sunflower pattern. Unfortunately two of the flowers have positioned themselves such that it appears her nipples have been framed by yellow petals.

I drag my gaze back to Penny. She grins. "Sorry for getting you here under false pretences."

She's not at all sorry. Oh, sod it.

"Harry, no..."

Everyone turns to stare. I strip to me Y-fronts and blush slightly when someone wolf whistles. I hold Penny's gaze. The grin returns. "Get you, big boy," she says with a wink, then her gaze drops. "Though you might want to get in before your stiffy becomes too apparent to everyone. It's not really the done thing in a communal birthing pool."

She splashes away as I hastily check. Bloody woman. I ease my way in and wade slowly over to Penny. "How did that thing with Soderberg go?"

"Ida? Oh, fine. Just prelims really, a few rushes, some silly poses and so on."

"You kept your kit on then?"

"So far. The photographer suggested I did a profile shot with my hands covering my nipples, then he saw how big they are and we decided that no one had hands that large."

"You showed him your knockers?"

"Christ Harry, I was changing into different maternity exercise gear all day long. It's what you do. You don't have the option to leave a lot to the imagination, it's just a studio."

"Did he film you?"

She glares at me. "Grow up, will you? He's a professional. I was surrounded by make-up people, Ida, two other models—"

"Were they involved as well? Naked?" I can't help sounding anxious or possibly pervy. It's hard to tell the difference sometimes.

"God, you are such a prude." She floats away to chat to Chrissy. That went well.

Everyone else seems relaxed. As I ease my way round to Mo, I bump into a small fishing net, floating on the surface, and pick it up. Mo, up close, looks less enamoured of the whole thing than me. That gives me a small boost.

"Having fun?" I ask him.

"You know, it didn't occur to me until Maddy asked Priscilla if they'd changed the water after the birth. Imagine if they didn't…"

I do well not to gag.

"Yeah, that's how I felt. She assured us they had, but how do we know? It's a bit murky, don't you think? And over there, where Penny is now, it's a bit slippery under foot."

"Christ, stop it Mo." I can feel my face turning inside out with disgust.

He looks at my fishing net. "What's that for?"

I wave it around and then shrug. "To land the baby I suppose."

Priscilla floats by at that moment. "Oh no, rather more banal. Giving birth is a major strain on the bowels and keeping control for Mum isn't easy. That," she points at the net, "is to fish out any little turds that Mum accidentally releases into the wild."

Mo spectacularly fails to keep his stomach in check; for my part I do what I've been anxious to stop Penny doing and that is exposing myself to everyone. As I hurry to climb out of the primeval swamp, my saturated and lightly elasticated underwear decide to remain in the claggy waters. With my tackle fully on display and my pants snagged around one ankle I stumble across the room, my ignominy complete.

If there is a good side to any of this, it's Penny's giggles. She just about manages to say something that may or may not have been a comment on its insignificance before she stops herself by clamping her hands over her mouth. Priscilla gives me a consoling look and hands me a towel. She really is a mother hen and I, for one, am grateful to her.

As soon as we get home, I decide I need a bath and Penny asks if she can follow me in. The bathroom is steamy – the way I like it – when we swap over. Her curves are magnificent and I say as much as she slips into the warm water.

She waves dismissively. "Maddy and Chrissie enjoyed your show. They think you're quite something." She gives me what can only be called a salacious stare. "You're pretty sexy, you know? For a lawyer, I mean." She reaches out of the bath and slips a hand under my towel, instantly triggering a reaction. "I can, you know? There's that cream…" She points to a bottle of coconut balm.

Charlie Jepson's suggestion comes back to me. I let the towel slip to the floor and kneel at the foot end of the bath. "Let me try something."

She's smiling though looking a bit confused. "Harry?"

"Shush." I gently massage her foot and then slip her big toe into my mouth, sucking on it gently. I instantly feel her tense and suck more, alternating with licking the others. It's like electricity surging through her legs and she's having trouble stopping herself slipping down into the bath.

I've barely been at it a minute when she pushed me off gently with her other foot and looks at me. In a breathy sigh, she says, "Fuck."

"Good?"

It's not easy to move fast when nearly eight months pregnant but Penny, naked and dripping, is on her feet in moments. I go to pick up a towel to hand to her but she puts a hand on my shoulder and stops me, then uses me to support her weight as she climbs out. I lean in and kiss her nipples and she grinds her fingers into my hair before pushing me back, out of the bathroom, along the corridor and into the bedroom.

Slowly she climbs onto the bed and I start over with the other foot. The middle toe on her right foot – not generally regarded by the cognoscenti as her best digit – is directly wired to whatever part of her brain it is that controls orgasms because they blast their way out of her, like the cannons at the end of the 1812 overture.

She's flushed, hot and loving it; me too, only my self-control is beginning to fade after weeks of abstinence. She meets my gaze the next time I stop for air and nods. And grins. "Damn you Spittle, where did you learn to do that? Geez. Come here, you wretched piece of man-meat."

An hour later she's on her side, stomach propped and snoring gently. The bed is a disaster: wet, sticky and with crumpled sheets. My cracked wrist is throbbing like my nob and we're both naked and drained. Somehow, despite recent convention, physics and planning we've managed to make love. Not very well and probably not often to be repeated but we've done it.

The doorbell goes, dragging me from my slumber. Rather to my embarrassment I've developed an involuntary stiffy that won't subside as I pull on some jeans and a T-shirt.

"What time is it?"

"Midnight. I'll go and see who it is."

"If it's Magda, tell her she's too late and you're all fucked out."

I'm smiling as I open the door to reveal Jan Kruis.

"I'm sorry Harry, but I need you to come to the station. It's about Barry Tritewell. There have been some developments. Specifically we've been sent some pictures and told your prints are on them and we just need to eliminate you from our inquiries. Do you want to get dressed?"

"What, right now?"

"I'm afraid my boss insists. Sharon Wallace? You may remember her."

As I climb the stairs to explain to Penny what I need to do I'm very aware my erection has wilted.

## *Chapter Fifty-Five*

If there is a small mercy in this nightmare scenario it is that Jan has arranged for us to go to the police station at Crystal Palace and not the one in the City of London. The duty sergeant is busy so we stand in the small reception areas, waiting for him to finish with a rather peeved member of the general public.

There's a silence before Jan says, "For now, it's just fingerprints. We will want a word later."

I sigh rather too deeply. "If these are photos of Barry and his room and desk then I expect my prints are on them. Who sent them to you?"

He looks at me strangely and then sags. "I hoped you'd know nothing about them. Anonymous. Did you take them?"

"Me?! God, no. How…?" I stop. It's obvious how they can think that of me, it looks dodgy as hell. "I picked them up at Boots. By mistake. The girl behind the counter gave them to me rather than my holiday snaps."

"When was this?"

The pit I'm in is getting deeper and deeper and I have no choice but to keep digging. "The same day he died."

"Why didn't you tell us?" He looks concerned and then seems to try to answer his own question. "Did you not know you had them until recently or something? Bloody hell Harry."

I want to lie. I want to cry. He sees the confusion. "We can pick this up when we speak. Tomorrow."

"It's complicated."

He nods but doesn't respond. Then, "You saw him in a dress? In the picture?"

"Yes."

"Do you know where it is now?"

I look to the ceiling. The light is swinging slowly in a wobbly ellipse. "I believe Mr Crout may have it."

That generates an even more peculiar expression. I wonder how many he has in reserve. "Crout – the senior partner?"

"The very same. I thought Barry died of a heart attack, Jan. I didn't think these would…" I stop myself. No point pretending any more. "What time tomorrow?"

The sergeant nods us over and we are shown into a small room where the process of taking prints happens. I feel like the criminal I probably am. Jan disappears while this is going on but reappears as the sergeant finishes up.

"We will call but I think we'll want that word after lunch. And this time you have to tell us everything, however small and insignificant it might seem. Yes? I'm being deadly serious here."

I manage a nod.

"That's it for now. I'll take you home and we can get these processed. You'll need to come to the Snow Hill nick in Farringdon. Is that okay?" He stares at me for what seems like ages. "I know you, Harry. You're protecting someone. Again. But you must also think of yourself. How's Di?"

The change of topic throws me. I'm about to say 'fine,' but stop myself. "I think you really should get back in touch with her. There's unfinished business between you two."

"Yeah I know, but it'll have to wait until this is sorted out. I can't get too close right now."

"I get that. She's pretty tied up with work anyway."

He takes me home, saying little on the way. When I get in it's really morning but a part of it I rarely see. Penny is at the dining room table sipping herbal tea. She makes me a builder's brew and sits opposite me. "Spill. And it better be everything or you're moving out tonight. Or this morning."

It takes an hour but I cover most of it. She doesn't speak or ask any questions. "I'll give you the benefit of the doubt and assume you didn't tell me this because of some misplaced idea of protecting me and Wigglet," she pats her stomach, "but hear this, Buster. Don't you dare keep such a big fucking secret from me ever again? We're in this together, you know. A team, a partnership and—"

"Will you marry me?"

"What?"

I wriggle off the chair and, holding the table to stop myself wobbling over, I kneel to say, "Will you be my wife?"

She narrows her eyes. "Now? You propose now? You were talking about this the other night when I was drifting in and out of sleep, weren't you? I thought I must be dreaming, especially as you never mentioned it again."

"I've been thinking about this for a while. It seems, I don't know, right?"

"This?" Another tap on her stomach.

"Yes. Well, that's part of it."

She appraises me for a while, tilting her head to one side. "I can think of two reasons for this proposition—"

"Proposal," I interrupt to correct her.

"Whatever. You don't want Wigglet to be called a bastard – which frankly is a little last century of you – and you want him or her to be called Spittle, which is hardly the greatest gift you could give."

"No… it's… I thought…"

"And then you get arrested in the middle of the night…" she holds up a hand to stop my obvious interruption, "or whatever just happened, and then tell me this extraordinary story you've kept from me. And after all that, you want some – what – absolution? By proposing? Not on your nelly matey."

I struggle back into my chair. "It's not like that, but I am being really serious. I'll talk to Crout in the morning, sort something out. And tell you what happens."

She reaches across the table and takes my hand, "I do not care about your partnership, okay? I don't want a ring on my finger, through my nose or stuck in, on or through any other fucking place. You've done nothing wrong and you've been pressured into hiding things you shouldn't have hidden. Just tell Kruis and that other policewoman. You don't need Crout's permission for any of this."

"No, but it would be best if he knew in advance. He may want to come with me, tell his side of the story from his perspective."

"All right. Just tell him, okay? Do not be persuaded to lie."

"And marriage?"

She holds my gaze for an age and then drags herself to her feet, heading back to bed.

# Friday, 2nd October 1987

## *Chapter Fifty-Six*

I don't really sleep but I do dream.

I'm with Crout and Kruis, and having told them everything I still find I'm sacked, removed from the Roll as a solicitor and thrown into jail.

This nervy, febrile state continues and by the time I make it into the office I'm drained.

What I don't need is Gloria waving at me rather frantically and looking like she might burst. "Did you hear about Mr Crout?" she squeaks, eyes panning across my face.

"Crout?" I immediately assume he's been arrested or at least pulled in for questioning.

"He's in hospital, in a coma. Someone said it may have been attempted suicide."

There's something about the way she says this, almost with a sense of excitement, like it's not real but a storyline from a soap, which makes me angry. "You shouldn't be talking about this, Gloria. If it's true, it's highly private and confidential."

For a moment she's nonplussed but then her own anger takes over. "Hey, smart boy, don't get all high and mighty with me. You're the one the police are interested in."

I must show my surprise because she goes on in a weirdly conciliatory tone, "Don't worry, I'm not one to gossip."

I go to my desk wondering who told her. Of course it has to be Greg. Yes, that makes perfect sense. After all he's the one who gave them the photos. He'd know that if he told Gloria it would be all round the office by lunchtime.

A call comes in as soon as I've sat down.

My new bike is ready. It's a Trek, with cool mountain bike tyres and a bright yellow frame.

Something of this newly-found street cred is, however lost when I collect it in my suit. Trying to avoid sweating as I cycle it back to the office, I narrowly avoid a post office van that pulls out in front of me - so much for the promise that 'no one will miss that bike' that the bike shop owner confidently predicted as I left. The subsequent swerve sends me into the kerb and into an undignified heap in front of two barristers, in full wig and gown on their way back to Chambers from some court appearance. One clearly calls me a wanker as I dust myself off. It's as I'm about to retort that I see Toogood watching from the other pavement.

He just stares but I know, I just know he too is thinking 'wanker'.

## *Chapter Fifty-Seven*

A message waits for me from Kruis: he wants me to come in at 12.30, although he doesn't specify whether that's am or pm. Sadly, I have no excuses, no competing meetings or critical research or drafting. The photos I do have – the ones that show Crout in the dress – are locked in my desk. I check them again, almost as if inspiration will come to me and give me a reason not to worry. I put the pictures back in my briefcase and study my to-do list to try to distract myself.

I've decided that to-do lists reflect your personality. Crispin's, which litter his desk and walls where they are stuck up with Blu Tack, are impressively detailed. Erica's, my articled clerk, are examples of the sparse minimalism that describes her own methodology. Mine? Rambling, incoherent and in the final analysis more or less useless.

I've various things to attend to: documents to read and a letter to draft, but I can't really summon up the enthusiasm. I need to update Chuck on our research – there's a complicated note from Doringo's team that I need to read. In the end I do the one thing I really don't need to do: go and see Crispin about Caldera. I'm not involved but still insatiably curious.

I find him with his head in his hands at his desk. "What's straining the brain today, oh wise seer?"

"Bugger off Spittle." He sits back and points at a telephone attendance note. "Read it for yourself."

It's in his secretary's tiny square hand.

*Mr MacT called. Says he wants to know why our firm is trying to screw him over, most irate. Some partner rang saying Newe Waters can no longer act because of a conflict of interest that was 'previously undisclosed.' He wants an urgent telephone conversation with you.*

"Has to be Toogood. What's he playing at?"

"Of course it's fucking Toogood. He called me," Crispin indicates a crumpled message that he's tossed – probably hurled – across the room, "...and said he'd be telling Frank about my 'poor performance.' Apparently I was wrong to accept the instruction to act for Caldera since the firm already acts for him from the time he bought his title for Lordship of the Manor. He says we need to withdraw and accept the consequences. He told me he has already notified the insurers of a potential claim – in that snake's words, 'if I was advising Caldera, I'd sue us for every penny' – and will let Frank know what he thinks of my work and the implications for my future." Crispin looks at me, wide-eyed. "What the fuck have you done, Harry?"

I'm stunned. "Toogood is using the potential for litigation against the firm for his own ends? Surely he can't be serious?"

"Very – deadly serious in fact. He even quoted Law Society rules on conflicts at me. You've completely fucked up my career with this oh-so-clever meddling. I told you not to interfere, but you knew better, didn't you? Well, if I go down then you're going down too, you twat." He stands and goes to the table in the middle of his room heaped with papers, collecting three fat files, then turns to face me. "You wanted to be the hero on this one so you can fucking bury it like it will do for both you and me."

"There has to be a way to sort this out. There just has to be," I say as I take the Caldera files.

"If you have any good ideas then feel free to share them because right now your input is about as conceptually brilliant as an ashtray on a bloody motorbike."

As I leave him to his gloom I walk right into Greg. "Harry, I need a word about those photos."

"You know what Princip, why don't you just go crawl under a bloody stone?"

Two secretaries are chatting outside their room. They stop mid-sentence and stare at me, but right now I don't care. I go into my room, dump the files, avoid any eye contact with Jonjo and Erica, grab my briefcase and jacket and head for the lifts.

For once, I suppress the urge to save money and instead wait for a black cab to come past. None are going in my direction, so I cross the road to see if I have better luck on the other side. As I walk slowly along the pavement I look back and see Gloria appear from the front door of the office and turn right. As she reaches the passage that leads down the side of our building heading towards the steps to the podium level, a young woman emerges from somewhere, gives her a friendly peck on the cheek and falls in step with her. She's familiar from somewhere, but I'm buggered if I can remember where. Before I have a chance to ponder an answer a cab appears and my mind turns to my upcoming interview with the police.

## *Chapter Fifty-Eight*

"Thanks for coming in Harry. How have you been?" Sharon Wallace is an inspector, still short and with a pleasingly pneumatic appeal, not that I focus on that too much. We first crossed paths over the mysterious death of Sven Andersen and subsequently the equally bizarre demise of Sir Penshaw Grimsdale, the man whose untimely death Penny was briefly suspected of being implicated in. She was helpful, sympathetic and clever. It's only now I remember fancying her when we first met, although since I was so on-off with Penny in those days I was apt to fancy any woman that smiled at me while equipped with a shapely bust, even a policewoman who was questioning me about a suspicious death. Maybe it was mutual because her greeting is oddly effusive. As we go through the pleasantries, if you can call settling into a windowless interrogation room in Snow Hill police station pleasant, I try to remember whether I ever asked her out. I realise I must be staring or at least looking at her in an odd way, because she stops saying whatever it is she's saying and asks if I'm all right.

"Yes, yes fine." Concentrate, moron.

"This is just an informal chat for now. Is that okay?"

"Yes. It might save time if I tell you what I know. Jan advised that I say everything that comes to mind, however small. Is that okay?"

Sharon smiles. "Perfect."

Nodding, I take out the wallet of photos and tip them out on the table.

Both Kruis and Wallace glance at each other; Jan pulls the nearest one to him. "Are these copies?"

"I'll explain everything as it happened, if that's all right?"

Sharon nods. "Do go on."

"As I told Jan last night, I collected Barry's photos in error on the afternoon he died. As you already know, I went back to the office after hours to collect a folder to work on over the weekend. It was then I realised I'd got the wrong snaps. I could have left them in my desk and swapped them on the Monday but thought it best to drop them off with Barry or his secretary, so I walked down the back stairs to his office."

"You went to his office?" They exchange a look that fails to hide their surprise.

252

"I found him. He was sprawled across his desk and wearing that dress." I point at the picture with Mr Crout in the garish frock.

Jan looks at it and picks it up. "Is this—?"

"Please Jan, I'll explain if I can, but it will be easiest if I go through it chronologically."

He glances at Sharon who confirms my plan.

"I was still absorbing what I was seeing when Mr Crout appeared. I've thought about this since and I think he may have already been in the room. He certainly made me jump."

"I bet." Jan colours at his own interruption. "Sorry."

"Mr Crout seemed shocked too but persuaded me that I should go and leave him to it. He'd sort out... yes?"

Sharon has raised her hand and asks me, "Did you make sure he was dead?"

"Yes, sorry – of course. I think I checked his pulse but his face was already blue. Mr Crout was worried about scandals – both for the firm and his family. He... that is..." How the hell do I explain this?

"Harry, you've done really well. Do you need a break? A drink or something?"

"No, no, let's finish this. I said he had on that dress, but it was pulled up and... and his buttocks were on show. It looked like... oh Christ. It looked like someone had taken him, you know – buggered him over his desk."

The surprise they'd shown earlier isn't so exaggerated this time. My story is so incredible they no longer know what to be surprised about.

"No one knew he was gay. I still don't know if he was fully living a lie with his wife and kids... something Mr Crout said made me think he was probably bisexual and... and he – that is Mr Crout – may have tipped the balance, so to speak... he and Barry..."

"They were lovers?"

I answer her quickly. "He never actually said so, it's just an impression he gave me."

"Okay. And what happened then?"

"I left. I was sick – really sick, in a bin – but he's my boss, he told me to go and he'd sort it out. I believed he'd arrange for an ambulance, even though we both knew he was dead and that he would call the police. He really seemed genuine that he didn't want me involved. I took him at face value. And he said it was natural causes – heart attack or a stroke or something like that. So despite the shocking circumstances I…" I hang my head. "…I wanted to believe him. I'm up for partnership next month. I need his support. I should have done what I knew was the right thing, but I didn't."

"You didn't leave the photos, did you?"

"No, after all that I forgot I had them for a few days. My secretary found them in my desk and looked at them out of nosey curiosity. It was then I realised how intimate they were. I imagine they're the ones you were sent if they have my prints on them."

Sharon reaches for a folder I'd not noticed and slips out some enlarged prints. "You mean these?"

I glance through them taking time to study the one of Barry in the dress. "Yes, I think so. I put them away quite quickly. I was horrified by it all but I knew I had to ask Mr Crout what I should do. Then work got in the way – please remember it was still being said it was a heart attack, a natural thing entirely separate to whatever else happened that evening. So a couple of days later I dug the pics out to take them to Mr Crout and realised they'd been swapped and those," I indicate the set in front of Jan, "had replaced them. Initially I thought they were from the same set but then realised that the man in the dress wasn't Barry but Mr Crout. After much agonising I told him what I had discovered and he seemed genuinely surprised. He told me – or at least confirmed what I'd guessed – that he'd changed Barry's clothes and taken the dress away. It was in a gym bag somewhere in his room. He said something about him and Barry, I don't really recall what but as I say I got the impression they had some sort of gay relationship. Maybe a love affair, I don't know. He told me I should tell you but then he asked for 24 hours. Then Jan gets sent the first set and Mr Crout tries to kill himself and—"

"What!?"

"Sorry, I thought you'd know that."

Sharon is shaking her head. "No, we'd not heard anything. Do you know how he is? Where he is?"

"He's in St Tommy's. All I heard was that he'd attempted it. Nothing more than that. It's been a tricky start to the day, as you can imagine."

Sharon puts down her pen; she's been taking notes. "Would you like some tea?"

I think I look stunned. She smiles; I remember that smile from before. "It's part of our ruthless interrogation technique. We offer you tea and then deny you two sugars and get stingy with the milk. Jan?"

When he's gone, Sharon studies the images. "Who hates you enough to do this, Harry? If what you say is true, then someone is setting you up to look rather shady. Do you think it has something to do with your career?"

"Yes, I think that's probably it. Gregor Princip. He's a colleague but these days more of a rival. He was there when I picked up the wrong pictures. And he knew about them being in my desk and what they showed. It makes some sense that… oh, and he was there that Friday night. He says he saw me on the Private Client floor. In fact," it suddenly comes back to me, "I think he was there too. I'm sure I saw him just before I found Barry's body. I'd forgotten. Sorry, that sounds stupid. I don't know it's him. It's circumstantial, isn't it? But I can't think who else it might be."

"Is he related to Piotr Princip?"

"Piotr is his Father."

A rather lovely eyebrow shoots up. "How interesting."

Jan comes back with the tea. Sharon says, "Can you just repeat what you just said to me while Sergeant Kruis was out of the room?"

I repeat my comments and then sip the tea. It could be part of a cunning plan to get me to confess because it is utterly disgusting.

Sharon and Jan confer in whispers. "What about negatives?"

I swallow and reamin silent.

"And you didn't remove any pictures when you opened the packet? This is correct?"

"Yes, yes, I think that's all I've seen." I cough and add, "I noticed how in the first set you can only see Mr Tritewell and in the second only Mr Crout, though if you have both you can see they are in the same dress. I assumed they all came from the same film but without the negatives…" I try a shrug but it feels like it is more a shudder.

She scribbles and nods but it's not a comforting gesture. Does she believe me?The questions continue for another three-quarters of an hour going over the details. Not much else comes out. They're interested in Gloria and Ronnie and what we did and said in reception, but that's it. I'd like to say they believe me, but in all honesty they could just be good poker players.

## *Chapter Fifty-Nine*

There's a message to ring Chuck, which I do.

"You got it?"

"It?"

"Don't be cute. The passport."

"No. I've been rather busy, you see, and—"

"Call. Now. Then call me back."

So I do.

"Another week," I tell him.

"Shit." He rings off then seconds later is back on the phone. "You've 48 hours." Once again he hangs up.

I should be terrified, but since I have no influence with the Home Office it feels like a stupid, if not idle, threat. The phone goes again. I snatch it up and bark, "Look, I can't…"

"Spittoon, are you normally so aggressive?"

"Dobbin? What do you want?"

"A pint. Several. And a word. I know it's late for lunch but are you free?"

"No. I… yes, sod it. Where?"

"Christ, you're the most indecisive man I know. How about The Goblet in Love Lane?"

We agree to meet in 20 minutes. Erica is hovering, clearly wanting a word. I say, "I really need to dash. Can this wait?"

"Very quickly. The records office rang about the Barrington Lord—"

"Things have moved on, now we know Toogood is—"

"He isn't. Well, not technically."

That stops me dashing out. I'm getting short of time. "Come with me and explain."

She grabs her jacket.

I shake my head. "Just to the lift."

Disappointment – oh Harry, so cruel.

She perks up though as we walk and inevitably wait for the lift. "The transfer of the Lordship is only valid if it's registered within a reasonable time and no application was ever made so it lapsed."

"Did we cock that up too? When we bought it for him?"

She can't hide her excitement. "No, that's just it. I looked at the file. When we bought it, he didn't actually want it. It cost £50 to

256

register and when we told him he said not to bother. There's a note on the file saying that he'll do it if and when he wants to."

"I don't suppose anyone has opined on what a reasonable time might be?"

She's almost quivering as she juggles some notes. "Not for this sort of thing – there aren't many precedents – but in the case of *Acme Sprocket and Spoke Construction Limited v Annerley & others* in 1931, Lord Justice Atkins said that there would have to be compelling reasons for any delay beyond a year to register any customary right, such as the death of the transferee and even then the courts would not look favourably on delays where the transferee had been professionally advised. This involved some very specific Royal Charter rights of turbary that exist in West Lawton on the edge of the Yorkshire Moors. I think—"

I hold my hand up. "That's great. Sounds like he truly shafted himself there. Didn't that historian say they were outbid? How did that work?"

"The previous holder – actually the current holder – is a Mr Featherstone, and he wanted to sell the villa and the lordship together; what Mr Melpot and his friends couldn't afford was the price of the property. It looks like he assumes – everyone does – that Mr Toogood bought everything and indeed he paid the price and took a transfer. But then he didn't go through with the formalities."

The lift grinds to a halt with a jerk. "That means Toogood holds the beneficial interest and this Featherstone retains the legal interest. Are we sure he can't just register late?" I hold the lift doors, which is a little like Canute and the tide because after a few seconds the bloody thing will descend to the basement anyway. "Come on."

"I'll tell you when you get back."

"Tease. For that you can look up conflicts. Toogood says that as we acted for him when we bought his house and those rights, we can't now act for Caldera. Can you see if it's a try-on?"

"Surely, oh great and wise master."

The doors try to close and I lose my grip. She's already skipping off to start the research as they shut and I head for the basement, accepting I'll have to take the stairs to the ground floor, since any attempt now to press the 'G' button will be futile.

## *Chapter Sixty*

Dobbin is waiting just inside the door to the salon bar. "You look frazzled. Would a pint help?"

"Please." We sit on stools by the bar.

"Bad day?"

"Just the usual: crashed my new bike, interrogated by the cops, career in ruins, Penny's turned down my proposal of marriage which means she may actually hate me. Oh, and I may want you to impersonate a solicitor again." Years ago, Dobbin pretended to be Penny's defence counsel; it lasted about three hours before we were rumbled.

"How very exciting. Leaving aside the idea that Penny has come to her senses about you being an unsuitable life partner and husband, why do you need me to aid and abet a crime again? Or maybe that should be: 'why should I?'"

"My sister is likely to go to prison and I may very well end up in the foundations of some new office building somewhere if you don't."

"Knowing you, that's entirely plausible. When do you want this favour?"

"No idea. Come on, cheer me up. How shit is your life?"

"First, have you signed those forms I sent you? About your investments. Remember? The market is so hot you're losing thousands a day."

"Seriously?"

"No, not really, but you are losing out."

"I'll do it tonight. What's second?"

"I spent most of the other night with Karen."

"Get you with a married woman."

"Shut up and listen."

I sit back, surprised by such vehemence from Dobbin.

"In summary, it's pretty clear Brenda still loves me—"

"Hold the front page. What have I been saying—?"

"Yeah, shut up. And I do her, but there's no way we're ever going to get back together." He won't look at me as he says this.

"Come again?"

He looks up, his face full of fury. "Don't you get it? You are the problem."

"Me? I don't fancy her and—"

"You really are a jerk. You want to know when it started to go wrong with Brenda and me? When you accused her of spying on you for that crook McNoble."

"She was!" I can't help squeaking and am conscious of one or two late lunch drinkers beginning to take an interest in us. "She nearly screwed everything up."

"Yeah? But she didn't, did she?"

"She deceived you as much as me. More so." I manage to keep my voice in a lower register, but it comes out as a hiss.

"Right. And you thought, I know what – I'll not only crush her but I'll make sure Dobbin is there too so he can watch while I do it. You knew, Mr Clever Pants, that I adored her. I was besotted, right?" He's beginning to cry, and I've never ever seen so much as a sniffle from Dobbin. "You didn't need to do what you did, not like that, did you? I sat there while you crushed her. And I couldn't do anything, could I? My best mate, the guy I'd rely on for my fucking life, is eviscerating my girlfriend, the woman I'm harbouring thoughts of a long-term relationship with. Right there in front of me. And you were right at the time. She'd been a total shit."

"I don't understand. She admitted it. And we sorted it out afterwards. We're all good."

The glare, when it comes, is so all encompassing I'm certain he's about to punch me.

"You fucking moron. You've never forgiven her, have you?" His breath is coming in short pants. "When did you forgive her, eh? When was the exact moment you said to yourself, 'It's okay Bren, I've punished you enough and now you're free?' And more to the point, when did you tell her?"

"I... that's..." He's right of course. I never really did forgive her. Sure, I've been polite, we've had dinner and been friendly but there has always been an edge. I've made an effort to do the minimum because I knew Dobbin wanted to get back with her, but really it was the very minimum. It's the least I could do.

"Look Harry, I'm not dumb." Harry? He never calls me Harry. "She did try to ruin things. We know why and the reason was understandable, but the fact is she treated you awfully." He shakes his head hard. "I'm sorry, but this isn't about you. Well it is, but it's not your problem."

"What's brought this up now? What did Karen say?"

"Just what I told you. She still can't get beyond me – us. And I realised it's the elephant in the room. She's right. In effect she's asking me to choose between you and her and she doesn't want to do that because she knows that if I choose her, I'll eventually resent her. And mate, she may be right. I just don't know."

"I never knew. Really."

"Course not. Every time we met she'd want to know what you'd said. She didn't make a big thing of it but it's obvious with hindsight that she was looking for a sign you'd moved on. You know how many years it took you to hug her when we all met?"

"I…" He's right about that, too. "I didn't think she wanted to. What about the politics thing?"

"It was never about that."

"No? She was pretty convincing."

"Yeah? Well it wasn't."

"It sounded plausible." Oh how pathetic I sound.

"None of us are heroes in this story. She thought – the other day, when you brought us together – she assumed you'd forgiven her, but I told her you were just doing it for me, not for you. I snapped at her then, gave her an ultimatum. Karen told me she's not coming back. Fuck Spittoon, it's a total mess."

"Is it? I'll go and see her, tell her—"

"It's too late. There's no point."

"I want to try."

He studies the mirror behind the bar for an age before nodding and leaving without another word. I stay for another 20 minutes, deliberately drawing out the dregs of my pint.

## *Chapter Sixty-One*

Erica is in a training session when I get back so I look for the file myself. Jonjo asks if he can help.

"There were some papers I gave her. Caldera Investments? Any idea what she might have done with them?"

"Ah, those. Chris Collins popped in and collected them. Said his team were taking over."

"Shit. Toogood's stooge. When?"

Jonjo is grinning. "Erica left you this."

All my remaining energy has drained away as I take the piece of paper and read it.

*I had a call from Chris C in lit. Says they are taking over the Caldera matter. Said Crispin had okayed it. My notes on what we discussed are attached. Nothing on the file so he won't know about the problems with the transfer. If you think he should know then send them on. Speak later or tomorrow.*

*P.S. No conflict when we took instructions. The potential now means we should continue with existing instruction – Caldera, unless they agree to go elsewhere. Chapter and verse in bottom drawer.*

I glance through her notes, focusing on this:

*...in Chaucer it's clear that the transfer of manorial rights is an exception to the usual rules on equities arising. Failure to register within a reasonable time is fatal to the transfer: see Hermitage v Nodule CA (1886 2 AER 56) therefore Featherstone retains all rights absolutely until registered. I looked at the purchase file and I believe he's too late to call for the new transfer either (a) because the obligation has been performed and it was his failure to register that's caused the problem; or (b) the obligation is now time barred and can't be enforced (see Acme Sprocket and Spoke Construction Limited v Annerley & others CA (1931 P&CR 342 at 374). therefore it looks as if there's no reason now why Featherstone is contractually obliged to transfer to Toogood.*

*P.S. I had a quick look and I think Featherstone is dead; I'll hunt out his executors and trustees.*

My head is still spinning when I get a call to go and see Frank. Can this day get any more complicated? All I want to do is go home and hide under the bed, but first the boss.

## *Chapter Sixty-Two*

"Harry, thanks for popping in. Close the door, would you?"

That makes me feel ill. I stand at the end of his desk, much like I used to with 'Birch 'em' Sackers my old headmaster. Frank doesn't offer me a seat either, but then again Frank isn't renowned as an administrator of corporal punishment.

"Seb… Mr Crout is in hospital. Had you heard?" he says.

"Yes. How is he?"

"Poorly. In and out of consciousness. Thing is, he's apparently mentioned you. Calling your name, that sort of thing. His family – he has a sister; they're very close – wondered if…" He rubs his face, fiddling around with things on his desk – straightening papers, moving a file, checking his Dictaphone, but eventually he looks at me. "Were you…? Did you and he… you know… were you in any sort of tryst…?"

"If you mean were we in a relationship, then the answer is no. I have a girlfriend and I'm about to become a Father." I try to remain cool, hoping my voice isn't giving away my nerves at this line of questioning.

"Yes, well, that's what I said but the fact remains…"

"Can I sit down?"

"What? Oh yes, of course. Sorry." He half-stands, as if he's about to find me a chair or catch me or something.

"Was it a suicide attempt?"

The way several expressions scud across his face tells me that it was, that I shouldn't know about it and if I do I shouldn't be saying it here out loud.

"It's all tied into Barry Tritewell's death," I say.

"Barry? What do you mean?" The expressions now inhabiting Frank's face are those of the serially perturbed. It's my turn to fiddle but all I have is my shirt sleeve. "I found Barry's body and… Mr Crout was there. He persuaded me to let him deal with it, but he didn't tell the police and it's now become clear to them they were lied to. I'm not sure why but this attempt has to be connected in some way."

"But why?"

"He said he was worried about the possible scandal for the firm and—"

Frank shakes his head so hard I wonder if something will snap. "Wait. Barry's death is – was – a tragedy, so what scandal? What are you talking about?"

Oh bollocks, I really don't want to do this. "When I... when we found him, Barry was wearing a silver and blue sequined dress. He was sprawled... Frank? Are you okay?"

The shaking has stopped probably because all the blood has drained to his legs and maybe even now it is seeping out from under his toenails, so white is his face. I can see beads of sweat forming on his forehead.

"Mr Crout said he would sort it out. I didn't realise that meant moving him and dressing him in his suit. Then there were ambiguities about his dress and some photos—"

"Someone photographed him?" It's Frank's turn for his voice to cross the alto threshold.

"No, not like that. Before. In that dress. He and Mr Crout, they—"

"Yes, yes we all knew they were lovers for a while. So what?"

"You did? Mr Crout didn't say. He said... he let me think it was a secret."

The laugh is harsh, quick and lacking any humour. "Sure. They were hardly discreet. But Seb isn't to be told, is he? Someone had a quiet word with Barry, said there was a risk his wife would find out if it didn't stop."

"Who?"

"It's really got nothing to do with you. Tell me about these photos."

In another life I may have wanted to debate my entitlement to know what the fuck has been going on since it's me who's been grilled, albeit lightly by the police, but I keep that thought to myself. "There are pictures of the two of them, both in that dress. Although not at the same time. Obviously. The police know about the snaps and that's... it was when I told Mr Crout I'd seen them and had to tell the police... I tried..." My throat suddenly lacks all moisture. There's a silence that hangs for a while as he stands and stares out of the window.

"Right. So the police know. That's good." His gaze suddenly returns to me. "If you're saying you weren't Seb's latest, erm, lover, then how do you come into all this? I mean, I understand you saw the body but how come you know about these photos?"

I sigh and explain what happened for what feels like the tenth time. "I picked them up by mistake when I went to collect some holiday snaps from Boots. I was going to give them back to Barry on that Friday evening and that's when I found his body. I didn't know at the start what they showed and when I did I agreed with Mr Crout to give him time to decide what he wanted to do. But some of them were taken from my desk and given to the police so whatever Mr Crout intended was pre-empted. They interviewed me and I told them all I knew and then I heard about him being in hospital."

"Someone stole them and gave them to the police? Why on Earth would someone do that if the death was innocent?"

"I suppose to embarrass him, and maybe the firm. And maybe to bugger up my chances too."

"Aren't you being a bit paranoid, Harry? It sounds like you were just in the wrong place at the wrong time." Another beady glare. "Do you have a suspect for this theory?"

Okay, well I didn't want this but now we're here fuck it. "Greg, I think. Maybe. He knew that I collected the photos. He was there when I picked them up by mistake. I think he made sure I had them. And he knew Mr Crout and I had found Barry's body. He was there too on the night Barry died."

Frank looks utterly confused. "Greg? What's he got to do with this? Why would he try to do that to you? Or Seb?"

"I don't know. When I told Mr Crout that I suspected Greg he said something…" What the heck did he say? "…something about things being different this time. Or him being different, maybe?"

Frank's collapse seems complete. "Christ. Surely not…" He moves abruptly, sending his chair careering back into the wall. He marches to the door and bellows for his secretary. Charity isn't there one second and is in front of us the next. This trick is so disconcerting Frank and I jump in unison. "Christ Charity, stop doing that. Get Sonia. Now. Tell her it's urgent. Tell her Project Wobble is back."

Frank doesn't elaborate for me and we lapse into another uneasy silence while she evaporates back to her room to find Sonia Porcelaine.

## *Chapter Sixty-Three*

To say Sonia isn't best pleased is a huge understatement. She's dressed in a dark navy power suit with shoulders as wide as the door and a slit in the skirt that reveals an awful lot of leg and some heels that in other circumstances would be classed as dangerous weapons. "What the fuck, Fr... what's he doing here?" she says when she sees me.

"Seb's in and out of consciousness and he's asking for Harry. Harry, tell her what you told me."

Sonia slumps into a chair, exposing even more thigh and the top of a stocking; she crosses them in a very distracting way and proceeds to light a cigarette. By the time it's fired up and glowing I'm into my story and from there it doesn't get smoked. Frank makes no pretence about his staring at her exaggerated limbs while I speak.

As I'm about to elaborate further on my suspicions of Greg's role in all this when Frank butts in. "Seems Seb thinks it's happening again."

"You don't know that."

"He said he'd not let it lie. He was quite clear it wasn't over."

"It was ten years ago Frank."

"We should never have taken him on. We knew the risks."

Sonia stops and looks at me, then Frank. "Does he need to hear this?"

"I don't see why not. They want to screw him too, although I don't know why."

Sonia's penetrating gaze makes me squirm. "Well? Why would the Princips give a fuck about you?"

"I don't know. Other than the partnership."

Sonia's barking laugh is harsher than Frank's but there is humour there. "Oh, come off it. It's not that big a deal and you two are pretty much shoo-ins, aren't they Frank?"

He looks very tired suddenly. "Until all this blew up, maybe."

For just a moment I want to cheer but then the reality of Frank's qualification hits me.

Sonia's expression softens. "I can see why you think you're being used Harry, although not why. Personally I think Frank – and if you're right, Seb also – are exhibiting typical male paranoia and letting two and two make an unfeasibly large number. Let me say this much. Newe Waters has had some awful publicity – as I'm sure you've heard and seen – and we can't really take much more without risking defections from some very important partners and clients. The whole sorry sequence began when we refused to act for Piotr Princip – or rather his vehicle – on a listed debt offering. He was trying to re-establish himself in the City and having our name attached to his bond issue would have given it extra credibility. One partner was very anxious we acted, pushed very hard, but we—"

"Don't be modest." Frank is smiling. "You were the reason."

Sonia shrugs. "I'm not one to do modesty, Frank. Yes, I told Crout that if we acted I'd leave and I'd use my contacts in the government to make sure the firm didn't so much as get a sniff of their work in future. Crout's a good man. A bit feeble, granted, but he understands the firm is bigger than one individual and he stood up to them both. It set Princip back and he was furious. All sorts of accusations were made against us and Seb. The Law Society investigated but the City grandees closed ranks and we were okay in the end. But we, and especially Seb, had made an enemy with a long memory who now has a lot of resources."

This is all news to me. "Why take on Gregor then? If there's some sort of family grudge?"

"He had a fair bit of support. He's one of the brightest young lawyers around, very dynamic and, well, it came from what appeared to be an entente with his Father. I wasn't involved. Frank?"

Frank is looking guilty. "I thought him excellent and I saw no reason to suppose he was like his Father. Indeed, the tensions between them were evident at the start. Mind you, from what I hear they have grown closer, Princip senior has encouraged some of his contacts – good ones – to bring him work. I promised Seb – God, why was I so naïve? – that it was a new start."

Sonia looks sympathetic and lights another cigarette. "Come on Frank. We debated it and agreed. It's not just on you. Harry, he isn't going to try to shaft you, at least not in such a clumsy way. He's too clever for that. But we need to think about what this all might mean." She tilts her head. "I wasn't sure about you, you know. Decent lawyer, sure, but partnership material? Well, I suggest you go back to being a fine property lawyer and let me and Frank worry about the firm and Seb. Answer the police honestly and keep your head down. And do not go spreading any stories about Greg. If there's anything in his being around at the same time, then Frank will uncover it."

We both look at Frank whose expression indicates he is far from convinced he is up to his newly appointed role as sleuth-in-chief.

"I have a meeting. I'll go and see Seb later, Frank. Ciao for now."

Frank seems to be in a world of his own and I start to slip away when Erica's notes come back to me. "By the way, I want to call out Toogood on his attempt to stop us acting for Caldera on their scheme in Barrington. He says there's a conflict but our research says not. I want to tell the client we will continue to act. Is that okay?"

I know I'm being unfair; Frank is barely functioning. He nods, not really appreciating that the wrath of Mervin scorned will be crashing about his ears sooner rather than later. It's the only thing that makes me feel marginally less miserable than Frank as I leave his office.

## *Chapter Sixty-Four*

It's gone four when I finally get back to my desk. There's a telephone note from Natalie asking if I'll go with her to see Amos on Sunday. I'm in two minds, but I can't say no given how he is. I ring and leave her a message.

Of more interest is a handwritten note from Erica:

*Featherstone died 14/2/1985; executors: G. Melpot, P. Oldcorn, T. Melpot. Chris asked if there were any other papers. I said no. I've kept the notes re. Featherstone on my desk as per our agreement. Hope that's okay?*

Sod Toogood. I'm damned if he's going to screw anyone on this. I push my other worries to one side and call Mr Melpot.

"Taddy speaking!"

"Mr Melpot—"

"I recognise your voice young man and I know I told you to call me Taddy."

"Sorry – Taddy. Can I ask about Mr Featherstone's estate?"

"Why should I speak to you when you work with that charlatan Toogood?"

"How do…?"

"I may have many failings Mr Spittle, but my ability to mine the facts are unquestioned. Are you speaking to me as Toogood's minion?"

"No, Taddy. No, I'm not. Far from it."

"Interesting. Divide and rule, eh?"

More like self-immolation, I think. "So, Mr Featherstone's estate?"

"Let me be clear. I will share publicly available information only. What do you want to know?"

"Who benefits from his Will?"

"Me and my brother and my cousin. We're his nephews."

"I thought you went up against him over the manorial rights?"

"Indeed. Making us his beneficiaries was his guilt money for the damage he did."

Interesting. I'm wondering if I should probe a bit more when he says, "I've done some further research about you, you know?"

"Me?"

"Your firm. I'm intrigued."

"Oh?"

"Toogood is a partner and has an interest as local land owner. Your firm appears to be acting for Caldera on their scheme. Do you know of its possible rival?"

"Thompson Greek? Martindale Cove?"

"Ah-ha! So you do. Good, good."

This is beginning to make me squirm.

"What do you know about it?" he asks.

"I..."

"Is Toogood party to it?"

"Sorry?"

"Martindale Cove. He'd have to have a role in it."

"Why do you say that?"

"His land controls access to Martindale Cove so he would need to be bought off or made part of it. That man would just love that."

Maybe that's what Jonjo's work on rights of way was really all about. I need to look at the file more closely to see if Taddy's assumptions are correct. Another point to follow up on.

He is still talking, "From the little I've heard, the Thompson Greek scheme is on a smaller scale and may be preferable to those of us who worry about over-development."

"So the council would be more inclined to favour the Thompson scheme?"

"Young man, are you being deliberately obtuse? Of course not. They want the income, the rates, the votes. They'll do all they can to assist Caldera."

"Oh. So you'd be one of the objectors?"

"I have made representations, yes. Caldera's plans are an absolute eyesore."

Damn, and there was me hoping to seek Taddy's help.

"Mind you, with some easy modifications it could be both stunning and of significant benefit to the community, not that they'd listen to me. Do you know much about the Martindale Cove scheme?"

"Only that it is a rival to harbourside. If that doesn't proceed then I've been told it has a chance of securing planning."

"Well, I know that young man. Is that the best you can do? Mind you, if that scheme was the one to make Toogood even richer I'd be happy to see it defeated, however good it might otherwise be."

That's more like it.

"Of course that's just me being silly. Come the moment I would rise above such petty personal considerations for the greater good."

Noooo.

"Young man, can we do without this cloak and dagger business? Does your firm act for Caldera, on this scheme, or Thompson… what did you say? Steak?"

"Greek."

"Greek. Yes. Or just Toogood, as he is a partner? I have no idea how you manage to avoid conflicts, but that's your domain."

"Er, um, yes. Caldera. That's our client."

"Well, I suppose that makes sense. You'd hardly be so ignorant about the Martindale Cove plans if you acted for them or Toogood, if he indeed does has a role. And you are friends with young Karen Thomas, correct?"

"I am." That's a bit of a non sequitur.

"I have been told she is a fine lawyer. Is she also acting?"

"I don't think so." My brain is feeling rather pummelled.

"Manorial rights?"

"Sorry?"

"Oh, do keep up. You asked about Featherstone's estate. Previously you asked about manorial rights. I assume there's a link?"

"I'd rather not go into det—"

"You don't have to. It hardly takes Lord Peter Wimsey's level of detective work to see the link, and from what I know of the Caldera scheme doing some deal with the current holder becomes critical. Toogood has the rights, as I think we have established, but I ask myself, given that fact and given your firm probably acted when he obtained them, why are you calling me?"

Bloody man is too clever for his own good. And mine.

On he goes. "While you do your lawyerly thing and concoct a plausible but essentially trite and incomplete answer, would you like to bear in mind – assuming you have any influence with MacThing – that I would love to sit down with him and his team? I'm sure I can help him come up with a scheme that would command local support. Right now, I fear his planning application will be rejected. If you are on your client's side – and I remain intrigued how your firm can have Toogood as a partner and yet act for this scheme – you'll pass that on."

"I will pass that on, Taddy."

There's a sort of hollow silence as I struggle to think what to say. It takes me a moment or two to realise he's rung off, clearly not expecting me to answer him. I've got what I need, but in doing so I have to wonder if I've given too much away. Bugger.

After I've put down the phone I sit and stare into space for a while, plucking up courage to call Gerry MacThing. This is one of those calls that are like a crap after being constipated; you know you have to but it's going to hurt. Part of me thinks I should bring Crispin up to date, but I doubt he will talk to me right now. It's nearly six and MacThing will probably have gone home but, oh hell, here goes.

"MacThing." I die a little when he answers.

"Mr MacThing, Harry Spittle here." I try for cheerful but I probably sound desperate.

"Yes Harry. And it's Gerry. Are you about to make or ruin my weekend? I bet you hoped I'd not answer and you could salve your conscience by leaving a message to ruin my Monday instead."

"Not really either. I wondered if Mervin Toogood had—?"

"He's a partner in your firm? Crispin told me he controls this Lordship business."

"Has he called you?"

"His monkey has. Collins. Says they want to talk about something of mutual interest."

"Did he say anything about us, about this firm acting for you?"

"No, should he have?"

"No, although he… can I be candid and ask you keep this to yourself?"

"You intrigue me. Go on."

"Mervin Toogood is a partner here and we acted when he bought his seaside home in Martindale Cove."

"Is he in with Thompson Greek?"

"No, I'm pretty sure he's not. He has suggested we, Newe Waters I mean, shouldn't continue to act for Caldera because we acted for him."

"What?"

"No, wait. It's up to you to decide. We aren't obliged to cease to act and I'd press on you to continue with us. I probably shouldn't…"

"Harry, what's going on?"

"I'll be honest and say I'm not happy if Mervin tries to suggest you should go elsewhere. We – Crispin and me – want to see this through, but it needs you to want us to do that."

There's a pause and I wonder if I've lost him. "He's the Lord of the thingy, yes? If so he can stop me, can't he? I need to buy him off. If I do that, then he's out of the picture and we can carry on."

I don't want to lie to him so let him work out his own logic. For now.

"Okay," he says. "I'll tell him I'll meet to discuss terms and if it makes sense then we'll carry on. If not then it doesn't really matter because there won't be a scheme." His voice drops as if I'm not meant to hear. "And I'll probably not have a job."

Christ, it can't be that bad – can it?

His tone changes. "By the way, is Crispin okay? I rather tore into him when it wasn't really his fault that there are all these problems."

"A little bruised but he'll survive. Can I ask that you talk to Mervin or Collins but don't conclude anything without talking to me first?"

"Why?"

"I'm looking into an alternative approach that might avoid the need for you deal with Mervin."

"That would be neat, but I'll believe it when I see it."

"Oh, and can I send you the details of a local resident, whose interested in your scheme and has some ideas for how it might be amended to overcome any local opposition?"

"Let me guess, Thaddeus Melpot?"

"Yes. You know him?"

"Not yet but I received a bizarre telegram from him. I haven't had a telegram since I was married in August '82 and my mother never forgave Thomas my best man for reading it out. He sniggers. "Sorry, but her face… Anyway, I thought he must be a bit of a crank, given what he said, about saving my face or some such. Is he?"

"Eccentric, yes, but he could be very helpful. Maybe if you can find the time?"

"All right. And Harry?"

"Yes?"

"You're doing well. Not many lawyers – professionals, actually – go this far out of their way to help a client."

I manage a smile, not something I've done much of recently. Time for a swift pint and then home.

Ronnie O'Porter is already on reception. He salutes me. "And will you be squiring our Miss Eagle this evening, do you think? Just for a drink, mind?"

"I wasn't planning on it."

"Oh, to be sure, I thought… It's just…." He seems to lose track so I wait to see if he can find his thread. "It's about Mr Tritewell…"

Once again my stomach does a flip.

"She's... I think... now let's see, I don't know if I should say."

"Say? Say what?"

I want to help him but it's like pulling teeth with a clothes peg – no traction.

"You being her friend and all that. I mean not like that, but you go back a'ways, to be sure? Proper friends, I mean?"

That's not how I'd describe us but I nod, thinking this is what Ronnie wants me to do.

He takes a deep breath, swallows, looks around for co-conspirators and says, "I think our Gloria and Mr Tritewell may have been more than just friendly, if you catch my drift? I'll not be wanting to get her into trouble, mind."

"No, right, of course."

"And the police asked but she said it would be embarrassing so I never mentioned it."

"Said? Said what?"

"She'd been with him that day. When you came back she'd been with him."

"Did she say as much?"

"No, but when we swap over on the front desk, when she's finished I mean, she sometimes goes down to the lower ground floor to use their ladies to change or else she just goes home. But that evening she took the lift up and got out on his floor. I shouldn't have looked, you know, but I was curious seeing as it was unusual. I couldn't think where she'd go. I mean it was before, long before, I got the call that he'd died so it had to be a coincidence, right? That's why I kept it myself. Never one to grass, me."

Blimey, so how does that fit in? A vague memory that someone said he'd had sex recently before he'd died comes to me. Is that relevant? Could that be with Gloria?

"She can do without the trouble, the poor thing. She's a good kid. She don't need the bother, not with her bloke being a bit rough."

This is taking a little time to compute. As a sort of holding statement, I manage to say, "I didn't know she had a bloke."

"No, well, I don't like to say. And... oh! Don't you look the business, to be sure you are quite a sight."

He glances over my shoulder and I spin round, much as I might if I'd heard a creaky floorboard in a shadowy cellar. Gloria is quite glammed up but looks most un-Gloria like given how she's usually fizzing when she's about to hit the town. She hurries across to me and takes my arm, squeezing it in a gesture of affection.

"Now there's a sight for sore eyes." She startles me by brushing my lips with hers.

Out of the corner of my eye, I see Ronnie's eyebrow do a knowing jig. God, what rumour will he now start?

Gloria taps me on the chest and straightens my tie. "Have fun Harry." She turns quickly and exits through the revolving door.

I glance at Ronnie. He just shrugs as if to say I should be the one 'squiring' her. I'm at a loss what to say and so follow her outside. She's already lit a cigarette. "How are you Harry?"

"Me? I'm fine. Ron says you're seeing your boyfriend tonight? You certainly look the part."

Something passes across her face before she wrinkles her nose and feigns a tired laugh. "He's an old gossip. I should be so lucky. Look, I gotta dash. I need to get home and then I'm off out. Duty calls" She grinds out the cigarette with her foot but doesn't elaborate.

I say, "You want to share a cab? Bit cold to walk or wait for the bus."

She puts her hands on her hips and pulls an offended face, more like the old Gloria. "It's not just you la-de-da fancy pants lawyers who take cabs, you know. And I'm not going your way." She winks before she turns and releases an amazing piercing whistle; the last time I heard that was when Gloria forced me to buy flowers for a young secretary I had inadvertently upset. A cab swings in a tight circle and pulls up next to us. She leans into the open window. "Dreyfus Place please." Then she opens the door, stops, blows me a kiss and disappears.

One heck of a woman that one, although what she was doing with Barry beats me. I do wonder if Ronnie has that right. Mum would call Gloria a gold digger, given how she's always targeted someone who might keep her in the style to which she wants to be accustomed, but Barry wasn't an obvious candidate.

I'm still pondering the mystery that is Gloria Eagle as I walk towards the tube when that bloody loon Jepson appears from a doorway, mimics someone about to be crucified and presses a card into my hand. It's one of those you find in phone boxes offering various personal services. I'm about to ask him what he means by giving me this when I see the name has been changed from Cathy to

Dina. Not very subtle. When I glance up he's running down the road; no, he's skipping. Bloody hell.

As seems typical of Jepson that he's caught me in exactly the right spot; there's a phone box next to where I'm standing. I call the number and it is picked up on the first ring. "She's gone." Dina.

"Magda?"

"Yes. I asked her outright if she was working with the Americans. She said no so I mentioned Streib's name. That made her squirm. When she still wouldn't answer I told her I'd need to tell my bosses and the next thing I know she's upped and left sharpish. Have you got that passport? Has she been in touch?"

"No and no. I have a call out to the Home Office. They claim the paperwork is nearly through, although it seems remarkably quick. Someone pulling strings?"

"Of course. Where the hell is she?"

"Search me. Streib threatened me again if I didn't get it sorted by tomorrow but he knew I wouldn't be able to. It's not like I can influence things."

"No, but he probably thinks I can. Any idea where that American is right now?" Dina is, unusually for her, sounding panicked.

"Last I heard he was staying at Natalie's club in a spare room. They may be having a bit of a thing as Mum would call it."

"He's behind this. Shit." Another surprise – she so very rarely swears too.

"Are you okay? You're not in trouble, are you?"

"You have no idea. If the Americans control Magda, promise her they'll get her sister out and she believes them, then we really have a serious problem. Where the hell is she?"

"I'll call Natalie if you like, ask her."

"Okay, but please don't do anything to make him suspicious."

# Saturday, 3rd October 1987

## *Chapter Sixty-Five*

This is how it's going to be. I was somewhere on a pebbly beach with Dina. We'd dug a hole and someone was trying to climb out, but was being pulled back in. Brenda, dressed as the punk she once was with her pierced nipples on display, is stood by saying if Dobbin cared he'd help. And then Penny is punching me awake.

"What? What time—"

"She's coming."

"Magda?"

"No, will you stop fantasizing and call an effing ambulance? The baby you moron." This last sentence was ended by a groan of epic proportions as Penny does something she's not done in ages – bends in the middle. And then farts. Although that word doesn't do justice to the exponential jettison of hydrogen, carbon dioxide and methane, combined with hydrogen sulphide and ammonia that accompanies the highly uncomfortable manoeuvre. I must have been staring because she jerks herself straight and begins berating me again. "What the fuck are you doing? Call a fucking ambulance!"

"That wasn't it?"

"What wasn't what?" Her tone indicates that if this is 20 questions, I'm not likely to make it to number three without some organ being extracted.

"The fart. It's not just wind, is it?"

Even as I ask, I know the answer won't be greeted with a considered tilt of the head.

I slip out and upright. "I'll call an ambulance. Right now."

The out-of-body way that things happen when you are dragged from deepest sleep to immediate action is fascinating – how everything blurs and slurs. Eyesight is compromised, like looking through heavily smudged glasses, sounds are distorted as if coming through a thick quilt and touch is oddly heightened, making the telephone feel oddly sensitised in my fingers. When I have explained the situation and where we live the dispatcher suggests it would be quicker to drive her to A&E than wait for an ambulance as they are all busy.

Putting a fractious and understandably scared Penny into the car and driving as fast as possible without causing any significant jarring or hitting any of London's many potholes is beyond my capabilities and she has twice divorced me and once issued a petition for my internment and possible interment by the time an orderly has her in a wheelchair and is hurrying her inside while telling me to move the car and park it somewhere sensible.

Now that Penny is in capable hands and I'm alone, the massed ranks of panic that have assaulted me over the last 20 minutes instantly subside. It's not quite 4.00 am and absolutely nothing is moving. It's all rather lovely in fact, and I sit in the car wondering how long I can get away with staying put without causing Penny to have an attack of the screaming conniptions.

Inside the over-bright hospital, the A&E department reminds me of the one time I watched a boxing match with Dobbin. Someone from his office was involved in an amateur bout somewhere in the wastelands of Shoreditch. By the time the fight finished, chairs had been upturned, blood from both the boxers spilt, the referee, canvas and some of the audience in the front row seats were splattered and adrenaline was in the air.

"Follow the red line." The receptionist voice is crisp and lacking any warmth.

A mix of several coloured strips head off along the floor and into various parts of the hospital. Yellow and blue divert first, leaving me speculating what they are for. Green is clearly x-rays as that line disappears through swing doors saying, 'X-ray Department.' In other circumstances this would almost be fun.

Eventually the red line I'm following stops at a lift. When the doors open I step in and momentarily dumbfounded I stare at the walls and floor and then the ceiling for clues as to what to do next. A voice behind me says, "Maternity?" and without waiting for an answer a hand extends to push the button for the third floor.

As I turn to thank this female presser of buttons I see that she is wearing a thick, possibly hand-knitted cardigan and a tweed skirt, which looks far too much for the over-zealous heating the hospital seems to employ. "First, is it?" she asks.

"Yes."

"I can always tell. No idea where to go and pathetically grateful to be told."

The lift stops and she stands to one side. "Off you go sunshine, and remember: from now on it's not about you."

The red line now reappears and takes me along a straight windowless corridor. At the end it opens out into a reception area. Penny is sitting on an uncomfortable bench looking rather sheepish.

As soon as she sees me, she stands and heads back towards the lift and I turn and follow her.

"What's going on?" She is already pushing the button by the time I catch up. Someone else is approaching and Penny shakes her head hard.

Back at ground level she turns away from the red line that I am intent on following and in moments we are outside. A suggestion of dawn is in the eastern sky.

"Well?"

She grins. "You were right, smartarse. Wind."

"I was?"

"Mostly right."

"Mostly...? Eww. Do you mean...?"

"A bit of a follow through? 'Fraid so."

"I think that's probably enough information. You're sure?"

"Yes. They suggest we ring the maternity ward next time. God, it was really embarrassing. They were very nice about it but I think they thought me a bit simple."

We haven't moved since we exited the building. Penny is bare legged, although her coat covers her modesty – she's holding a clear polythene bag in which her pyjama bottoms seem to be stuffed and she's wearing ankle boots with no socks. To me she looks as sexy as all hell. She gives herself a hug and shivers against the early morning chill.

"You up for walking? The car's round the corner. Did I ever tell you you have the world's most fabulous legs?"

"No, and shut up. And I know what you're thinking and no, you don't get a reward." But she winks and is grinning broadly.

"Come on. What do you say we see if we can get a cup of tea and a croissant at the Magpie?" This is our local bakery that has a cafe attached. I've heard they serve customers from 4.00 am when the first loaves start coming out of the oven as that time appears to be the ideal hour to cater for drug addicts, prostitutes and road-traffic accidents. And possibly us.

"I've just shat myself and you want a date?"

"I'm game."

"Mum warned me about men like you." She shakes her head but is smiling.

I'm obviously lucky; they make a real fuss over Penny and when they hear of our escapade we're offered a free breakfast. Patrick – the owner – asks about names.

Penny looks at me; this is a topic we have both been avoiding ever since she said she liked Timothy, and I said the only Timothy I'd known had been both smelly and covered in acne and I'd never be able to shake the association. She called me infantile and wanted me to list all the other names that I had negative associations with and I said I'd only be able to say when the name was mentioned. She then asked about girls names and I'd said that was easier because the links would be different and she'd asked why and I'd said it was because it would be determined by those I'd fancied and she'd said she didn't want a daughter named after someone I had failed to bed. By the time we've explained this to Patrick we are all laughing, which is suddenly interrupted by a gargantuan fart from Penny and uncontrolled giggles from the bakery staff.

"You know, we should go and see your parents. Before I pop," she says with a wry smile.

"Like you did just now?"

"I'm rather hoping for that to be a phase."

"I think the whole of Herne Hill will buy into that. We could go next weekend?"

"I think I'm getting my hair done. What about the one after?"

"I'll call Mum. She's sure to have a spare room."

"How are the extension plans coming along?"

My parents' B&B is in a large rambling 10-bedroomed house near Lymington in Hampshire. Since they took it over six years ago they have gradually converted several of the garages and outbuildings into small cottages that can be rented and the works on the last three were due to be completed in August. However, parental incompetence knows no bounds and they were delayed until last week, just as the high season comes to an end. I think it likely they'll have more space than they know what to do with.

"Should be ready for a viewing. Mum always welcomes your ideas for décor and furnishings and whatnot; you could have some fun. Although there is one thing…"

"Yes, I know, I won't ask her to cook."

"Thank you."

When we get back home there's a message on the answer machine. Or rather there's a whispered voice that isn't at all clear followed by a loud 'put that down!' and a click. The shouty voice is Chuck Streib and I'd lay even money on the whisperer being Magda. "Are you okay if I go and see Dina?"

"Of course. I think I'll try to get a bit more sleep. The nurse suggested I rest a bit more. Did you find out where your sister's living?"

"Not exactly, but I can contact her."

"Oh, Okay. I think I'll pass on seeing Amos tomorrow. I'll call Natalie and tell her."

"Do me a favour. Find out if that American she's screwing is still staying in her apartment, will you? And if not where he is staying. I may need to talk to him over the weekend and I don't have a contact number."

She pulls a face. "And you said property lawyers would never fall into the trap of working weekends. How the mighty tumble."

"I'm sorry, but the—"

She presses a hand on my arm. "Shush. If you're lucky I may even wash my toes today. Don't forget to give your sis my love."

## *Chapter Sixty-Six*

Using the convoluted message system to get hold of Dina is beyond tedious but I have no other way of speaking to her. I'm just grateful the classified department is manned although the woman who answers sounds suspicious that I keep advertising the same improbable egg. "Doesn't anyone want it?" she says in a sarcastic voice. While I wait to be called back I make a quick call to Brenda and agree to see her at noon and then call Mum.

"Harold. How are you? And Penny?"

"It's about Penny. We just had a bit of a scare and—"

"Oh my. I hope—"

"She's fine. Just trapped wind. Speaking of which, she suggested we might come and see you before we're trapped like all new parents are, so what about next weekend – say the 16th? If you've space that is."

"Oh darling, that would be wonderful. Your Father will be delighted. And yes, what with the garage conversions causing chaos we've been running at about a quarter capacity since the end of the school holidays. So bring a crowd if you like. It will be good to be full again. What about your sister? Have you spoken to her recently?"

"I'll mention it if we speak."

"She works so hard, doesn't she? No peace at all."

I try to smile but inadvertently Mum has triggered a surge of jealousy. It's ridiculous of course, but when I started training to be a lawyer they were immensely proud and used to irritate Dina with invidious comparisons between us. I, of course, did nothing to stop them. And then she put herself through university and into the civil service and the balance of pride shifted. If I pointed it out they'd be mortified, but still.

After an hour the familiar figure of Dina in a long red mac and black boots appears, walking towards me quickly. She doesn't stop but just walks right past and I hurry to catch up.

"Well?" She's tense, her enunciation crisp.

"She called. I'm pretty sure it was her. Then I heard Streib's voice telling her to put the phone down. Penny is speaking to Natalie, so I asked her to ask about him – mostly where he's staying. I thought it might be a little less suspicious if she did it."

Dina barely reacts.

"The passport will be ready on Monday," I add.

"Things have gotten complex."

"More than they already are?"

"We think the Americans want to 'eliminate' Orik and to do that they're likely to want Magda apprehended with her sister. They'll have enough to make a convincing case that he's a spy. If that happens we'll not see either of the sisters again. If they've got her, it's a matter of time before they sneak her out of here and then that'll be that."

I let that sink in, not sure I have anything to say. Finally I ask, "Isn't there something you can do? Raid the embassy or something?"

"My boss is in cahoots with them, I'm sure of it. It's hardly a surprise, given how much we rely on them, but it really makes me sick betraying someone like Magda who's done so much. If only we could find her."

"Could you get her out of the country? If I got you the passport and you found her?"

"I doubt it. If Magda travels there on her passport, they'll be monitoring her as she crosses the border. After that she's probably had it. Let me know if Streib keeps hassling you for her passport."

"Can't you just stop it being issued?"

"Of course we can, but if he still wants it that will just alert them. And if he doesn't it probably means he's got rid of her already. We need to get to her before they get her abroad."

"I thought we were on the same side."

"Ha." She stops and looks around. The street appears empty to me. "If Natalie comes up trumps then let me know."

"Is there an easier way to get hold of you? Staff at the *Echo* are getting suspicious of the number of Fabergé eggs I seem to want to sell in Bournemouth."

"Sorry, not yet."

"Penny and I are going to see Mum and Dad the weekend after next if you're free. Mum asked me to mention it to you."

"I wish. If I can sort this out, then maybe."

"Okay. Look, take care."

We hug and she goes, head down, the mac flapping behind her.

"She's wonderful," a voice says.

I glance to my left, not surprised to see Charlie Jepson.

"She is. You ready to see your son yet?"

"Harry, I've wronged you and your family." He takes me by the shoulders and holds my gaze.

If I'm honest he looks pretty demented and a close proximity to a member of the less than great unwashed, and after my experiences with Penny earlier he isn't doing my nasal passages any favours. I chide myself for my less than charitable thoughts, telling myself to remember he's probably homeless, however bloody awful he's been to my family in the past.

"I've not been a good Father. You understand?"

My volatile intestines do a summersault. Around 10 years ago I was certain he was my real Father following an affair my Mother had with him in the mid-1950s. His ex-wife told me I couldn't be because he'd lost a testicle in a shooting accident that had rendered him impotent, but I was never entirely convinced about that. I wish I had the courage just to ask but it's one thing to think the thought and entirely another to articulate it.

He seems to be waiting for an answer so I say, "I'll tell Stephen you want to see him, shall I? Where shall we meet?"

"Your parents are the same. They also feel guilty. We all need cleansing."

"Right ho. Does that mean…?" I stop as he's rummaging for something inside his shirt.

When he pulls it out, it takes me a moment to recognise it.

It is a pencil drawing that Sven did as part of a set of clues about who was to inherit the proceeds of his Father's criminal empire. This one is of my Mother in her garden at our then family home.

He taps the background.

I say, "You want to meet Stephen at my parents' house?"

He smiles and up go his arms in thanks.

"That'll go down well. All right. I'm going to see them soon – the weekend after next in fact. What about that?"

By way of an answer he takes my hands and spins me round. In a cartoonish accent that reminds me off some TV comedy, he says, "The lady you seek is where no lady should be. Look for the lady where no lady should be."

Having made me dizzy he then leaves.

Goddammit, what did that mean? What lady? My Mother? Or Dina?

Then it dawns on me. In his silly voice he had said, 'Allo Allo' in a cod-German accent. Magda. He means Magda. But where shouldn't she be? And why tell me and not Dina?

I look up, prepared to chase after him and demand an answer, but as always he's disappeared.

## Chapter Sixty-Seven

Time is getting on so I have to hurry to the tube. There's a wine bar off Kensington Church Street called Jimmy's where Brenda and I have agreed to meet. She has been shopping with her Mother, Zenda; I hadn't exactly counted on an audience.

As usual, Zenda is lovely and greets me enthusiastically; Brenda says hello and goes to the bar to buy us all a drink. As soon as she's out of earshot, Zenda's expression changes. "She's been utterly distraught these last few days. About Gary I mean. I thought they'd finished but something's happened and she can't seem to stop moping about him. Do you know what happened?"

"I think so. Let's see… thanks." Brenda puts down the drinks.

We take a few minutes, each of us apparently reluctant to speak. Finally Brenda says, "What do you want, Harry? Because if this is about Gary, don't bother."

"He said the same thing."

"You should listen to your 'friend.'"

I think she emphasises the 'friend' but that could be my imagination. "He explained that I've been stupid, not understood the dynamics between us. You think you need my forgiveness—"

Brenda begins to stand but Zenda stops her. "Hear him out, dear. Please. For me?"

She glares down at her Mother, "Did you set him up to this?" But she sits back down.

"No one set me up. Gary Dobbs is the best friend I've had, will ever probably have. And I wouldn't hurt him for the world. And yet for the last, what, six years he's been waiting for me to forgive you for what you did. I mean really honestly move on. Because he thinks if I do that, then you'll not feel he's being asked to make a choice between us. And you'll be happy then to acknowledge you can get back together. Can you see it that way?"

Brenda says nothing.

"You nearly fucked everything up six years ago by telling Stephen McNoble what I was trying to do to sort out Sven's Estate without giving Miles Tupps any leverage but you didn't and it was hardly your fault given how you were being blackmailed. The thing is, in your shoes I'd do the same as you did. Bren, we don't need to like each other, do we? What we need to do is do whatever it takes to make sure he doesn't feel torn between us. I love him. You love him. Isn't that enough? I for one will do what it takes. And if that means getting on my knees and begging for forgiveness in front of him and whoever you like, then just say so."

She's still not spoken. After an interminable silence that I'm determined not to fill, she gets up and walks round to my side of the table. "Stand up."

Not understanding, I do as I'm told.

"Kiss me."

It takes a moment but then I hold her arm and kiss her right cheek.

"No, properly. On the lips. Imagine I'm Penny."

"I…? What…?"

She turns away and begins to pick up her bag. "Exactly. You can't, any more than I could have if you'd asked me to. He'll know." She's standing right in front of me; she reaches up and puts a hand on my cheek. "You're a good friend to him, a good person, and I'm not. Never will be. Thank you for trying, for wanting to try but we can't unpick what happened and it's better if we all move on." She looks at her Mother. "I'll see you in the salon."

Left alone, I look at Zenda who is smiling.

"I'm glad you're happy," I say sarcastically.

"Oh, I'm not really but this is progress."

"Really? It feels like hitting the buffers to me."

She pats my hand that's resting on the table. "If you had kissed her like she was Penny that would only have made it worse. So how do you think we're going to get them together?"

"I've no idea. If I invite Brenda anywhere she'll smell a rat."

By way of an answer, Zenda pulls a little diary from her bag and taps it with a pencil. "You know her friend Karen? The one she'd like to come and work for us?"

"Yes."

"I thought I'd invite her and Brenda for a weekend away in the country. I'd like to help with some money – I think that's the issue, not that Brenda tells me much. Could we maybe find somewhere where you could bring Gary?"

"You met my Mum and Dad, didn't you? How about their B&B? It's empty with plenty of room, and I'm going there the weekend after next. I'm pretty sure I can get Gary to come along – I'll invite Karen's husband John. Might make it easier if I do. It'll mean bringing Karen in on the subterfuge."

"Oh. Will she be happy with that?"

"Sure. She wants what's best for Brenda and I'm pretty sure she thinks that means Gary, just as we do."

"Well, if that's all right? Yes, let's do it. Although Brenda may recognise the address. She's been to your folks' house before, hasn't she?"

"Once or twice, but they were living somewhere else then. I'll give you the directions… actually why not let me give them to Karen and get her to sort out the invite? If we can get them into the same room and I can tell them what I want, what I'll do, well, I can't do any more than that."

# Sunday, 4th October 1987

## *Chapter Sixty-Eight*

I've agreed to meet Natalie at Waterloo Street station – she's been visiting some ancient relative. She's dressed in a long coat and a sort of furry Cossack hat and her expression tells me she's in something of a mood. She pecks me on the cheek and says nothing as she leads off towards the hospital. After a few minutes of head-down walking she says, "Chuck wants a word."

"Chuck?"

"He's been so good to me. For me. I'm not sure how I'd have coped."

"I didn't know that you'd become close."

"He kind of understands me. He's also been divorced twice, you know? Made some stupid decisions." She stops mid-stride and takes my arm. "We need to have a talk. He made me see that."

Is she scanning my face? It feels like it, like she's looking for something. Before I can say any more she's off again at a furious pace that it takes me a couple of hundred yards to overhaul her. When I do I say, "I find him a bit odd, frankly. You find out anything about him?"

"I know he works for the CIA if that's what you mean. He said he'd told you."

"Okay. Yes, well, there is that. Cindy told me you two had become, you know, an item?"

"How quaint, Harry. Yes, we've had sex. So?"

"None of my business?"

"Quite. You made yourself pretty clear. About us I mean."

"Is this the 'word' you wanted?"

"No. Let's see Amos first."

St Tommy's is pretty quiet today. The reception desk where Jackie helped me is manned by a woman with dreadlocks pulled into a fluffy ponytail and the brightest red lipstick I've seen since Brenda was a punk, although that may have been blood. She has a note of Natalie's name, so we are given details where to go even though it's unnecessary. As we traipse along the corridors I go back to the subject of Chuck. "And has he moved in too?"

"No, Harry. God, you're nosy. He's using the spare room, okay? He says he doesn't sleep well with anyone else and anyway he's on the phone to America a lot until pretty late so it makes sense."

"Saves him money too."

"He's paying rent if you must know. And anyway, he's kept the apartment in Shepherd Market that Cindy negotiated for him as an office and a place to crash if it gets too rowdy for him to work. The bar is a bit noisy for him sometimes."

"Typical Yank flashing the cash. Two apartments, aren't I rich?"

"What's wrong with you? You don't normally take against someone like you seem to have taken against Chuck."

"Just having a bit of a tough time. Ignore me, okay? Look, I think that's the place."

The ward we want looks very sombre. The signs outside make it clear we need to wash our hands to minimise the risk of infection. There's the same careful check when we enter, and we are asked to wait after they take our names. We sit on moulded blue plastic chairs, staring at various posters that are deliberately of the unscary kind, unlike those that are doing the rounds on TV right now.

Conversation has stopped; I feel oppressed to be near so much sadness. Instead I try to make sense of Charlie Jepson's latest message. I'm still in a little world of my own when Chuck arrives in a flurry of apologies and handshakes. Before I can wonder why he's here, he asks if we've seen Amos yet and we say no, he turns and heads for nurses' station.

My stomach does its usual trick of flipping summersaults. "Why's he here?"

"I told him about Amos and he said he'd lost friends to AIDS and wanted to come."

"Why? Is he a ghoul?"

She glares at nothing in particular. Before I can press, a doctor appears and after a brief, animated conversation with Chuck they both head towards us.

The doctor says, "You friend has had a difficult 48 hours."

I look at Natalie, expecting her to look worried but she's nodding, like she knows.

He continues. "He has a chest infection and we're worried his ulcer and the operation has weakened him. He also – how to put this – he doesn't seem to have much fight left." The doctor looks suitably sad, but rather fidgety.

She says, "I understand. Is it okay to see him?"

The doctor and Chuck exchange a look.

Natalie's face expresses a new level of anxiety. "What? What is it?"

Chuck speaks first. "He's not here."

I can tell Natalie is certain he's dead. Her face drains of colour. I'm trapped in my seat. Chuck is quickly at her side. "He's not dead, Natalie." He crouches in front of her taking her hands. "He's discharged himself. Against advice but a cab came and picked him up."

Her tears are slow moving and large. I watch as I might a TV drama or stage play; this isn't real. Chuck however is perfect – just the right mix of clarity and sympathy. The doctor excuses himself.

"They're not keen to let us have a forwarding address so I said you were his sister and next of kin and you needed to know where he said he'd go. He said he'd see what he could do."

Natalie nods. "Sorry about losing it. I think I'll go and wash my face. Do go, will you?"

It's not clear who this is aimed at but we both nod. As soon as she's gone, Chuck turns to me. "She told you?"

"Told me?"

"Yeah, I thought not. She may have AIDS."

"What?! How?" My voice is all over the place and he shushes me.

"For the love of Christ, Harry, keep it down. We were talking about Amos and she said that when she was looking after him he had a haemorrhage and covered her in blood. That was months ago and since then she's started to look... well, you know. I think she knew it was a possibility but couldn't bear getting checked." His gaze is piercing, mesmerising. "She said you two had sex after. You should get checked, yeah?"

I pull my gaze away to the poster above a table covered by three vases of flowers.

"You can't blame her. She didn't know he had it. Not then. Just shitty luck, that's all."

My brain is spinning out of control. I can't begin to form a reply. Natalie chooses that moment to reappear, walking back towards us. "It's why I came, to make sure you knew. I suggest you don't say anything right now, okay? She said she'd tell you and she still might but, hey, I thought you needed to know right away and I guessed she'd find it difficult. Given, you know, all the history between you and your girl too...?"

She is stopped by the doctors and listens to what he has to say without speaking. When he's finished, she nods and says something which he writes down, then she joins us. "He's going to call me if they can find out any more. Come on, there's no point staying and you both look like you could do with a drink."

# Monday, 5th October 1987

## *Chapter Sixty-Nine*

After Chuck's bombshell the drink was awkward and almost poisonous. Why hasn't Natalie said anything? What if she speaks to Penny first? That seems too horrid to contemplate. Chuck didn't mention the passport issue or Magda, which I suppose isn't surprising in one way but in another feels out of character. He's not someone who strikes me as particularly empathetic. I need to get checked, that much is plain. After that I can decide what to tell Penny. If anything.

When I returned home I found her in a happy mood, spring cleaning the bathroom. Her reason for such an unusual burst of cleanliness was an article in the Sunday paper about how physical activity in the last weeks of the final trimester can help ensure a painless – or at least a less painful – delivery. I tried to join in with her enthusiasm but clearly failed since she told me I was draining her karma and why can't I 'just sod off somewhere else,' so I did.

Now I'm at my desk which is a bombsite. Friday's to-do list has grown to a size to rival the sort of tracts on which religions are formed. Even Dobbin at his most morose would show more enthusiasm for life than me right now. And just when things truly cannot sink any lower, Greg appears – more like explodes – into my room.

"You are a complete shit, Spittle, you know that? What the fuck did you say to Frank?"

At that precise moment my conversation with Frank on Friday – that may have involved Sonia too, though that seems a blur as well - is so far back in the mists of time as to be more like an implanted memory from childhood.

I think he must assume my silence amounts to a confession of guilt. "If this is your attempt to screw up my chances of a partnership, then it won't work. Wait and see. You just bloody wait and see."

And he's gone. As the papers fall to the floor in his wake – he's moving at such speed he's created a vortex that has drawn everything from my desk after him – I go down on my hands and knees to retrieve them. When I look up Crispin is staring down at me. Even at the odd angle at which I take in his expression it's absolutely and completely plain that he too is livid. What is going on this morning? "Are you determined to get me sacked? Toogood was waiting for me and told me – in a voice that probably drowned out Big Ben – that I'd undermined his negotiating position with MacThing, we are conflicted and why did I tell him we weren't and if I've lost him money he'll make sure I pay for it. What the fuck have you done?"

If Frank's conversation is a blur, any call with Gerry MacThing's doesn't even register. Did I speak to him? If so, what did I say? "Crispin, really, you know I'm trying to help. I…"

He too has gone in a rush. As he leaves he says, "I'll talk to Greg. We need to work together, just as he said we should."

Bloody hell. As I get to my feet I feel my stomach flip. I don't need to check my watch: it's half past nine. Whatever else might be going on in my life, my Mother's training stands for no delays or interruptions. I consider the detritus for a moment before leaving it where it is and hoping Chloe will pick everything up when she gets in, and with that I head for the gents.

Without delving too deeply into the mysteries of my bowel movements, let me just say that some mornings things are more urgent than others. Having the various scares I've had recently, including Chuck's and the haranguing from both Greg and Crispin already, this one is at the top end of the range.

I'm already undoing my belt as I enter the loos, which comprise two cubicles and two urinals. Both stalls are taken. This happens occasionally and, in the past, a cheery 'will you be long?' gives me enough guidance to decide if I should stay and hop or hightail it for the ninth floor.

In truth the pressure is such I'm not sure I could make the ninth and the only realistic alternative is to head for the ladies with all the embarrassment and opprobrium that that would entail. I try my 'will you be long?' to which the replies are 'maybe' and 'soon.'

I don't recognise the voices, but then again I'm not really concentrating. I'm about to ask what 'soon' actually means when something shifts down below, and with a cold and rather soft and squirty certainty I know that things are about to happen.

I spin and lean against the door; the ladies will have to do.

As I do so there's a cry, something like 'Oi!' and a noise like fists hitting a wall. The door doesn't move so I push again, creating a small crack. Outside I can see a pair of grey trousers and a slew of documents blocking the door.

"Can you shift?"

"No I bloody can't. You've made me drop all these files. Just hang on."

It is probably the one thing I can't do.

In true desperation, I manage to squeak as I rattle both stall doors in turn, "I really really need to use the loo. Please." But there's no reply from one and a snort-cum-sneeze from the other.

There are moments in life when choice is stripped away, and the answer is plain if utterly unpalatable. In the most unseemly rush I drop my trousers and pants and plant my arse over the sink, letting go of the last shred of resistance.

The relief as the faecal confection explodes out of me is accompanied by a mix of guilt and disgust at what is occurring, coupled with unreasonable anger at whoever has blocked my access to the cubicles and the exit. My mind is focussed on what I will say to these two miserable bastards when the door to the outside world flies open and Frank stands in the doorway. He takes in me, my trousers and pants around my ankles, a rank smell that speaks of only one possible source and the sink that is now full of something that has no right to fill it.

His eyes narrow and then harden. "Are you responsible for that?"

In a way it's a rather stupid question, given my undress and the lack of anyone else who might have just shat in the sink, so I hesitate to answer.

"Christ, you did it, didn't you? You put that turd on Seb's desk? Is this all part of a plan? Undermine the senior partner and your rivals to ensure a partnership?"

Then it hits me. He's referring to Cyn's parting gift alongside her resignation. He's making a link that has no right to be made.

"No, come on Frank. I was desperate. The cubicles are occupied and—"

"Christ Harry. You're not four. Surely you can go to another toilet. They're down one flight of stairs."

"But the door was blocked. I couldn't—"

Frank is clearly irritated. "If it's blocked then how did I get in?"

Just then the left toilet flushes and Crispin appears, followed shortly by Greg from the other. They all stare at my grotesque offering in horror.

Frank takes charge. "Just clean this up, Harry and then come to my office. I think you two might want to go downstairs to wash up."

## Chapter Seventy

Frank takes his time to finish whatever it is he's writing before he turns to me and points at a chair. While I wait I think about the odds on this whole thing being a dreadful chance accident versus a campaign to get at me by Greg and Crispin. Conspiracy easily beats cock-up by two conniving bastards to nil.

Finally Frank says, "I spoke to Greg. About what you said on Friday. Did he mention it?"

I nod.

"He denies everything, of course. Says all he's tried to do is help you and everyone else. He mentioned you had some grudge about a client he has brought in. Tupps? Says he tried to involve you but not only did you refuse to help but you've gone out of your way to try to smear his reputation."

"Miles Tupps is a crook. We shouldn't be acting for him."

"And how do you know that?"

I begin to give Frank a potted history of what I know about Miles' past. Frank holds up a hand. "Yes, Greg mentioned this. He also made a fair point. If you thought he really was still involved in crime why didn't you raise it with me or another partner rather than let Greg continue? He also—" I try to interrupt but he speaks over me. "He also mentioned the fact that you and his ex-wife are lovers and that this might be colouring your judgement somewhat."

"I'm not... we're not..."

"You've not had an affair with this woman?"

"No... yes... well, not like that."

"Not like what? I may be a bit old fashioned but how do you have an affair other than it involving having sex with someone who's not your wife?"

"She's my girlfriend, my partner – not my wife."

"Christ Harry, she's having your kid. It doesn't matter what label you put on your relationship." He's shaking his head in slow arcs, avoiding making eye contact.

I can feel my feet losing grip on the carpet as if I'm about to fall through a rather large hole in the floor. "Did he say why he was there? Greg? The night Barry died? Why he was in the private client department?"

"He was dropping off some work. He never looked into Barry's room as he went past – he says he thinks the door was shut. He went down the back stairs so didn't come walk past his room again."

"But he refused to do any work for the private client partners. What work? And since when does he use the back stairs? He hates the smell."

"Stop this. He told me he was trying to help you with those photographs. He said he knew the assistant at Boots and she'd alerted him to the police call. They were trying to help you. He said he told you this. Yes? Is that correct?"

I nod.

"So why didn't you believe him? I thought you two were friends."

I have no answer, not at that moment. After another couple of minutes of swaying heads and 'oh Harry' reproaches I'm dismissed with the lament, "I need to think about this. It's a shame Crout is still in a coma. Let's hope he comes round soon because right now I'm beginning to wonder whether any of what you've said is true."

My head is spinning. It feels like the immediate sack is the most likely outcome. What I don't need right now is to speak to anyone else in the department, so I head for the stairs. The back stairs.

If you descend them you have a choice at ground level: one door takes you back into reception and the other takes you through a fire exit and into a staircase that leads down to the car park in the basement. I decide I need a coffee and head for reception, although before I get there I push the door open a fraction to see if anyone is hanging around as I'm determined not to bump into anyone I know.

I pull back, glad of my caution because standing by the revolving door to the street is Greg with Miles; Greg is frowning and Miles is smiling broadly. Their conversation is short and soon Greg turns away, nods towards Gloria and heads round the corner to the lift. As I watch, Gloria waits until Greg is out of sight and gives Miles an enthusiastic thumbs-up; in return he strangely appears to blow her a kiss.

I'm still absorbing this scene when one of the messengers carrying a sack of by-hand deliveries comes whistling down the stairs behind me. As he sees me, he says in a cheery voice, "Coming through!"

I hold open the door for him and follow him into reception. Gloria is back at her desk and smiles up at me. "Hiya lover boy. How's Pen? You all excited? Must be days away now, right?"

I manage an unconvincing nod and something simple but, in the current circumstances very tricky to get right, such as, "Yes," and hurry out onto the street. Miles is hopping into a cab and I hear him say, "Dreyfus Place."

Now why does that ring a bell?

# Tuesday, 6th October 1987

## *Chapter Seventy-One*

I usually quite like Tuesdays, mostly for no other reason than they aren't Mondays. Sitting on the toilet at 6.00 am and waiting for the painkillers I have just taken to dull the ache behind my eyes, I can't help but review yesterday. Not great what with the toilet farce et cetera. In fact I never went back to the office after that episode – I told Chloe I had a doctor's appointment and wandered off, ending up in Dreyfus Place for no other reason than I wanted to know why it rang a bell. I did see Miles briefly as he jumped into a Daimler or Jag or Bentley or something expensive-looking with a vanity plate of PYP 001 – I'm guessing it belongs to Piotr Princip – but something else still nags at me, which isn't good for my hangover.

At least I avoided being home early enough to tell Penny that (a) I might have AIDS (b) so might she (c) so might our unborn child and, oh by the way (d) it's likely I'll be sacked for shitting in a sink at work. To do that I undertook a sad solo drinking session – two in fact – that ended up with me watching some well-dressed young women appear to proposition a couple of posh-sounding young men – they looked like they might be fellow lawyers, although I'm not sure why. It was while I did my lonely people watching that I thought about Chuck and the office flat and the prostitutes who used the other rooms. I wondered if that was what Charlie Jepson meant when he talked about Magda and his cryptic clue.

\*\*\*

When I wake up and stumble to the toilet the sun is streaming into the bathroom and I really, really do not want to go into the office. I can hear Penny snoring – advanced pregnancy has given her the most thunderous farts and guttural snores – and know I can easily sneak off without waking her but by doing so I'll feel even more guilty than I do already.

From where I perch I can see the sun draw a sharp line through the gap in the curtains and across our bed. The line has been gradually moving up the duvet and will soon reaches her face, which will wake her. Maybe I should bring her tea, tell her what Chuck said and what happened at work and make some plans. Maybe—

"Ow, you vicious little fucker!"

Pettifore digs his claws into my bare calf and makes me stand up quickly, kicking him away. A line of blood spots has already welled up on my leg. Penny doesn't stir and the feline psycho, having asserted his authority over me, hops onto the duvet and heads for Penny's hair, purring like a haunted dial tone.

Penny mimics the purr and gradually turns over, letting the moggy increase the density of its contentedness at the same time as dripping salty cat snot onto her chin.

I hop back into the bedroom and begin a hunt for some pants. "Why do you let him do that?" I say as Penny regains consciousness.

"I'm getting used to having disgusting substances dribbled all over me in anticipation of motherhood. Anyway, you pick your nose and eat the contents."

"I bloody well do not. Well, not since you told me I did anyway."

"If you say so. What happened last night? You sounded pretty plastered. Celebrating some deal or something?"

"Not exactly. I'd better get on. Lots to do today. There are few things I really need to sort out." I hop with one leg in my underwear towards the wardrobe.

A hand shoots out and grabs my leg. "Stop."

I stop, but I don't look at her.

"I told you – no more secrets. So spill it. If it had been a celebration you'd have sought absolution. If you've been playing Harry the Hero with Dobbin or whoever, you'd try to coyly extract some praise from me. If it wasn't that, then what?"

Taking a deep breath, I recount my confrontation with Greg and Frank and Crispin, the unfortunately badly timed evacuation and the resulting mess. Having finished I realise she is laughing.

"They really did that? Deliberately blocked you? What a cracking trick."

"I don't know. It could be coincidence but Frank is convinced I'm some sort of phantom shitter that he's uncovered."

"It'll blow over. You did the right thing by telling him of your suspicions. And you're not to blame for Mr Crout's suicide attempt, if that is what it was about." She's studying me. "I'm glad you told the police too. Honestly, you may be right about Greg as well. I've always liked him, but as you say he's got a dodgy background, hasn't he? And he oozes ambition. But if it's not him, then who?"

"It has to be someone in the office, someone who has a grudge or is help… shit." It's like I've been slapped.

Penny's right eyebrow lifts in a question. "Are you going to explain?"

"I'm often wrong but I have a feeling that darling Miles Tupps may be behind all this somehow."

"Miles? I thought you said he'd turned over a new leaf. And wasn't it Greg who introduced you to him?"

"Yes, but…" I'm already climbing into my cycling gear that's piled in a heap on the bedside chair. "I'll tell you later, really." I reach over and kiss her on the lips. "You are the sexiest woman alive, and I truly mean that. That's why I have to go."

I'm running down the stairs as her voice floats after me, "And when you get back maybe you can explain why Natalie left a message and asked if I'd spoken to you yet?"

## *Chapter Seventy-Two*

I reach the office in pretty much record time and ignore the shower, merely having a quick wash and a brief ten minutes on the loo to compensate for my performance yesterday. I then grab my jacket and a cab and head back to Dreyfus Place. I'm hopeful that it's too early for Miles to appear.

The block of flats where I saw him is accessed by a large black door that has a keypad and an entry intercom – all very modern. Natalie once lived in something similar and there the last button on the entry system allowed access for tradesmen. Nothing seems to work here so in the end I press the first three buttons and eventually someone lets me in when I say I have a delivery to drop off.

I guess I have about two minutes before the occupier becomes suspicious. Scanning the hall, I am disappointed there aren't any letterboxes, but on the table there are several letters – mostly junk. I'm flicking through when a voice above my head says, in a rather pre-emptory tone, "Did you just ring the bell?"

Bingo! I've found what I'm looking for, but the resident isn't happy with my ignoring her.

"You. Yes, you there! You can't just come in here and start rifling through other people's post. I'm going to call the police."

She begins to return upstairs.

"Before you go, do you know this woman?"

One of the recent innovations at the office is the introduction of a photobook; in it there are pictures of every member of Newe Waters' staff. I have the book open to the penultimate page.

The woman stops and comes down a flight. She peers at the grainy image then she sneers. "Yes. Awful tarty creature, always with her cleavage hanging out. Stays with that unpleasant man on the third floor. Tupps. I have no idea why Piotr allows them to stay. Relatives, I suppose. They'd have to be foreign, wouldn't they?"

"Thanks. Oh, and if you do call the police my name is Spittle, Harry Spittle. Be sure to mention it."

I'm rather pleased to find she looks utterly nonplussed.

Well, well, Miles Tupps and Gloria Eagle – it appears they are an item. I wonder how that came about.

## *Chapter Seventy-Three*

I'm suddenly popular. Chloe has left me a bundle of telephone messages. The most urgent seems to be from Gerald MacThing. Otherwise, in no particular order, Crout's secretary asks for a word, Greg and Crispin both need a chat, Chuck wants me to call him back and a woman who didn't leave her name would like to speak to me. Natalie? Dina? Maybe even Magda? I start with a really difficult one. I'm expecting to have to leave a message again but to my surprise the light tone of Jackie answer.

"Hi Jackie. It's Harry."

"Hi. You after that drink?"

"An even bigger favour."

"Shoot."

I take a deep breath. "You know my friend, Amos?"

"The AIDS patient?"

"Yes."

"He's been discharged."

"I know. Shit, how do I explain?"

"Usually it helps if you start from the beginning, preferably with short easy to understand words, yes?" I can sense she's smiling but I hope she understands this is a struggle.

"Natalie may have contracted AIDS from him and given it to me so I need to be checked." It comes out in a rush and stuns both of us.

"I thought… isn't he gay?"

"Yes, but he haemorrhaged and she got covered in his blood. Since then she's become really thin and looks awful."

"That doesn't mean she's contracted it." She sighs loudly. "And you and Natalie…?"

I don't need to explain since her tone tells me she's made the leap. Not that it needed much of a leap.

"Penny and I were on a break, okay?" Why do I need to defend myself?

Her tone hardens. She's definitely judging me and I'm found to be wanting. "Yes, I know about you and your 'breaks', don't I?"

"It's not like that. Can you get me checked?"

She doesn't sound happy. "Go to your GP, Harry like everyone else does. It just requires a blood sample."

"I can't. He's Penny's doctor as well and she sees him a lot, what with the baby nearly due. I know you think I'm a shit and I probably am but I can't dump that stress on her right now, especially if I'm in the clear."

She releases a humungous sigh that feels like it's going on forever. "It's most likely not a problem, but come to the hospital at three. I have a break then and I might be able to swing it."

"Can you keep it anonymous? You won't call Penny, will you?"

There's a short silence. It's her turn to sound defensive. "Why would I know where to call her?"

"True, and sorry – it's not that I don't trust you or anything."

The silence grows. "All right," she says and the line goes dead.

Next I call Gerry MacThing. I'm put through immediately.

"I spoke to that Collins chap and then Toogood himself. I said I'd been told your firm was happy to continue to act for Caldera but that if we needed to talk about related matters I would only do so if you were at least listening in so you knew the context."

"Great." I manage about two on the enthusiasm scale and he picks up on it.

"Harry, I'll be honest. You are the one I trust. Not Crispin and certainly not Martin. And I don't think I've ever spoken to the partner who took this over. I understand if this is awkward. Do you want to do this? If I have to instruct someone else I want to do so in the next couple of days. You understand?"

"Yes. How did Toogood take it?"

"Oh, he laughed. Said he didn't think the property department wanted to act anymore and he'd make sure we were all clear about that. His arrogance is rather breath-taking and that makes me want to continue to instruct you, if possible. As you'll fully appreciate, he tried to pressure me to talk details but I told him that I was too busy and would get back to him in a couple of days."

"Well done. Thanks."

"He is one smug sod, isn't he?"

"Among a few other disarming and delightful character traits, smug is definitely on the list, yes."

"He said he holds the key to both our and Thompson's schemes and while he considers ours to have the greater potential to secure planning, he'll deal with whoever shows him the most commitment. By which he means money."

"Did you say anything about that?"

"No. You told me not to."

"Right. Of course. You've been patient, Gerry. I'm pretty sure you're in a stronger position than he suspects but I need to do some more work on it."

"And you can't tell me why?"

"I don't want him trying to pull rank. I'd prefer it if you could continue to plead ignorance."

He laughs. He actually laughs. "You really want to screw him over, don't you?"

"In career terms, I'd like you to screw him, but I'm happy to try to set it up so you can do it."

"Bloody hell, and I thought I'd instructed a law firm. Instead it's like working with the Borgias."

Now that's done I'm feeling rather exhilarated, like I've climbed one impossible mountain but have several more to go. I shuffle the messages and dial the woman who didn't leave her name. It's Natalie sounding upset. "What did he tell you?"

"Chuck?"

"Of course Chuck! He had no right to say anything like that."

"He was trying to help, Nat—"

"He's a shit. I thought he was different. Why am I such a rubbish judge of men?" Her breathing changes and I realise she is gulping back sobs.

I die a little inside. I am so bad with tears, even if they are over the telephone. "Deep breath, Natalie. I'm getting a blood test myself. We'll know soon enough." I'm about to ask about her having a HIV check when Erica walks in and dumps a file on her desk, sighing as she sits. Fuck, go away can't you? I silently plead.

"He's trying to get at you, or you and me. It's rubbish, Harry. I never said I had HIV or AIDS or anything. Yes, there was a haemorrhage but I never absorbed any of Amos' blood. Not really. It just got on my skin."

What does 'not really' mean? "But Chuck said you told him—"

"It's a lie, Harry."

How would she know? I want to cut the call and find somewhere private to continue it but I say, "Did he tell you? That he lied to me?"

"What? No."

"Then how…?" Erica looks over at me, picking up on the anxiety in my voice. I turn away from her, no doubt making her even more suspicious. "How do you know what he said?" I say in a hoarse voice.

There's a pause and it sounds like she says something to someone in the background. I strain to hear but the voices are disembodied, remote. "Natalie, are you still there?"

When she comes back on the line her voice is almost a whisper and I clamp the earpiece to the side of my head to make out her words. "There's something... not right about him. I think he's planning something. He keeps asking all these questions about you and Dina. I thought he was just being curious but they are sort of odd, like 'where does she work' and 'how often do you see her'. And he wanted your home address. Then Cindy told me he's got this woman at the apartment he uses as an office. From East Germany she said. I wondered if that was Magda. You said she was staying with you."

She stops, sounding rather breathless. It's what I'd wondered after Jepson's recent message. Something doesn't ring true. I'm sure I never mentioned Magda. Maybe Penny did. I'm trying to frame a question when she starts coughing, apologises and abruptly rings off.

It's only as I put the phone back I realise she never explained about the AIDS and whether she knew for sure she'd not got it or if she was just guessing. Do I still go ahead with the test?

I need to distract myself so grab my jacket and say to Erica, "Come on, we need to find Crispin."

She's delighted to get away from whatever is covering her desk. "Was that Chuck? About the securitisation?"

"No, just... come on, I'll explain later."

Crispin is at his desk, looking thunderous. When he sees me, he turns a remarkable shade of cerise and then starts hiccupping. "Harry, I..." he sees Erica and stops. "What?"

"I need 30 minutes. Out of the office. You free now?"

He looks bemused but nods.

"Erica, can you go and get a table at the Sense of Hummus? We won't be far behind."

As soon as she's gone, Crispin starts over. "About yesterday and all that nonsense. It was Greg's... well, we were both furious and we know how you like to go on. It was a spur of the moment thing. We just thought we'd make you squirm. I had no idea that Frank would think... that it might end..."

"Okay, I believe you. Tell Frank. That's all. I think he's already made up his mind anyway. It wasn't about that."

He starts to ask what it is actually about but I hold my finger to my lips. We leave the office and I don't speak until we each have a drink and are sitting in a corner of the café with my back to the wall where I can see who comes and goes. "MacThing," I finally say.

"Good God, Harry, I'm done with that. It's damn nearly cost me my chances at the partnership."

"I know, and this is how we restore them."

"Are you serious?"

"Never more so. I heard today that Toogood has asked MacThing to make him an offer to save his scheme. He's told him he controls both the harbourside development and the rival Thompson scheme at Martindale Cove but he's giving MacThing the first chance to bid. I think we all know he'll then start playing the developers off against each other."

"Does he control both? How? The Lordship is only relevant to Caldera, isn't it?"

"He thinks he has the answer to the access issues at Martindale Cove as well as building onto the foreshore at the harbourside for Caldera."

"Oh great."

"The thing is, his pet rat Collins took the files and has been using the knowledge gained from our work on Caldera to improve his negotiating position."

"Can you prove that?"

"Maybe, maybe not, but I bet we can make him squirm."

"Toogood inflicts squirms, he doesn't squirm himself. Trying to threaten Toogood with, what? Misconduct? That's not going to work."

"I know. But what Toogood isn't aware of is that he doesn't have the key to both schemes. Possibly the Thompson one – in which case not our concern – but not Caldera's."

By now Crispin's face is a picture of confusion. "I'm sorry Harry, I know you're clever and I'm slow but please, in words of one syllable, what do you mean?"

"I've spent a bit of time talking to a local historian, a character by the name of Thaddeus Melpot. That and Erica's genius for research has shown us that our darling Mervin Toogood did not actually become Lord of the Manor when he bought his estate in Barrington because he forgot to register it."

"But surely he can..." Suddenly Crispin beams. "No, he can't, can he? He can't register late. The transfer will have lapsed."

Erica goggles at him. "Did you read my note or did you just know that?"

Crispin looks surprised. "Doesn't everyone know the exception relating to manorial incidents and other rights? Acme something or other in the 1930s?"

I have to laugh. "I don't know about me Crispin, but the partnership needs a mind like yours. When we acted on the purchase Toogood took the matter over – I've put the purchase file somewhere safe, so he can't fiddle with it and blame someone else – and he's clearly failed to register it despite being told to do so. The previous holder of the title died years ago and his executors hold the rights on trust. One such is this historian who is also a beneficiary. He happens to hate Toogood and I'm pretty sure he'd happily screw him over."

"Toogood can't force a late transfer? Brilliant! "

Erica nods.

"Even if it isn't then what was the consideration for the transfer of the rights? If there was none the only consideration being imputed is because of the affixing of a seal, then he could seek damages if the contract isn't completed but I think the Courts will not grant specific performance." He looks at Erica. "Yes?"

She nods. "He is time barred but yes, if he wasn't that is probably true as well. He can't enforce."

Crispin face twists into a frown. "Doesn't the Lordship depend on owning land within the Manor?"

"Yes," she says triumphantly, "and Mr Melpot complies even if the other trustees do not."

"And he's definitely a beneficiary too?"

"Yes. The Will makes it clear the executors are to split up the residue as they see fit between them and only in dispute do they have to sell and split the proceeds. There's a deal to be done there."

"Does this Melpot character know he has control?"

"No, he doesn't. He's convinced dear Mervin is the Lord and holds the rights. The thing is, he's quite keen on the Caldera scheme but only with some modifications. By the sounds of them they aren't ones that MacThing will object to but that needs some careful handling. As does Toogood."

"Why tell me? You've sorted it."

I shake my head. "It's your deal. We just stumbled on a solution. You need to take it forward."

Erica is more a defender of my position than I am myself. "Harry, why—?"

My hand on her arm forestalls her. "I put him in a mess with MacThing and then Toogood. If Crispin speaks to Taddy – that's what Mr Melpot likes to be called, don't ask – I'll sort out Toogood."

Crispin's face is a veritable picture. On the one hand he can't really believe I'm giving him an olive branch so heavy with juicy fruit; on the other he looks a touch guilty that I might be about to self-immolate when I tell Toogood that his greedy plans are well and truly buggered.

"I'm not going to talk to Toogood today or tomorrow. He expects MacThing to make an offer, although in typical fashion he hasn't said what for. What he might try to do is get a recording of the conversation, but Toogood is too clever. One reason I thought we needed this chat outside the office is I don't trust that place not to be full of spies right now. If you speak to Taddy and then try to set something up with Gerald, feel free to take Erica – it will be great experience for her – then let me know and at the right moment I'll puncture Mervin's bubble."

"Harry, I don't—"

"Neither do I. Now I need to do some work."

## Chapter Seventy-Four

Back at my desk I spend half an hour returning various calls. Jonjo happily agrees to deal with a couple of client matters, leaving me free to head out once again. This time I meet Stephen McNoble at the tube station. "Well? I'm meant to be chasing a two-timing wife in Ealing so be quick," he says.

"I think Miles is living with the receptionist at my firm, a woman called Gloria Eagle. I was trying to work out how they might have met and realised that she was once the mistress of my ex-principle, Jeremy Panther—"

"Panther? That wanker?"

"The one and same. He probably took her to Miles' old club to impress her. Miles makes a great pretence about being loaded and if there's one thing that attracts Gloria it's the smell of money, so it feels utterly natural they'd get together. Can you pop into my reception and see if you recognize her?"

"Won't she recognise me?"

"I hope so. I hope she looks terrified, especially when you say Miles sent you to collect the photos."

"Photos?"

"I may be wrong but Gloria is very shrewd. She got hold of a film that I was set up to collect from a nearby branch of Boots. Gloria and the assistant there are friends. I saw them together the other day but couldn't place the face immediately, but then I realised Gloria and Miles had a link and it was a light-bulb moment. But the thing is I'm fairly certain only some of the pictures that were on that film were included in what I was given. I think she'll have kept some back, maybe the negatives too. And – and I accept this is a bit of a long shot – it wouldn't surprise me if Gloria kept them rather than gave them to Miles. She's canny, so she might see them as insurance."

"Bit of a leap Harry."

"Maybe, but I've a fairly shrewd idea of Gloria Eagle's character. If you do your old-school heavy impersonation and give her a little bit of a fright, then I think she'll probably cough up."

"Wouldn't Tupps have demanded she hand them over?"

"If he knew there were more, then yes, but she may never have shown him everything. Let's find out."

"And if I do get them?"

"Give them to me. Just try to avoid getting your fingerprints on them as they'll be going to the cops."

"So you're in trouble?"

"You have no idea."

"Anything I can do?"

"Really, you're doing enough. And I think I may have arranged for your Dad to come and stay at my parents in Hampshire the weekend after next. Why don't you come too?"

"Because your parents hate me?"

"That's true and neither are exactly keen on your Dad, but I think this is the time to let bygones be bygones. I'll square them away."

"You don't believe that, do you? About bygones?"

I manage a smile. "We're getting there. Slowly. Maybe."

"Where will you be if I get anything?"

"I'm off for a hospital visit. I'll be back later. Just leave a message with Chloe where we can meet."

As I begin to go he says, "Does this have anything to do with Princip?"

"Which one?"

At that I leave him looking confused.

***

Back in the office and before I can leave to visit Crout I call the Flaming Flamingo. Cindy answers and is half way through telling me Natalie is out when Chuck seems to grab the phone and call me an interfering shit. "For her sake, just fuck off. I'm trying to help you both."

Before I can answer he rings off and when I call back Cindy tells me he's also gone out. I stare at the phone. Who do I believe? Probably Natalie, but she's not making much sense and it wouldn't surprise me to find out she was trying to avoid the possible implications of getting Amos' blood on her. I'm wondering if I should call Jackie when another thought occurs. This is the second time I've spoken to Chuck and he's not mentioned the passport. And just recently it was all so very important."

I pull out my address book and dial the number I have for the Home Office. It takes me 20 minutes to reach the right person but finally I'm put through. There's a rustling of paperwork before the person – Colin something – says, "I don't think we have an application for a Magda Kleinkopf."

"You must. I spoke to someone about it – it may have been you – only a couple of days ago."

"Can you spell that?"

"K-L-E-I-N-K-O-P-F."

Another minute. "I'm sorry. I'm afraid you will need to reapply."

"Reapply? Does that mean you've lost it?"

"Apply. I meant apply."

My last conversation with Dina comes back to me. "All right. I'll look into what's happened."

He seems very quick to end the call.

I take a couple of breaths and then put out a call through the classifieds to get Dina to ring me. "Tell her I'll be free in a couple of hours."

## *Chapter Seventy-Five*

Even though he's still in a coma the SP is clearly a man of influence. He is in a private room off a rather plush corridor in a recently opened and very expensive private hospital in London Bridge. This nurse-cum-bouncer, who is apparently half-woman half-Rottweiler, eyes me with a look that suggests it's nearly dinner time and I might be the starter. However, the mention of my name changes her mien, if not into something recognisably friendly then at least herbivorous. I'm told to go through and not to tire him out.

As I head for the room she has pointed me to I realise I hadn't expected to be allowed in, at least unaccompanied, although quite why I thought that I don't know. There is a glass panel in the door and I glance at the man propped up in the bed. If I am expecting a different person to the one I know I'm disappointed. But for the red and white stripped pyjamas he looks as he always does at his desk. As I study him from the safety of the anteroom, I wonder how he tried to kill himself. I can hardly ask and I don't suppose anyone will tell me, though the rumour factory will be hard at work in the office by now. I knock and enter.

Inside things are very different. The heat is the first thing I notice and then the sour smell, like the room needs airing. But the biggest surprise is the SP. Only his eyes move; these and two fingers on his left hand that's resting on the blanket. And even they seem exhausted by the little wave they manage to give.

"Harry." His voice is fractured and he motions me to a glass. This feels so strange but I fetch it from the table next to him and hold it out. It is immediately apparent I'll need to present it to his lips and then it is clear I have to help him sit forward to take a sip. This means actually touching the Senior Partner, which is beyond intrusive. It's like being told to grope royalty. All the while this is happening I feel like I've intruded on some very private grief.

Once he's composed himself he tries again. His voice is clearer and stronger, more like the SP I know but the only animation is his mouth and, to a lesser extent, his eyes; his body seems immobile. "Harry, I'm sorry that you have to see me like this but I needed to clear up a few things with you. I understand you went to the police—"

"Yes, sorry. I did want to wait until we spoke but then this, you know, you had this, your, erm, this…"

He waves me quiet. "I know it looks like a suicide attempt, but it wasn't. Not really. More a thoughtless playing with fire." He seems to hesitate and then adds, "Though I'm sure the stories will make it sound like I've lost the plot. Still, I'm sure you don't want to know, do you?"

Is that an invitation to ask? Surely not but the pause seems to be intended to encourage me.

"The burns will heal though apparently it's unlikely I'll be able to enter any more point to points." He smiles. "More importantly, though, you did the right thing. I had concluded that that is what we needed to do and I would have organised it the next day but for this. Sonia told me about your conversation with her and Frank. Do you really think Greg is behind this?"

My mind is still struggling with what he did to cause burns somewhere in the saddle area but I force myself back to the moment and say, "No, I'm not sure I do now. But I do think it stems from his Father. Greg and I aren't exactly on friendly terms just now, not after my rather hasty accusations, but I'm pretty sure he and his Father have a strained relationship. He may be as much a victim in this as you are."

"And you?"

"Yes, well, there is some history there. Are you well enough for me to explain?"

He nods and says, "First, ring that bell and ask for some tea and cakes if you'd like them. I'm told by my daughter they're pretty good."

"Daughter? I didn't know you had a daughter."

"No, well, until this happened I'd barely seen her in 12 years. She was at university when I divorced, because… well, maybe you can guess. She didn't take the news very well. Every cloud, eh? Go on, tell me your theory."

I'm wondering at what the 'news' might have been but try to answer his request. "Before I joined Newe Waters I was executor of a friend's estate – Sven Anderson. It was complicated and involved some illegal business interests that were formerly owned by Sven's Father."

"Goodness. Did you tell us about this when you joined?"

"In a roundabout way, yes. One of these was a chain of estate agencies run by a man called Miles Tupps. Sven's plan, which I carried out, was to close him down and get him to move to the north which he did for a fee. I'd not seen Miles for an age until he appeared a few weeks ago as a new client of the firm introduced by Greg. He seemed to have turned over a new leaf because he used to hate me and threaten he'd find a way of paying me back."

The SP might be ill, but he is utterly engrossed by this tale. "How did Greg know him?"

"Through his Father who is behind a new business venture, financing it. I've a theory I need to check about that when I get home. I can't be entirely sure but I think Miles managed to find a way to put someone into the firm, someone who got sufficiently close to Barry to dig up some dirt on him and you. Someone who knows me and who has maybe inadvertently helped involve yours truly in this whole set up."

The SP's face is a picture, but I'm beginning to worry all this might be putting him under a strain that I shouldn't be doing. "Did this person – Tupps? – and their co-conspirator kill Barry?"

"It seems a bit far-fetched. Maybe they blackmailed him with the pictures and his heart gave out. Probably not deliberate. In my life all the biggest disasters have usually been on the cock-up side of the conspiracy/cock-up continuum. I think they may have wanted to photograph him in a compromising situation, maybe even with you in the room. If you go to the back stairs you can see into his office. You were already there, weren't you? When I turned up I mean."

"I'd had a message he wanted a word. About us. About a problem."

"Who was it from?"

"Just a written message. It didn't say. I assumed it was from Barry. I did wonder if he'd committed suicide when I found him."

"You didn't mention that."

"I don't believe I was thinking much more clearly than you at the time. And I doubt anyone was hanging around to take photos that night. After all, why didn't they take a shot of you and me together with him?"

"That may have been because I know the person who could have been poised to shoot and they had an attack of conscience."

"You originally thought it was Greg, didn't you?"

"Yes. I knew he was in the office and if he was setting me up then it made sense. Not that I had any reason to think it beyond the partnership race and, anyway, he couldn't have known I would have gone to Barry's room so even I thought it was a long shot."

"If he was working for his Father it could have been to maximise any scandal. Piotr Princip has not been our friend for a while but this seems so, I don't know, elaborate."

"The police did say they were doing further toxicology tests. He may have been drugged so they could take that picture with you and inadvertently the drugs killed him. When I say it out loud it sounds crazy. I don't suppose we'll know either way."

He shakes his head wearily, the first real movement since I came in; indeed, the colour seems to have come back to his face a bit and his voice sounds stronger. "Have you told the police all of this, including any speculation?"

"Not the speculation, no. Do you think I should?"

"Definitely. Especially if this Tupps man is as bad as you say he is. Although that might compromise the person who you are still trying to shield."

I don't reply; he's still shrewd and perceptive despite his current condition. I half want to tell him about Gloria and what I've asked Stephen to do but somehow I think using a thug to try to extract evidence against Miles might not go down well with the ethics of the SP.

He sags back into his pillows. "Thank you for telling me this. I saw Frank yesterday and he expressed some reservations about your, hmm, character. Something to do with a stool? Of the turdiferous variety?" I detect the semblance of a grin and that must be good, surely?

"Maybe that's for another time. And Frank might be right anyway. There are only two slots at best in property right now and after what they've been through I think Greg and Crispin probably deserve the places," I say.

"Let's leave that where it is for now, shall we? But don't give up hope."

"Sir. Mr Crout. Seb. There is one thing. Mervin Toogood."

"Not your biggest fan."

"That is mutual. The thing is I need some guidance, help if you like."

"I doubt you'll get him on side this late in the day."

"No, no, this isn't about me and the vote. Not directly anyway. I think I am going to have to report him to the Law Society for gross misconduct and I'm not sure of the best way of tackling it."

A bushy eyebrow shoots up and then settles above a more serious and rather intimidating expression. "What are you talking about here, Harry?"

"We act for a property developer, Caldera Properties. They have a scheme at Barrington, on the south coast near his—"

"Where Mervin has his house?"

"Yes. Mervin believes he has the key to Caldera's investment, as well as a rival scheme, and is negotiating with them to get the highest price for his co-operation."

"I assume you are worried about a conflict? If he isn't represented by the firm then it shouldn't be an issue. There's nothing to stop a partner making an income from a client."

"No, but Mervin's assistant took our files in order to understand exactly what Caldera's position was and find out the details of the rival scheme so far as we had them, which is very private."

"You know that? For a fact? And can prove it?"

"Pretty much. I thought it might happen, so I introduced some fictitious elements to each scheme and both have been raised in the negotiations. We have also discovered that Mervin's negotiating position isn't that strong after all, and since we aren't conflicted from continuing to act for Caldera I intend telling the client what he can do to stymie Mervin. He won't be happy when he finds out."

"I'm not sure I understand what you want me to do."

"On Thursday or Friday he will realise he can't do what he wants to do. He'll be pretty furious. I'm happy to cope with whatever he throws at me – honestly, after my previous experiences I've faced worse – but I really don't think either of the likely winners in the partnership race should be penalised, especially Crispin. I wondered if maybe you could have a word with him."

"How do you think that will help?"

"Maybe if you explained that you are prepared to persuade me not to proceed with the gross misconduct allegations."

He smiles, the first sign of any sort of proper animation. "You have great faith in my ability to persuade people, Harry."

"I think, from what I've heard, you have many powers of persuasion. Sir."

He regards me steadily for a long time; I try not to blink even though I'm wondering all the time if maybe I've gone too far. When he does speak it is encouraging. "You will make a fine partner…"

But then he has to go and ruin it.

"…somewhere. Maybe you could leave me now?"

I ease my way out, wondering – not for the first time – if I've been a little bit too clever for my own good.

## *Chapter Seventy-Six*

I'm a glutton for punishment so I head to St Tommy's. Jackie's left a message and I follow the instructions to get my blood extracted. I want to see her, given it now feels like it might be a false alarm, assuming Natalie isn't in denial. Why I should feel the need to explain beats me. It's not like Jackie is trying to protect Penny, although maybe the Guild of Womanhood demands a certain fealty even between exes and I've broken some unwritten rule. For my part, I just want it over. While I'm waiting I reflect on the strange call with Natalie. How did she know Chuck lied to me, unless he said he did and why would he do that? Although I need to follow up on the idea about Magda being in that flat. Mind you, I can feel the stress levels building up to dangerous levels every time I think about spies and whatnot. How on Earth does a boring lawyer get sucked – or is that suckered – into such a situation?

This part of the hospital is hotter than the London Bridge one where I visited the SP and my head is beginning to throb. I do suffer from the occasional wretched headache that requires me to lie in a quiet and dimly lit corner and make small mewling sounds. Nibbling digestive biscuits also seems to help, coupled with whatever strong pain relief is available. Maybe I've got one coming on. Hardly surprising given the stress I've been under lately.

Having apparently had a vein drained I head home – I can't be bothered to go back to the office to check on my post or pick up my bike. By the time I reach the front door, all I want to do is throw up and go to bed, which I do and then I shiver and sweat under the duvet in neat 20 minute sessions throughout the evening and into the night. Penny takes her pillows and heads for the spare room. I can hardly blame her. I know I should tell her what's going on but I really am not in any condition to explain anything just now.

# Friday, 9th October 1987

## *Chapter Seventy-Seven*

God, I feel terrible. I've barely been able to move, let alone get to the office. Penny has been a real snarling guard dog, keeping everyone at bay and feeding me dry toast and soup and odd coloured medication that has turned my piss green. At least I hope it's the medication and not some awful warning sign.

Penny brings me tea just after the phone rings.

"Who was that?" I gasp.

I can see she's thinking about what to say. "Cindy. Works with Natalie?"

"Did she want to talk to me?"

"Why would she?"

"I… no reason. Everything okay?"

"Sure."

There's something in her tone that makes me think she wants to say more but right now my head is too full of crap to think about things too hard. She must pick up on it. "Natalie has taken the till money and not banked it."

I bury myself deeper. "Oh?"

"Get some rest. I'll bring you more toast in a bit."

It's as I'm drifting off that I wonder why Cindy would tell Penny about the money. I manage to snooze, drifting in and out of weird dreams. I'm vaguely aware of Penny moving about the room and the cat joining me. Pettifore likes to sleep at the end of the bed, only stirring to check on what food I've been left and usually ending up disappointed.

I wake with a start. The light is seeping through the closed curtains making it seem like late afternoon, but it's just two. There are wisps of dreams that I can't catch as I blink and realise Penny is watching me from the door. "Sorry. Didn't know you were there."

"You've been talking in your sleep."

"Have I?" I pull myself upright. "Hope I was lucid."

"Well, you didn't make much sense." She comes and sits on the end of the bed. "You said something about finding Magda."

My mind is suddenly crisp and clear. Jepson's clue. And Natalie's suggestion about Chuck's apartment. "Oh shit."

"What is it?" She perches on the end of the bed.

"I need to think."

"You promised to tell me what's going on. Why are you trying to find Magda? What aren't you telling me?"

"Nothing."

"I'll make you some sweet tea while you get your brain straight."

When she returns and gives me the tea she says, "Cindy told me that Natalie took the money to help Magda. She says she's been staying with the American you mentioned. Chuck?"

"What?" I begin to get out of bed but she presses me back.

"You're going nowhere. While you were asleep Natalie called. Magda told her the American has promised to help her get out of England and over to see her sister in East Germany but she doesn't trust him. That's why Natalie took the money but she called because Magda needs a passport and she said you were sorting it out."

"I was, but it's been blocked or something. I suppose I'd better get a message to Dina."

"Magda said no one should call Dina. Does that make sense?"

"Nothing makes sense. Magda is desperate to get away." I rub my face. "I don't know how to help without a passport."

"What about those men who worked for Sven? You called them the Boulders."

"The Grates? I don't know. They certainly knew how to get things done in rather nefarious ways."

"Can you call them? See if it's the sort of thing they can help with?"

"I think she'd be better off with the Americans. We—"

She shakes her head. "Magda isn't happy. At least give the Grates a call. It would be good to do what we can."

"I hope she can get away. I was worried that Chuck might have locked her in."

"I think we need to move her, but first things first. The passport. Oh, and the visa."

It's rather nice to have Penny directing me as I feel washed out after whatever bug I've struck down by. Still, as I begin to stand I sway alarmingly. Despite this the combination of stress and terror do wonders for my sinuses, if not for my ability to think logically. She eases me towards the small third bedroom and the old-style bureau where we keep important paperwork.

Somewhere in the bureau I have a file with all the clutter I accumulated while sorting out Sven Andersen's estate, although my fear as I pull down the roll top is I'll have left it somewhere safe and not be able to find it. Luck is on my side; clearly I've moved things around a lot but the phone number is sitting on the top of a pile of financial papers. It takes a ridiculous amount of effort to dig it out and focus on the writing which must be mine because it really is terrible.

Grant Grate answers on the second ring. He is as I remember him: too many haitches in his replies and a calm manner that nonetheless makes me think he is also wondering whose head to rip off next. The good news is that he can sort out a convincing passport and visas in about a week. For the right money of course. "Don't worry, 'arry. We'll sort hout the money side later."

At least I have some spare from Sven's estate that I can use if necessary.

In the file there's a list of people in Natalie's tidy hand. I was going to dig this out the other day – another thing I forgot to do. Sure enough, in among the gamblers listed as using Miles old club is one Piotr Princip. Back in 1981 Miles Tupps and Piotr Princip knew each other through the club and another guest there was one Gloria Eagle who was invited by my old principal Jeremy Panther. Coincidence? Yeah, right.

Penny comes in with more tea and toast. Pettifore follows and jumps on the desk.

"Grant says no problem."

A smile breaks out on her face. "Wonderful. And you a respectable City lawyer." She leans forward and kisses me on the mouth, proffering a smidgen of tongue. "I love you, you know?"

"Thanks. I hope this works."

"Finish your toast and then let's go and get Magda. She needs somewhere safe where the American won't bully her to leave on his terms. It'll be good to free up Natalie too. She's sounding pretty overwrought. Not surprising given everything that's happening."

I immediately think about the word 'AIDS' which bounces around inside my head, making me wonder if our love will survive that cold dose of reality, depending on the results.

"We'd better go."

I have to drive since Penny finds wearing the seat belt at the same time as managing the steering wheel a struggle.

Every time I climb into our car I'm reminded why I hate them. Leaving aside the fact that you could have a dial on the dashboard spinning faster than an industrial washing machine and still it wouldn't accurately represent the loss of pounds per minute that owning a car and living in South London involves, this specific example of its type it just so annoying. Irritation number one is the fact that we bought it in the summer when the heated seats were in the 'nice to have' category. Come winter they seemed like a Godsend until we actually turned them on for more than five minutes, at which point the residue of whatever incontinent mammal had sat and defecated in them became only too apparent. Irritation number two is the need – if opening the bonnet to check the oil/top up the radiator/ditto the screen wash and/or generally stare at the engine in the hope that by making it feel uncomfortable and shaming it, it might spontaneously repair itself – to pull on the lever under the dashboard at the same time as holding down the bonnet, thus rendering the idea of opening on one's own redundant. I have 17 other irritations of different magnitudes but listing them all is a recipe for self-harm and I'm rather pressed for time.

"This is exciting, isn't it?" Penny's face is glowing. Her gaze is fixed ahead, which happens to be the back of a white van with the word 'wanker' smeared in the dirt on the rear door. I glance at her bump.

"Are you sure you should be doing this? It's not putting Wigglet under strain?"

"It might loosen the little bundle." She runs her hands over the smooth curve. "I love this, Harry. Don't you?"

Does she mean our baby or this sub-James Bond nonsense? "No. I'd prefer to be back home."

She puts a warm hand on my forehead. "You okay? When we get to the flat you should stay in the car and I'll go and sort out Magda."

"You can't do that. What if he's there?"

"He won't know me, will he? I can say I got the wrong address. Or offer him gravid sex, given the rep of this whole area."

"It's strange, isn't it? A posh area like Piccadilly and it's basically a red light district."

"It's meant to be high class. I guess they use condoms with a Royal crest."

"Was that in that film? Half Moon Street?"

"Maybe. I thought we saw it together."

"Nope. You didn't think I was old enough."

She punches my arm but at least she's smiling. "Seriously, you should let me get her. I'll attract far less suspicion."

We bicker for the 20 minutes it takes to get us to the apartment block. She wins. Of course.

I'm getting anxious when no one has appeared after what feels like an age. Then first Natalie, then Magda and finally Penny emerge. Magda has a holdall and if anything looks even grumpier than normal. "Iz your idea, 'arry?"

Penny speaks before I can think of what to say. "Get going and we'll talk about it later. Go on," she urges when I look at Magda and Natalie in the rear view mirror. As I pull away, Penny says, "Harry has organised a passport and tickets to France. Natalie has some money. It'll take about a week."

"'arry?"

"I…" I don't know what to say.

Magda sighs. "Penny say American is bad. What about Dina? She say trust him then not trust him." Another sigh. "I just wanna see my sister. I not care how."

Penny rubs her hands together. "Good. So this is the plan. We will take you to Hampshire where we will be able to collect the passport in a few days. We will put you on a ferry to France and give you money to travel to Germany. We hope to have a visa to the East and after that…"

"Ja. I know."

I look in the mirror, uncertain at what's happening. "You don't have to do this. You could stay with Chuck."

Natalie slams a hand on the back of the front seat, speaking for the first time since she emerged from the flat. "Fuck it, Harry. He can't be trusted, okay?"

There's an awkward silence and everyone seems to be looking out of the windows. I'm about to respond when I see a layby ahead and pull into by it braking sharply. Before anyone can say anything, I unclip my seatbelt and turn round. "Enough. Chuck Streib works for the CIA. You don't piss around with these guys, okay?" Magda's wide eyes stare back at me. God how I wish Dina was there. "Where will you stay?" I hold up a hand to Penny. "And no, not at ours."

"Grant Grate's." Penny says it like it's obvious.

"What?" My brain is really moving very slowly.

"While Magda packed I called him. He'll look after her. They need to take some photos and will doctor one so they can make a passport for her sister. He'll meet us at Fleet Services in an hour." She gives me a huge smile.

I narrow my eyes. "You planned this?"

"I wrote down the number. It was obvious we needed to get her in front of a camera for him so it made sense."

"You okay with this?" I say as I look at Magda.

"Ja. Iz what you say. Penny say it good plan. I happy." She looks anything but.

"What about you? Won't Chuck suspect something?" I look at Natalie.

"Maybe. We did argue when we last spoke. He's let me down badly." Her face is hidden behind her fringe as she stares at her hands.

I jump slightly as Penny puts her hand on my thigh. "I spoke to Veronica."

"Mum?" I suspect I look quite manic but she is the epitome of calm.

"The reason we took so long to leave back there was partly persuading Magda it was a good idea and speaking to Grant, but we also thought it might make sense if Natalie got away for a few days. Cindy can look after the bar and Veronica is happy to put her up." She lowers her voice a little. "Amos too."

I slump back in my seat and close my eyes. I must be delirious and any moment I will wake up, bathed in sweat in my own bed. I open my eyes, conscious that both Penny and Natalie have lent in close – I can feel their breath on my neck. Penny speaks slowly. "After Natalie spoke to you, about what Chuck said, she called me. She thought you'd have told me."

Oh fuck, that's just fucking great. I think Penny reads my thoughts as she squeezes my hand. "I get why you didn't say. Natalie does not have AIDS. She was tested."

There's an intake of breath from Magda's direction and a 'shush' from Natalie.

"So don't worry. The thing is we managed to trace Amos. He's not at all well but he's staying with a friend. He's desperate to see the sea one last time so I thought... we thought if we can get him to your parents, settle him in we can give him a final picnic. He can see the hotel – he loved it there – see some of the old faces: Terry, Christian, even Cyril. He won't be strong enough soon."

I start shaking my head and the swings get bigger with each new suggestion. "Wait!" I thump the steering wheel. "Stop. Just stop. Mum and Dad won't take Amos. He's dying of AIDS. You know what they're like. They think condoms are strange party balloons."

"Your Mum is fine about it—"

"What?! You've told her!?" My exhaustion roars back and I can feel the sweat beading my temples and neck. "I can't take this."

She sits back in her seat, glancing at me. "Are you going to be okay? Because we don't need you fainting on us."

"Oh great Yes, I'll be fine, only please stop springing this stuff on me."

"Please, just trust me on this. If you drop me at a tube station I'll go home and collect Amos tomorrow and bring him down. Cindy's dropping a bag off for Natalie with some clothes. They'll stay until the passports are sorted and Magda has caught the ferry. Grant will make sure it's okay—"

"What about the money? It'll cost a bloody fortune."

"He told you not to worry, didn't he?"

"Yes, but—"

"So stop fretting. Go on, you know London. Where's the nearest tube?"

I stop to drop her at Hammersmith. When I've pulled in I climb gingerly out of the car. The transition between sitting and standing makes me swoon but I use the side of the car as a support. I slide around to her side, making sure the doors are shut so we can't be overheard. "About Natalie and the… you know."

She reaches up and kisses me. "I love you, you useless, gormless wonderful man. Make sure you tell your Mother exactly what's wrong with him. You're just like her. She'll want to help."

"Do you think I should I call Dina again? She didn't want the Americans taking over but…" Deferring to Penny seems to be the right approach.

"We can talk about that tomorrow, but I doubt it." She hugs me hard. "Let's just get her away and try and do something for Amos." She holds me at arm's length. "And make sure you let your mother spoil you. You look like an extra in a Hammer Horror film. Though, obviously don't let her try and fatten you up."

The drive to Hampshire is easy and silent. Neither woman says a thing. Grant is brilliant. He and Graham Grate meet us at Fleet Services on the M3 as arranged. He explains what they are going to do very calmly and carefully. "The passports will take habout a week, 'arry. I'll let you know, ho-kay? We'll see 'er hoff, probably stick her hon the Cherbourg boat. Once she's hin France she'll be fine to find her own way."

I look at Magda. "Are you okay for money?"

Grant puts a hand on my shoulder. "I'll make sure it's sorted, 'arry."

"No, you shouldn't—"

"We will talk later." Grant has a face that stops avalanches so my pleadings aren't going to wash. I still worry that Sven's contingency won't be enough.

Grant looks at Natalie. "You staying with me?"

She sighs. "I'm staying at Harry's parents' place."

Grant nods. "Nice. Right, time for ha pee."

Magda smiles, the first smile I've seen from her in an age. "I vanna pee too." She follows him towards the cinder service block. Graham walks away whistling.

"We need a word." I take Natalie by the arm and lead her out of earshot

## *Chapter Seventy-Eight*

I head for a patch of scrubby grass but on reaching it I realise it is the preserve of dogs in need of bowel evacuation if the substantial covering of squitty turds is anything to go by. I move us towards some pine trees but the ground underneath isn't much better. In the end we perch on the edge of the kerbing and stand shoulder to shoulder, staring back at Grant's van. I can feel her eyes turn towards me and I twist to look at her. Her soulful brown eyes appraise me warily as she says, "I'm sorry. You shouldn't have had to go through that."

"You're lying about something, but I don't know what." I can feel my rage bubbling up.

She frowns and begins to mirror my anger. "How can you say—?"

"You told me Chuck lied to me about you getting covered in Amos' blood, but how could you know that? How could he know any of it unless you said something?"

"I don't know what I said, just that he took it on himself to scare you, make you get a blood test—"

"How do you know that?"

"You told me you were going to. Have you?"

"Yes, but—"

"He's a shit. He wants to hurt you." She folds her arms and defies me to argue. Then her shoulder slump and she looks defeated. "I'll go back. It's too much to ask you to ask your parents to put up with me." She's instantly on the verge of tears and I take an involuntary step back before I remember what's behind me. The squelch reminds me. "Fuck."

"What?"

"Nothing," but since I begin scraping the turd onto the kerb it is immediately apparent what's happened.

She laughs. "Typical you."

"Exactly. In the shit again."

She steps to me and holds my arm, making me look at her. "I'm sorry. I never meant to hurt you. I just thought Chuck could comfort me. I was stupid." A tear leaks out and she hurriedly scrubs it away. "I'm in such a bloody mess." Her sobs are silent and for once engender my sympathy rather than panic and/or irritation.

"You are among friends, you know? We all care about you," I say.

"Do you?"

That throws me. She begins to turn away and without thinking I grab her arm and spin her back to me. We are kissing in moments and it's electric, though the wafting stench of dog shit rather detracts from the moment.

She breaks off and holds my gaze. "You have no idea how much I wanted to do that."

I'm utterly torn and have no words. That's when I look up and spot Magda standing like a statue halfway back to the van. She's obviously seen us and from her slack jaw I'd hazard a guess she is failing to compute what she has just witnessed. When she registers I'm looking at her, she drops her gaze and hurries to Grant's van, where Graham let her inside. He looks at me, raises an eyebrow and winks.

"She saw, didn't she?"

"Yes. Oh fuck."

"She won't say, if that's what's worrying you."

"Partly. But also… also…" I don't know how to explain.

"Don't say. You don't need to explain. It's my fault. I… I—" She is turning away.

I take her arms and pull her to me. "Stop it. I wanted that as much as you."

She touches my cheek. "I know and so does Penny."

"What do you mean?"

She shrugs like it's entirely natural. "You love us both, don't you?" She waits and then hugs me. "You can't say and I doubt you'll ever be able to admit it but we, Penny and me have known it forever." She puts a hand behind my head and pulls me down for another, gentler kiss and then lets me go. A slight smile flits across her face. "But you're not going to do anything that might piss her off, are you? Any more than I am. You and she are made for each other. You'll make great parents and I'll be a god-mum or aunt or whatever you need and I'll never come between the two of you. But it'll be easier if you accept your burden, Harry. It's never going to be easy for you."

The combination of the bug I've had and the emotion of the last few minutes makes me want to sit down but fortunately I remember in time what's behind me. "Oh Christ, what a mess."

"Only if you want it to be. We won't do this again, so don't think you're getting some sort of free pass here. I'll tell Penny and—"

"Fuck! No!"

She grips my arms hard. "Listen. We've always told each other. She knows you'll probably slip occasionally and relies on me to make sure it comes to nothing. Sometimes, like now, I need to give in a bit but mostly... let's say this isn't going to happen again." She puts a finger on my lips. "Thank you, Harry." She rubs my arm. "Are you sure you want me at your parents? I can find a hotel."

"No, you're coming to mine. It's time I grew up a bit, don't you think?"

"Don't do that. Come on, you need to clean your shoes or no one will want to get close to you again." She takes my arm and leads me back to the car, all the time pulling me close.

Grant is waiting. "I'm hoff then. Take care, 'arry." He hesitates. "...Natalie."

We shake hands. He nods at Natalie and spins away.

"Do you think we embarrassed him?"

"More like he's trying to decide if he should kneecap me or not. I think he always found Penny easier to deal with." I try to put on a confident face; it's something I will have to master if I'm to be a successful partner. "I'm sure it will be fine." Somehow, I manage to cross my fingers behind my back.

"I'm so sorry Harry. I'm trouble, aren't I?"

"No. You're beautiful and beguiling. And a good friend. What we need to do is get you well."

"I wish."

"You hop in and I'll go and wash my footwear. Maybe Mum can make something that'll be a cure for whatever is afflicting you."

"If I remember your mother's cooking that's of the kill or cure variety."

"Yep, pretty much but in this case that might work best."

We watch the van drive slowly towards the exit. As it passes us and I see Magda's profile staring determinedly ahead I realise I may never see her again. I should have said goodbye.

Oh well...

# Saturday, 10th October 1987

## *Chapter Seventy-Nine*

Having kissed Natalie and understood something of Penny and Natalie's relationship that I never suspected, we both seem much more relaxed. I must admit to having had a small sex-based fantasy as we passed Winchester but that's all. It feels like we have cauterised a wound. For good. I think. Last night we talked into the wee hours. She admitted to not knowing what was wrong with her and being frightened she might have all sorts of terminal illnesses. She also told me about her attempts to find someone to share her life with. 'I even gave Cindy a go'. That caused us both to laugh until she embarrassed me by asking if I'd fantasied about sex with her and she meant Cindy and I thought... anyway, she told me that she had this fixation with me and that the last few men she'd dated she'd compared them to me, including Chuck. 'He's a good lover', she said, which I didn't want to hear, it being implied (or so I thought) that that meant he was better than me. Finally at about 3.00 am, we went to our (separate) beds and I at least slept badly.

I eventually give up at just before seven. That's when I find Mum and Mrs Ohja doing breakfasts for the four guests, two of whom are also up early and chatting amiably about the birds they hope to see on the salt marshes. Mum and Mrs Ohja are like conjoined twins, finishing each other's sentences and laughing at jokes even before they've got to the punchline. And to think they hated each other when they first met, not that they'd admit it now.

The business is very well organised. Given its size, it can handle up to 20 guests right now with a maximum, when all the building work is done, of 29. It takes a lot of work and they currently employ seven people, a mix of full- and part-time staff. The gardens are being worked on under the supervision of Cyril Larrard, a local whose penis I inadvertently caused to be amputated while he was the pervy gardener at Hemingways when Penny, Natalie, Magda and I worked there in the seventies. It sounds as if finally Mum will have a kitchen garden to be proud of and they aim to be self-sufficient in veg in three years.

Mrs Ohja explains how they feel the reception rooms in the main house, which are very grand, are wasted and while they don't want it to be a hotel they like the idea of creating a restaurant that focuses on locally sourced food and - I did well not to laugh when Mum told me -

wine. It is while we are in the massive kitchen drinking tea that Mrs Ohja asks about Natalie.

"What's wrong with that girl? She used to have a lovely figure, now her titties are more shrivelled than mine." She laughs; Mum laughs; I cringe. 'Mrs Ohja' and 'shrivelled titties' have no place in the same sentence.

She does have such a smooth, sing-song voice though – I always feel like I'm being soothed – and listening to her, even if I'm being told off, remains a pleasure.

"I don't know. We're all worried about her. She's a bit of an exercise obsessive but I'm pretty sure it isn't that."

"How long will she stay?"

"No idea. I'm hoping at least a week. Her friend Amos needs some looking after and until he's too ill – if and when that happens – I hope she may stay. But she runs a bar in the West End and I doubt she'll want to be away for too time. Her staff are great and I'm pretty sure they'll not let her down, but you two know better than most what it's like running your own hospitality business."

Both women nod in unison. Mum says, "Oh goodness me, yes. Pritti and I try to make sure at least one of us is around or we'd feel the place was falling apart."

"What about Dad?" We'd barely mentioned him last night beyond Mum saying he was at a meeting in Lymington. He still hasn't appeared so far today. Another look is exchanged between the women.

Speaking slowly Mum says, "Well, I won't be disloyal, but let's just say his mind is... elsewhere right now."

Pritti claps her hands, a sign of mild impatience. "Come Vee, tell the boy. He ought to know."

"What's the silly old sod done now?" I say.

"Now, Harold, don't be rude about your Father. He's become a stalwart of the local Conservative Association and, well, he's hoping to stand as a councillor. He's become very passionate about local politics."

"Dad? You haven't remarried have you, Mum? Because the last time I checked he was the last person to champion a cause."

"You'd be surprised. I'm very proud of him, even if... even if I'm not so sure I agree with his ideas."

"I take it his version of being a good Tory is to reintroduce transportation for the crime of watching ITV and to have the unemployed resolutely birched for not having a job?"

"It's really not funny. He is very anti-immigration and, well, he's said a few things that have caused some upset locally."

Mrs Ohja has become rather fascinated by the sink.

"When you say 'locally,' do you mean here?"

"He suggested that Papaji move into a room at Hemingways rather than live here without contributing."

"Bloody hell, Mum. It was only because of Papaji that he didn't go bonkers and do something stupid when the B&B nearly folded. Has he forgotten all that?"

"He just gets a little too passionate about things now and again, that's all."

"Maybe I should have a word?"

Mrs Ohja rubs my arm, "Or maybe you should let things lie for now, eh? We will work this through."

I pull her into a hug and then Mum. Both woman respond as I'd hoped. I say, "Just as long as he stays put, okay, because if there's any suggestion of Papaji having to go then I will be down here like a shot."

"Just like his Father, eh Pritti?"

Mrs Ohja pinches my cheek. "Oh completely Vee, completely."

I kiss them both on the tops of their heads. "Bloody women."

Mrs Ohja lifts the kettle and begins to make more tea. "I'll see what I can do with that young woman. I wouldn't be surprised if she has a dietary problem. We will experiment, Vee. Yes?"

Mum nods, giving me a sideways glance; we both understand that involving her directly in any kitchen capacity is more likely to cause than eradicate dietary problems.

When Penny arrives – without Amos – at about one, there is a lot of smiling and talking. It may be because Mum is close to becoming a grandmother for the second time, but Mrs Ohja is clearly intent on sharing the spotlight.

About Amos, Penny says, "He's really not too good today. He wanted to come but we decided it was best to leave it for a few days. He'll be along soon, I hope." Her smile for the two older women is genuine enough, but I can tell there's more there than meets the eye. Since they have now moved onto a discussion about the imminent birth, details of which I really can't quite stomach, I leave them to it and go for a walk around the grounds. It's inevitable I find myself walking up to the bungalow where Sven lived. In the back garden is a swing where I had my first sexual encounter with Natalie one hot July evening in 1976. That didn't end well. What is up with her? If—

"Halloooo."

"Christ, Mr Jepson. Charlie. Why do you have to do that? You'll give me a heart attack."

He joins me on the swing, staring at the house. "Do you remember that party, Harry? Back when you worked at the hotel?"

God, he never saw me getting frisky with Natalie, did he? No, he couldn't have.

"My wife came onto you. Do you recall? She wore that white sheer dress and no underwear. I saw her playing with you out here. I was furious with both of you. I didn't realise what a temper I had back then. I did some awful things. Stupid things. Monica is a good woman and I never really realised. And you were barely more than a child. You probably didn't understand."

For my part I can't get the memory of Monica Jepson's rivet-like nipples out of my head. She was indeed quite something.

"She forgave me a long time ago by the way. She told me one thing, though." He turns and faces me. "She said you feared I might be your Father." His stare is intense.

Oh Christ, why now? "How did you know to come here? To find me?"

"I misunderstood what you said. I thought you were coming down this weekend with Stephen, but I understand from Dina that it's next week."

"Dina? Where is she? I tried to speak to her."

"She drove us. She's up at the house now. She said she can't stay long – she has to set off for Cheltenham."

"Oh shit. Look, don't go away. I'll be back in a jiffy. Okay?"

I need to catch Dina while I can but I really do want to finish this with Jepson.

Dina's car is outside the main house. If in doubt, head for the kitchen. Sure enough everyone is there, including a bleary-eyed Dad. "Harry my boy, good to see you. Hope you voted?"

"Monster Raving Loony Party as per your instructions. Dina, can we have a quick word?" Penny is sitting at the table and she fires me a warning look.

Dina nods and we head out front and into the woods that lie away beyond the manicured lawn, still set up for croquet. "I got the messages but I was too busy."

"Have you spoken to Penny?" I ask.

"Penny? About what?" She laughs sourly. "Being a Mother? Oh yes, I'm so very good at that."

"You are but… stop changing the subject. Magda."

"What about her? She's made her decision to go off with the Americans."

I stare at her profile, wondering what I should say.

Abruptly she turns and hugs me, which is still something of a novelty between us. "Don't worry, she knows what she's doing. I probably shouldn't say, but since I involved you…" She pauses, apparently struggling with what she's about to say. "Oh, bugger it. I heard the Americans have taken over her handling and I expect she's already on her way to Leipzig under their care. It's been made completely plain to me that while I did my best, I should now back off if I know what's good for my career. Yesterday afternoon I was told to pack up and head back to Cheltenham. It seems I need more training and some desk work."

"She's in Leipzig?"

"As far as I know, yes. I failed her but there's only so much someone of my rank can do. I have been assured she will be looked after but, well, I'll never know now. I've said enough. Just forget about it, okay?"

"But what if—"

She squeezes her eyes tight shut. "Can we talk about something else please?" She smiles at last. "At least I will be able to come down next weekend and spend some time with you, Penny and George. I've decided to let him go to school here. He's so settled. Mum's suggested I use Sven's bungalow as a base for weekends."

"You'll go round the effing bend."

"Sometimes that is the best option and it's time I took motherhood a bit more seriously. If this partnership stuff doesn't work out for you, you could always move here and take an apartment in the main house."

"That would last about three weeks and then I'd murder Dad and off I'd go again, running from then law. Speaking of which, I saw Jan Kruis again. He's still investigating the death of a partner at my office. Remind me to tell you about that."

"Before you do, just let me say that Jan and I met and we're definitely over, okay? I don't need those sorts of complications right now. So spill. What's this death in service mystery?"

"Oh, it's a great… shit – Jepson."

"Charlie? He's down here, you know. I brought him with me."

"I saw him. He thought Stephen would be here, but that's next weekend."

"Do Mum and Dad know?"

"Not yet."

"They'll love that."

"Look, I need to have a word with Jepson. Are you staying long?"

Dina checks her watch. "Too late. He told me he was off to meet up with Mr Hemingway for lunch. They were close once. You can catch him later, maybe. He's not said what his plans are. He never does."

"Oh buggeration. It's surreal, you know, how he keeps popping up everywhere? I know you've used him as a messenger, but how do you get in contact with him?"

"Same as with you. He's just there when I need him. I heard he had some sort of mystical experience on a retreat. Found God and developed special powers or something. Sounds rubbish but it's very strange. Anyway, your mystery death…?"

"Oh right. Well, this partner died at his desk. I found his body. He was in a dress and looked like he'd been buggered. Turns out he may have been drugged and then had a heart attack. The senior partner was his lover and there are these incriminating pictures that have reached the cops. There's a chance they might make the press. Right now with the government handing out all this privatisation work, the last thing we need are salacious headlines about senior staff. It looks likely that Miles Tupps – remember him? – and his latest backer Piotr Princip—"

"Now there's a crook."

I stare at my sister. "Why does an MI5 operative say that? What do you know that I'd like to know but probably shouldn't ask?"

"He's one of those names you hear mentioned. Nothing specific that I know of but then again there are rumours about all sorts of public figures. Maybe a whisper that links them to the secret services or a backer of some IRA affiliate or a sympathiser with the USSR. The more respected, the greater the risk…" she says cynically. "As one of my mentors said, the sooner the knighthood the bigger the blackmail…"

"I have no idea how all this works."

"It's not difficult. Let's say he's well known, moves in what are called the right circles but he also has contacts with some of the less acceptable faces in society, mostly in his past. Just the right mix makes him both seen as being grounded and having an interesting history. He will avoid the risk of being suspected as 'too good to be true' so conversely he's more respectable than those with an impeccable past. But also that someone may be incredibly useful to us. Because he's known not to be squeaky clean there's no real mileage in pointing it out so he can float around places where people will say, "Oh that's just Piotr," like he's a bit of a scallywag, whereas if it's someone else with a whiter than white rep the tabloids would make a meal out of it of any dodgy connections. Remember how Sir Penshaw was flayed in the red tops for being found dead as a result of some weird sex game gone wrong? And taking part in illegal gambling? Piotr used that club as well, yet no one bats an eyelid. Of course, if he really does do something wrong then no one saves him but while he keeps floating along like a buoyant little turd, he's fine."

"Goodness, so much deep-seated hypocrisy."

"Democracies depend on hypocrisy to keep going; you can't keep all the bad guys out by the rule of law, Harry. The end truly justifies the means. Western democracies are mostly ruled by the consent of the people but there are times when that consent has to be guided. Look, watch out if you're getting close to Princip, okay? It won't end well as he does have friends in high places."

"And does your radar extend to his son?"

"Nope, I didn't know he had any offspring. Probably completely corrupted or completely disgusted. Like Sven. How is Princip involved anyway?"

"I don't know that he is, but there's some sort of long-term grudge against the senior partner, not that I know the details. I'm doing my best to find out – using Stephen incidentally – but I don't expect I'll prove anything. It's a sod really."

"Stephen McNoble? Since when did you and he work together?

"These are strange times."

"Tell me about it."

"God, we sound like two old geezers. Come and give me a hug."

She does, nestling into my shoulder. "There was a time when this would have made you gag."

"As I said, strange times."

She pulls away. "I've promised to go and see Jim and George and I need to get a move on. Love to Penny and hopefully see you next weekend."

She wanders towards her car. She's taller than I remember – probably the heels – and is quite a glamorous woman these days. I just wish her life was more settled. Shame about Jan Kruis. He would have been good for her.

# Monday, 12th October 1987

## *Chapter Eighty*

Back in London I feel good about myself as I cycle to the office, which is truly strange given all that's going on in my life just now. The weather is hardly conducive to the mood either; it's intermittently wet and mild – Mum would call it mildewy. A lorry has shed its load near the Imperial War Museum and the traffic is clogged and the drivers are fractious. As I sail past two cars with the drivers hanging out of the windows, red-faced and remonstrating with the other, I feel rather smug. Then I realise one is Mervin Toogood and I feel especially clever at avoiding such a self-defeating mode of commuting. I wonder if MacThing and Crispin have spoken. Having had three days away from work followed by an out of body surreal weekend it feels like I'm returning not so much from a break as a previous life.

It is only as I approach the slope up to Blackfriars Bridge, an incremental incline that on windy days eats away at your energy and momentum like dry rot at a wooden building, that I remember the partners are going to meet this week to thin out the candidate list. If Greg is to be believed, and increasingly I think he is, the 'cull' – on Friday morning – will leave only those in the paddock whose chances are better than 50-50. The only reasons why the next vote – on Monday evening 19th October – on those remaining runners shouldn't go in their favour is if some last-minute disaster pops up – like a rogue turd in a sink for instance. It's an historic anomaly, this need for a second vote, and was originally to allow for 'mature reflection' to ensure that if anyone has a concern that they don't feel capable of raising in the open meeting, they can raise separately with the Senior Partner, or, in his absence, a member of the senior management team who will then 'take soundings' to see if the worry has merit or if it can be dismissed prior to the meeting. I still harbour hope – I don't know why, maybe the slightly encouraging comment from Crout rather than the damming negativity from Frank – but I'm prepared for the call on Friday to be told the vote went against me and I'm already out. In anticipation, I've got John Thomas' number to invite him and Dobbin to my parents for the weekend, as planned with Zenda but also to begin discussions of an alternative career path. I just know I'm going to need it.

Penny has made me promise to book a holiday for Friday – she has this thing about watching the Farming programme on Sunday morning TV and they predicted strong winds for the weekend. "I don't want us driving down with all the Friday night rush and branches flying everywhere, not with me like a space hopper. Can we go on Thursday and make a long weekend of it?" She adds, "And that may be the only way we can get Amos there. I'm off to see him again today and I'll be able to update you later on."

"Where is he? You've not said."

"He's fine. Staying with a friend, that's all."

Our relationship has reached that fine-tuned stage where she says this last sentence in a way that implies, 'and don't ask about the friend, okay?' which is fine by me as I need to get on with my day. As for the holiday, well okay, she's a bit of a wuss, but I have a few spare days so why not? It'll be good to be out of the office when word spreads that I've not made the shortlist. I've never been good with pity, especially when it's aimed at me.

At my desk there's a message from Stephen McNoble. He wants a word about Gloria. I have Chloe call him back; we will meet in the Bow Tavern off Bow Lane at lunchtime. Erica isn't at her desk when I arrive but appears at 10.30, flushed and clutching two fat files. "You feeling any better?"

"Thanks, yes. Anything happen?"

"Mr Toogood got wind of the problem with his claim."

"Did he demand my head on a platter?"

"No, he went looking for Crispin's."

"And?"

She won't meet my eye. "I think he wants to explain himself."

"Okay. Do you now if the Senior Partner had a word?"

"Mr Crout? Isn't he unwell?"

I don't press the subject.

She's still hovering. When I smile, assuming she'll take the hint and go away, she says, "And Greg was looking for you on Friday."

"And how was he looking?"

She effects a sheepish grin. "A bit like Mr Toogood."

I manage a nod, not trusting myself to speak.

"Crispin stepped in on a meeting with Mr Tupps."

"I hadn't heard of any meeting."

"It was last minute. Greg asked him to go along."

Just then Chloe interrupts to remind me of a meeting with Doringo about the mortgage business. Greg and Crispin will have to wait.

The update is short and well-managed; it's really prep for tomorrow's full meeting. Nothing for me to do but it does remind me I've heard nothing from Chuck Streib for some time. He must be aware that Magda has moved out although who knows if he has linked it to Natalie's absence. The fact he's not threatening me is some sort of comfort, but he'll be in tomorrow's meeting so any relief on that front will be short-lived.

By the time I've finished I grab my jacket and head out to meet Stephen for lunch. When I arrive he looks serious, pained almost. "That woman Gloria, she's not to blame."

It is my turn to frown. "She has to have known what's going on. Did she have any photos?"

He nods. "Yes. Graphic too."

"Graphic? How did she get them printed? Oh, of course. Her friend works at Boots."

"It's her sister."

"Sister?"

"Tina Eagle. Her younger sister."

"Okay. Fine. It sort of explains why they might work together, but you just said she's not to blame."

He looks irritated. "I think Tupps is blackmailing her."

"But... but I thought she was his, you know, girlfriend?"

He shakes his head. "She said she was but I didn't believe her. Not now, anyway. Maybe once. She's protecting her sister from being ruined by Tupps. I don't know their background but Tupps is behind setting up that man Tritewell. That was the main aim of this – the scandal it would cause. It seems that involving you might have been a bonus to him."

"Did she say if Princip is involved?"

"No. The name meant nothing except in so far as it links to the Princips and this Church."

"Church? You've lost me."

"I've fixed to see her – Gloria, I mean – again. Me turning up and asking about the photos scared her witless, so I took a chance and said I was working with you. She seemed relieved and terrified in equal measures."

"When?" My heart is pounding at the thought that she might even now be warning off Tupps and Princip.

He manages a smile. "Who'd have thought of us working this through together, eh? I'll let you know when later on today."

"Thanks. This is really helpful. I think. In other news, I saw your Father again. He's already in Hampshire and knows we will be down at the weekend. Can you make it? I'm pretty sure he wants to see you this time."

By way of reply he nods but doesn't say anything. He orders a salad, which he barely touches and scuttles off before I can suggest a coffee. He looks very worried about something.

Back at my desk, I'm finding it difficult to concentrate. I manage to get hold of John Thomas and invite him for the weekend. I leave a message with Dobbin, reminding him of the invite and suggesting he and John come together on Friday in Dobbin's new car – a treat to himself he said, some fancy BMW thing.

I circle the floors a couple of times, hoping to catch Greg and Crispin but they are both away from their desks and I leave none the wiser about how things stand.

## *Chapter Eighty-One*

Penny has made me a stew for dinner. She looks flushed and rather damp about the temples. The smell is wonderful. When I've dumped my cycling jacket and less than fragrant trainers I head for the kitchen and a glass of wine. We have agreed on a rule – one glass every other night so as not to make her too jealous. She is wearing a silk kimono her Mother gave her years ago and is barefooted.

"You been washing your feet?" I struggle with the cork, which is rather too dry to be a good sign.

She turns slowly; the kimono is undone and she is naked underneath. Her rounded belly forces the material to flap away from her breasts and there is a fluff of pubic hair just visible. With a sly grin she manages to lift a foot and put it on the nearest chair. "If you're offering."

I meet her gaze. "What brought this on?" I concentrate on the wine, at least mostly.

"I had another session with Ida and her crew today. We did this set with me naked, one hand here," she turns sideways and covers her breasts making a poor job of hiding her nipples, "and one here," the other slips between her legs and covers her pubes. "Everyone said I was very sexy." She lids her eyes and mimes what is probably meant to be a sultry pout but I can't help but feel horrified. They are setting her up.

Suddenly she is in fits of giggles. She ties up the kimono and comes over to me. "God, your face. I didn't believe Dina when she told me she'd a copy of that old video I made."

I'm speechless but manage a squeaky, "She told you? Why did she mention that?"

Penny holds my face and seeks out my gaze. "She apologized for putting you through things for Magda. The tape? I made this silly soft porn thing, not that there was any sex, not even simulated, just a bit of oily cavorting. I'm proud of it, in fact. I liked my body then. Real curves. You liked it too if I recall. Dina thought I should know what she'd done and why, okay?"

"When did she tell you?"

Penny looks uncertain. "At your parents? In the kitchen. Does it matter?"

Something is bugging me, but I can't think what. "No, not really I suppose."

"I told them about it at the shoot and everyone thought it a hoot. They're very professional and this isn't their thing, okay? And anyway, if someone showed my parents, Dad would have a heart attack and Mum would tell me to go for it. Do not worry your pretty little head. Go on, sit down and drink your wine and tell me about your day. And after, assuming I've not shocked the bejeebers out of you, you can have a bath and we'll see if you can't loosen up this bloody child."

# Tuesday, 13th October 1987

## *Chapter Eighty-Two*

If I'm being honest I've been dreading the meeting. I've convinced myself, since I handed Magda to Grant and Dina said the Americans were in charge of her, that either the CIA and Chuck know what's happened with Magda and will jump on her sometime soon or, if they don't, they would have been all over me about what I know. But this silence is unnerving. The urge to call Grant to check everything is okay is becoming overwhelming but what if they are bugging my phone? And now I'm meeting him, I'm certain I'll inevitably give myself away.

There is no way to avoid it though, so at 10.20 I take the stairs to the fourth floor and head for the meeting room. This one is really made to hold eight people, but Doringo can never host a meeting with less than 12, or so it seems, and every chair is taken. When I appear his articled clerk – Albert Twencross, a spotty chap from Liverpool who was once in a band that went on to have a number 20 hit after he left; such is his fame – disappears to try to find me a seat. The result is a lot of shuffling and people having to lean backwards and forwards when they come to speak.

To be fair to Doringo, he understands his brief and commands it well. Erica has already contributed the summary of our research into the Land Registry's requirements and an outline of some of the technical issues around transferring the legal and beneficial interests in the mortgage pool – I'm only needed to deal with strategy, which they've begun to discuss. Chuck is seated about four people to my right. He's in shirt sleeves with a pad in front of him. He doesn't acknowledge me as I enter and continues to discuss some point on bond structures that goes way above my head.

For an hour or so the meeting works its way through a detailed agenda and at just before midday Albert summarises what has been agreed and the next steps. There are lots of them. He completes his list and looks at Doringo.

"Okay. So that's it for today, Chuck. We'll have the regulator's initial views by next week I hope and have a first draft of the suite of documents available for a first pass on Wednesday of next week. Have you decided who is going to be running it from here?"

My ears are obviously blocked or something, but I must be the only one since no one else jumps or starts or makes any movement that suggests surprise.

Chuck sniffs, "It'll be a Vice-President for now. Dolores Sanchez is due this Friday and I'll fix for her to meet you guys on Monday or Tuesday."

I'm pleased to see a frown on both Doringo's and Albert's faces. "Friday?" Doringo sounds concerned. "How will that work? If you're going at the weekend? We need to have a proper handover, Chuck."

He sounds unconcerned, breezy almost. "I gotta get back. Just the way it is. There's some real important business that means I have to be on the East Coast come Monday without fail. Meantime she's up to speed, okay? And I'll be back by the end of the week. Just need to bury a problem or two and then I can refocus on this."

Doringo laughs. "I thought you people had other people to bury your problems, Chuck?"

Does he glance my way?

I'm sure he must as he says, "Some need a little personal attention now and again."

The meeting begins to break up, but Chuck stays in his seat re-reading something in front of him.

I'm desperately hoping he'll go but in the end I have no excuse but to stand and move down the table opposite him.

Albert has a mountain of papers he is gathering and Erica is waiting for me. I manage a cough and say, "Hope you sort things out, okay?"

He nods, not looking up. Then he smiles and turns to me, "Sorry Harry, I wanted to tell you. It's been mad. You seen Natalie? Cindy said family but I guessed it's that friend Amos. I wanted to tell her that I'll be away for two weeks or so. I'll be running around for the rest of this week so might miss her. Can you pass on my thanks for all the help so far?"

"Sure. Of course. When are you off?"

"Late Friday. And thanks Harry. You've been amazing. I really appreciate everything – really everything – you've done." He bends back to his notes and it's like I'm dismissed.

As Erica and I climb the stairs to our floor she says, "Are you all right? You look rather ill." After a rather heavy silence she adds, "Did you speak to Crispin?"

"No. And I think everything is great, but it might just be absolutely awful."

"Sometimes Harry," she pulls open the door to our floor, "you are as clear as mud."

I let her go. That clear? I'm doing better than I think.

## *Chapter Eighty-Three*

It's about 2.00 by the time I am aware that Crispin is back in his room. He's recently learnt how to use his conference phone – the squawk box as he calls it – but it does mean that at times we all share his calls.

Since I'm not due to be in my next meeting for an hour I go and sit opposite him while he explains to some misbegotten client why the lease he's acquired is the worst possible thing in the known universe. The call ends with the client absolutely eating out of Crispin's hand. As the light goes out on the phone he looks over at me and grins. "You really tried to screw Greg, didn't you?"

"No. It wasn't like that. What's he said?"

"He just said you were an unrepeatable word that rhymes with hunt, but that he'd spoken to Frank and things were settled now. I guess you two can sort it out. Anyway, what can I do for you?"

"Caldera. Erica suggested you had spoken to Toogood. Sorry I wasn't around to deal with him."

"No problem. It's all in hand." His smile stays put but he is clearly not offering any more details.

"You going to explain?"

"I'm a bit busy. The client is pleased, so that's good."

"What about Mervin?"

"Ah, yes, well there is that. I think he might be best placed to explain."

"Explain? Explain what?"

"Why he wants to see you leave."

Shit. "Come on, I sorted out this mess so—"

His expression darkens. "You? Erica's fabulous research and Gerry's discussions with Mr Melpot have led to a plan that will give Caldera a real prospect of success at planning and he is confident the financiers will be happy. Mervin, it is fair to say, isn't… but he is a commercial lawyer. He grasps that Caldera will progress without his needing to intervene and the Thompson scheme probably won't. He and Gerry have spoken and agreed to put their previous differences to one side."

"It's Gerry, is it? It was Mr MacThing last week."

"Come on, Harry. You needlessly got Mervin's hopes up then undermined them. You might have ruined the relationship with the client too."

"What?"

Crispin sighs. "We think you've let this partnership ambition cloud your judgement."

"We?" I can't hide – I don't want to hide – the sneer in my voice.

"I think I've said enough. If you need more then maybe you should talk to Frank. He's still upset by Turdgate."

"Oh, drop it. That was—"

"He's wondered out loud whether in fact it might have been you who left the turd when Cynthia got the blame."

"But she admitted it!"

"Did she? That's the story, but who actually spoke to her about it?"

"That's ridiculous."

"I must get on. If you—"

I lean over his desk so he has to sway back. "What. The. Fuck. Is. Toogood. Saying?"

He looks rather pale, which is pleasing. "As far as I understand it he believes you were trying to blackmail him into getting an unfair advantage."

"And what's that mean?"

"He is of the view you wanted to use his mistaken belief in his entitlement and his negotiations to concoct a story about miscon—"

"You know what he did was wrong. You said it yourself."

"He's a partner, Harry. One of the management group. You can't go around threatening him and hoping to use your influence with the Senior Partner to get a partnership by the back door."

It's my turn to sway back. "That's insane."

He blows out his cheeks. Then he starts counting on his fingers, "One, you tried to scupper my relationship with the client when you found out about the issue with the Lordship. Two, you didn't warn me about the financing deadline and that way you got control of the files. Three, you then told Chris about them so Mervin would feel he had to see for himself what the problem was with his title and then hid the research Erica did so he'd make a fool of himself with the client. Four, that then looks like he is using confidential information for his own gain whereas he was trying to understand if you were in fact using your knowledge of his conveyancing to improve your position with the client and thus look a better candidate for partnership. Five, you tried to undermine Greg by suggesting he was involved in Barry's death—"

"Wait. What's that got to do with Caldera?"

"It shows you'll do anything to get this partnership. At least that's what Frank thinks. Why don't you ask him?"

My head is spinning and I stagger away. This is truly a Comedy of Errors. Mostly mine to be fair. Whatever happened to Crout's word?

Outside his room, I hesitate. I don't know where to go or what to do. I know I tried to help and handed the solution to Crispin because I thought he ought to sort it out, having felt a little guilty – maybe very guilty in truth – about not telling him the deadline for the refinancing was approaching. But to end up with Crispin smelling of roses, a happy client and Toogood determined to ruin me is not what I expected out of all this.

Why don't good news and bad news attract each other – like opposites attracting? Frank appears from his room, sees me and marches down the corridor. "Harry, a minute of your time." Here we go. It's that 'Perkins we need a futile sacrifice' moment and I'm to be left in a locked office with a loaded revolver in the drawer to do the decent thing.

Before explaining what he wants, he puts his head round Crispin's door, "I just had a very satisfied client on the line. Mr MacThing. Odd name, but there you go. Said you'd done a fine job and had smoothed things over with Mervin. So well done." He looks at me but is still talking to Crispin, "Always an excellent idea to keep the firm's good name front and centre with clients like him."

After some modest acceptance of the compliments by Crispin, Frank pulls Crispin's door shut and looks at me. "We need a word. Sebastian will be back on Thursday and has suggested we all get together ahead of the first vote on Friday. Are you free?"

"Yes. Yes, of course."

He looks like he wants to say something more but after chewing his bottom lip for a moment he simply nods once and turns away. I watch him disappear down the corridor with a growing sense of imminent disaster.

Oh shit.

# Wednesday, 14th October 1987

## *Chapter Eighty-Four*

Last night Penny told me Grant had rung. He told her that everything is going okay. I'm still convinced the CIA will descend on us and spirit us away to some disused industrial building and wire my testicles to the National Grid while tickling Penny's feet. For a brief moment I wonder if they are running Grant or if Natalie is working for Chuck in some way and I've been duped. Again. I haven't told Penny about my conversation with Dina – I don't know why but something doesn't add up. Anyway, she was told that the fake passports will be ready on Friday afternoon or Saturday morning and he will personally put Magda on the Cherbourg ferry on the afternoon sailing on Saturday, from where she can catch a train to Paris and on to Dusseldorf and then get a coach into East Germany. He's organised the train tickets and everything, although I'm beginning to wonder what this is going to cost me. He says that Magda is happy with everything and a bit nervy but basically okay.

In other news, Amos is really not well and she's been told by the friend who's caring for him that it may not be wise to take him with us on Thursday. She says they're looking into how to do it safely, because he's now desperate to go.

In truth I'm happy to leave that to her what with everything else that's going on. As I leave for the office she frowns. "You look really tense. You going to be okay to get away tomorrow?"

I look at her wide soft brown eyes. What have I to worry about? The partnership and Frank's concern over my scatological propensities; Mervin's plans to have me for blackmail; the ongoing worries about Gloria and Barry and Miles and how that might unravel; Greg's obvious determination to avoid speaking to me – he's planning to shaft me, I'm certain of it. I smile and say, "No, I'm fine. Everything's fine."

"This partnership decision, I expect?" She kisses me. "I'll still love you whatever way it goes."

And with that she pushes me out of the front door. It works. I smile a proper smile. Not much but just enough to get me moving.

I managed to speak to Mr Crout's secretary – she's the only person who has actually been nice to me this week, or so it seems – and she told me he has spoken to the police. They haven't asked to see me again so I'm taking that as a good sign, too. After all, he was in Barry's room when I turned up so he can vouch for me. However, I really do want to know what's been going on and why, so when Chloe tells me Stephen McNoble has fixed up a meeting – she doesn't say who with but it has to be Gloria – I head out. Unlike Greg, McNoble's venue of choice is a pub, the Admiral Pensive, halfway down Haircutter Lane that wends a tortured path to the river from behind Cannon Street. The salon bar is the very definition of snug. McNoble is already there with Gloria who jumps when I enter.

After I fetch us both pints and her a gin and orange and Stephen's scared away a hopeful punter attracted by the cavernous cleavage on display, he pulls out an envelope, lays it on the table and puts a hand on top. "Have a look."

Gloria's hands can't keep still. She says, "I never meant to hurt you, Harry."

I ignore her and open the envelope. There are about 20 pictures, some involving Crout and Tritewell. The only way to describe the images is that they are compromising. And graphic. Especially graphic. They make the ones I've seen look like innocent family snaps.

"Shit." I look at her then. "How did you get these? Did you take them?"

She looks away. "Miles had the film. Tina printed them at Boots, when no one was around."

I shake my head, trying to free up something that makes sense. Nothing works. When I look at her again she starts talking, fast and in broken phrases.

"I thought he and I... We were... I thought we had something but he... He found out about Tina... he said... she couldn't..." She says this like it explains everything.

"Tina? She's your sister? What about her?"

She looks at Stephen, confused. "Didn't you explain?"

McNoble tugs at his ear. "You can."

"No, I can't." She shakes her head hard.

He looks irritated and goes on. "Tupps is blackmailing them. Their old man is this lay preacher or something and he's put the fear of all wotsits into Tina – hell and eternal damnation – if she goes the way of Sodom and Gomorrah." I must look confused because he adds, "She's a dyke, yeah?"

"She's gay?"

Gloria winces. "I hate that expression. She's so confused, poor thing. They gave up on me – I couldn't get out quickly enough – but Tina believes. She's very devout. She hates the way she is, wants to have some sort of medical intervention to save her. I don't like it but she's so determined. If Father found out she'd do something stupid. She believes his every word. I told Miles. I thought he'd help me, sort things out. He said he would but… Oh what have I done?"

"He's your boyfriend? I thought he was married and living in Leeds or Newcastle?"

She looks pained. "He is but he spends a lot of time in London on business. He told me we'd be together but… I'm such a fool."

So much for my plans to get rid of him. Yep, that worked well. "Okay, but how does this lead to Newe Waters and these photos?"

Stephen makes an impatient noise. "From the start, okay?"

She nods. "It was early on. I'd known him a while but we were just friends. Then Mr Princip appeared and I told Miles how I knew him."

"Greg?"

"No, his Father. He's really nice, generous. He's been a good man at the Church. Where my Father preaches, where Tina goes."

"Okay." Things are a little clearer.

Stephen finishes his pint and sighs. "I'll get us another drink."

Gloria continues, "Mr Princip is a patron of the Church where my family have been members for years. He's helped Father. I was surprised to see him at the club; I didn't know he knew Miles. A short while later and Miles suggested I applied for the receptionist's job at the firm. I said you were working there and that made him even more interested. After that we became close. It all seemed to be going so well."

"Has Greg been giving you instructions? About the photos?"

"No. Not at all. Greg's a good man. Why do you think Greg is involved? I thought you were friends?"

So did I. I wave her on.

"No, it's Miles. After a time, he asked me to get close to Mr Tritewell." She looks down. "I'm good at that. It was always Barry he was interested in."

"Did you know why?"

"No. I told him I didn't want to." She shakes her head vigorously but soon stops. "But he made it clear I had to. Because… because of Tina."

"He blackmailed you?"

It takes her a while to nod. She seems reluctant to say any more. Stephen has been watching us. He taps the back of her hand and prompts her. "The photos."

She swallows and picks up her glass before putting it down without touching it. She looks very pale. "Miles told me I needed to find out about Barry and Mr Crout. I didn't understand but eventually Barry and I... he and I..." She looks mortified.

I look at Stephen, not sure what to do. I really don't want to hurt or upset her any more than she already is. Stephen sighs. "You had an affair, didn't you?"

She looks furious. "No, nothing like that. I... He..." Then she collapses back. "Miles wanted me to. Insisted. But he just wanted to talk. One afternoon I got him drunk and he told me he liked to dress up in women's clothes. He told me about him and Mr Crout. Miles knew something but not that. Barry showed me the dress. He tried on a pair of my heels." She laughs briefly at some memory. "He said he was an Ugly Sister because he couldn't get them on." She stumbles momentarily and then picks up the thread again. "Miles wanted me to get him to dress up, in the office and he'd then photograph him. Miles took these. I don't know how he got them I let him into the office a few times. I... Oh god Harry, I'm such a fool."

"Come on, he was blackmailing you. It's not your fault. It..." I stop. She's almost shaking her head off.

"It's so easy to let people in when you're on reception. They can come and go via the stairs to the basement car park. They come to the front and you give them a few minutes, until the coast is clear and then open the fire door to the rear staircase. After that they have the run of the place."

"Did you know what he planned to do with the photos?"

"No. When I saw them, I guessed he wanted to embarrass Barry, or Mr Crout or the Firm. I never realised he planned to involve you. That was a total shock."

I look at Stephen who shrugs. I do my best to work out what he had in mind. "I suppose he might have planned to have me deliver the images and somehow implicate me. If Tritewell or Crout thought I was involved it would ruin my hopes too."

"He hates you, doesn't he?"

"Oh you'd better believe it. But then Barry dies before it pans out and after that it's a case of damage limitation. If you tell the police then…" Her horrified expression tells me what she thinks about that. "You think he'll still tell your Dad about Tina?"

She nods, not exactly happily. "Will you tell them?"

"I don't know. I don't see why Miles should get away with this. What will you do about Tina?"

"We'll sort something out." She sounds defiant but looks defeated.

"Did Tina know what was in the packet? When she swapped it with mine?"

Gloria shrugs her shoulders. "She printed them. At work. She had to. But I don't know if she knew what was in the packet she gave you."

My brain is working overtime. "Did you tell him I was going on holiday?"

She nods. If her chin is any lower it will pierce her chest bone. "I told him you always go straight to Boots to get your holiday snaps developed. You probably don't remember me asking you when you came back. I told Tina and she was ready for you."

Very clever. "And your church. Greg goes there too, doesn't he? That's how he knows Tina."

She nods.

"And you're sure Greg isn't involved in this? With Miles? He was there when Tina handed over the pictures. Was that coincidence?"

She's momentarily very angry. "He's a good man. Why are you so against him? He's a stalwart of the church, like his father, but his father is a cold man. Greg is lovely. He's been good to Tina. He… I think he understands about her, but I'm not sure there's much he can do."

Stephen stands and looks like he wants to leave. "I need to get on. What are you going to do, Harry?"

I look at Gloria. "You swapped the photos in my desk, didn't you? Why?"

"Miles told me to. He wanted a set with your prints on them. That's why the packet you picked up only had a few prints in it. He didn't say why but I suppose it was for the police. He wanted me to give you the really awful ones but I couldn't do that. That's why I still have those." She indicates the envelope on the table. "I didn't want to, Harry. You must believe me."

"I do. And has he got the negatives and other prints?"

"I don't think so. Other than then one's you had that I swapped and gave to him."

"They're with the police. He sent them to them anonymously."

"He's very nervous, Harry. Especially when we heard about Mr Crout trying to… you know?"

"Yeah, well. I doubt he's too worried. It's not in his nature. We will have to try and find a way to sort this out."

"You're going to help me? Me and Tina?"

"Of course. You're a victim too."

"You are such a nice man, Harry but I don't think there's anything that will help. Not while Miles can ruin Tina."

Is that a compliment? 'A nice man?' Oh well, I guess I'll take it. "Are they all the photos you've got?" I point at the envelope.

"I gave them all I had to him." She indicates Stephen. "He scared the living wotsits out of me, the shit." She manages a smile towards McNoble. "I'm pleased, really. It's been such a burden."

I sit totally still, trying to process all this. "Can Tina and your Father be reconciled?"

"Hell freezing over comes first, Harry." There's a tiny bit of the confident Gloria poking through in places.

"Would Greg help?"

She looks horrified. "I couldn't presume."

"No, but I could. Would you let me try?"

She looks doubtful.

"I'll not tell the police or Crout unless you say I can. But I think Greg's a good lad. Probably. If he knows about Tina, then I'm sure he will do what he can to help. He's very persuasive. He may know how to approach your Father."

"I don't know if he does. Know, that is. About Tina. It's just a guess."

"Is it okay if I try to find out?"

Eventually she nods.

Stephen, who has watched us both intently, looks at me when it's clear we're done. "What about Tupps? And Princip?" He glances at Gloria. "Senior."

"I think we have to let that play out. I'll tell Crout that Tupps has a set of pictures and he'll do what he needs to with the press to minimise any adverse publicity. I don't suppose Miles'll want to use them in case his role in all this comes out so careful management might sort out that side."

"Princip won't care, will he? It's his vendetta. He'll happily screw your firm and Crout."

"Vendetta?" Gloria looks from one of us to the other.

I wonder what I should say and then decide there's no point hiding anything now. "It's just rumours but there's ill-will between him and the firm. It goes a long way back. That's why I need to prepare Crout. But I haven't proof of Miles involvement unless you want me to say and I won't put you through that, okay? Unless you say I can."

She nods while Stephen looks disgusted. He says, "You're not letting him get away with this, are you?"

I smile. "That will always be the difference between us, Stephen." I push the pictures back across the table to him. "You keep them."

"Me? No, you're the noble one. You can decide what to do with them. But don't get caught with them if you want that partnership."

I raise my glass and chink Gloria's untouched glass on the table. "They'll be another partnership. Somewhere. Don't worry about me." Penny's smile of earlier comes back to me. Yes, we'll be okay, I think.

Stephen grabs the door handle but stops before pulling it open. "Christ, you really piss me off, Spittle. Where's you fucking spine?"

"Search me, Stephen. Miles Tupps is a client of the firm and no one believes me when I say he's a crook. I'm sure something will turn up."

This time he does pull open the door. "God save me from fucking optimists." The door bangs shut behind him.

"Yep. Hopeless." I swivel so I'm facing Gloria. "Other than warn Crout, I will talk to Greg. If he can help he will. And we need to get Tina some counselling. She can't go chasing after some stupid therapy that won't work."

Gloria looks unconvinced. "If Greg will help, he may be the only one to persuade her. She dotes on him. You know, like a big brother."

"He's a man of many parts. I think I should get to know my colleagues better." The photos are still on the table. "Will you take these Gloria?"

She leans away as if they'll burn her. "No. No way. Stephen's right. You decide. I want nothing more to do with them." She frowns at them. "Stupid." Then to me. "Give them to the cops, Mr Crout, whatever. Tina and me, we'll be okay."

"After I speak to Greg."

We part outside the pub; she kisses me on the cheek and hugs me but doesn't say anything. I walk slowly back to the office, clutching the envelope. Why does the mess always end up in my hands? Greg isn't about and his secretary doesn't know if he's coming back. I suppose it will have to keep until Monday. It's not going to change the next few days anyway.

# Thursday, 15th October 1987

## Chapter Eighty-Five

When, eventually, I reach my desk - I almost can't be bothered - I find a message telling me the meeting with Frank and Sebastian Crout is cancelled as Crout is still too unwell. I'm still staring at the note, wondering if I have the energy to go back home when the phone goes. It's Frank, sounding very tired. "I'm sorry about the meeting, but t doesn't really matter. Not now. I'll speak to you tomorrow. Or Monday." He says this as something of an afterthought. I don't bother to tell him I'll not be in the office tomorrow and, depending on the news probably Monday too.

I'm on my way out when Greg emerges from the lift. He smiles at me but looks rather frazzled. I'm about to move into the vacated lift when I stop. "Have you got a minute?"

"If it's about what you told Frank, then—"

"No, but I was wrong so sorry about that. I've told him. Crout too."

He turns to face me while I stick a foot to stop the lift door closing. Any moment now it will default to the basement. "It's about Gloria. On reception. And her sister Tina."

His eyes narrow. "What about them?"

"You all go to the same church and—"

He turns away. "What I do in my private time is my business, Harry."

"You can help them, you know."

Again he stops and half-turns. "Help?"

The lift has a distinct personality, sort of passive-aggressive in a mechanised way, and the doors are now bouncing against my foot, desperate to close. "Monday. Can we talk on Monday? It's important."

"What can I do?" He looks genuinely worried as the lift car gives an almighty shake and I withdraw my foot before the whole edifice explodes or eats itself or something. I know better than to choose a floor and let it deposit me in the car park.

As we descend, mortifyingly slowly (I'm half expecting Greg to beat me to the bottom) I have to wonder if I've done the right thing. What if he asks Tina on Sunday in front of her Father? Not that she'll know what he's on about.

Dobbin has been nagging me about the investments he wants me to take out to make the most of the highly volatile and hot market just now. He's even organised a loan, pending a re-mortgage of the house so I can maximise what I do. The forms have been on my desk for a week, but on the basis I might be unemployed next week I've signed them, his words ringing in my ears: 'I have a good feeling about these, Spittoon. You'll be amazed what they'll look like when the markets wake up on Monday.' Gloria organises the by-hand deliveries – we have an in-house courier who takes letters around the City at 10.00 and 3.00 every day – and I give her the envelope to put in the three o'clock bag. She gives me a feeble smile. No one else is around. "I spoke to Greg and I'm sure he will help."

She looks really hopeful. "You did? What did he say?"

"We're going to sort things out on Monday. It'll be—"

"He knows about Tina? Is it common knowledge? Did he say?"

"No, he didn't." Bugger I hate lying by omission, "but he's a good chap. He'll know how best to sort things out."

Another client arrives and prevents her giving me the third degree. I slip away, not at all sure this is going well.

I have agreed to collect Amos at 2.00 pm from an address in Putney. Penny has been talking to him and from what I can gather he's being well looked after but may not last long. Last night I voiced my rumbling fear that he should have proper end-of-life medical care. She smiled, I must say a little too cavalier for my liking, and said, "Oh don't fuss. It's all sorted." And when I asked how, she just waved away my questions.

The roads in Putney are awfully narrow and full of parked cars with a surfeit of BMWs such is the affluence. But when we pull up in Glencoe Terrace it's full of small terraced houses that were clearly made for poor and very short workers. It feels like a model village. "What number?"

"That one – 17. There."

I glance where she points, not sure how she can spot a house 50 yards ahead as being the right one. And then I see Jackie and realise she is waving at us. I do an emergency stop, which gets me a 'fucking moron' from Penny followed by a barking laugh. "Your face is a picture."

I'm fuming as I double park and get out. Both women are grinning manically and watching me. "I suppose the joke is on me. This is the 'friend' is it?"

Jackie walks round to my side and kisses me on the cheek. "I'm sorry, but this was a long time coming."

"Long time?" Then it dawns on me. "This wasn't just because of Amos? You knew each other before this?"

Jackie shakes her head and nods, a most confusing combination. "Five years, do you think Pen?"

"Five?!"

"When we split, when you went back to Penny, a mutual friend put us in touch. Penny and I needed to clear the air. For your sake."

"Me?" Why does it feel like I'm some sort of invalid and others are happily discussing my wellbeing without involving me?

"She didn't want me to resent the fact you'd gone back to her and she wanted to thank me for doing what she should have done in supporting you while you unravelled Sven's estate. All a bit of a sisterly soul searching."

"And this mutual friend? Natalie?"

Jackie shakes her head. "Dina."

"Dina! Shit. Who else is in on this conspiracy?" I look at Penny. "Is she part of your girls' drinking group?"

Penny nods. "There are about seven of us. Jackie fits right in."

"No wonder you never want me around when you get together." Back to Jackie. "And how did this come about?" I wave at the terrace of houses.

"Penny asked me to help him. Amos was on the verge of doing something stupid in hospital. This is where I live now. He's lovely, no hardship, but he could really do with that break." She lowers her voice. "I doubt he has long left." She shakes her shoulders and gives Penny a large hug and kiss. "If she lets her standards slip with you, I've told I'll be right in there."

Penny uses her bump to push Jackie away. "Hey, sister, that's not happening."

Jackie sticks out her tongue. How did they get to be so close without me knowing? "Penny was brilliant when I broke up with my ex. We never told you, well, because we knew you'd find it weird."

"It is weird. Horrid."

Penny holds me tightly. "You should be flattered that you have exquisite taste in women."

I'm not sure it's the flattery or the ego boost that softens the blow; why should it matter that they get on? The mood drops several degrees when we go to collect Amos. I have to carry him to the car. Jackie has a bundle of medication and takes an age to get him settled and tells me to take my time.

We're nearing Kew when Amos asks if Natalie will be around over the weekend. "Yes, and Magda if I can organise it. There are some other friends coming too. Dobbin, my old flat mate, his ex, Brenda, her Mother, another couple of friends from Law College by the name of John and Karen. Oh, and Dina hopes to be there on Saturday as well."

"Brilliant Harry. Thank you. A real party. Just what I want. I promise not to be a misery. Unless I snuff it." That causes him to laugh, which morphs into a cough and no one speaks for an age.

I turn on the radio that is full of contradictory messages about the weather. Some say a storm is coming and some say it will batter north France. Nothing is going to spoil our fun, I think. I need something good to happen this weekend.

## *Chapter Eighty-Six*

When I look at my watch it's just before midnight.

"What's that noise?" Penny sounds as awake as I feel.

"The wind. Sounds like the woods are exploding. I… shit."

There is the most enormous splintering noise. A light comes on in the hall and there are whispers outside.

"I'd better go and see what's happening. You try to sleep."

There's a groan and a whump of air as she sits up. "I need a pee." As Penny heads for the en-suite I head outside onto the landing. The voices are now downstairs, and I can see someone is standing by the front door as I turn to head down the main stairs. My parents' house is a grand New Forest Villa built in the 1920s. The west wing, added in the 1950s, is where the B&B rooms are; Mum and Dad used some of the Sven legacy to add en-suite bathrooms to each bedroom. Last night when we arrived the wind was picking up and there was a real buzz. Dobbin and John arrived late at about 10.00 which caused a bit of thing with Brenda who went to bed immediately – she, Karen and Zenda had already arrived when Penny, Jackie, Amos and I drove up about 4.00. Mum and Pritti Ohja were in their element, serving everyone tea and scones and then an enormous dinner in the kitchen. This is a huge room with a scrubbed pine table that must weigh a couple of tonnes in the centre around which we all easily sit. Dad, Asoka and Ravi had already left for the Conservative Club debate in New Milton where apparently Dad is speaking on the subject of reforming the rating system. Sounds like one of those topics that will never generate any interest.

Outside the house and across a rather splendid croquet lawn there are about 15 acres of woodland, and to one side is a line of larches that are probably what I heard. The person at the front door is Dobbin, already dressed for the weather, with Dad in some awful bright red silk pyjamas blocking the door. Mum is standing to one side, arms folded and glaring at all the late-night drama.

Dobbin sees me and gives me an exasperated look. "Will you please tell your Father to let me pass? I need to move the car." Dobbin has driven down in his new BMW, which he proudly showed off when he arrived, something that I suspect irritated Brenda and was part of the reason she went to bed so early. She really doesn't like conspicuous consumption. "Arthur told me there were still two garages I could use."

"That was earlier, Gary. It's dangerous."

"It's on my head, Arthur. I'll take my—"

"Listen to it, Gary, it's like a cacophony of banshees out there. Branches are flying everywhere. It's not safe."

"Arthur, please. It's exactly because I can hear debris hitting the house that I want to put her indoors. You said I could use a spare garage."

"Let him Dad. Despite appearances he is actually an adult and capable of making his own stupid decisions."

"Sod off, Spittoon... sorry Veronica."

"That's all right, Gary. Just please be careful."

Dad stands reluctantly to one side letting Dobbin open the door and step outside. The wind that hits us nearly knocks us off our feet and redistributes a pile of magazines that are on the welcome table where guests wait to be checked in.

Dobbin smiles and heads outside. Behind me a voice says, "What's he doing?"

It's Brenda. She comes and stands next to me. "Is he leaving?"

"Moving his pride and joy to a garage. I'd better go and help him. I expect the doors will be a two-man job."

"Harold, is that wise? You're about to become a Father."

I give Mum a hug, promising myself that once I am a parent I will not let myself worry quite as constantly as my parents do about me and Dina. I take a Barbour jacket and my shoes from by the door and hold the handle. I grin back at the three anxious faces. "I am just going outside and may be some time."

As I slip out, I hear Mum say, "That's not funny, Harold. That poor man never came back."

As the door closes I hear Brenda ask who the poor man was. That'll keep Dad busy, I think, telling her all about Captain Oates. Now, with my back to the front door I take in the mad world that is southern England. The weather man said there was no hurricane coming and it may be it isn't technically one but the wind is mental. I can see the largest larch by the corner of the house whipping back and forth like a crazed headmaster beating an errant pupil. The sky is oddly lit and all around me is a vortex of leaves like psychotic murmurations and bits of tree and other debris hurtle past. Dobbin is almost bent double as he approaches his car, like a man being pulled back but fighting against it.

When I try shouting at him my voice is whipped away. Pointless. Instead I head towards the garages, keeping as close to the house as possible. There is a gap between the corner of the main house and the start of the garage block that I have to cross. As I approach the space, the wind is making the most peculiar noise, like 1000 sopranos having plasters ripped off some sensitive body part. I don't have a choice so make a dash for the gap.

One minute I'm astride, upright and heading for the garages, the next I'm four feet in the air and dropping hard. Another moment passes as I consider flight is an interesting option, before it ends with my face planted in a flowerbed, having rather neatly and painfully pruned a hybrid tea rose 'Autumn Glow' with my arse on the way past. I take a moment to triage myself – yep, perforated but more or less in one piece – and crawl the way I was headed until I'm past the end of the garages.

Back on my feet, I can see Dobbin has started his BMW and is manoeuvring it towards me. The first three garages have been converted into small one-bedroom cottages. Amos and Jackie are in the first one. It's dark and it looks like they're both in bed although you'd doubt anyone is capable of sleeping. The next four are empty and in the process of being converted and the last three remain as garages. It's the end one where we are headed. I wave Dobbin towards me and hear the car crunching across the gravel drive, the stones on which are dancing like an agitated hive.

He's wound down his window and is finding it hard to force his head out so I can hear him. I ease forward.

"This is bloody ridiculous, Spittoon."

A tug of wind makes me grab at his wing mirror. "Geez. Look, I'll only open the doors at the last minute, okay? If you reverse up, I'll rap on your back window in a lull and you can slip it away smartish."

"I'm not sure…"

"Fuck's sake, Dobbin. Let's just do this, okay?"

I bend almost double while he slowly turns the car around and begins to back it towards me. The door latch is smooth when I test it, but even opening it a crack lets the wind give it a yank and I have to use all my body weight to close it again.

He's a few feet away and braking when I feel the wind ease a little and reach forward to tap the back window.

This is where things go wrong. I manage to open the first door and fix it on its hook, but when I let go and head for the second door, which is already vibrating alarmingly in the gusts, the hook gives way and it takes all my strength to catch it and force it shut again.

Dobbin is trying to see what I'm doing. I pull myself alongside his car.

"I can't do this on my own. The hooks aren't tight enough to hold the doors open and I can only hold one at a time. We need another pair of hands. I think you'll have to leave it where it is until this dies down."

I think he understands because he's shaking his head like it's caught in a gust. "Get Jackie."

"No, she's asleep. Just leave it."

"If you're not going to help then I'll do it. You can just bugger off."

"How will you manage that, oh weedy one?"

"I'll sort it. Go on, go and snuggle up with Penny and leave me to it. If you want a job done properly…"

"You are a pain, you know that? I'll try to persuade Dad to help."

He lets me go. Somehow I reverse my route, crawling between the buildings and entering the house. Inside, once the front door is closed I realise my ears are ringing and my skin tingling from the pummelling. The hall is empty but low voices come to me from the small sitting room to the right. Brenda, Dad, Mum and Zenda are gathered round a radio listening to the local news reports of devastation around southern England. As I walk in, the man says, "I can't emphasise this enough: stay indoors."

The serious faces look up at me; Brenda is the first to react. She laughs. "Christ. Worzel Gummidge lives." Then her expression changes. "Where's Gary?"

"Sitting in his stupid car. I need a volunteer to come and hold a garage door or he's going to do it all by himself and almost certainly get himself killed." I manage a huge smile that isn't reflected back at me. Mum is on her feet. "You are not going out in that again. It's utter stupidity."

I hold up my hands. "It won't take long. Dad, are—"

Brenda is already halfway to the hall. She doesn't say anything but by the time I join her by the front door she's put on her coat and conscripted a pair of Wellington boots. She looks grim. "Let's do this and get him indoors. Bloody show off." She does manage a half-smile.

"Okay then. Follow me. You'll need to do as I do or you'll end up in the Solent."

It takes us several minutes but finally we are hanging onto the side of the car. Dobbin looks annoyed. "Where's Arthur?" He won't look at Brenda.

"You've got me, okay? Which door, Harry?"

I'm about to point at the one that didn't break its latch when Dobbin heaves the car door open. "You drive," he says to Brenda. "You'll never hold it in this. And be careful." They manage to exchange a look then he says, "Please."

She nods, climbs in and guns the engine. He waits by the car window until he's happy she understands the controls and heads for the second door while I take the first.

It's rather difficult to describe what happens next. I manage to get my door open but holding it in place takes all my strength. I can't do anything expect concentrate on this wriggling and vibrating wooden planking. I'm vaguely aware that Dobbin has unhooked the bolts that hold his door in place and is pushing it open when there is a fearsome cracking noise and a flurry of something blue. It take a moment to understand it's the door with Dobbin holding on to the handle; it flies maybe 15 feet and comes down on top on him.

Brenda sees this disaster too and is out of the car in seconds. We both run in a crouch to the now flattened door and lift it up. Another gust catches it and it flips out of our hands and cartwheels off into the dark as if it's returning to the wild. Dobbin is spread-eagled, like he's been caught in the middle of a star-jump and then put through a mangle.

The headlights show he's got a horrid cut on his head. He is groaning and looks awfully pale. Brenda has fallen to her knees and is sobbing into his chest. I can't hear what she's saying. I take the other side and crouch by his head. An eye flickers open, looks at me, looks at the top of Brenda's head and – bugger me – he gives me a salacious wink. I wink back, and he closes his eyes again, pain suffusing his face. I whisper in Brenda's nearest ear. "Keep him here, Bren and I'll get Jackie."

It takes us half an hour to get him back to the main house and stop him bleeding. Mum makes a sofa up as a bed while Jackie bandages him. She wants him to get x-rayed, but the phone lines are down even if we could get an ambulance out. By now, Mum is utterly insistent that no one is going out again tonight, which we all accept.

Brenda, meanwhile, won't leave his side, holding his free hand even if he's drifting in and out of sleep. Natalie has got up and is wrapped in a blanket, twitching at every rattle of the shutters. Because Jackie was using the second bed in the cottage, Natalie has a room in the main house which is probably just as well; she'd be completely spooked otherwise.

Mum, Pritti, Zenda and I adjourn to the kitchen where Jackie expresses her concerns about his injury. "I don't know if there's any internal bleeding. We need to keep an eye on him and get him checked out as soon as we can. When's this bloody storm going to end?"

"The radio says it will have blown out by morning, but the roads may be blocked. If it stops we might be able to get out but if not there's a small hospital in Lymington and the local doctor lives about half a mile towards Milford. We might be able to walk to one or the other when it gets light."

She sighs. "I think Brenda will make sure he's okay. I'd better go and stay with Amos."

"You can't go—"

She puts a finger on my lips. "I can. Now stop fussing." And she winks at me, reminding me of Dobbin's dirty little wink of earlier. Something stirs inappropriately down south but I push all smutty thoughts away. There are times when being me is a real disappointment.

Zenda smiles. "I might get her to rest for a bit and I'll take over. I think they both need a break."

We follow her back into the little sitting room. Brenda is curled up in a chair and Karen is sitting next to Dobbin, reading a large book. She holds it up. "Hope you don't mind, Mrs Spittle. It was in my room."

Mum peers at the spine. "Oh please, my dear. Feel free. This is Harold's home and having so many friends is, well, a real treat. Now unless anyone needs me I'm off to bed. I think it might be best for a latish breakfast. Maybe 8.30?"

Penny would think that early, but she seems to have managed to get some sleep so I accept on her behalf.

"Hopefully the storm will have finished and we will all still be in one piece."

No one speaks and we all listen. The wind is howling down the chimney and it appears that the roof tiles are dancing across the rafters.

Mum shudders. "Not that I'm likely to get much rest with that going on."

# Friday, 16th October 1987

## *Chapter Eighty-Seven*

When I wake it is to Mum bringing Penny and me a cup of tea. Penny manages some sort of greeting and rolls over to re-establish her right to doze while I drag myself upright.

As she pulls back the curtains, flooding the room with light, Mum says, "Southern England is a mess. Everything is shut down – airports, railways, roads are blocked. All sorts of famous trees and buildings are destroyed."

"Blimey. Was it a hurricane then?"

"Apparently. Your Father has gone out to assess the damage and to see if we are blocked in. It certainly looks that way. We have a tree leaning on the second garage conversion – fortunately not the one with Jackie and Amos in it."

"I hope they're okay. Thanks," I take the tea cup she's offering me, "maybe I should go and help the old boy."

"He'd like that." She stands by the door. "You have some interesting friends, Harold. Lovely but, well, different."

"How's Dobbin?"

"He's complaining he has a headache like he used to get listening to Brenda's band." She looks concerned. "Did I hear their name right? It's rude isn't it?"

"It was, Mum but she a fine upstanding young woman now."

"Well, good. Her Mother seems very, um, worthy. A little muttonish, perhaps."

"You don't approve of the green streak in her hair?"

"She was rather underdressed this morning I thought. You know?" Mum shuffles her bosoms to indicate, I think, that Zenda may be braless.

"Mum, you are lovely but a prude."

"Maybe, though I like to think of it as maintaining standards. You'll be pleased to know that your Father is doing the breakfasts with Pritti's help when he gets back – she can't get back to the hotel. And with the phones still down we will have to make do on our own."

"I wonder how we're going to get Dobbin seen."

"At the moment he seems to be rather busy with Brenda and Caroline."

"Caroline? Oh, Karen. Is she acting as referee?"

"They're not playing games, Harold. The sitting room is covered in paper. Poor John looks utterly bemused. You might have a word and see if you can ask them to allow Gary to get some sleep. He does look a little overwrought."

She smiles at Penny's profile. "If you can wake the dead, breakfast will be in an hour."

I pull on some clothes and head downstairs. Voices – animated and excited – float up to me from the sitting room but before I can ascertain what is happening the front door opens and Dad steps in. He sees me and beckons me over.

My Father is on the small side – five feet eight or thereabouts – with a balding pate and round, fleshy cheeks. He has a glass eye, poor hearing in one ear and something of a limp. And the smile that usually accompanies his greeting is missing.

"What's wrong? Have we lost the roof?"

In a whisper, while glancing at the sitting room he says, "You'd better get your boots on and come and see."

It doesn't take long to find the source of his worry. Standing where we left the car, Jackie and a heavily wrapped Amos look like they are in mourning so low are their heads bowed. Even from the front door it is clear Dobbin's new pride and joy is no longer a thing of beauty.

It appears that the errant door that did for Dobbin must have bounced off the bonnet and then the roof as there are deep jagged grooves of torn metal in both. Meanwhile slates that have been ripped from the garage roofs seem to have made a beeline for the windscreen and side windows, destroying them all and filling the car with slate shrapnel, woodland debris and rainwater.

Dad watches me, his look askance. "You never put it away, then?"

"I was more concerned to get him indoors. I completely forgot."

"I hope he's insured."

"Oh, he's sure to be," I say, with a silent prayer to a Dobbin that is sensible and cautious, not the version who his friends would immediately recognise. "Shall we have a wander and see what else has happened? Unless you need to do the breakfasts?"

Jackie catches my eye. "Can I come? I'll just get Amos indoors."

Dad nods. "Okay, we'll wait." He faces me, his hands on his hips. "It's good to see you Harry, old chap. And breakfast will happen when it happens, yes?"

While Jackie takes Amos to the main house Dad says, "So can you explain who's who? That young woman? Is she Amos' private nurse?"

I manage a laugh. "She's an ex-girlfriend of mine who Dina introduced to Penny and they hit it off so well that until yesterday I didn't realise they were happily having a separate social life with a group of other women without telling me. And yes, she's a nurse. She agreed to help get Amos settled, but then she'll go back to London. I think she was hoping to catch a train this afternoon, but it doesn't look likely now, does it?"

"No, probably not. And Amos. He worked at Hemingways?"

"Yes, that's him. You know he has AIDS?"

"Oh yes poor man, though now Our Glorious Lady has embraced them, I think it only right we do our bit."

"Diana?"

"Princess Diana, please, Harry my son. We need to maintain certain standards around her."

"Mum said that earlier. I think I must be a disappointment again."

"Hardly." Dad looks around as if we are being listened to, "not with your forthcoming good news."

"Your grandchild?"

He shakes his head, his face carrying an expression like I'm a halfwit. "No, no your," he barely breathes the word, "partnership. I am bursting to tell the committee."

"Committee?" I already feel sick but can't help wondering about this body who are waiting for news.

"The Conservative Club Main Committee. I have felt that they are somewhat less than accepting of me as a full member – being as we are in the hospitality business – but having a member of the family a partner in such a prestigious law firm will make all the difference." He really couldn't look prouder. "And when I tell them we have hosted a dying AIDS victim's last wish, well, I think I can fairly say the nomination," Dad has decided to speak in a sort of crypto-parent, because he sounds out nom-in-a-tion as four distinct words, "…is in the bag."

The front door opens and John and Jackie emerge. Dad rubs his hands and explains. "The drive is blocked and the telephone lines are down but fortunately the power line is untouched. I think this tells me we need to get it buried in the near future; another storm like this and we'll lose power for sure. And get a generator as back up."

John is looking back at the main house. "Much structural damage?"

Dad pulls a face. "About two dozen slates have come off. Apart from the tree that's resting on the roof of one garage and the doors we lost last night, the other buildings look pretty unscathed. Come on, we'll have a quick peek in the woods and then have a look at the bungalow. From all the detritus on the drive it looks like it might have taken a battering."

The three of us follow Dad as he heads off at a steady pace. It's remarkable, I think as I watch him explain to John about the history of the house and the extensive grounds and their plans for it, how he has changed in the last few years. Even the idea of him in conversation with the local Tories and their committee takes some getting used to.

There are several trees either wholly or partly blown over and many branches down. Approaching the bungalow from the drive we can see Dad is right. It has practically been cut in half by a giant ash tree and looks completely wrecked. We start to circle round to the back, which is when we all notice someone on the swing that is remarkably in one piece.

As soon as Dad spots the trespasser he speeds up and raises his voice. "I say. Excuse me but what do you think you're doing?"

John goes to follow him, but I hold him back. "I think those two need to have a moment together before we interrupt."

John gives me a curious look but I shake my head and we stand still and watch.

Dad is in full 'aggrieved of Lymington' mode but before he can confront the man on the swing, the man stops the motion and looks up. With his face clearly visible, it's Dad's turn to stop but that doesn't really do justice to the abrupt way the identity of the man hits him; it's as if he's run into an invisible wall.

The man then stands and walks towards Dad, who initially at least seems to start to back away but who then propels himself forward. Dad stops a few feet away and the man hesitates before lurching in and hugging him, the man's frayed poncho enveloping the old man so he almost disappears. Then he falls to his knees and taking Dad's limp hand, presses it to his lowered forehead.

I can feel John and Jackie looking at them and then me. He asks, "What the hell is that all about?"

I have to smile. "Absolution. Many years ago those two were best buddies. Then that bloke – Charlie Jepson – tried to steal Mum from Dad. Also Dad was the victim of an accidental explosion for which Charlie was responsible. He lost an eye and his hearing in one ear. If that wasn't bad enough, 10 years ago Charlie reappeared and almost ruined Dad's marriage again as well as pretty much financially crippling him. Recently though, Charlie seems to have reformed and when I last spoke to him he was keen to try to obtain Dad's forgiveness. I'm not entirely sure prostrating himself will do it but I suppose it's a start."

"Goodness. What about your Mum? What will she say at this turn of events?"

"I've no idea. If anything, her relationship with Charlie has been even more of a roller-coaster than Dad's. She knows Charlie isn't trustworthy and she's been duped by him more than once, but I'm not entirely sure she's ever completely got over him. That is Dad's main concern, really."

Jackie and John make appropriately amazed sounds. Part of me would like to go on and say that I'm still trying to find out which of the two men – currently creating an informal diorama that is a pastiche of a Crusader seeking his Monarch's blessing before heading for the Holy Land – is my Father but I still can't admit the fear to myself let alone others.

Jackie moves first. "Come on. Let's get back. I think they may need more than a moment."

Indeed, Charlie is leading a clearly shocked and stunned Dad to the swing where he seems to have a bottle of something brown and probably alcoholic.

Breakfast – cooked by Zenda and Brenda – is marvellous, an antidote to any nerves that Charlie's presence has engendered, which when coupled with what may at the very moment be transpiring in London makes it surprising I'm capable of any social interaction.

Dobbin has gone back to his room, his headache roaring back to life after apparently being much better when he woke up. Jackie gave him a good inspection, much like a vet might a horse with Brenda in attendance like a worried owner. When they come back into the kitchen and join the table Jackie says, "I really would like to get him to see a doctor. Is there any way we can get in touch with someone?"

Mum, who has accepted my explanation that Dad wants to spend more time checking the grounds for damaged trees, suggests we walk along Silver Street to see if Dr Trebushay is available.

"Is he new?"

"She is excellent. Polly knows her stuff. Even your Father is happy with her advice."

The door opens and we look up; it's Pritti, flushed and carrying a huge bag accompanied by her two children, the gorgeous Noor, now nearly qualified as a solicitor, and the strapping and seemingly newly confident Sajid, who has just started at uni. He beams at me and then he sees Brenda. Years ago, he had a rampant crush on her when she led the Twats, her punk band. Unbeknownst to his parents I even got him a poster of her, on stage, ripping her T-shirt off as part of her famous closing performance. When I introduced them he could barely breathe let alone speak but now he squeals with delight. "Vera! Goodness. I've died and gone to heaven."

Brenda looks up, startled then smiles. Zenda looks across in surprise but Mum's expression is a picture. "Who on Earth is Vera?"

Sajid has crossed the room to Brenda who has stood and offered herself for a hug. Sajid points at Brenda and bows low. "This woman is a musical goddess."

Mum looks confused but is determined to cover it by saying, "Oh, were you in…?"

It is only at that moment she must put two and two together. The colour drains away as first Brenda and then the rest of us laugh. Mum has many faults but being able to take a joke against herself – unlike Dad – is very much ingrained. "Well, I won't ask you to play if that's all right. I've only just cleaned the floor."

Pritti bustles her assistants into the huge larder. "They've brought supplies."

"How did they get here?"

The hotel where they live is two miles away and has to be as trapped as we are. "Ravi managed to get the Land Rover across Jollife's fields and dropped the children by the water tower. They wanted to see you all. I told them they shouldn't be so reckless but you know what Ravi's like."

"Any phones?"

"None that I know of. Now what shall we have them do?"

Mum gives Pritti a hug. "Thank you, my sweet. What would we do without your family? Now Harold, I'd better find your Father and then you and Jackie can go on a doctor hunt." She looks at the end of the table where Natalie and Amos are in close conversation. "Those two look like they could do with some help." Mum indicates Jackie to Pritti. "Jackie is a nurse and is helping Amos but frankly it's that young woman who needs more assistance if you ask me."

As Mum heads for the door, Mrs Ohja says, "It's all right Veronica. Arthur is outside talking to a vagrant. He said he'll be in in a moment."

"A vagrant? Oh, poor man has probably been made homeless by the storm. I'll go and fetch them."

"No, Mum, wait it's—"

"Phooey, Harold. You'd better get going. We'll keep the patients alive while you're away."

I watch her go. Cripes, how is this going to go down? Pritti is in conversation with Jackie; they are both looking at Natalie, who seems oblivious to the attention she's attracting. Brenda and John are talking with Sajid while Penny and Zenda are deep in discussion. While I wait for Jackie to be ready to go, Karen catches my eye and waves me over. As I reach her seat she stands and I'm given an enormous hug.

"That's lovely if unexpected."

"You are a clever, cunning man Harold Spittle."

I wince. "Please. I can cope with total strangers and my parents calling me Harold, but for everyone else it feels like I'm being told off. But leaving that aside, why the unnecessary compliment?"

"When I woke up this morning, Brenda and Gary were lying on the sofa. They had spent most of the night deciding how to restructure her law business and shelter with his money. They then told me that Gary had agreed to join John to run the agency, which would free me up to join Bren."

"Is Gary putting money into Brenda's business? I thought she wasn't happy about that?"

"That's the neat bit. Gary buys me out and I buy into Brenda's firm."

"But she doesn't have a firm."

Karen points at a heap of papers next to her. "She does now. Well, the outline of one. We'll set it up on Monday or whenever we get back." Karen picks up a slice of toast and waves it at the big picture window. "If we hadn't been trapped; if Bren hadn't thought Gary was about to die, we'd never have had the chance to talk this all through. You made us all come for the weekend and you probably somehow whipped up the storm and had Gary topped by a flying garage door. As I said, *genius* planning."

I pull a face. "I haven't told him about his car yet."

She nods and looks serious. "Yes, that was probably the only thing they disagreed about. She told him that if he didn't get rid of it she would total it."

"Ah, right. Well, I might be a little ahead there. Why were you still writing, by the way?"

"I can't stop being the boring lawyer. Brenda said she wants to sign something with him before he snuffs it so I agreed to put together some heads of terms for when he's awake. Poor lamb really doesn't look well."

"Yes, well... oh shit." I'm still looking out of the windows at the sloping lawns where three people appear round the side of the house. Charlie Jepson is walking backwards his hands held high, not in adulation but as a defence, followed by Dad who is trying to push Charlie away with his right hand while holding Mum, waving a large umbrella wildly, at bay with his left.

Everyone in the kitchen stops talking at the same moment and stares. Dad notices the sea of faces first and must say something because then Charlie turns and Mum follows to look. Almost together everyone drops their arms and, in Mum's case her weapon.

"I'll go and get them. If I leave them alone, they'll kill him."

It is inevitable that the remaining guests are fascinated by this unexpectedly violent tableau but, being British, can't find a way to ask what it's all about. Well, Pritti, showing her Kenyan roots, can. "What are you doing Veronica? Violence is never the answer."

Mum looks sheepish but says in a rather defensive squeak. "But Pritti, this is that man I told you about. Charlie Jepson."

Do I imagine Pritti's look of horror as she glances over at me, like it's my fault before she strides forward to where the three of them are standing just inside the garden door.

Crack. She absolutely larrups Charlie on the right cheek. That's evened things up.

I'm aware of everyone holding their collective breaths. They are fascinated and intrigued to see what he will do. To everyone's surprise he looks stunned, shakes his head and then falls to his knees. "Thank you, Pritti. Thank you so much. You at least understand." He looks at me. "And thank you Harry for making this happen."

It's Mum who turns on me first. "Did you invite him here? Is this your doing? You of all people should know better than to let him back into our lives."

Dad joins her, facing me down. "Yes Harold. How could you have your Mother so upset by asking him of all people to come and visit?"

Behind me Zenda – who is Charlie's sister-in-law – begins to say something and probably trying to support me, but I hold up a hand. "No, it's okay Zenda. They're both right. This man has singlehandedly tried to scupper my parents' marriage on more than one occasion. All I can say, Mum, Dad, in my defence is he has changed. He wanted the opportunity to apologise. You don't have to accept it and I know he'll go if you insist but you both taught me to be forgiving and move on."

They look speechless. Both turn and look at Charlie who nods and then they turn back to me. Mum picks up the brolly and hits me on the arm. Not that hard but hard enough to make me jump and yelp. "You shit. Don't you ever surprise me with that sort of trick ever again. He can stay for lunch and we will listen to what he wants to say but then he goes and I don't care if the roads are blocked and full of dangerous trees and marauding footpads. He's not staying here. Right Arthur?"

"Completely Veronica." The glare is intended to be of the stone-forming Medusa sort but is more Bash Street Kids.

I rub my arm ruefully.

Mum tut at me. "Don't be pathetic. You and Jackie had better get a move on. Lunch will be at two. The rest of you can help tidy up and sort things out."

Everyone stands and looks ready to leap into action.

Mum scans the room. "Zenda, would you clear up in here please, and maybe Karen and John could help? Penny needs some rest I think, as do Natalie and Amos I expect. Why don't you go through to the conservatory Penny and see if there's any warmth in the sun? Amos, dear, there are some maps in there. I heard you'd like to have a picnic. If we can get out of here, maybe today or tomorrow we might go and enjoy something, yes?"

He nods and offers her a bony hand.

She takes it lightly. "And if you tell Penny what you'd like to eat, I'll see what I can rustle up."

Dad and I exchange a look, which Mum doesn't miss. "Oh for heavens sake, you'd think my food was poison. Now stop it. Pritti will do it if you're going to be like that. It's not as if my food will kill him."

Dad's expression mirrors mine.

We can't be too sure.

## *Chapter Eighty-Eight*

It takes Jackie and me about an hour to battle through the fallen trees, rogue dustbin lids, smashed flowerpots, a random sign advertising Shell Oil and other natural and manmade obstacles to reach Polly Trebushay's cottage. She's in her mid-twenties, four feet and not much more and very nervy. She and Jackie speak in a code, while I take a bow saw and make a path from her house to her garage and then on to the road. Dr Polly is about to walk to her practice in Lymington, which is on the way back past our house so she comes with us and accepts the offer of coffee en route. She checks Dobbin's vital signs and pronounces him very lucky – he's back in the sitting room with a probable concussion – and then disappears with Jackie, I assume to see Amos. But when I follow them through to take some orders, it is Natalie with whom they are talking; Pritti Ohja is also involved.

Everyone congregates in the sitting room; Polly doesn't stop but swigs her coffee and heads off. The rest of us take whatever seats are available. Penny comes in with Jackie and breaks off to sit with me. "What's up with Natalie?"

"I think they've found out what's wrong."

"Oh God, she doesn't have AIDS after all, does she?"

"No, coeliac disease."

"What's that?"

"Haven't you heard of it? It's when you take in gluten – from wheat and flour, mainly – and it sort of jams up your stomach. Pritti suspected it was dietary and Jackie's confirmed it could well be. Natalie is going to make a diary of what she eats and then get tested when she's back home."

"How did she catch it?"

"She didn't. You can develop it at any age. Poor thing has really been worried that she has caught something deadly and given it to you and anyone else. To say she's relieved – assuming this is what the problem is – would be quite the understatement. It's a pain in the arse – sometimes literally – but coeliac disease can be managed."

"What a grand day. First Dobbin and Bren sort themselves out and now this."

Penny looks across to where Bren is sitting with Dobbin resting against her shoulder. Karen is explaining something to them. She raises her voice to get their attention. "What have you two been up to then? Harry says you've sorted yourselves out."

Dobbin manages a smile. "Karen's just putting the finishing touches to things. We're going to sign. Come on Spittoon, you can be the witness. You've passed all the exams to let you sign your name— oh damn. Shit."

We all look at him with varying degrees of concern. Penny speaks first. "What's up? Left some beans on the hob?"

He's focused on me; that's the look that says I may think I'm covered in pigeon shit but it really isn't that lucky. "Sorry, mate but you'll not believe it. I had those forms you signed and I was going to buy the stock today. My spies told me it was going to be the best day to get in and you'll now have to wait for Monday and hope the stock market doesn't explode. God, I'm really sorry. That's incompetent of me. I hope it doesn't cost too much." He manages a laugh. "If it's really bad, if it does take off then I'll give you the car. Bren insists on me getting rid of it anyway." He narrows his eyes when he catches my expression. "What are you not saying, Spittoon? I know you too well not to be worried when you make that face. Was it scratched when you put it away?"

"Um, well, not exactly."

"Why isn't that comforting?"

"In the circs – you're nearly dying, yeah? – I sort of forgot to put it in the garage."

"Okay, so it stayed outside and… it got a little bit scratched?"

"More like a lottle bit scratched."

"Would you like to define 'lottle'?"

"As in a total wreck. Trashed. Undrivable. Good as a hen house but not much more."

For one long moment I'm grateful that he's sporting an enormous bandage and still appears to be managing the most humungous headache because I'm pretty sure he's about to leap up and tie several complicated knots in my windpipe. Then he laughs, makes a face like he has ingested adder's sputum and throws up.

When he's settled himself and, in his newly patrician way allowed Brenda and Karen to clear up his vomit, he says, "You are a wonder. I can now claim on the insurance rather than sell it. Perfect. Let's sign this thing before any of us change our minds or Spittoon wakes me up and tells me I'm really him."

Later, Mum, Dad and Charlie Jepson (who by some miracle of etiquette hasn't been thrown out) call me outside. Mum and Dad still seem wary and leave Charlie to speak. "I will go now. Cuthbert

Hemingway is expecting me. But thank you Harry for facilitating this meeting." For a moment he looks a little like the old Charlie, sort of ready to see if he can find an angle to exploit. "I'd like to say a 'reconciliation' but maybe not quite yet."

Neither of my parents react. Good for them. He no longer has any hold over their marriage. "Mr Hemingway? How is he?"

Up go the hands and on goes the beaming beatific smile accompanied by the slightly vacant eyes, which I'm beginning to suspect is a bit of an act. "He is embracing his own personal Nirvana."

Mum dusts her hands and coughs. "That's sounds lovely. I must get on. Harold, why don't you see Charles out?"

I do as I'm bid. "How are you getting to Mr Hemingway's?"

"He's in Lymington. By the Quay. He has a boat – he adores the water – and we are going to enjoy the Aqua of our Existences together."

"Right. Good for you. What if Stephen makes it sometime this weekend? Is that where he can find you?"

We are halfway towards the front gate; he stops and points at a watery sun. "Stephen will find his own way but you, Harry, you have others to show. And their path is mined and deadly unless you find their way for them. Your lady needs to channel her fears."

To my surprise, he turns round and runs off towards the woods rather than to the road. He's singing at the top of his voice and it takes a moment to realise it is The Marseillaise. "Formez vos bataillons! Marchon! Marchon!" floats back towards me. Then he's lost among the trees.

What a barmy man. And what did he mean this time? Although his use of 'lady' brings to mind his last clue about Magda. I realise that Grant's plans may have been undermined by the storm. Oh bollocks, when will I ever get a run of good luck? Oh well, no doubt Grant will sort it out in his inimitable way.

# Saturday, 17th October 1987

## *Chapter Eighty-Nine*

If Thursday night to Friday morning was extraordinary, then last night was the epitome of ordinary. Amos sat in the centre of the group leading us in reminiscences of our time together in the seventies. He was happy and engaged but on a few occasions he lost the plot and everyone held their breath. We all agreed that, everything being equal, we'd have that picnic tomorrow.

Breakfast is my favourite meal of the day. For one thing bacon and coffee and fresh bread are better when the smells of the day haven't upset the nasal equilibrium. But mostly it's because people haven't had the time to get upset with each other and are generally more relaxed. That is if you don't get visitors. The first knock came at 8.20. Mum answered it and came to find me – I was eating with Brenda and Zenda, the other early birds.

"There's one of those thugs the Andersen boy set up. He's waiting for you at the door. Grant, I think. He said you were expecting him."

I wasn't, but given the disruption I'm not as surprised as I might have been. "I'll have a word."

As I stand she adds, "The old receptionist from the hotel is with him. Maud? Martha? She has a bag. You didn't mention she's staying."

"Magda?" A bag? Does he want her stay and catch a ferry from here? "Don't worry, I'll go and sort it out."

It is only as I'm opening the door to the hall it occurs to me that there is no reason why Grant would know I'm here, let alone think I'm expecting him. He is filling the hallway with a sort of awkward malevolence and Magda has sat on the very edge of a chair, looking worried.

"'arry. 'ere," he holds out a brown envelope. "Passports." He glances at Magda, then back to me. "Hi've called your sis hand—"

"Mine? Dina?" If I was frowning before – and I know I was – this news makes it feel like my forehead wants to fold in half.

"You hain't hanother, 'ave you?"

"No, but why? I mean, did Magda say to call her?" Another thought follows the first. "Does she have her number?" How come Magda knows how to contact Dina and I don't?

He looks like I'm speaking Swahili. "She told me to call. Hin case there were problems, like."

I'm confused. Behind me, the stairs creak. Penny.

"Hi. Grant, is it?"

"Penny?"

She stretches out a hand. "What's happened?"

"There hain't no ferries today so Di said come 'ere. Hi tried—"

I grab the sides of my head and groan until he stops talking. "Will someone tell me what is going on here?"

Penny takes my hand. "In a moment, love. Trust me, please?" Her eyes implore my agreement. The curve of her stomach is pressing against mine and, just then there is the most enormous volley, exploding into the back of the net and making me suck in a rapid breath. My surprise is echoes in her face. "Blimey, he… or she is keen to get out."

"Me too, matey. One minute." She kisses me, and I step back.

"You got through to Dina?

"Took hages. There's a working phone hon the 'igh Street. Lucky she's hat work. She's hon 'er way though doesn't know 'ow long hit will take 'er." He indicates Magda with a flick of his thumb. "She hain't 'appy, mind. She's desperate to get going and thinks there's a conspiracy ha'foot."

We all look at Magda. Yep, that is indeed the face that uncovered 1000 conspiracies.

"How was Dina? She did say not to call work unless it was an emergency."

"We 'ave a code, right? She hunderstood, said she'd sort hit hout. She," he indicates Magda, "his keen she leaves today. Hor," he lowers his voice, "she says she'll go hon 'er hown."

Penny nods and thanks Grant who gives Magda a clumsy kiss on the cheek.

"Hi'd better go. Hi got some herrands to do for Di."

Penny eases Magda to her feet and leads her into the kitchen where all faces turn to us. Amos has appeared with Jackie through the garden doors. When he sees it's Magda he makes a beeline for her. They hug in silence, both quietly crying. Mum makes a sort of ferrumping noise but no one else seems to notice. I go and hold her round the waist, and whisper, "It seems Dina might be coming. Maybe later."

That makes her turn and smile broadly. "Oh, that would be so lovely. Today?"

"I think so, but she might have to work a little when she gets here."

Magda makes an effort to look pleased to be here, but as each guest appears, she glances nervously at the door and when she sees it's not Dina, she looks away.

As I chew a piece of cold and soggy toast, I run through the last few days. The oddity of Penny's behaviour, Natalie too now I think about it, begins to make sense. I know I've been set up but not how. In particular the conversation I had with Dina last weekend, when she told me the Americans had taken over, comes back to me. She should have been more worried. That's it.

I watch as Penny sits with Magda, talking to her in a low voice, once or twice glancing at me. I'm utterly confused but in a way relieved that my sis is back and involved. Although Penny's role is making me feel angry again. But there's nothing to do and no point making a scene until Dina arrives.

Mum and Zenda are having something of an argument over the picnic; I hope Zenda wins. The good news is that the sun is out and warming up; the not so good news is there are no tree surgeons or indeed anyone with a chainsaw available to clear the drive. Dad springs a surprise when he appears at 10.00 to tell us that if we can cross the fields at the back of the house – there's a little used footpath there, Ravi will meet us with his Land Rover to ferry us to the beach.

"Did you walk to Hemingways?"

He nods and says, "I needed the air."

Since when did he do exercise willingly?

## *Chapter Ninety*

Ravi has just left with a group comprising Mum, Zenda, Brenda and a still-groggy Dobbin – they are the second phase; the first phase comprised Amos, Jackie, Natalie and Pritti. I'm about to turn back to the house to assemble phase three when a Mercedes appears round the corner and honks. Two men peer at me through the windscreen. One is McNoble who I was expecting; the driver is Gregor Princip who I most certainly was not. They park and step out. I nod at Stephen and say to Greg. "Come to gloat? You know what happened?"

He looks about to argue when Stephen says, "Leave it, Harry. He's one of the good guys."

"Like you'd know. If you're coming to the house you'd better park and follow me; the drive is blocked. You staying the night?"

Greg shrugs. "Up to you." He heads back to the car to park it somewhere out of the way.

Stephen says, "Depends on Dad." He stops me as I begin to climb the stile back into the field. "Is he about?"

"Down in the harbour with Mr Hemingway. You remember him?"

"Cuthbert. Yeah, he was okay. Tried to keep Dad and Monica from falling apart. Dad spent time with him when they split."

"Here?"

"Yeah, I think so."

"I'm not surprised. Things seem to happen around me these days and I have no idea who's telling me the truth and who isn't." I smile at Stephen. "Oddly, I think you are one of the few who are completely honest. Although why you're with him, I have no idea."

He follows me over the stile into the field. "I wouldn't bet on it." He falls into step with me. "Should we wait for Greg?"

"Fuck him. Let him work it out."

"He's not what you think."

"I know. It's me, not him. I thought he was crooked or at least duplicitous but he's just ambitious, like I guess we all are. I misread him and it pisses me off."

"I don't think I've ever heard you so angry."

I let out an unnecessarily dramatic sigh. "Do you remember the gay waiter, really camp from when you and your Dad stayed at Hemingways? Amos?"

"Vaguely."

"He's dying of AIDS. Wanted to come back to the Forest one last time so he's here. We're all going to the beach for one final picnic. Rather poignant."

"Sounds like a right giggle but I'll give it a miss if that's okay. I really want to find Dad. Do you have Cuthbert's address?"

I give it to him. "It's a two, maybe three-mile walk. I wouldn't use the car."

"That's not mine. The walk is fine. Do me good. Will your parents mind if I stay?"

"Yes probably but please do, I want you to. We need a good chat about Gloria and all that. I assume that's why Greg's come down?"

"Partly. He's worried about you. He thinks… ah, here he is. He can explain."

I sigh. "Give me your bag and you can head off. It's back to the road and then head left. After that, turn right and follow the road until you are at the bottom of the High Street by the Quay. I'll wait for our city boy."

"I'll just check he's okay then I'll be off."

Greg is not a country lover, that's for sure. His expensive brogues seem to have attracted an unconscionable quantity of mud and cow shit in the few hundred yards since he parked his car and if his expression is anything to go by it's not an enjoyable experience. He's lifting his feet in large deliberate steps, as if the speed and height will make a difference to the mud's viscosity and adhesiveness.

"It'll wash off, for Christ's sake."

"Please Harry, do you have to blaspheme?"

That makes me start. Without thinking about it I say, "Sorry, but really – don't be so precious. It's just mud." And as a reaction I assume to his snotty putdown I add, unnecessarily, "Put here by your precious God no less."

He shakes his head, a more effective remonstration than any words. "What have you told him, Stephen?"

"Nothing about our conversation. Up to you. I'll see you two later." McNoble lifts a hand. "Don't kill each other."

"If you can make it back for dinner, it'll be about seven."

"Let's wait and see."

We watch him go then head off towards the house. We're soon on a gravel path and Greg visibly relaxes. I'm feeling rather put upon, what with Penny and Dina's trickery over Magda, leaving aside the twisted way in which my role sorting out Caldera has been exploited by Crispin and how my partnership prospects have been undermined by rogue turds. So while I do want to help Gloria, right now I'm buggered if I'm going to be the one to speak first. I last about a minute before I ask, "Did they drop me?"

"The partners?"

"No, moron, the Tiller Girls. Given all Frank said and how I got it wrong about you and those photos, I imagine—"

"The meeting didn't happen. Not quorate. Given the chaos that's only to be expected. They're planning on using Monday to decide so for now everyone is still in the frame."

"Only another two days until my fate is sealed." I kick a convenient pebble that sits up in front of me, just asking to be booted. I'm halfway through my back swing when I think of Wigglet kicking me earlier and lose my footing. Greg shoots out a hand and stops me toppling into an embarrassed heap. "Thanks."

"I thought you were the country boy."

"The truth is I couldn't leave soon enough and I'm still coming to terms with the wasted teenage years I spent trapped down here."

We've walked out of a birch coppice and stop above the back lawns that sweep down to the house. If it is impressive from the main drive it is even more so from here. He says, "Well, you were hardly a pauper."

"This place? Hell, I didn't even know this place existed back then. My folks acquired the house six years ago."

"I heard. Via your friend Sven?"

"You know about that? I don't talk about it much."

"No, but Natalie does. Miles too."

"Yeah, well, I doubt that crook has a good word to say about me."

"No, that's true. He loathes you, as I have now found out." He takes my shoulder to stop me marching ahead. "I made a grave error of judgement with him and I'm sorry."

We exchange a look. I'm not convinced he's genuine, but he does look solemn. As if that counts. "It's a bit late."

"Not necessarily. I spoke to Gloria after our brief conversation on Thursday and she and Stephen told me the rest. Especially about him and Tina."

"Really? And?"

"I knew she was having doubts about something – I suppose I assumed it was her faith – but her sexuality makes more sense. She is a credit to the church, that girl. You know we belong to the same congregation?"

"Yes, Gloria said. She also said the problem was her Father."

Greg's eyes go up dramatically and not in a sign that he is looking for Divine guidance. "Pat Eagle isn't a bad man. Old fashioned, for sure, but he's a good Christian. He might not approve but he does forgive. Maybe it's easier when a relative stranger explains."

"You've talked to him?"

Greg doesn't show any sign he heard me. "Tina wants to dedicate her life to the church, but feared if Miles told her Father she was gay, he and the other elders would have her ostracised. When I found out, I managed to broker something of a rapprochement. An understanding." He shakes his head. "This has been very painful. Especially," he swings round until he is right in front of me, "will you promise me to keep this to yourself?"

Goodness. I wasn't expecting that sort of confessional. "Of course," I say, not knowing if such a promise is either possible or sensible.

"My Father is one of the Elders. I could see his hand behind all of this after I spoke to Gloria and Stephen." He smiles. "He prefers Steve, doesn't he?"

"Does he?"

"I thought…?"

"What? We're friends? I'll tell you about him and me sometime."

Greg shrugs. "Anyway, I now see what the introduction of Miles, getting close to you, him asking about you, what it all meant and—"

"He wanted to shaft me."

"Yes, but that was incidental. When I joined the Firm, my Father seemed genuinely interested in my colleagues in ways he had never been with my friends before, but looking back, it was you he asked about most. He said you were quite an example of someone who stuck to their principles."

"Me? What bloody principles?"

Greg manages a laugh. "That's what I told him. He put Tupps up to it. I'm bloody sure of it. I confronted him yesterday."

"God… sorry. How did that go?"

"As you might expect." He laughed. "'Just business' he said. Told me that it really didn't matter, he'd screwed Crout and that was the aim and Miles was a waster anyway so he was pleased to be shot of him." He shuts his eyes again; I really believe this is painful for him. "You know, part of the reason I went to Newe Waters was because of Father. I now wonder... ah, never mind. I called the policewoman who interviewed me. Wallace, I think. I had Gloria with me and we went through everything. The other pictures Gloria had—"

"They're in my desk."

He grins. It's good to see. "Not any more. You are such a creature of habit. Chloe unlocked your desk and I took them. The police have now seen everything and are planning on re-interviewing Crout. I suggested she might want to talk to Toogood—"

"Merv... sorry. How's he involved in this?"

"Toogood? Oh he and my Father go back a long way. I'm pretty certain he's the reason the firm took me on. Didn't you know my family home is on the south coast? The Toogoods and Princips are close neighbours. Somehow, I suspect darling 'Uncle' Mervin has a role in all of this. Even if he doesn't where's the harm in stirring up that old rattler, eh? You know the reason why my Father and Crout are at loggerheads is over a financing?"

"I knew there was history."

"When Crout was the head of the Company Department – before he was SP – it was on his say so that the firm refused to act for my Father's company. Apparently Toogood threatened to resign and Crout stared him down, called his bluff. But after that, he sort of promised he'd help my Father. One was with my Articles. This whole game may have been another. That at least is what my Father implied."

"But Barry's death was an accident, wasn't it?"

He shrugs. "I suppose. They'll be a coroner's hearing at which some of this may come out. Miles' role in blackmailing him might be uncovered but if there's one thing Crout is good at it's minimising bad news. I can't see any criminal charges being laid. It's just going to blow over. I hope that at least Tina, Gloria and their Father come out of this well. I'll do my best to make sure they do."

"Good." I don't feel great in truth, given I should have done more and earlier to be open and honest. "I'm sorry if I tried to make you out to be the baddie here."

"Baddie? Very possibly. I fear my 'enthusiasm' for a partnership coloured what was important."

"Yes?"

"Our friendship, Harry." He holds out his hand.

We shake. "Well, at least that slimeball Tupps has had to go elsewhere. That is some consolation for this mess. I'm sure I've not heard the last of him and his need for revenge, though."

"I think I'm officially at the top of his hate list right now."

"Welcome to the club."

Maybe he detects something in the sombre route that our conversation seems to have taken. He looks at the sunshine, sparkling through the trees. "There's everything to play for, Harry. Don't give up. We'll make this the best property department in the City. That's partly why I'm here. I want you to promise me you'll keep pressing. You'll not do anything stupid, such as hand in your notice."

I pull a surprised face. "Hand in my notice? Where'd you get that idea from?"

"The head-hunter's card on your desk? Crispin said you looked like you'd pretty much given up when he spoke to you about that thing you sorted out in Barrington."

"Yes well, the last I heard was Toogood intended to blackball me. If he's adamant then even if Crout wanted to support me he couldn't overcome that."

"That's not what Frank told me. The client – Caldera – told him it was you who put it all together and explained, with Crispin's help, what Toogood had tried to do. Frank said that if he tries to object Frank will raise the Barrington business and seek to have Toogood recused from the vote."

"Blimey. Can he do that? Would he?"

He shrugs. "We'll find out."

"What about you and your Father?"

He takes a while to speak. "I expect we'll work things out. I have a lot of admiration for how he's made himself what he is but, well... I have to think of my Mother and sister. I can't just abandon them."

I'm taken back as he talks to Sven Andersen and how he worried about protecting his sister. I hope he has more success. I tune back in.

"I'll have to find another church, though. That will be a wrench." He holds his face up towards the sun and shuts his eyes as if absorbing the little heat. Then he points in the direction of the house. "Time we went and sorted out those people who appear to be waiting for us." He motions towards the B&B. I'd clean forgotten about our trip to the beach.

"Yes, come on. Rest assured, I'll see it through and take my final humiliation like a man. Anyway, I don't think Frank is minded to help as you suggest."

"Frank? He loves you."

"Maybe he did, but that was before Turdgate."

"Tu…? Oh that. You being serious?"

"He's sure I'm the phantom stool-dumper. That it was me and not Cyn who'd added the rather graphic full stop to her resignation. Since I can't prove it's not me and he was pissed off that I tried to dump a load of shit on you, I don't think he'll be pressing my case very hard. As you've always said, there are two places at best in property and in a fair fight, currently the odds have to be on your two. Frankly, I think you two deserve it. I might stay one more year and give it one more go, but I doubt we have the business for a third extra partner."

He looks serious, staring away over the tree tops as we head for the small knot of people. "You heard the markets have shut for the entire day? And New York plummeted? Everyone is expecting a nightmare on Monday, a proper crash when they open. If that tips us into recession then we'll be lucky to have any sort of department whatsoever."

"There you go. Is it any wonder I'm not holding my breath?"

The others are nearly with us, so we stop our gloomy discussion and I introduce Greg. He declines to join us, which I'm grateful for since we don't have the space in the Land Rover and I don't really want to debate my failing legal career anymore.

"We'll talk later but I can't see how it will end well on Monday," he says with another shrug.

He walks off, his head down in a familiar pose, like he's composing poetry. It's going to take a stroke of magic to get us out of this one.

## *Chapter Ninety-One*

The picnic is a great success. Amos, although unable to do much and clearly tired from the short walk to the pebbles – Hordle Cliffs aren't known for glorious golden sand; none of the beaches hereabouts are unless the tide is so far out it's tripping – is the life and soul. Even Natalie seems more engaged in proceedings, although Jackie says it's more psychological than physical since she's hardly had time for the dietary changes to begin to work. At one point, Natalie and I find ourselves near each other and no one else around. I say, "I'm glad you've got some idea about what may be causing your problems."

"You?"

It takes a moment to get the joke. "I'm sure you can do better than me."

She runs cold fingers down my left cheek, an oddly intimate gesture. "You know you are most men's envy? There are at least three women around who fancy you, Bren too probably. Zenda and your Mum both think you're adorable and—"

"I think I can correct that impression, leave it with me."

"You don't realise, do you? Poor bloke. When you do it'll probably be too late."

"Too late for what?"

"To take advantage." She bites into a scone carefully, as if she's aware of the possibility that Mum may have cooked it. "All that free sex you've missed out on. Ah well! Although that's it, isn't it? You've always been the least likely bloke to take advantage, which is what attracts the girls. Still," she peers at the inside of the scone, "Do you think your Mum used flour or some sort of plaster?"

I give it a sniff and then taste it. "I think maybe she's used beef suet rather than butter. Toss it for the gulls?"

She smiles and throws it towards the water. "Silly me!" She brushes crumbs from her jacket. "Still," she goes back to her previous line of thought, "Penny deserves you for her patience and tolerance." She takes my arm, as she did in the car park at the service station a few days ago. She squeezes me hard. "I'm over you, you know."

"And for a moment I thought you were flattering me. Tolerance indeed." I squeeze her back. "But good. You deserve to find the right person."

We both look across to where Penny is sitting on the rug with Amos on a foldaway chair next to her. As we watch Penny says something and rolls onto her knees and stands. She takes his hand and together they waddle to where the waves are lapping at the grit that demarks the shore from the sea. Penny takes off her shoes and then helps Amos out of his and together they paddle, splashing and laughing.

Natalie shivers. "Bloody cold, I bet." She loosens her grip and turns me towards the base of the cliff, where Brenda, Karen and Dobbin are looking at something. "I'm sorry I didn't realise that Chuck was going to make things so difficult. I thought he was sweet, but I'm a shit judge of men."

"That puts your early compliments into perspective then."

She snuggles in close. "Yes, probably. And I'm sorry about the tricky business with Magda."

"Yes, well, that's Dina's problem now. Not that Penny's told me much about how she organised it." I give Natalie a chance to speak but she ignores me. "Bloody hell, maybe that's what you're really saying. Women like me because they can manipulate me."

She shakes her head. "That's a very unappealing characteristic in a man, frankly." She goes quiet and bows her head, as if she's being careful where she's treading. We reach the others to find Dobbin pontificating on the likely fossils that are hidden in the gloopy mud that the storms have brought down. He has almost persuaded Brenda to have a dig with her hands when we arrive. Brenda looks relieved. "This is your home turf, Harry. Will I find fossils in the mud?"

"Quite possibly but you'll also find it is as sticky and glutinous as any known substance and you'll be digging it from under your nails for weeks. A classic risk-reward dilemma."

For a moment she looks torn then turns on Dobbin. "You sod. You knew, didn't you?"

He shrugs but can't hide the smile. "I—"

We are interrupted by a cry and a shout. Amos has fallen over and pulled Penny onto her knees. They are both floundering in the shallows. They're not in danger of drowning but it is Karen who first realises what it might mean. "Come on. They'll freeze. We'd better get them dry."

Neither Amos or Penny is concerned, but Karen's supposition is correct and they are shivering by the time we get them into Ravi's Land Rover and on their way home. Jackie and Zenda go too while I help Mum and Pritti clear things up and move everything up to the car park to await our lift.

Mum says, "You're friends are a lovely group of people, Harold. I'm very pleased." I recognise the unspoken wistful note that hangs between us.

"Dina?"

"I wish she'd settle. Jim was never going to be a long term – what's the expression? Soul mate? But there must be some other eligible men out there who are self-sufficient and still have their own teeth."

I love Mum's criteria. "Sure. There was a nice policeman for a while but that's fizzled."

"What about one of your lawyer friends? They must be of her sort."

"Probably too boring." I try to imagine Crispin with Dina. His intellect would appeal but his limited horizons would drive her to a justified homicide very quickly. "Let's hope she does make it for dinner. It'll be good to see her." And, I think, find out what her game is.

When we get back, the sky is darkening and the wind has picked up with an easterly bite to it. Happily, Dina is there having somehow hitched from Cheltenham. She must have spoken to Penny by now, not that she shows any sign of embarrassment. Indeed, she seems quite relaxed and happy, chatting with Greg. Mum's words come back to me. Greg would be perfect for her although his status is opaque. I realise that until a couple of days ago, the only personal information I knew about Greg Princip was the gossip about his Father. I don't even know which way he swings, although there's something in the white-blond hair, chiselled jaw and striking blue eyes that's screams 'hetero' at me. I'm probably completely wrong, of course, and am merely evidencing a bundle of unacknowledged prejudices.

I'm wet and muddy so leave the kitchen's snug warmth and head for my bedroom to change. The en-suite bathroom looks out over the back, from where we returned a while ago.

As I stand at the sink and have a wash, I see a movement in the trees. A torch flashes once.

I stop my ablutions and stand back so I'm hidden by the curtains. From below me an outside door opens and closes. It's Magda. She looks left and right and hurries across the grass to the tree line where the torch flashed. As she reaches the edge a man steps forward and offers her his hand. I may not have the greatest eyesight, nor is the light brilliant, but I'd recognise the pudgy form of Chuck Streib anywhere. That and the globular torso and tree stump legs.

They talk for a minute or so. Mostly Chuck does the talking and Magda nods before she turns back to the house.

# Chapter Ninety-Two

"What's going on Di?"

Dina smiles at Greg, apologises and walks past me towards the hall. "What?"

"You're using me."

"Oh, don't be so paranoid. You wanted to help and now you're helping. You didn't specify how and it was easiest, in case anyone asked, that I wasn't involved and you didn't know."

"But you are involved. You set this whole thing up. The message from Charlie, Magda's disappearance, the worry about Chuck, the…" And then it clicks. "Fuck, are you working with Streib? How come? Is that why he's outside at this moment giving instructions to Magda?"

She squeezes her eyes shut but doesn't react with any sort of surprise. "Things have gotten a little complicated." She looks drained, unlike a moment ago when she seemed full of life.

"How come he's out there now talking to Magda?"

"It'll be fine if we can just get her on her way."

"What about the ferry?" I grind to a halt. "Has it been cancelled?"

"This bloody storm has been a bloody nightmare. The ferries have been cancelled and there are no flights. Chuck is trying to find another way out but the options have narrowed. It's a risk, her still being in the UK."

"But I don't understand why you used me? Me and Penny?"

She sighs. "Magda trusts you. She blamed me for the passport fiasco and because I told her to use the Americans' offer she didn't trust that either. Getting you involved, using Grant and—"

"You set that up? I… shit, Penny suggested him, didn't she? And coming down here. It just seemed like it came from me as well. No wonder Grant didn't worry about money. Bloody Americans flashing the cash."

Just then there's a knock at the door, making us both freeze. When I answer it, it is McNoble looking rather windswept. He steps in, sees Dina, smiles and gives her a hug. "Long time no see."

"You well?"

"Dandy."

Since when does McNoble say 'dandy'? I interject. "Did you see your Dad?"

"Yes. It was... interesting. We talked a lot. He apologised, sort of. So did I. Cuthbert took us out on his boat. He's a lucky chap as many of the yachts in the harbour were damaged but he was in France and sailed back on Friday morning so rode it out."

"Did he say why he's been avoiding you?"

"Yeah, well, hints. I'd rather not say just now. Why are you here? Any reason?"

"Just having a catch up. It's pretty full."

"Did I see Magda from the hotel? She was in the garden with that chap from Natalie's bar. The American. He a friend?"

"Yeah. Sort of." An idea is forming. "Is Mr Hemingway going out again soon?"

"Tomorrow. He's taking Dad to France."

I glance at Dina. "Can we have a quick word? Outside?"

Stephen steps back. I add, "Go through and say hi. Greg's there for introductions. Brenda and Zenda too."

"They'll be delighted. I don't think Brenda will ever forgive me, not that I blame her. What about her boyfriend?"

"Dobbin's there too."

"Don't be too long. I may need some back up." Stephen offers me a hand and we shake. "Thanks Harry for sorting out Dad. You too Di. He told me how good you've been to him."

We separate and I watch his back as he straightens his shoulders and pushes open the double doors to the sitting room."

Dina says, "I'd love to be a fly on the wall right now. So what's going through your tiny mind?"

"Sending Magda on that boat with Hemingway and Charlie. She'll be in France, but via some obscure port rather than a main terminal. Anyway, she's got a false identity. By the time anyone realises she can be across France and West Germany."

"There's another problem. The entry requirements have been tightened. I don't think the visas Grant sorted will do. That's really why Chuck is here – to sort that out. He's talking to Magda."

"Not you?"

"We are trying not to speak. Not until she's gone. Then... I can't really say but once Magda's in East Europe something will happen. This is all about plausible deniability Harry. The fewer official lines that are used the better. Can you ask Hemingway? I mean you know him, don't you?"

"Can I involve Stephen? He and his Father might be able to persuade him."

"If you trust him."

She gives me such a look, a mix of surprise and scepticism that I burst out laughing. "I know, I know. Me trusting McNoble. Who'd have thought it? But I do."

"Okay. In that case the sooner the better then."

"I'll talk to him tonight and see if we can't get things moving in the morning."

# Sunday, 18th October 1987

## *Chapter Ninety-Three*

The night is rather disturbed; Penny is awake at 4.15 with a gripping stomach pain, positive she is about to give birth but after the last false alarm we stay in bed and wait to see if there are any other developments. As the sky lightens in the east, we talk about Magda and Dina and Chuck. I say, "I spoke to Stephen and he's keen to help. He's pretty sure his Father will be, too."

"Why is Chuck here? Is he after Magda?"

"They're rather coy but they now seem to be on the same side. It's Dina's boss who's the problem."

"I'm glad I don't work in that line of business. I hope Magda is okay."

"Indeed. I think Dina's had enough too."

"Will Dina get be in trouble?"

"God knows. Chuck seems very impressed with her. That might help I suppose." I roll over and rub her back, triggering a groan. "How come you were involved? And why not tell me?"

"Natalie called and said it was very important. When we met Dina was there. She sketched out what to do. Sorry, but your ignorance was vital."

"Yeah, because I'm George Washington and 'I cannot tell a lie.'"

"No, it's because you're a crap actor."

"Same thing."

"I think Nats has fallen for Chuck, despite the excess poundage."

"That's not what she told me."

"When has she ever really told you what she's really thinking?"

I think back to the conversation on the beach. Yes, that's probably true.

"It helped that you happen to have contacts in the criminal underworld too, of course."

"Yeah, great. What a CV. If I have to find a new job, it'll be up there with my degree and cycling proficiency certificate. Couldn't they have asked Grant directly?"

"Dina sounded him out, but this was about persuading Magda."

"She could have said. You too."

"Stop whining. And if you knew? Would you have done it? You'd have over-thought it. Scared yourself and made yourself believe that whoever told you to do it could do it better themselves. But if you thought only you could do it, then there was a chance you'd pull it off."

"You played a very neat hand to get me to involve Grant."

"Why thank you kindly."

"You put Grant's phone number on the top of the papers in the bureau, didn't you? Had you already rung him before I called?" She doesn't answer but I can feel her smiling. I stop rubbing her back and flip over. "I hope it works. Sounds like Dina's career is hanging on this going through."

Penny slowly rolls over to me, groaning a little. She kisses me. "You'll sort it out." Another groan and a reverberating fart follows and she sighs, easing herself back onto her side of the bed. "I think I'll sleep now.

## Chapter Ninety-Four

My alarm goes off at 6.30. I crawl out of bed and dress quickly. A wash can wait. Stephen is already in the hall and Magda appears a minute later. He says, "Di's gone ahead to find the Yank. She said to meet by the parking spot."

There isn't a lot of conversation. Chuck grunts when we get in his car, some non-descript Ford saloon, and resumes his whispered conversation with Dina. Magda sits in the middle between Stephen and me. He dozes with his head against the window, while she sits bolt upright staring ahead and, it seems, barely breathing. I desperately want to hear what Chuck and Dina are discussing but without any luck. I give him directions and sit back, watching the countryside give way to the outskirts of Lymington and then the shops of the High Street as we drive slowly down the hill, past the Angel Inn and Kings the bookshop. Mr Hemingway's cottage is smaller than I assumed but neat in a classically English, roses-round-the-door sort of way. It faces out to sea across the Lymington River. Today it is sleepy and quaint; two days ago during the height of the storm I imagine it was terrifying.

To my surprise the be-ponchoed Charlie J is leaning against the front wall. He is eating something and pushes himself upright when he realises we are stopping. Stephen does the introductions at which point Charlie holds his hands in the air and turns his face towards the bleary-eyed sun that makes a belated appearance from behind some clouds. "Oh joy!" He drops his arms, bestows on each of us a wide smile and adds, "This way!" Once again he skips towards a group of moored boats. Chuck catches my eye and raises an eyebrow.

Hemingway's boat explains the modest cottage. It is large and shiny and seemingly well-equipped. I know diddly-squat about boats and sailing, and despite spending many years by the sea I never developed any part of my body as seaworthy, especially not my legs. If we were meant to be aquatic we'd have bloody gills. And didn't our distant forebears make real efforts to leave the sea for the land? I see no reason to reverse hundreds of millennia of evolution.

Hemingway appears on deck. Since I saw him last the tight grey curls have been allowed to grow and lose their shape, his face is bronzed and he's also lost weight. The effect is to transform a 50-something going on 70 into a 40 year old. There's also a little of the jaunty Ted Heath about him, which isn't especially appealing.

He smiles at us all and especially Magda for whom he makes a beeline. As Hemingway talks to her and shows off his boat, Dina, Chuck and Stephen have an animated conversation is low whispers and so I gravitate to Charlie. "Did you sort things out with Stephen?"

He nods once, his gaze out to sea, beyond the Isle of Wight. "It's been a long time coming Harry, there's a lot to resolve."

To my surprise – actually horror wouldn't be far off the mark – he turns quickly and takes me in a firm grip, kissing my forehead like some religious ceremony has been undertaken, cleansing me of sin or somesuch. When he lets go, he says, "I'm done now Harry, all thanks to you and your sister. Time to leave."

Echoes of a fear someone expressed about him committing suicide come back with a shiver. Who said that? I say, "Where are you going?"

He points at Magda and then Stephen. "To restore some pride. For all of us. This is both a happy and a sad day, especially for you and your friends."

I feel duty-bound to nod, although the idea of him going off with Stephen and Magda doesn't make me especially happy or sad. I hesitate to say 'indifferent' but in truth that's probably accurate.

"We will always be close Harry, wherever you and I are in the world. We have a bond, don't we? A special bond."

He holds my gaze. I'm completely sure in that moment he's telling me he's my Father and I just have to make some sign, frame the elephant-sized question and he will confirm it once and for all. But Sod is up and about, even this early on a Sunday, and Chuck decides that that is the moment to clap and bring our attention back to him.

"Okay, listen up folks. Stephen and Charles will accompany Magda across Europe as part of the disguise. She and Stephen are in a relationship for this purpose. The plan is they separate in Berlin after they have secured an up-to-date visa and exit permit for Magda and her sister from the US embassy. I just want to say, even if you're not completely clear about why this is happening, it will all become very clear in the next six months or so, maybe a year. Harry, Dina and I need to scoot off and get her to Cheltenham. You okay to be dropped at the top of the High Street and make you own way back?"

"Of course," I say. "And thanks Chuck. Will you be back for the home loans?"

"Yeah maybe. I've unfinished business on a personal side too." He winks, a gesture guaranteed to turn a man's stomach.

As we watch from the dock Hemingway decides it is time to go to catch the tide, which he makes sound like he's catching a cold. We stand back while he busies around using Stephen as the crew. Soon enough they've lifted the sails – I've no idea what you call that manoeuvre – and are bobbing along at a fair old lick towards the mouth of the river and the sea beyond.

"Where are they going? Which port?" I'm standing next to Dina; Chuck has gone back to the car to wait.

"You don't need to know. Really. And don't even ask which country, okay, because I don't know and I didn't ask."

"I thought they were heading for France?"

She smiles enigmatically and takes my arm in both her hands before pulling me in close. "I may have made a dreadful error, you know. Or possibly a stroke of genius. It's hard to tell."

"Yep, you could have allowed the Spittle genes to come roaring through, but I doubt you have, and anyway Chuck thinks you're the business."

"Maybe. I think he's just weighing up the odds. That man calculates every advantage, every angle."

"Like Greg." I glance across, wondering if I'll get a reaction.

She takes time answering. "He's nice. He's asked if he can see me when I'm next in London. That's rather old fashioned, isn't it?"

"You want me to chaperone you?"

"Do you want to chaperone me, you perv?"

"Not a chance, thank you. My retinas would rather develop cataracts then be exposed to that sight."

"He trusts you, you know. And he understands why, given his family links, why you'd be suspicious."

"I know. I'm sure now – belatedly – that he's one of life's good guys, but he'd grind me into the dust if I stood in his way to a partnership."

"And you'd not reciprocate?"

"You know I wouldn't. I've never had enough self-belief to put myself forward as a better candidate than someone else. Stephen said it was one reason why I used to piss him off so much."

"It pissed me off too. Anyway, listen to Greg. He makes sense. And if we go on a date? You don't mind?"

"Not at all. It will get Mum off my back if you start dating again."

"She's doing well, isn't she? It's good they're having some success at last."

"Chuck's waving. You'd better get off to Cheltenham. I think I'll walk from here. It's going to be a nice day and I imagine I'll be allowed some scraps for breakfast. When will you be up in town?"

"Wednesday. Greg's taking me to the National."

"Bloody hell, that's quick. Will you want to stay with us?"

She reaches up and kisses my cheek before moving towards the car. Halfway there she spins round. "If everything works out then I hope not." She blows me a kiss. "Love to all."

I shudder; Greg and Dina kissing is a bad enough image for a sunny Sunday, let alone... I wait until the car has disappeared and then set off on the three mile walk home. I'll be back by about 9.30 and plan to have a nice quiet day. I buy three Sunday papers and smile. What could be better after the last few days?

## *Chapter Ninety-Five*

I guess I should have known better. When I push open the French doors to the kitchen the small group around the far end of the table: Dobbin, Zenda, Brenda, Karen, John and Greg look sombre. Racks of toast are untouched and cups of tea stand cold and ignored.

As soon as she sees me, Karen stands and comes over. "It's Amos. Jackie's with him and that doctor. They're waiting on an ambulance although no one thinks it can make it up the drive yet and he's… he's not well enough to be carried."

"Where is he? And what about Penny?"

"Penny went to lie down. She's upset, of course." This from Dobbin. "She looked awful. Your Mum and Pritti are with Natalie and Jackie. Your Dad is trying to organise some people with chainsaws to clear the road."

I dump the Sunday papers, no longer interested in the Leader writers and their prurient interest in the damage the storm has caused. I can't decide in the immediate moment what to do. Dobbin stands and takes my arm. "Go to—"

I don't give him the chance to finish. I run out of the room, up the stairs and into the bedroom. Penny is on the bed, her legs spread at about 45 degrees and her head is bent forward, like an inadequately designed rag doll, trying and failing to flop over.

"You okay?"

That's a daft question given I can hear her moaning and see she is rocking. If I still wasn't sure, to increase my understanding of the tableau I'm seeing she says, "Of course I'm not fucking okay, you fucking moron."

I begin to pivot back the way I've just come. "I'll get help."

"COME HERE NOW!"

I can't see her face for the mass of hair that's fallen forward but I can recognise the hand reaching out for me. I hesitate only briefly and her fingers do a grabbing, flapping thing to indicate I need to take it pronto or consequences will follow. Necessarily those consequences aren't spelt out but the increasing speed of the grabbing and especially the flapping makes it pretty plain they will be swift, dire and recurring.

"What…?" Truly I intend to say, "What can I do?" but as I finish the 'what' my hand touches her fingers and something extraordinary envelopes them, a flesh coloured anaconda-cum-vice and various bones are reorganised in an egregious and excruciating way. Thus the "What...?" becomes "What the fuck? Sheeeeeiiiit!"

Nature has designed us to remove ourselves from pain in an instant, but nature hadn't considered the incredible strength of the pregnant and fearful woman that is sat opposite me and is currently reeling me in like an inadequate sprat to her great white apex predator.

Closer now, I notice in a sort of abstract out-of-body, pain-induced hallucinatory state that she is pouring sweat, as am I. I can see her face through a matted tangle of hair. Her eyes are wild, manic and more white than brown. "Never," she is hissing, "ever," it is malevolent and uncompromising, "get your dick anywhere near me ever again. Capiche you bastard?"

If the searing agony being inflicted on my unsuspecting and largely innocent metacarpals is a guide then I too want nothing to do with the creation of new life again.

Abruptly she lets go and collapses back into the pillow, panting.

"Was that a contraction?"

One eye has appeared through her wild tresses. It regards me with contempt. "No, it was fucking performance art. Did you count it?"

"From where?"

"If you make me say 'the start' I will rip your dick off with my teeth."

"I mean were you in the middle of whatever it was when I came in?"

"And where the fuck have you been?"

"I went—"

She lurches forward and groans again, reaching out her hand. This time I take her by the elbow and slide next to her, rubbing her back. The pain doesn't last, as in what seems like a very few seconds she stops and lets go, pushing her hair off her face.

I look at her, the pain lines deep-embedded around her mouth. She smiles and strokes my cheek. "Kiss me."

I lean away. "Only if you promise not to bite off my tongue."

That releases a laugh and she pulls me close and we have the softest sexiest kiss imaginable. Well, considering the circumstances.

It seems as if the tumult of a moment ago has dissipated for now. "You were saying where you'd got to?"

I explain about Magda and how Charlie and Stephen went too. "It felt like it was all planned but I'm probably wrong about that. Oh, and Dina fancies Greg and has wangled a date."

"Yes, he told me. I think he's quite smitten."

"Are you okay? Is Wigglet on the way?"

"Just a warning, sort of a hello. Getting ready I think." Her face darkens. "How's Amos?"

"I don't know yet. As soon as I got back I heard that he'd taken ill but you'd come up here and Dobbin was concerned about you so…"

She pats my face. "Go and find out. I think you can rely on me to scream if anything happens."

"If you're sure?"

"Go. And hurry back."

Outside there is a smattering of rain. I turn towards the converted garages – Mum and Dad will have to think of a better name soon – only to see Dad standing by the gap where I was blown off my feet in the storm. Dobbins' BMW hasn't been moved and in the mid-morning light it looks vaguely alien. Dad spots me as I spot him and hurries towards me. "Your friend is on his way to hospital. He's had a haemorrhage that caused some issues because of his… you know… condition. Anyway, they managed to get an ambulance halfway up the drive and we used the hostess trolley to get him to them."

Dad's eyes are almost swivelling he's so nervy.

"What's wrong? You look awful."

"I think he died, Harold. On the trolley. No one said, and your friend Jackie has gone with them, but they were doing all that foot and mouth thing… No, that's not right." He frowns and I want to correct him, but I know he hates that so I bite my tongue. "Foot in mouth? Help me Harold, I'm going mad here. No wait. Mouth to mouth. Of course. She was trying to get him to breathe. Something about clearing his airways."

We aren't a demonstrative family but an arm round the shoulder seems appropriate. He leans against me, making me stagger slightly. "Goodness, how I've missed you and Dina, your good sense and encouragement." He pulls away and stares at me. "We – Veronica and I – are tremendously… is that snot on your cheek?"

It is and it is almost certainly Penny's. I wipe it away as discreetly as I can while he pulls a moue of distaste. "Where are the others?"

"Your Mother and Pritti are cleaning up. Your friends – Gary and those young women – are having breakfast. Or maybe it's brunch. I've not seen your sister and that awful lout hasn't appeared. Why did you invite him? Him and his Dad are nothing but trouble."

"Dina's had to go back to Cheltenham. Work is crazy for her right now. Stephen has left, fear not. His Father too."

Dad shakes his head looking sorrowful. He says, "Your work colleague Greg asked about her. Are they, erm, stepping out together?"

"So far as I know they met for the first time yesterday."

"Goodness. I gained the distinct impression that they were, well, quite intimate. Parents are the last to know, I suppose."

"I suppose. Has the drive been cleared now? We can't really get back until it is."

We automatically turn to the wrecked car. "So much for German engineering. The men are working to clear everything. Mr Garrett has promised not to stop until there's some sort of passage through. I mean it's been brought home by your friend that we need access in case of any more accidents or emergencies.

"Penny's having some contractions. Maybe you'd tell Mum and I'll go back and spend some time with her."

"She's grown, hasn't she? Have you had one of those skins?"

"Skins?"

"Where you can look at the baby inside Mummy's tummy."

"Scan. Yes, three."

"And is yours huge?"

"Not especially. I think it's just an early play to get me to build a swimming pool."

"Where would you put it? Your garden surely isn't large enough."

"You'd be surprised what you can do these days, Dad. Have the telephone lines been repaired yet?"

He brightens a little. "Now that was a pleasant surprise. A man from the GPO was up a pole on the S bend while I waited for the ambulance. I told him I was impressed he was working on a Sunday and you know what he said?"

"Go on, Dad."

Dad effects a Hampshire burr. "I'll lose me job, what with that witch in power if I don't." Dad chortles. "Maggie as the White Witch. What a lovely idea. I must give you a copy of the talk I gave at the club. I think you'll find it interesting." He moves away towards the garages, chortling.

This probably isn't the day to challenge him on what shade of witch Maggie is. I know I'm a hypocrite since my job and salary are a function of many of her policies but I have principles even if they're compromised. And Dobbin says he'll make me even richer with these fantastic investment opportunities. In all honesty I should give it to charity.

Back inside Greg is waiting for me. "I saw you talking to your Father and didn't want to interrupt. I assume you'll be staying?"

I'm confused and must show it.

"Penny. You can't think of driving if she's about to give birth."

I try to look relaxed, but I do have a nagging worry. "She's got over a fortnight to go, so I expect we'll drive home later. It depends on the roads. Dad has people working to clear a passage through."

"Fortunately I can get away. Your friend Gary is coming with me, as is Brenda. Is that his car? What on Earth happened? Do you have trolls wandering the grounds?"

"Did he show you his head wound? Both he and his car were attacked by some garage doors during the storm. I wonder what he plans on doing with the write-off." I take his proffered hand. "Thank you, by the way. And I thought about what you said. I won't give up. If as is likely, and fair, you and Crispin get the available slots tomorrow then unless Frank tells me my chances are less than hopeless I'll stay for one more year. If we can make more progress then maybe another place will become available."

He smiles enigmatically. What is he thinking? "All I'd say is stick by the phone. If it's repaired."

"Are you winding me up? Do you know something about how they'll vote?"

He holds his hands up defensively. "No, no, not at all. But there's one thing I need to do first thing and I think we ought to go soon."

At that moment Dobbin appears. He's clutching his bag and a section of the paper. "Spittoon. I need to get off. Did you read this?" He is holding the business section. "All sorts are going on in the US and with the stock markets shut here on Friday, I have a feeling Monday is the perfect day to buy."

"Really? How are the stocks you didn't buy for me doing?"

"Until the market opens, I can't know but you may have been very lucky. I'll know better tomorrow. Right, I'll just get Bren."

While we wait for him to return, Greg asks me what I'm planning on investing in.

"I have no clue. That man is a genius. He's made himself a fortune, sold his business a few weeks ago and wants to use the cash for some good causes. If he says I'll make a fortune then maybe I will."

Greg keeps looking at the stairs. "Sounds like he's someone I should spend time with." He peers across at me and then away. "Like Dina."

"Are you fishing?"

"Fishing?"

"You know what I mean."

"You two are close, aren't you?"

"Very. She's a genius, calmly logical, clinically insane and if you so much as make her look even slightly sad—"

"I would never—"

I stop him with a flat hand like a traffic cop. "…I'll be amazed. She'll run rings around you and you'll adore her. If she turns out to like you, then you won't know how lucky you are. You know she's got a kid?"

"I gathered. Is the Father around?"

"Yep. They're still close and will remain so. Just don't try to get between her and her lad or make things difficult with Jim and his family. She knows she owes them all."

"Thanks."

I wonder if I should tell him she is a card-carrying atheist; no, let him find out after they've had some fun.

"Your parents have done an amazing job here, too. You can see where she gets her talents from."

"I still find it difficult to see my parents as competent, but Dad always said Mum just needed the right opportunity to make it big and he's right. She's thriving on the pressure of this business venture and he's content to let her be the successful one."

"Gary said your Dad is going into local politics?"

"I heard that too, not that I'm about to discuss it with either of them. I hope it remains a pipe dream. To say we are politically opposites doesn't really do justice to the distance between us."

Dobbin, Brenda and the others all appear at much the same time. Hugs and goodbyes and thank yous are liberally distributed. Mum returns and there are more of the same, but by 2.00 Greg has led the first party away with Dobbin promising to have the garage recover his car inside a week. At about five, Dad announces the drive is clear enough for Zenda to leave with Karen and John. "Are you and Penny going as well?"

Penny has emerged from her nesting to sit in front of the large fire in the sitting room. I look at her and she says, "We'd better stay until we know what Jackie plans. We need to take her with us and, well, there's Amos…"

Mum looks suitably sheepish. "Oh goodness, how silly. Arthur, they can't go yet, can they?"

"No dear, they cannot. Do you two want a job?"

Penny pushes herself to her feet. "Why not? I'll get fat if I just sit around."

## *Chapter Ninety-Six*

I've never been in the attic in this house. It is enormous, easily accessed by a door on the top landing that I must have seen but never registered. It is lit by two swinging bulbs caught in draughts from heaven knows where.

Mum stands just inside the door, hands on hips, and Penny is to her right. "If you go over there," she indicates vaguely to her left, "you'll find all Harold's clutter. I meant to sort it out when we left Hordle but there never seemed to be the time. Dina's heap is to the right. And while it's very tempting, don't go wandering right to the back. That's all left over from when the Andersens were here. I dread to think what's in it. I wanted it chucked out, but your Father is terrified it might be," here she drops her voice to a whisper, "evidence of criminality, so we just pushed it all to the back. Anyway the box thingy is locked so unless we take a crowbar to it, we'll never know. I don't suppose it matters now but he's worried it might lead to a scandal and that's not what he wants, not with the hustings due soon."

Having dropped that temptation our way, she brushes some cobwebs from her hair and leaves us to it. "Pritti is making something yellow and minty for about seven. Don't overdo it, darling."

"I won't."

She looks at me like I'm a halfwit. "I meant Penny."

As the door shuts, Penny turns and kisses me. "Shall I give birth here? We could call him or her Wigglet Atticus if I did."

"Or Lofty."

"With your height genes I think something less aspirational might be better. Okay, let's see what she's saved from the boy-genius' past."

While Penny heads over to the boxes and bundles indicated I ignore Mum and go in search of the previous owner's – Robin Andersen's – remnants. I am awfully curious but also - and this is a natural state for me - more than a little anxious that there will be some dreadful piece of compromising evidence that shows I too am a criminal even if I was unwitting.

There are folders and files and all sorts, making me wonder if indeed it could be a record of his criminality. I pull one out at random: it appears to be receipts for things as mundane as lawn mower servicing, supplies of oil for the central heating, a bunch of keys, a plan of some industrial buildings and, bizarrely, a repair bill for a glass toucan.

"Bloody hell!" Penny's voice drags me back to her rummaging. "Amanda!"

I put back the keys and the folder and crawl back to where she's now stood. Next to her looking dusty and faded is the cardboard cut-out of a bikini-clad blonde advertising Boots photographic printing services. Penny points to her bikini bottoms and the hole Stephen McNoble carved with his knife and through which, in an experiment I will live to regret forever, I once stuck my penis.

"You remember?"

"How could I forget?"

"You going to try again? See if you still fit?"

"You are beyond tasteless."

"But admit it, you were wondering if you could."

"Stop it. I'm amazed Mum kept it."

"It's what Mothers do; keep what they can to embarrass their offspring at some point in their future. It looks like it's working. Shall we take it so Wigglet can play with it?" To add to my clear discomfort, she picks the cut-out up and peers at me through the hole.

"Come on. Leave her until they start biology lessons. What else is there?"

"I found some children's books we might take but while your Mum and Dad have all this space for all your school reports and medals and certificates we may as well leave most of it here – you never said you had passed your Sunday school exams?"

"Did I? I have absolutely no memory of that."

"Let's go down. Hopefully Jackie will be back soon and we can get going to London."

## Chapter Ninety-Seven

There is still no sign of Jackie but the telephone is working again. I call the hospital – Southampton General – to be told Amos has been admitted but nothing more. At least that must mean he's probably still alive.

We eat an early supper and play Scrabble. The place seems awfully quiet now that it is just we four. Dad tells us about his speech to the Tory club and Penny opens a can of worms by asking about his political aspirations.

Mum and I leave them to it and slip away to watch the TV, where I fall asleep, dreaming about toucans flying south for winter carrying Amanda, with Barry's photographs spilling from its beak and cascading down in a torrent of bizarre imagery. Someone is shouting at the bird, telling it to do something. It takes me a moment to realise the shouting is at me and it's Mum.

"Harold. Now I need you to keep calm. Penny's waters have broken and I think this is it. Unfortunately the phone has gone down again but your Father has gone to use the call box and then fetch Pritti."

I'm discombobulated by all this. "Pritti? Mrs Ohja? Why?"

"She delivered several babies in Nairobi before they moved to Uganda. It's only a worst case scenario."

"In case of what?"

"In case we can't get an ambulance to take her into hospital." There's a knock at the front door. "Now what has your Father forgotten. Silly man." Mum sounds rather panicked. While she goes to answer it I head upstairs.

Penny is on the bed, surrounded by more towels than I've ever seen. "Oh Harry. This is a disaster."

"It will be fine." I do my most calming voice. It's the equivalent of fingernails down a blackboard even to my ears.

"If you think the definition of 'fine' encompasses you delivering our baby, you're fucking mental." She's stopped from her snarky diatribe by a wave of pain that causes her to lurch back into the pillows like she's attached to a rope and some moron is yanking her through the wall.

Just then the bedroom door opens and Jackie hurries in. I'm not sure who is the more relieved: me or Penny. No, okay, it has to be her, but I'm a short head behind.

She starts doing nursey-type things with wrists and watches and so on and then says, "Your Dad has managed to get through to the emergency services and an ambulance is on its way. Now let's see how dilated you are." She looks at me. "You'll probably not want to see this. I've been told that for the Father to be it's a bit like watching a favourite toy ripped apart by a demented Rottweiler."

She goes to what Dad would call the business end and lifts the sheets.

If I thought I was free to feel faint in my own time, Jackie has other ideas. "Grab that table lamp, will you?"

"What? Why?"

"So I can see, numpty."

"But how? I mean, it's too…"

She laughs. "I don't need to go inside, you nit. I'm just going to have a peek at her cervix."

Yes, I'm definitely about to faint, but needs must and I surprise myself by doing whatever it is Jackie needs. After a quick inspection she visibly relaxes. "Not too far gone, Penny. I'm sure you'll be okay to get the ambulance. I don't suppose you packed just in case?"

Penny looks sheepish. "It's still another couple of weeks; I kind of assumed I'd be back at home."

I watch the two of them chat; my girlfriend and my ex. There's something oddly surreal but comforting to know they are in control of this and my role is now reduced to cheerleader and…

"Tea? How about I make a cuppa?" I say brightly.

Yes, I'm happy with that. Char-man.

# Monday, 19th October 1987

## *Chapter Ninety-Eight*

I'm sitting in the reception of the maternity ward of Southampton General hospital. It's somewhere between 3.00 and God-knows-what-o'clock. I briefly wonder how many times I've been awake at this time of day. A handful I suppose. There's not a lot to recommend it. I've tried to read the magazines and made conversation with a Father of four who says he usually ends up counting the pleats in the curtains to stop himself going mad. I don't say anything but surely counting pleats is one of several definitions of madness?

Penny is in room four, three doors and half a power scream away. There's been a lot of shrieking and I'm currently here because the midwife thought my presence not conducive to her mental health. All I did was ask how much longer. It was an innocent question, one I get asked all the time – 'when will we exchange?' The clients – my clients – know I can't say for sure but I try to be open and give them a reasonable estimate. That's all I wanted. But it led to some sort of metamorphosis in Penny, much like a sudden transition from human to werewolf in the light of a full moon. "Are you fucking rushing me? Do you think I want to be in this fucking abattoir you utter fucking moron? You come here and try to force a fucking basketball out of a space even fucking Thumberlina would say was cosy and see if you want to fucking rush it."

Then the tears came, and she was offered more drugs that rather worryingly she accepted very readily. It's was when the nurse who was trying to ease the gas mask thing away from her; all I did was try to help. "Come on Pen. Give it back."

That was when she swung it and clouted the midwife who had turned to shush me and didn't see it coming. In the ensuing kerfuffle I was told to wait outside. Which is where I currently am.

The serial parent – his name is Trevor – is waiting for the birth to be announced. I asked him why he wasn't present and all he could do was swallow a lot and shake his head hard. It seemed as if he couldn't actually say why, like the words might eat him if he let them go.

Jackie has disappeared. She's been gone quite a while in fact. She went to find Amos and Natalie and hasn't come back. That must have been two hours ago. Or maybe it was 10 minutes. I've begun to hallucinate. Trying to close one eye and focus on the right curtain makes the pleats seem to vibrate. Or is that a wobble? When does a wobble turn into a vibration? Is there some wave length thing that you have to measure, like light? I—

"Mr Spittle?" A young man in a white coat who can't possibly be a doctor and must be someone just here from a fancy dress party is standing in front of me. I nod, wondering how he knows my name. Did they give me a sticker?

"Penny – Mrs Spittle – is asking for you."

"She's not... we're not... we should be, but I never..." He's ignored me and has already disappeared back down the corridor. Maybe he's the son of some doctor on work experience. I go to follow; Trevor won't meet my gaze, rather like you'd look away from someone about to die out of politeness.

In room four, all is calm although the midwife winces as I step inside. The teenager is still very serious, standing next to Penny and talking to her in a quiet voice. I glance around for the doctor but he or she much have popped out. I walk over to the bed. "Mr Spittle, I was just explaining to Penny that we think we should consider a C-section."

Penny doesn't look fazed; probably the drugs.

"Shouldn't we wait for the doctor?"

Penny's eyes roll towards the ceiling. The midwife was right to try to restrain her usage of the gas. "He is the bloody doctor," she hisses.

It must be the lack of sunlight or maybe I've accidentally ingested too much of some sort of airborne opiate but they both look like she's telling the truth. "Er, really? Okay. Why do you think she needs a C...?" I can't actually say that word as the idea, even though it is something we often talked about in the NCT class has now moved from the abstractedly theoretical to the bloody real and very possible and I now know what Trevor feels like.

It seems like a good question, but it fails the acid test of the capable barrister – one reason why I decided not to pursue that line of career option – that you shouldn't ask a question where you don't know the answer. In this case it's more you shouldn't ask a question where the answer is given in a strange pidgin Martian. Most sentences contain words I can't begin to spell, and some contain familiar words but used in a sequence with which I'm utterly unfamiliar. I cast a look at Penny, assuming she will be equally mystified but she's nodding along at what appear to be appropriate pauses. Suddenly he stops;

there's an awful hiatus, during which I can feel his confidence draining. I manage a, "Right. Okay. Thanks. What do you think, Pen?"

She rolls her eyes again. "Of course. There's no decision, is there?"

The doctor says, "It is a big decision. I understand you might want a word together but we really should get to it shortly."

He steps away and leaves me gawping at Penny. "I haven't the first clue what he said. Is he really a doctor?"

"Yes, and go and tell him we want to get on with it. I don't think I can put up with this for much longer and they said Wigglet is getting distressed."

In the next 30 minutes there's a lot of action, during which I get in the way four times and am made to feel utterly useless. Someone – I have no idea who – suggests I wait in yet another windowless, magazine-strewn room devoid of curtains. It's 4.17 am and I can feel my eyelids drooping.

## Chapter Ninety-Nine

I'm shaken awake with daylight filtering into the small waiting room and a lot more noise than I remember when I rested my eyes just a moment ago. Where did the window come from? I'm sure it wasn't there when I sat down.

It's the doctor, smiling. "You're a Father, Mr Spittle. Congratulations."

"Harry, please."

"A boy. Mother and baby are doing fine, although Penny is going to be rather sore for a while. They're in recovery. Would you like to see them?"

Trevor's terror makes a brief visit to my imagination, accompanied by awful Hieronymus Bosch pictures of tortured souls skewed on tridents before I manage a nod and follow along the corridor. How do I feel? I'm a Dad, a Father, a pater familias. It occurs to me as we turn a corner and then another that I've just accomplished the first really adult thing I've ever done in my entire life. And that means it is utterly irreversible. I will always be a Dad whatever else I do.

The doctor – has he even told me his name? – stops and indicates a door with a glass panel in it. I begin to bend to look through when an arm snakes past me and he pushes it open. I stumble forward and enter Penny's new domain at a half-crouch, half-trot.

I must be maturing because my momentum carries me to the side of her bed where I stop and stand and look down on a clearly exhausted Mother. Mother! I say the word. I say it again. Penny opens her eyes and hisses – what is it with this hissing? – "Do not call me 'Mother' ever! I have a name. I will not be a label."

The doctor is just behind me. I can hear his feet shuffling. He says, "Here is your son."

And there he is. Brown-faced, like tea on newspaper, with a head shaped like a walnut with large blue and unfocused eyes. He is also huge. No wonder he wasn't coming out the traditional way. And bald. His hands seem to be on small springs and he's cut his cheeks with his fingernails so they've put him in small white boxing gloves.

Penny's sounding a bit slurry. "Is he beautiful? Cute?"

I know honesty is not what is required just now, but the truth is he is… he is…

"He's a right little character. It's like he wants to conduct an orchestra."

That works. "You think he's musical?"

"Or interested in a career with the traffic police."

She slips back down, wincing slightly. Her voice comes from far away. I think she manages to say, "Wanker," but that might be the drugs.

"Why don't you hold him?" A nurse expertly picks up Wigglet and shows me how to manhandle him, cradling his head. I'm rigid with fear and she laughs. "They're built to survive unsure Fathers you know. Try to relax or you'll be next under the knife with a seizure or hernia or heart attack or something. Do you have a name in mind yet?"

There are many decisions you make in life, some of which you regret and of those a few that can haunt you for ever. But bequeathing your child with a name that might lead to teasing, some awful diminutive or acronym is up there with the top three long-term life mistakes. "No. We thought we'd wait until we saw him and then decide."

"And what name springs to mind when you look at him?" the nurse asks.

"Walnut."

She laughs and I relax a little.

Over the next couple of hours, Penny comes to and the nurse encourages her to try to breastfeed. At seven I go and find a phone and call Mum – delighted – speak to Dad – ecstatic – then Penny's parents, Peggy and Axel – also over the moon – and Pritti who asks how I'm doing – I love that woman. At nine I call Chloe with the good news. She squeals with delight and says she'll make sure everyone leaves me alone. I want to remind her that at some point today Frank will want to call me and tell me I've been passed over, but I can't be bothered. "If you need to get me, ring my Mum and leave a message. I'll be speaking to her and be back home at some point."

"Have you decided on a name? The girls will be dying to know."

"Nope, not yet."

"Oh." She couldn't sound more disappointed. "And how heavy was he?"

"Nine pounds seven."

"Oh, how awful. Poor Penny."

She doesn't ask about me.

The nurses change at 11.00 am and Penny dozes off. I've still not seen Jackie or Natalie who have been with Amos all this time. I go on a hunt. I'm feeling buoyant as I check with the nurses' station how I'll find out where he is. The directions take me all over the place before I work out he's in an isolation ward, and when I get there I can see Natalie sitting on a plastic chair with a stare that says despair as clearly as if she was screaming it at the top of her voice. She's holding a plastic cup of something at the sort of angle that any sort of shock will surely tip it everywhere. I carefully take it from her, making her start.

She looks at me as if she's never seen me before; then she stands and throws her arms around me so hard and so tightly the rescued coffee flies from my hand anyway.

"What's happened? How's Amos?"

She tries but can't speak. A nurse sees us and comes over, asking if she can help. It turns out that Amos is on life support in intensive care. Jackie has gone back to my parents exhausted.

"What's the prognosis? How's he doing?"

The nurse shakes her head. "I think you'll need to wait for the doctor. They're with him now." She won't be moved on the subject of imparting any information. Natalie isn't any more capable of telling me. It occurs to me that Jackie may be better informed so after promising Natalie that I'll come back soon, I go looking for a phone.

"Lymington 697262."

"Mum, it's Harry. Is Jackie there?"

"She's gone to bed, dear. She's very tired."

"Did she say anything about Amos? I'm struggling to find out what's going on."

"No. Sorry. How's Penny? Have you chosen a name?"

"She's asleep. Pretty exhausted. And we've not had a chance to talk names yet, no. When we know, you'll know."

"Yes, of course. I hope Amos is going to be all right."

"I get the impression that it's unlikely. I'll call again a bit later."

Back with Natalie, I tell her where Penny is and offer to take her. She looks around and shakes her head.

"I'll stay. You go and see her and Wigglet. If anything changes I'll come and get you," I say.

She isn't sure but eventually heads off to visit Pen. I hope it might cheer her up a little.

The waiting room here is similar to the maternity ward, but the atmosphere is completely different – it is pervaded by a sort of miasma of gloom. Everyone – the medical staff, the porters, the visitors – all have their eyes downcast, averted like too much contact might be inappropriate.

I check my watch. It's just after midday and the sun is out. The real world is out there somewhere but it's dull and unimportant right now. Amos is barely 40 and should be at some sort of peak. The idea pings into my head that we should give Wigglet 'Amos' as at least one name but I know I'll hate it, although I'll never be able to say that without upsetting someone. 'Amos Spittle' sounds like some minor character out of a Harriet Beecher Stowe novel, alongside Seth Bribbet. I should mention it to Pen but I know I won't. I hate being a coward. Will Wigglet be any better? Will he have Penny's ballsy gene or my ineffectual 'he meant well, but…' version?

"Excuse me, are you a friend of Amos? Ms Pendant mentioned to the nurse that you were here with her." The doctor is more informally dressed than the last one but with a trademark stethoscope around his neck.

"How is he?"

"I'm afraid it really isn't good news. Is Ms Pendant about?"

"She's with my… my partner? In maternity. We've just had a baby."

It's clear this juxtaposition of life and death is outside his experience. He looks totally non-plussed.

"Is he conscious?"

"He's heavily sedated. He has brief moments of lucidity. Would you like to see him?"

"I think maybe I should get Natalie."

"He may not have that long."

I get it, I think. Having washed my hands and put on a mask and gown I follow the doctor into the ward. Amos is a small shrunken almost two-dimensional sliver of flesh on the pillow. I sit next to him and touch his fingers. There's a flicker of recognition in his eyes and a bleary glance. He tries to say something, but there's no sound to accompany the moving lips. All this effort must exhaust him and his eyes close and his breath slows. I'm watching to see if I can register each breath when a finger rubs along mine. And then it stops.

Is he dead? The doctor has left me but comes back when an alarm goes off. I'm moved away and ushered outside as curtains are pulled round him.

It feels awful to be in the presence of an untimely death on the day I want to be joyous and celebrate life. I don't know how to deal with either emotion. I hesitate for just a moment and then leave to go and find Natalie.

In the maternity ward, Penny is sitting up with Wigglet in her arms. He is sleeping and looks content, as does she. Natalie is sitting next to the bed smiling. When she sees me, Penny beams. "It's all happening, lover boy."

I'm not sure what my face shows but it causes her to laugh. "They brought me a phone. Your Mum called. It seems that a Mr Crout rang her and wants to speak to you as soon as possible. She wanted to know if he was important. It's about the partnership, isn't it? And Gary also rang. Apparently the world is crashing and burning, or maybe that's the stock markets. He said it's brilliant news that he never managed to invest your money last week and given the falls today you'll make a killing in the near future. And Dina called to say there's good news from a foreign land – poor Veronica was completely baffled by that, but she means Magda, doesn't she? It's all going well, isn't it?"

It's understandable but none the less it's difficult to deal with all this right now. Natalie picks up on my lack of animation. "What's the news with Amos?"

Both Penny and Natalie's expressions change in an instant. I'm crying. Uncontrollably. I hate crying when others do it but in myself?

This really sucks.

# Two Weeks Later

## *Chapter One Hundred*

Amos died peacefully in the end. He never regained consciousness. His funeral was an awful affair, but we spread his ashes across the lawns at Hemingways with Ravi Ohja's permission. Wigglet was finally named John Arthur Axel Spittle and will be christened soon (Mum insisted and Penny didn't have the heart to fight it). Natalie, Jackie, Brenda and Dina (who also blanched at the idea) are godmothers; we decided to drop godfathers when Dobbin made it clear he wasn't keen. He lost a bundle on the crash, but his incompetence saved me a fortune and he still hopes to help me cash in later. I don't really care in truth. Ironically his loses enamoured him to Brenda even more, although he insists he'll still have enough to buy out Karen as planned. My sister's boss is under investigation but Dina has decided to resign anyway. Partly that's because she had begun to hate the politics, partly it's to give her more time to see George, but if you ask me it's to give her more time with Greg as well, on whom she seems very keen.

And the partnership? Yep, for some reason they offered it to me. And Greg and Crispin. Martin the serially incompetent junior partner resigned to pursue a career as a reflexology and reiki practitioner, which he assured me was his real passion. I had to look them both up. I'm not entirely sure how it all came about but Frank made an effort to forgive Turdgate, although he does eye me suspiciously if we're ever in the loos at the same time.

"I've been thinking." Penny has taken to motherhood with a passion. I'm more circumspect but I love that she won't do any of the baby caring stuff for me. It's just after five in the morning; it's still dark and the rain has only just stopped. John is asleep on her chest, having just fallen off her exposed boob. I look longingly at the nipple that has taken a pounding over the last few weeks.

"Hmm? What about?"

"Marriage."

That wakes me up. "You want me to propose? I haven't got a ring."

"We were never going to get engaged if you thought you could buy me a ring. No, I was talking to Bren and she and Gary are thinking about getting spliced."

I stretch myself and swing my legs off the bed. "I'll make us some tea."

"No wait. Do you think we should?"

I roll back and look at my lovely little family. "Can I nuzzle your boobs please?"

"Later. Do you?"

"What's this about? Are we in competition with those two all of a sudden?"

"Not exactly. We thought a joint wedding might be nice… Harry, where are you going?"

Printed in Poland
by Amazon Fulfillment
Poland Sp. z o.o., Wrocław